1 MONTH OF
FREE
READING

at

www.ForgottenBooks.com

By purchasing this book you are eligible for one month membership to ForgottenBooks.com, giving you unlimited access to our entire collection of over 1,000,000 titles via our web site and mobile apps.

To claim your free month visit:

www.forgottenbooks.com/free164727

ISBN 978-1-5280-8928-9
PIBN 10164727

UNDER THE TREES.

BY

SAMUEL IRENÆUS PRIME.

NEW YORK:

HARPER & BROTHERS, PUBLISHERS,

FRANKLIN SQUARE.

1902

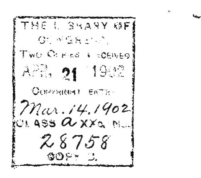

Copyright, 1874, by HARPER & BROTHERS.

Copyright, 1902, by WENDELL PRIME, MARY PRIME STODDARD, and LOUISA PRIME.

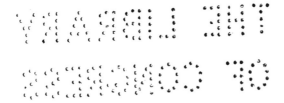

TO

Lily Prime

THIS VOLUME IS

LOVINGLY INSCRIBED.

NOTE.

Many of these miscellaneous letters and papers were written out of doors, and the writer yields to the request of others in putting them under the cover of a book.

CONTENTS.

UNDER THE TREES.

I.

OUR TENT PITCHED.

It is said that fools build houses and wise men live in them. This is not true of the place where we have now set up our household gods, and in the midst of confusion yet feel already a sense of at-home-ativeness, never enjoyed more completely since the sunny days of childhood. For it was a wise man who chose this spot for his house, and here made for himself a home. His judgment, taste, and skill are seen all over it, and if in this changing world it has finally fallen into our hands, we will not call him unwise, but rather be glad that he was led to make it what it is, that it might be all the more enjoyable for us.

It is on the banks of the Hudson. From this rustic seat where I am writing you might throw a stone far into the river. Twenty miles or more of this glorious stream, embracing the whole of Tappan Zee, lie in full view, and from the house some forty or fifty miles of river, forest, and mountains spread themselves continuously at our feet. Between five and six acres of land, chiefly covered with old trees, a wild glen crossed by rustic bridges on the southern side of it, walks winding through the woods and in constant sight of the waters, garden and fruits and flowers, which for many years have been coming to their present condition, ornamental shade-trees, and evergreens arranged to give effect and beauty to the lawn and land-scape, are the outline features of the place. It is the midst of spring. The cherry-trees have been in full bloom, and the apples and pears are now getting to blows. The birds have a carnival of song all over the woods, and about sunrise they seem to meet for morning praise, and hold a concert near the house.   Three pairs of them have built their nests in the piazzas, and are as much at home as any of the family. They shall have their board and lodging without charge, and the longer they stay, the bet-ter we shall like it.

   We have not been here a week, and have yet to learn by experience the various inconveniences which every place in this world has ; but just now every thing is around us to make up the comfort and beauty of a rural home. It is about twenty miles from the city, and the railroad and steamboat take us to town or from it a dozen times a day, if we should wish to go so often.   It is about three miles below the Sunnyside of Washington Irving, and in the midst of scores of our fellow-citizens who have found on the eastern bank of the Hudson River the most ele-gant, costly, and healthful situations for their summer res-idences.   Every part of the Hudson River is so beautiful that each inhabitant of the shore and the adjacent hills thinks his own spot the most beautiful, and he can make a very good argument in support of his opinion.   But the region that we are in, and which is in full view of the old arbor under the trees, has been made classic by the pen and the life and death of Irving, whose placid and genial humor has rendered every subject and every place that he touched immortal in the affections of his countrymen. This Tappan Sea was the terror of the early Dutch navigators, who made its perilous passage with more fear and trembling than their children feel when crossing the ocean. It is the widest portion of the river, being three or four miles. We are constantly tempted to look out on the ever-changing surface of the water. The steamboats that pass, more than hourly, enliven and diversify the view. A lady sitting by me was a passenger on the first steamer that ever disturbed the waters of the Hudson, and of course the first in the world! What changes have since come over the shores and over the world! Yet she is only —— years of age, and has seen all the progress of the country and the age since that experiment of Fulton's was made, revolutionizing the commerce and intercourse of mankind.

Those who have been on the Rhine delight to speak of its romantic beauty, its vine-clad hillsides, its castle-crowned crags, and mighty fortresses. A day on the Rhine is a lifetime picture of beauty and grandeur. But it is not patriotism alone that challenges the Rhine or any other to compete with this tranquil river in majestic scenery and picturesque effects. Long may it be before its heights are crowned with citadels, and its people fortified against their neighbors. A few miles of the Rhine are exceedingly lovely, but a day's voyage on the Hudson furnishes far more enchanting scenery, and to a dweller on its banks it spreads a perpetual feast.

And here we have pitched our tent. Strangers and pilgrims on the earth, as all our fathers were, it is well to feel that "this is not our rest." We have no continuing city, no abiding-place. Others have been in these beautiful groves. This rustic summer seat, falling into decay,

speaks of former possessors who doubtless here sat down
to stay, but the places that then knew them will know them
no more.   It may be so with us, even if the stream of life,
like this bright, clear river, should flow on these many
years.

The current of thought has been broken by a thunder-
shower that drove me to a better shelter.   The sight and
sound were another of the entertainments to which we are
invited.   For an hour or two I had been observing the
clouds in the upper bay, and around Mount Taurn they
were black with signs of a storm.   The sun was obscured,
but this was pleasant toward the close of a warm day.
Presently a sharp crack of a thunderbolt and the glare
of the lightning filled the air, and the rain came in torrents.   It was short and sweet.   The dark cloud pursued
its path down the river, its footsteps in the deep ; and
soon the sun tricked his beams and stood out in the western sky, more lustrous than before the rain.   He has just
sunk down into a bed of golden clouds, that lie on the
hills directly in front of us.   A broad belt of sunlight
stretches across the river ; the whole western firmament
is aglow ; the vessels that cross the track of the sunshine
are covered with the light of it as if they had been suddenly set on fire, and all nature at this evening hour
seems to rejoice and be glad in the beauty of its fresh
verdure, refreshed with showers.   It is very still now.
Nothing breaks in on the silence of the hour and the
scene but the murmurs of the tree-tops, and the gentle
wash of the water on the shore.

> "The time, how lovely and how still,
>   Peace shines and smiles on all below ;
> The plain, the stream, the wood, the hill—
>   All fair with evening's setting glow."

It is hard to make it real that so much calmness, peace, and beauty can be and abound in a world with evil in it. It is a beautiful world; and the true heart swells gratefully to its Maker in the midst of loveliness and glory like this. "Every prospect pleases." The earth is going to rest, and soon the voices of tired nature will be silent. But the praise of God goes up with evening hymns from all the dwellers on the river-side, and from those across the stream, and from these crowded steamers that are rushing by on their journeys. Who can be thankless in such a world, with God all around us, and a better world than this to come?

II.

THE GARDEN AND GARDENS.

It is high time that the gardens were made and the vegetables fairly on their way toward perfection. But we were so late in coming into the country that we can make no attempt this year to have things early.

While out before breakfast this morning among the roses, radishes, and cucumbers, it occurred to me that the first labor of our first parent, father Adam, was something of the same, for he was placed by his infinitely wise Creator in a garden to dress and keep it. When he awoke from one of his earliest sleeps, and found by his side a full-blown bride, he had such a vision of beauty as his eyes afterward never saw in the fairest flowers that sprang beneath his fostering hands. And when they went together to their morning work, in that Eden which the Lord made *for* them before he made them, they found it of all conceivable employments the most congenial to their innocence and purity. I believe in the garden of Eden; the tree of knowledge of good and evil; the tree of life; the serpent; the temptation; the fall that "brought death into the world, and all our woe." It is a thousand times harder to believe the miserable substitutes for the history of the Bible, than to take it as it is and admit that the greatest miracle was creation. After believing that the world was made out of nothing, it is easy enough to believe all the rest.

Out in the early morning upon the paths of nature, and communing with God in the works of his hands, it is sweet beyond expression to *feel* that the same hands which fashioned the heavens, and hung out the stars, and decked the earth with loveliness, what time the sons of God shouted for joy, made the first garden, and planted the flowers and the fruits, watered them with the rivers of his pleasure, and made for his creatures a Paradise in which he himself loved to walk in the cool of the day and converse with them, his loving children, as friend with friend. There was some wise design in this arrangement of his; and from that glad morning in which our primeval ancestors began their work to the present hour, no employment on earth has been found to combine more completely the idea of the useful and the beautiful than this, from the effect of which just now I confess some aches and pains that are hardly in harmony with that last line. But we shall get used to it shortly, and then the work will be more like play, and leave only pleasant reminders in renovated health and increasing vigor.

And since those good old times when Adam and Eve were alone in their glory of innocence and beauty, their children have in all ages spent their highest skill and strength in the embellishment of the garden. Among the wonders of the world were the hanging gardens of Babylon. With what a lavish hand did King Solomon adorn his gardens, pursuing the study and culture of plants till he knew them all, from the cedar of Lebanon to the hyssop on the wall. Yet a greater than Solomon has told us that in all his glory he was not arrayed like one of his own flowers, and that one of the most delicate —the lily. Ten years ago I was climbing up the hill of Samaria, where even now, after the rains of two thousand

years have washed its terraces, we can yet see the remains
of magnificent beauty that once environed its slopes and
crowned its summit, making it a gorgeous spectacle, probably unsurpassed by any thing on the earth in the days
of Herod the Great.   And· away on the banks of the
Bosphorus are "the Gardens of the Blessed," where the
daughters of the East, more beautiful than the flowers,
may lay aside their perpetual veils, and wander and·waste
their indolent lives.   Every city of Europe that aspires to
rank has its broad acres in public gardens for the instruction and delight of the people, where bands of music entertain them ; and to their credit let it be said that, while
thousands walk for hours among beds of tempting beauty,
not one will put forth his hand to pick a flower.   He feels
that it is his where it is ; it grows and blooms there for
his pleasure, and to pluck it would destroy his own and
others'.   This is a popular education we have not attained
in our free and enlightened country.   There is not a city
of this land where the people could have free access to
a public garden without a strict police, to see that the
sovereigns do not steal their own property.   The " Central Park" is by far the noblest public promenade in
America, resorted to already by thousands daily—yet even
here, in our great metropolis, ladies are desired not to
carry flowers into the park in their carriages, that the
police may be able to take it for granted that any one
with flowers in his hands has stolen them, and is to be
treated accordingly.   Even in our rural cemeteries, where
the flowers cover the ashes of the dead—emblems of the
loveliness and frailty that perishes below, and emblems,
too, of the beauty of the love that cherishes the memory
of the departed—even here our fair countrywomen—not to
say the men, of course—will steal flowers.

In the city of Florence, the fairest city in beautiful Italy, the city of art and song, some of the masterpieces of the great masters of sculpture, such as the David of Michael Angelo, stand out in the open street, exposed to the hazards of accident or to wanton recklessness; yet there for centuries may stand the delicate marble that a stone from the hand of a rude boy would mar forever, and yet it is safe as in the halls of the Pitti Palace itself. Universal homage protects these memorials that genius has left for posterity to cherish and admire. In a little village, the name of which is so obscure that I have forgotten it, the "Common" was a beautiful garden surrounded by numerous marble statues of poets and artists and patriots, evidences of the spirit and taste of the people who thus delighted to adorn their rural neighborhood.

On the banks of Lake Como, in Northern Italy, there are hundreds of palaces, the abodes of men and women of wealth and genius and fame, some of them artists, others celebrated singers, and others whose riches have come down to them by inheritance, and these people or their predecessors have made the shores of this enchanting lake a garden, or gardens, of surpassing splendor. You may stop, almost at random, and be charmed with the scenes of loveliness that meet your eyes as soon as you step ashore. And instead of being warned off by a sign-board that "all persons are forbid trespassing on these grounds," you are kindly admitted through the hospitable gates, and permitted to enjoy at your leisure the feast of beauty that is here spread at your feet. One of these gardens is around a hill—a steep and high hill— terraced from the sole of its foot to the crown of its head; and each successive terrace is adorned with flowers and plants in luxuriant growth, representing different climes,

B

so that the visitor, as he walked around and gradually ascended the hill, was cheated with the illusion that he was reaching a colder and still colder region as he climbs. Toward the summit the hill is pierced with a tunnel three hundred feet long, and wide enough for a coach to be driven through; the path is curved like a rainbow, and standing in the centre of it, you can look out both ways on lakes that lie on opposite sides of this remarkable garden hill. And this splendid spot, on which wealth is freely lavished with taste and toil, belongs to a gentleman whose duties in the army keep him almost constantly from home, and he rarely visits the place on which he expends his ancestral treasure ; but he freely allows it to be thrown open to travelers, who delight to carry away with them recollections of its beauty, and liberality of its princely proprietor.

No memories of England are more delightful than those of her parks and gardens ; art has made castles and cathedrals and libraries, and yet art has no power to please like that of nature in the hands of art. We have a vivid idea of Westminster Abbey before seeing it, but Chatsworth is a world of whose existence we have no conception till its cultivated grounds are all around us.

III.

THE ROSES.

JUST now there are at least a thousand, perhaps two thousand roses in full bloom in sight as I sit on an old tumbledown settee under a tree in the midst of the garden. They are of all known colors for roses, and their names are far beyond my attainments in the science of flowers. Beautiful exceedingly, we can repeat again and again as we look at them, but even as we look they are passing away. Beauty soon decays. And this led me off into a meditative ramble on the old question of the distinction between the useful and the beautiful, as if beauty were not useful, and the useful necessarily not beautiful. And it occurred to me that there is another question to be answered first, on the answer depending the result to which we shall come in looking after the comparative merits of cabbage-roses and cabbages.

If we live to eat, and that is most to be desired which gives us food; if we live to dress, and that is best that yields us clothes, we shall very soon have a standard by which to measure the value of every thing within our reach. But by so much as the inner life is more than the visible, and the enjoyment and advancement of the soul more to be desired than the lust of the flesh or the pride of life, so is the gratification, the cultivation, and perfection of the higher tastes to be esteemed of more account than those which man has in common with the brutes that perish.

Horne Tooke defined virtue to be any thing that answers its purpose—certainly a very low and disgusting conception of the term. But we may say that every thing beautiful is or ought to be useful, and if it is not so, it is either neglected or abused. Because more than one half of the world go through it without a thought of the charms with which its face is clothed, we often fall into the mistake of thinking that beauty is thrown away on them, and reserved only for those whose eyes have been anointed by culture or association. But when I was in New York a few days ago, in a part of it where poverty alone would be content to dwell, and the last place in the city where one would look for taste and beauty, I saw the third-story windows of one of the houses filled with pots of flowers, set out on the sills to catch the sweet influences of the spring-time sun, and it was pleasing to reflect that up in those small, unventilated rooms, where the poor women must spend the whole year and never once get out into the country to enjoy such a wealth of floral beauty as this sweet June unfolds, they can and will have their few pet flowers, on which to lavish their affectionate care, and get the return that beauty gives to its humblest lover. Coleridge was admiring a waterfall, and overheard a man near him who said "Majestic." The poet turned to him, and said, "That is the very word." "Yes," continued the admiring rustic, "it is jest the purtiest, majesticest thing I ever seed." He had the soul to admire and enjoy it, but rhetoric was not his forte. One of our greatest heroes and statesmen had been neglected in the days of his youth, and he never recovered from the effects of such neglect. Some of his words were quite as peculiar as Mrs. Partington's. Yet he loved flowers and had a glorious garden, in which he was walking one day with a friend who admired its splendor, and said to him, "You have a fine taste for horticulture." "Oh yes," said he, "I was always fond of horses."

The ox looks out on a green meadow and admires it as it is good for food. Is he any better than an ox who sees in a rose only what it will bring in market? Beauty certainly has higher uses than to enrich its owner. The value we set on a painting or a statue has no relation to the price it will bring, unless we are in the "picture line." I was looking the other day at a painting—a single portrait —that the owner will not sell for $10,000. Mr. Church painted his last Niagara, the "Under the Fall," in six hours, from the white canvas to the last touch. I was unwilling to believe it, till he told me so himself. Mr. Roberts, the liberal gentleman for whom it was painted, gave him $1500 for it. The amount of time and labor expended seems to be in no proper proportion to the price paid; but the possessor has value in it far beyond the money that he parted with to secure such a "thing of beauty" for himself and friends. Every body can not have Niagara or a Church's painting of it. When an American lady was visiting England a few years ago, she was asked "if she had seen Niagara Falls." "Oh, certainly," said she, "I *own* them." She was, indeed, one of the owners —Miss Porter of Niagara. But if we can not own all the beauty and glory in the world around us, we may enjoy it, and so make all the earth our own. The possession of it sometimes poisons the enjoyment. Lady Coventry was so proud of her beauty that she always sat with her mirror In hand; when sickness made ravages in her charms, she had her windows darkened, that the wrinkles might not be so palpable; and when she grew worse, she received her food and medicine through the closed curtains of her couch, refusing to be seen even by her most intimate friends—and so she died! This is the madness of beauty, of which we have another example in the case of a young lady who admired her own beauty so much that she could not believe it possible for her to die, and when she was wasting away with consumption, she had a mirror always before her that she might delight herself in the charms that were fading from all eyes but her own. She died raving mad because she must die.

The love of beauty is not a fault. The love of being admired is not a fault. God himself, all holy and the perfection of beauty, loves to be admired in and by his saints. And in the ranks of all his sentient beings, how far down we can not say, this love reigns, a common, perhaps universal law of being. Some plants shrink from the touch, and we call them sensitive; and these flowers seem to smile in the morning sunlight as if they took delight in the beauty with which the hand of God has clothed them. The love of the beautiful is a virtue; it is useful in itself; it makes a people more gentle, refined, courteous, and happy. It is to be encouraged, stimulated, and developed.

It is a good, but not *to kalon, the* good—not the highest good. It may exist, and it has been, in the midst of the lowest moral debasement. The love of the beautiful in nature and art never flourished more luxuriantly in Greece and Italy than in the days of their vilest corruption and degeneracy. Kritobulus at one of the banquets of Xenophon said: "By the gods, I would rather be beautiful than be King of Persia." And a modern writer says that "the four things most desirable as a crown to the happiness of life are beauty, riches, health, and friends;" placing beauty at the head of the list. I would reverse the order precisely, and first ask friends, then health, then wealth, and then beauty. Before all these, of course, a right mind would have One Friend, and if the rest were added, what more could heart desire! If we put beauty last, it is because it is the crown and glory of all the rest. Hence, woman was made last, and the last becomes first. Anacreon sings of woman endowed with beauty, in which she is stronger than lions or men. Beauty in nature is woman in creation. Our sweetest Christian poet, in his "World before the Flood," recounts the work of creation, day by day, and in language of high poetic fancy speaks of the several parts of the work as done by the various energies or faculties of the Creator: thus He *looked*, and "sun and stars came forth to meet his eye." And last of all when he comes to the creation of WOMAN, the poet says:

"He made her with a smile of grace,
And left the smile that made her, on her face."

Thus beauty is the smile of the Lord; the charm of being; the fertile garden in the desert of life. We might live without it, and so we might live if we were blind. But what the earth now is to the blind, it would be to all if nothing grew but what is good to eat or wear. If "that reforming ass" who wished to "take down the sun and light the world with gas" were to root out all flowers in the pathway of life, and plant it with corn, he would prove his wisdom by the length of his ears.

IV.

THE BIRDS.

OUR daily and constant companions, as we sit under the trees, are the birds in the boughs overhead. I have tried several times to reckon the number and varieties of feathered songsters who are part and parcel of the household. We allow no gun to be fired on the premises, no bird to be disturbed in the pursuit of an honest living, or in the care of his own family, and consequently the birds are very familiar and abundant. Besides the sparrows, cedar-birds, yellow-birds, orioles, robins, phœbes, wrens, thrushes, quails, and larks, we have the mocking-birds in great numbers, whose music is wonderful for its sweetness and variety; misleading us often into the idea that the various tribes have gathered about us to give a grand concert, the finest singers having "volunteered their services for this occasion." But after watching to see as well as to hear, we find that most of the music comes from the mocking-birds, whose skill is so remarkable as to deceive the best ear. It becomes a curious question, Why do the birds sing? Have they themselves a musical ear, an organization peculiarly favorable to the enjoyment of song?

It is mentioned in an interesting work, entitled "Miscellanea Curiosa," that Mr. Clayton and Dr. Maudlin discovered a remarkable peculiarity in the structure of the ears of birds, particularly those distinguished for their

song.   Contrary to what takes place in man or in quadrupeds, there is in birds almost a direct passage from one
ear to the other, so that, if the drum of both ears be pricked,
water will pass, when poured in, from one ear to the other.
There is, however, no cochlea, but a small cochlea passage, which opens into a large cavity, formed between the
two bony plates of the skull, and this passes all round the
head.   The upper and external plate of the bone forming
the skull is supported by many hundreds of small thread-
like pillars or columns, which rest upon the lower and
interior plate, immediately over the brain.   Now, what is
worthy of attention is that this passage between the outer
and inner plates of the skull was observed to be strikingly
larger in song-birds than in birds which are not possessed
of musical powers.   So very remarkable is this difference
described to be, that any person to whom it has been
once pointed out may readily pronounce, upon inspecting
the skull of a bird, whether it was a bird of song or otherwise, though he might have no previous knowledge of the
bird or its habits.   No other animal, examined with a view
to comparison in these particulars, was found to have any
resemblance of conformation, except the mole—an animal
reputed to be very quick of hearing.   This singular construction of the skull in birds is evidently conformable to
the known principles of acoustics, and is, in fact, a sort
of whispering gallery for increasing the intensity of the
sounds conveyed to the ear.

It would be worthy of the investigation of anatomists
to endeavor to ascertain whether the skulls of celebrated
musicians have a greater interval between the outer and
inner tables than the skulls of those who are deficient in
musical ears.

The inference to be drawn from these facts would be

that birds, whose music is far more exquisite than that of the human voice, and therefore far beyond any instrument of human contrivance, have joy in their songs even more keen and perhaps exalted than we who sit under the trees, and imagine that they are making music for our delight. We have read of a canary-bird that sang itself to death. Birds often die of apoplexy, overtasking their energies, or exposing themselves to the sun.   There is something very like human nature in the birds.   They have warm and tender affections.   Mrs. Monteath's poem, in which she tells of the death of two doves who could not survive the death of a favorite child, is one of the most touching and beautiful things in the language.   A solitary gentleman, whose principal delight it had been to observe the conduct of animals, gives the following account of the affection of two birds:

"They were a species of paroquet called guinea sparrows, and were confined in a square cage.   The cup which contained their food was placed in the bottom of the cage. The male was almost continually seated on the same perch with the female.   They sat close together, and viewed each other from time to time with evident tenderness.   If they separated, it was but for a few moments, for they hastened to return and place themselves near to each other.   They often appeared to engage in a kind of conversation, which they continued for some time, and seemed to answer each other, varying their sounds, and elevating and lowering their notes.   Sometimes they seemed to quarrel, but their disagreements were of momentary duration, and succeeded by additional tenderness.   The happy pair thus passed four years in a climate greatly different from that in which they had before lived.   At the end of that time the female fell into a state of languor, which had all the appearance of old age. Her legs swelled, and it was no longer possible that she could go to take her food. But the male, ever attentive and alert in whatever concerned her, brought it in his bill and emptied it into hers. He was in this manner her most vigilant purveyor during the space of four months. The infirmities of his companion increased daily. Becoming unable at last to sit upon the perch, she remained crouch- ed at the bottom of the cage, and from time to time made a few ineffectual efforts to regain the lowest perch. The male seconded her feeble efforts with all his power. Sometimes he seized with his bill the upper part of her wing, by way of drawing her to him ; sometimes he took her by the bill, and endeavored to raise her up, repeat- ing these efforts many times. His motions, his gestures, his continual solicitude, expressed an ardent desire to aid the weakness of his companion, and to alleviate her suf- ferings. But the spectacle became still more interesting, and even touching, when the female was on the point of expiring. The unhappy male went ceaselessly round and round his mate, and redoubled his assiduities and tender cares. He tried to open her bill, designing to give her some nourishment. His emotion increased every instant. He paced and repaced the cage with the greatest agita- tion, and at intervals uttered the most plaintive cries. At other times he fixed his eyes upon her, and preserved the most sorrowful silence. It was impossible to mistake these expressions of grief and despair. His faithful com- panion at last expired. From that time he himself lan- guished, and survived her but a few months."

We know less of the habits of birds than of almost any other animals, because they are generally out of sight, though very near us. Only one man ever lived

who had the patience, perseverance, and fortitude to study
the ways of the birds. He has left a name that will always be associated with them, and with this region of the
Hudson River. While the upper part of the island of
Manhattan was almost a wilderness, he came to the spot
which is now known by his name on Washington Heights,
and there cleared away some of the forest, and built a
house which still stands in the midst of " Audubon Park."
The city is rapidly crowding in and around it; but the
park holds its own, and the birds hold their own in its
venerable trees and in the forest cemetery adjoining,
where lie the bones of John James Audubon. He was
born of French parents, near New Orleans, in 1780. His
father, an enthusiast for liberty, was with Washington at
Valley Forge; and the Audubon family still possess the
portraits of both, painted in the camp; that of Washington being the first ever taken of him.

"At a very early age, Audubon was sent to France,
and educated in art and science under the best masters,
among whom was David. The love of birds, which became the passion of his life, manifested itself in infancy;
and when he returned from France he betook himself to
his native woods, and began a collection of drawings
which made the germ of 'The Birds of America.' His
father gave him a plantation on the rich banks of the
Schuylkill; and luxury and fortune offered their bland-
ishments to wean him from his love of adventure. But
his heart was in the forest; and in 1810, with a young
wife, an infant son, and his unfailing rifle, he embarked
in an open skiff on the Ohio to find a new home. The
mellow lights and shadows of our Indian summer had
fallen along the shores of that queen of rivers. At long
intervals the axe of the squatter was beginning to disturb

the solemn reign of nature. He settled in Kentucky, and in the central region of that vast valley through which the Mississippi rolls on to the sea he pursued his studies and roamings. He has spent more years in the forests than most men live.

"Among the great lakes of the North, he saw beyond the reach of his rifle a strange, gigantic bird sweeping over the waters. He hunted for that bird ten years, and found it again three thousand miles from the spot where he first saw it. Meanwhile he had been chilled with eternal frosts, and burned with perpetual heats. He slept many nights across branches of trees, waked by panther screams; and many nights he passed in cane-brakes, where he did not dare to sleep. He saw the knife of the savage whetted for him; stepped on venomous serpents; started the cougar from his secret lair; swam swollen streams with his gun, ammunition, drawings, and journals lashed on his head; on equatorial rivers alligators stared at him as he landed; in polar regions the water turned to ice as it fell from his benumbed limbs when he struck the bank; his tongue was parched with thirst on deserts, and he laid himself down famishing to wait, like Elijah, till he was fed by the birds of heaven. This was his history during the life of a generation. And yet, through this long period of peril and suffering, which Cæsar would not have borne to have heard the tramp of his legions in three quarters of the globe, his courage never failed, his love for nature never cooled, his reverence for God— whose illimitable universe he was exploring—deepened the longer he gazed. Nor did he lose a throb of humane feeling for civilized men, from whose habitations he had exiled himself."

Such was the man whose "Birds of America" are the

memorials of his enthusiasm and heroism. His wander-,
ings over, he came here to the banks of our own river,
and with that devoted wife who started with him on his
pilgrimages he spent the evening of his eventful life, and
died in 1851. She still survives him, an elegant, accomplished lady, ninety years of age, more active in all the
duties and enjoyments of life, in walks of charity and usefulness, than thousands of the young ladies of our day.
She is a model of the virtues and graces that adorn her
sex.

When a copy of the " Birds of America " was received
by the Royal Academy of Sciences of Paris, Baron Cu-
vier said, " It is the most magnificent monument which
art has ever raised to ornithology."

Four beautiful brown birds, each with a top-knot on his
head, are sitting on a tree close by me, and flooding the
grove with their rich melodies. I do not know them
even by name. But if I had " Audubon's Birds of America," I should find them colored to the life.

V.

INSECT LIFE.

You can not live under the trees without a "realizing sense" of the variety and wealth of life besides your own. Just now an eagle came to us from the rocky palisades across the river, or perhaps he had wandered from the Highlands above us—a majestic bird; he soared over and near us for a few moments, and then took his way slowly to the North, leaving our birds to the enjoyment of the quiet he had disturbed. And he was no more to them than they are to the millions of insects that swarm in the leaves, and the air, and the earth we tread. For

> "As naturalists observe, a flea
> Has smaller fleas on him that prey,
> And these have smaller still to bite 'em,
> And so proceed *ad infinitum*."

The flight and fright of the birds when the eagle comes near, and the gathering of the chickens under the mother-hen when the hawk appears, remind us of the fact that multitudes of the tribes of animals live on one another, the work of destruction going on so constantly that the world would be depopulated if the arrangements of Nature for re-supply were not ample to meet all the losses. The fish multiply rapidly in the little pond at the foot of the lawn, yet the little ones are devoured by the larger, and millions of eggs are eaten up almost as soon as they are laid. The birds that farmers and gardeners make

war upon, and would gladly exterminate because they eat
a share of the fruit, are the fell destroyers of myriads of
insects and worms that would doubtless be far more de-
structive of the good things we wish to preserve for our
own use. Every thing has its use. Some things, if they
have any good in them, have a very poor way of showing
it. What these rose-bugs are made for, at least what useful purpose they answer, is far beyond me to imagine.
They come in troops, a flying artillery, charge upon one
bed of roses, and, like the locusts of Egypt, devastate the
whole, and then pass on to another. Beauty perishes before them. The flower of the field, the pride of the garden, the hopes of bouquets to come, fade as they approach.
It requires a large amount of perseverance to destroy
them, and more patience to submit to their ravages.

What on earth, or rather under the earth, does the
ground-mole live for? Blind to all the utilities of walks
or beds, he pursues his subterranean route of ruin, so silently, so obscurely, so rapidly, that the work of destruction is done before the presence of the enemy is suspected. "Wherefore do the wicked live?" is a question asked of old ; and we may inquire, and in vain, why moles
and rose-bugs, to say nothing of curculio, the weevil, the
musquito, have their existence in such a beautiful world
as this? Are they part of the curse under which creation
groans, waiting to be delivered? And will there be any
musquitoes in the millennium? For however we may assure ourselves that every thing is made for some useful
purpose, and therefore ought to be regarded with a sort
of complacency, even when we can see no good of it now,
there is no one who does not wish for that "good time
coming," when not only the lion and the lamb will lie
down together, but musquitoes will cease to bite. Hap-

pily we are free from this curse here, if it be one ; but I speak with a deep sense of the evil, from the memory of summers spent in a place where musquitoes most do congregate ; where living is cheap, but the musquitoes sent in their bills, so many and so long that we were glad to escape, with the loss of some blood, to a land of pure delight, where these disturbers do not bite nor give us songs in the night. Yet they are only the small annoyances of life. They are tests and trials of one's patience. If properly borne, they are as good for the temper as Spanish flies for a blister. Learning to bear the ills they bring, we may be fitted to bear the many greater ills that flesh is heir to, and so musquitoes may prove to be a blessing, not indeed in disguise, but a friend instead of a foe.

We have been more interested in the ant race than in any other of the insect tribes that abound. It is even more difficult to study them than Audubon found it to learn the habits of birds. They have the family and community system with a general government, more thoroughly established than any other tribe except the bees, whom they resemble in many of their habits. The system of slavery prevails among them, under some mild and wholesome laws that might with advantage be imitated by the human race where that unhappy system prevails. The workers or servants perform all the hard service of the family, while the winged heads of the household live in idleness quite unworthy of the name that has been a synonym in all ages for industry. Indeed these idle ants are often disposed to leave the premises, but the workers who have no wings keep watch of them, and bring them back to their duty of presiding over the establishment. Curiously wrought beneath the surface of the earth is the house in which these little creatures live, with galleries connecting various apartments, stored with food collected by the servant class, and fitted to survive the ruin that often overtakes the little mound or portico on the surface that is only an entrance to the palace below. Here they have their "insect life," perhaps more perfectly domesticated than any other of the many families into which the animal creation is subdivided. They have a rapid mode of exchanging "ideas," if that is the word by which to designate their mental operations; and the evidences of their capacity to adapt means to ends is far ahead of many more exalted races. Their sense of smell is very acute, and by it they are guided to distant places for food, and led back on the same trail to the little home they are bound to supply. If each ant in these myriads have his own house to care for, and the family relation is preserved, as it is among birds, the organization must be very perfect to enable them to distinguish each other and their respective dwellings. The discipline is perfect, under a monarchical form of government, administered by a queen, whom the workers carry on their shoulders from room to room, and to whom they yield the most profound respect and obedience.

These are the lowest forms of life that we can study with much success, without some aid to the naked eye. But take the microscope, and worlds of new life and beauty are unfolded within and beneath the humblest insect that flies or creeps. The atmosphere swarms with animals where we do not suspect it; and huge monsters play in the crystal water. The wisest of men has said, "Go to the ant, thou sluggard, consider her ways and be wise;" and even if I were lazier to-day than usual—for it is the hottest day in many weeks past—I would not have

far to go to get the lesson of wisdom which Solomon rec-
ommended; for as I was coming out to this rude writ-
ing-chair under the trees, I passed and paused to admire
a huge hillock, a dwelling-place for ants, who were running in and out, a busy race, within whose city no man's
eye has seen, though in all ages their habits have been
studied by thoughtful men.   These ants are not so great
as those mentioned by Herodotus and Pliny, which were
" not so large as a dog, but bigger than a fox."   Some
other early writers speak of ants that rival the wolf in
size, the dog in shape, the lion in its feet, the leopard in
its skin, and from whose fury the Indian has to fly on the
back of a camel.   That must be an exaggeration.

Within this heap of sand is a miniature house of many
mansions or apartments: yes, many houses, a village with
streets and galleries, which the workers of these tribes
have toilfully and skillfully excavated with their little
mouths.   They have made mortar by moistening clay
with rain drops, they have used grass covered with this
paste for columns and arches and roofing.   Others pene-
trate a tree and there hew out a home, with walls as thin
as paper, separating the residences of the several inhabitants.   They paint these walls black sometimes; others
leave them the color of the wood.   Froebel, in his " Travels in Central America;" tells of a species of ants in New
Mexico who construct their nests exclusively of small
stones of one kind, chosen by the insects from the sand
of the steppes and deserts; in one part these heaps were
formed of small fragments of crystallized feldspars; and
in another imperfect crystals of red transparent garnet
were the materials of which the ant-hills were built, and
any quantity of them might there be obtained.

In Southern Africa the ants raise solid nests of clay,

shaped like a baker's oven. The Caffrès, when first permitted to settle here, converted these nests into ovens.
Having expelled the ants by smoke, they scooped out the
nests, leaving the crust a few inches thick, and then used
them for baking their loaves.

"Another African species is described by the Rev.
Lansdown Guilding as 'parasol ants.' 'In Trinidad,' he
says, 'we may see marching legions of these creatures
with leaves elevated over their heads, like a London crowd
on a rainy day following the Lord Mayor's show with innumerable umbrellas; or, rather, as they observe the order and decorum which the crowd despise, they represent,
on a Liliputian scale, with their leafy screens, the enemies of Macbeth descending from 'Birnam Wood to Dun-
sinane.' These leaves are, however, probably collected
to cover their nests rather than to 'shadow the number
of their host.'

"Madame Meriam describes the 'visitation ants' of
Surinam, which appear only at certain seasons, or about
once in two or three years. These multitudes receive a
cheerful welcome from the natives, who throw open the
doors of their houses, when the ants enter, traverse every
part of their dwellings, and, after destroying all the vermin
secreted therein, take their departure.

"Dr. Poeppig described the ants of Peru as most numerous in the Lower Andes: they are from an inch in
size, and of all colors between yellow and black. In the
huts only are seven different species, and in the woods
of Pampayaes six-and-twenty species. One of the very
useful kinds, which does not attack man unless provoked,
is the Peruvian wandering ant, which comes in endless
swarms from the wilderness, where it again vanishes; it
is not unwelcome, because it does no injury to the plan-

tations, but destroys innumerable pernicious insects of other kinds, and even amphibious animals and small quadrupeds. 'Of these ants,' says Dr. Poeppig, 'the broad columns go forward, disregarding every obstacle, and millions march close together in a swarm that takes hours in passing; while on both sides the warriors, distinguished by their size and color, move busily backward and forward, ready for defense, and likewise employed in looking for and attacking·animals which·are so unfortunate as to be unable to escape, either by force or by rapid flight. If they approach a house, the owner readily opens every part, and goes away; and all noxious vermin that may have taken up their abode in the roof of palm-leaves, the insects and larvæ, are destroyed, or compelled to seek safety in flight. The most secret recesses of the huts do not escape their search, and the animal that waits for their arrival is infallibly lost. They even, as the natives affirm, overpower large snakes, for the warriors form a circle round the reptile while basking in the sun. On perceiving its enemies, it endeavors to escape, but in vain; for six or more of them have fixed themselves upon it, and, while the tortured animal endeavors to relieve itself by a simple turn, the number of its foes is increased a hundredfold. Thousands of the smaller ants from the main column hasten up, and, in spite of the writhings of the snake, wound it in innumerable places, and in a few hours nothing remains of it but a clean skeleton."

But I am much more interested in the ants that live under the trees with me than in their cousins of Peru or Trinidad. Here they are a very orderly community, with laws and government, perhaps, in common with all the tribes of ants the world over. I have never seen them milking the aphides, or slugs, that infest the leaves of trees, but Linnæus says they do. I have seen them often carrying their food into their granaries, though some learned ant-writers affirm that they do not lay up stores for the winter, but lie dormant in cold weather. That they have foresight enough to provide beforehand food for rainy days when they can not work is very plain from what we see them doing daily.

The accounts of the wars and expeditions of ants read like pages of man's history. "Ants of different species assail one another in their foraging excursions; and pitched battles are fought between the colonist ants. Huber describes thousands of combatants thus engaged, with great carnage; and a naturalist has seen fifty wood ants fighting within a few inches' area of what were supposed to be the boundaries of their several territories. Their bite is so sharp, and the acrid juice which they infuse is so deleterious, that many are thus disabled or killed outright. Huber also describes the exploits of the warrior ants, which almost exceed belief; but in 1832 such accounts were verified in the Black Forest and in Switzerland; with respect to the 'Amazon ant,' and on the Rhine as to the 'sanguinary ant.' Both these species make war on the ants of other species, particularly the 'dusky ant,' not for mere fighting, but to make slaves of the vanquished, to do the drudgery of the conquerors' ant-home. They are as cunning as diplomatists: they do not capture the adult ants, and carry them into slavery, but make booty of their eggs and cocoons, which, after the contest is decided—and the warriors are always conquerors—are carried off to the Amazonian citadel, and being hatched there, the poor slaves are probably not aware that it is not their native colony. Huber testifies to such expeditions for capturing slaves; and a living naturalist witnessed, in a great number of instances, the slaves at work for the victorious captors."

It fills me with wonder to think that under the surface of the earth we tread there is a miniature world of life and motion, *so like our world*, where there is no speech nor language that we can understand, but where there is certainly thought and purpose, the adaptation of means to ends, and a display of skill that no human ingenuity can approach.

Yesterday I was studying the far-down depths of animal life with the aid of a microscope, that brought into view the active operations of a living creature in the sap of a bit of grass. Its motions as it turned a wheel to draw up its food were so *natural,* it was hard to believe we must have a glass to magnify the object six hundred times to bring this infinitesimal being within the reach of mortal eye. And so it is with the whole world below us. There is a distance down as far and as densely peopled with sentient inhabitants as there is above us. Indeed, the angels are not farther removed from man than this animalcule, and, physically considered, they are perhaps nearer. Such lessons we learn from ant-hills : at least we began with one of them, and have ended with the angels.

VI.

SUNSHINE.

THE trees clap their hands to-day. The rocks and hills, the green grass in the meadows and the silent river, are all vocal and musical with praise. It is as if the spring-time had suddenly leaped out of the bosom of winter, in its beauty of leaves and flowers, with songs of birds and glad warmth of summer.

There is great power in sunshine. It is life for plants and life for animals. There are some of both, doubtless, who can live in the dark, but nature loves light. Put a plant in a dark room, and then admit a single beam of light into it, and the plant will grow toward it, twisting itself out of shape for the sake of getting into the little gleam of sunshine. Some of these apple-trees are one-sided because the forest trees have overshadowed them, and, instead of growing up and extending their branches symmetrically as they should, they creep out laterally to get into the sun. The question often comes up for consideration, Shall we cut down the trees to let in the sun, or keep the trees and live in the shade? We compromise the matter, and have a fair proportion of both, just like life itself. And there is this analogy too, that you may have whichever you choose to make for yourself. Plant trees and you have shade. Cut them down and the sun will come in. It is just as easy, and indeed much easier to regulate this matter in the house and in the heart. It may not be well for us to have sunshine always. It is wisely arranged that night follows the day in regular succession. It would be tedious to have daylight always. Providence is very kind in ordering it, that this change shall give us just what we need for rest and labor. So all things are adapted to each other, just as this green of the trees and grass is a color that suits the eye better than any other : it was made for the eye, or the eye was made for the color, it is no matter which. The change from sunlight to darkness is a type of the change that most of us find in our daily experience of life. Few if any are always in the light. The days of darkness are many. It is good for us, doubtless, that the sun is not always shining.

But too much shade sours and kills us. There is far more of this in the world than there ought to be. It is very much as one pleases, whether he will be gloomy or glad. One man will make perpetual sunshine wherever he goes or stays. Another will carry a pall with him, and spread it over the faces and spirits of every company he enters. And this is more true of the family than of society.

There is my old friend Longface. He is never pleased with any thing that any body says or does, or if he is pleased, he has a way of hiding his pleasure that makes his family feel that he is out of humor all the time. The breakfast is late, and it does not suit him when it is ready. He meets his children without a smile or a word of morning welcome, and leaves them to go to his business as if he had no interest in what was to be their business through the day. Longface has no small change to pass among his acquaintances in the street or in the market. A stranger would suppose there had been a death in his

family, or his business matters were in disorder, he looks
so glum when all around him is so cheery. Longface
seldom speaks but to grumble. He finds faults where
there are none, and speaks of faults that do really exist,
when other people would say nothing of them. For it is
making matters worse to be talking about troubles, unless
talking will cure or help them. But Longface never sees
a bright side to any thing, because he is in the shade, and
no sun shines on any thing he sees. If there is a bright
side, he turns away from it as if the sun hurt his eyes.
It is hard to say whether Longface have any sunshine in
his heart or not ; if he have, it never comes to the surface,
and his wife and children, who ought to feel it and see it,
have never had a glimpse of it playing around them.
They do not know any reason why he should not be a
happy man; but if he is happy, he takes a droll way to
show it, or, rather, he never shows it.

Of quite another pattern is my neighbor Blithe. He
rises with the lark, and has a heart as full of praise. All
things work for good with him, and his principle is to
make the best of every thing. In the house, at the table,
and in the evening circle, he is always cheerful, and his
sunny smile and pleasant words make good cheer continually. He thinks no ill of any one, or, if he do think so,
he keeps it to himself. Every one loves Blithe, and a
few such men would make the neighborhood a joy in all
this part of the earth. I wish he would go about as a
sort of missionary, not to tell people any thing, but to
show them how to make the world happier and better by
the power of their own cheerful living. In the best of
times, and under the most favorable circumstances, we
shall have clouds and storms, and cold, damp northeast
winds enough in this world, without any artificial means

to make uncomfortable weather. And there is plenty of trouble, vexation, disappointment, and loss to try the faith and patience of Job, or any other man of patience, without our adding to the stock by our own sulks and selfishness. When Lady Raffles, in India, was smitten by the death of a favorite child, she shut herself up in a dark room and refused to be comforted. A native servant woman rebuked her ingratitude and repining, and said, "You have been here many days shut up in the dark— for shame!—leave off weeping, and let me open a window." That was good counsel. Open the window. Let in the sunshine. It is good for plants and good for people; good for them in health and sickness, in sorrow and joy. Children ought to be in sunlight every day. The nursery should be the sunniest room in the house. It is not healthful to keep the little ones in a room where the sun does not shine directly. I love to sit under these trees and write while the warm sun is above them and me, and its beams are falling and lying all around in a wealth of glory. I know my favorite poet has said,

> "The sun is but a spark of fire,
> A transient meteor in the sky."

But he is God's great dispenser of light and warmth; a giver of good to every son and daughter of man; a fountain of blessing to every leaf and flower and herb, the source of life to animated nature; and I wonder not that Persian pagans paid divine honors to him who is the brightest manifestation to their eyes of the Infinite God.

VII.

SHOWERS.

SUCH a day as this for sunshine and showers we do not remember, and our out-of-door habits make us mindful of remarkable days. We have had so much rain lately that the seeds, rotting in the ground, have failed to come up as they were expected. And we could readily have dispensed with these showers to-day. Indeed, according to our way of thinking, this weather was not wanted at all; but we have long since learned that the Lord of the Harvest has a much better idea of what is best for the crops and the people than we have, and so we trust Him to take care of the weather. We have never yet attained to the contentment of the shepherd who said the weather would be just such as pleased him, because whatever pleased the Lord would please him. But we have found that there is no good in fretting about weather or any thing else. It will neither rain nor shine more or less for any thing we can say or do. Fretting only wears out the soul and body both, while the seasons come and go without regard to our impatience.

If we had no rain till all were agreed to have it, the ground would go dry. Even a drought would not make the people unanimous as to time or quantity. When his congregation wanted Pastor Jones to pray for rain, he told them he could have it whenever they were agreed as to the time. One farmer had his hay out, and it would be bad for him if it rained to-morrow; and another would be very much put out by wet weather the next day; and so it went on, until it was found that unanimity was out of the question.

A traveling preacher on his journey called at a cottage where the good woman entertained him with dinner; and when he asked a blessing, she inquired if he were a minister. He told her he was, and a Methodist. She said her little garden was nearly perishing for want of rain, and she wished he would pray for it. He did so, and went his way. Soon the heavens gathered blackness, and a terrific shower came down, washing her garden so badly that she suffered more by the freshet than the drought. "There," she said, "that's just like those Methodists: they never can do any thing in moderation." We must learn to take things as they come. Our way is not always the best way, and never is unless it is God's way also; and we may be very sure when we have a plan or purpose or an expectation that fails, there is some wise and good end to be answered, for the Lord makes no mistakes, and his love never fails. It seems to me that my Lima beans are to be a total failure, they are so slow in coming; and when I have tried to look into the root of the difficulty by disinterring some of the seed long buried, it proves to be rotting instead of germinating. But there is yet time to plant again; and I reckon that the future of the season will be so favorable to the growth of the garden that we shall have a fair supply. Even if we do not, there will be something else abundant.

For after these showers there will be warm, sunny days, in which vegetation will rush on apace. Rainy days are reckoned dark, sad days, and they are apt emblems of the sorrows we suffer, emblems in more ways than one.

The skies weep, and so do we. But weeping endures for a night, and joy comes in the morning. These showers are good for the earth, and our tears are good for the heart. Out of the depths of sorrow spring up the fruits of holy peace and solid comfort, such as they never know who have not mourned. Some good people—real Christians, no doubt—have long spells of bad weather, in which they suffer deep spiritual depression, losing all enjoyment in divine things, and seem to be shut out from the sunshine of their Father's face. There is very little of this experience on record in the Bible. David was often in deep water, all the waves and billows went over him. But the cause was some obvious sin into which he had fallen. Modern saints are often under a cloud, and sin probably makes the cloud; but the sin is so concealed even from themselves that they do not know what it is. Dyspepsia is a great foe to grace. It darkens the sky and shakes the hope of many Christians, sometimes sinks them into despair. They think the trouble is in their hearts, when it is in their stomachs. It was always strange to me that David Brainerd was so miserable, so long and often. Dr. Payson had awful times of spiritual darkness and distress. The sweet poet Cowper was a wretched victim of religious melancholy; and after one of his worst attacks, he wrote—

> "Ye fearful saints, fresh courage take;
> The clouds ye so much dread
> Are big with mercy and will break
> In blessings on your head."

Perhaps the causes were more physical than moral. God never sends his children into the dark. They go there, and weep and fast and pray; but He would have them in the light of his countenance, rejoicing always before him.

The sorrows of the good are the same that other men have. Sickness, death, care, disappointment, break in on the enjoyment of the saint, and he sits under a cloud, and the storm beats on him, and the clouds return after the rain, as they have done all this day. One trouble follows on the heels of another. But the sun is shining behind the cloud; there is a "silver lining" to it, and by-and-by the light will burst out in beauty and great glory, and the afflicted one will rejoice that he has been afflicted.

And so we will wait patiently till this wet weather passes by. It will be all right in a day or two, and very likely we shall be wise enough to see that it is better so than otherwise.

VIII.

BUGS.

WALKING under the trees, I found in the path a robin partially under the ground. He had not been drawn into a hole, but the earth had been removed from underneath him, and his head and wings and tail were resting on the walk. I examined him, and finding him dead, and evidently in the hands of some animal who designed to make use of him, I left him. Returning to the same spot an hour or two after, I found him drawn into a hole, head first, and it required some little effort to extricate him. Throwing him aside, I left him for the day, and toward night he was drawn in again, and was now so nearly buried that only part of his tail was above ground. Once more I rescued him from the grave, and leaving him in the walk, went away. Again he was carried to the hole, and I found him with the tips of his wings and his tail protruding, and these were quivering, as the body was being drawn with considerable force into the earth. The gardener was sure it was a snake carrying the bird under for more convenient mastication; but when we struck with the spade below so as to cut him in two, we found nothing. Once more we made the ground smooth and hard, and throwing the bird aside, left it. The next morning it was again going under. I drew it out suddenly, and found the beast. It was a bug, about an inch long, and slender, yellow, with black stripes. His strength was amazing, when his size was considered ; and as he seemed to be the only engineer and power employed in moving the bird, which was twenty or thirty times as large as he, and was drawn by it into a hole requiring great extra force, besides what was necessary to overcome the weight, it appeared to me almost incredible that he could do it. Some friends wishing the beetle to be preserved as a curious specimen in natural history, I performed for the first time that barbarous operation so common with naturalists : I put a pin through him, and fastened him to a board in the barn, designing to present him to some museum with a statement of his exploits. I left him there to his own reflections, and the next morning, to my surprise, as Samson walked off with the gates of Gaza, even so had this beetle taken himself off, not with the board, but with the pin, and I have heard and seen him no more. But another and smaller beetle of the same description is now making arrangements to bury a dead mole in the garden ; and if the beetles would kill all the moles, I would not disturb them.

It is the instinct of this bug to take a carcass, and, having covered it with earth, to lay its eggs in it, which are hatched during the decomposition. This is any thing but a pleasing operation, and is one of those remarkable arrangements of nature that defy all human reason to explain the why and wherefore. But it is so with many other habits of the lower orders of creation. They have a world of their own to live in, far below ours ; and yet they are so well adapted to it that they are doubtless able to enjoy it. No creature of God is made to be miserable. And if we can not see what comfort a beetle can find in a carcass, or what pleasure a mole gets in burrowing through the earth in search of his food, or a toad in his sedentary habits, we may yet believe that in their own way they answer the ends for which they are made, and take as much enjoyment, or at least suffer as little, as the circumstances of the case admit. It is quite likely that they all answer some useful purpose. If man is the highest order of animal on the earth, the ultimate object of insect life may be found in what the lower orders do to promote his good. But happiness is not man's highest good ; and the bugs that vex and bite him, when they fail to make him happy, may yet be doing him good.

I have spoken of the naturalist Audubon, who, pursuing the work of his life in studying the habits of birds, would sit or lie all day under the trees in the forest, watching, in seclusion and silence, the motions of a little bird, that he might record its manner of life. And with equal interest one might study the ways and means of a beetle, and make notes of his habits. Entomology is a subject that invites the student into a wide and beautiful field of investigation ; and if it were studied in the school, it would bring children into the habit of regarding insects with more respect, and then they would cease to persecute them, as they do now, in mere sport or thoughtlessness. The mote that floats in the sunbeam has life, and a complete world of its own, as truly and perfectly developed as the eagle or the lion. Cowper said :

> "I would not enter on my list of friends
> (Though graced with polished manner and fine sense,
> Yet wanting sensibility) the man
> Who needlessly sets foot upon a worm."

Uncle Toby lifted the window and put the fly out of it, saying, "There is room enough in the world for you and me." It was bloody Nero who delighted in torturing insects. I would have a child familiar with the living things around him, and fond of playing with them—finding enjoyment in friendship with the animal world, regarding all as the creatures of God, and working out after their own order his praise.

I was speaking of Cowper just now. As I sit here, and the squirrels run up the trunks and leap from tree to tree, or sit on the steps as if they were part of the family, I recall his familiar lines:

> "These shades are all my own. The timorous hare,
> Grown so familiar with her frequent guest,
> Scarce shuns me, and the stock-dove, unalarmed,
> Sits cooing in the pine-tree, nor suspends
> His long love-ditty for my near approach.
> The squirrel, flippant, pert, and full of play,
> He sees me, and at once, swift as a bird,
> Ascends the neighboring beech, there whisks his brush,
> And perks his ears, and stamps, and cries,
> With all the prettiness of feigned alarm,
> And anger insignificantly fierce."

The British squirrels must be more demonstrative than mine, for they certainly do not carry on in this style, but disport themselves more quietly as they pursue their own pleasures, heedless of the human company that intrudes upon their domains without disturbing them. Cowper, more than any other, is a friend and companion for the fireside in the winter and the shade in summer. He is just the man you wish when saying,

> "But grant me this in my retreat,
> One friend, whom I may whisper, Solitude is sweet."

It was he who said,

> "'Tis pleasant, through the loopholes of retreat,
> To peep at such a world; to see the stir
> Of the great Babel, and not feel the crowd;

> To hear the roar she sends through all her gates
> At a safe distance, where the dying sound
> Falls a soft murmur on th' uninjured ear."

And without a tinge of his melancholy, the bane of his
life, but in sympathy with him in his love of nature and
his fellowship with beauty, we may take him into the
country with us, and always find company and counsel in
his pure leaves.

IX.

AN ARROW-HEAD.

WE are in the garden, and among the flowers and straw-berry beds, and rejoicing in the morning of another res-urrection. I think this has been as perfect a day as the Lord ever gave me to enjoy. Would such weather be well for us all the year round? Probably not. But it suits me exactly, as any weather suited the shepherd.

The gardener handed me a flint arrow-head to-day, perhaps once used by the Indians, when they hunted the forests on these shores of the Hudson. It suggested to me that on many a field in our country the laborer will find implements of war, rusted or buried, fallen from the hands of our countrymen. Skeletons, too. How many shallow graves will be plowed over! It is .sweet to think that the days of warfare are accomplished, the flowers are blossoming on the field of the crushed skeleton, and peace reigns again.

But this flint set me thinking of those very learned men who prove that man has lived on this earth thousands and thousands of years before the Bible record fixes the date of his creation. They prove the Bible to be false be-cause in the valley of the Somme, in France, a vast quan-tity of these flints have been found, which appear at first sight to have been fashioned by human hands, and they have been found buried under such conditions that geol-ogy assures us they must have been there many ages on

ages before the Bible period. A work has been published in England to show the " Flint Implements from Drift
not Authentic." Some kind friend has sent me an anal-
ysis of the argument. The writer remarks with equal
point and truth :

" Sir Charles Lyell and similar writers devote the whole
of their energies to proving the almost immeasurable ages
that must have elapsed since the deposit of the flints recently found in Picardy and elsewhere ; and on deciding
that question to their satisfaction, consider it a necessary
and unquestionable conclusion that man has been for all
these tens of thousands of years a denizen of this earth,
and that without leaving any other traces of his existence
than a number of flints, chipped about in the most incon-
venient way possible for the purpose for which they are
supposed to have been designed. But they appear to
overlook the prior necessity of proving that these 'flint
implements' are really the handiwork of man. The only
foundation they have is the mere opinion of a few scien-
tific men, against which is to be set the verdict to the
contrary of other men of science equally learned ; and
yet with this slender lever they hope to overthrow the
credibility of the infallible Word of God.

" A few of the arguments adduced against the theory
that these chipped flints are human productions are the
following : There is no *necessity* for the belief that they
have been artificially formed, inasmuch as flint has a
natural tendency to break into shapes similar to most of
those that have been found. The writer of the pamphlet
has picked up numbers of most perfect 'knives' and
'arrow-heads' among flints that have been broken up
to mend the roads, and has also produced them — by
heating a flint in the fire and then cooling it suddenly—

quite equal to those discovered in France. They are utterly unsuited for use as arrow-heads. The conical bulb at the lower end would be a difficulty in fastening them to their shafts, the curved shape of many of them would render it impossible that they should fly straight, and the point is in some the most defective part.

" The good and the bad are found indiscriminately mixed together; from some so imperfect as to make it impossible to ascribe them to human hands, to others which might from their appearance have been so produced. There often appears to be most chipping on those most entirely unsuitable for use, and among the rest are many so small as to be quite worthless for any purpose whatever. This is just as we might expect to find them if formed by natural causes, but quite inconsistent with their being artificial.

" They are none of them at all ground or polished as the Celtic flint tools are found to have been, but produced by the simple fracture of the flint and the chipping of its side ; nor do any of them bear the slightest trace of ever having been used. As to the almond-shaped flints, found in such numbers in France and supposed to be axe-heads, how is it that they are the only tools or similar utensils to be found there ? Surely the axe could not be the only thing used. And to what use could axes have been put by them ? The climate at that period is known to have been as cold as Iceland is now, and consequently could produce no trees—nothing larger than bushes and shrubs. It is suggested that they were used for cutting holes in the ice on their rivers ; but it would have been impossible to cut through a massive coating of ice, such as must then have existed, with an implement the size of a man's hand.

" The immense quantities in which they are discovered renders it impossible that they can be any thing else than natural formations. From the large number that has been found in three acres of land, and the great area which the 'implement' beds are known to cover, there must be along the banks of the Somme rather more than *twelve millions* of them. And we are asked to believe that these are just the lost axes of such a population as could have been supported in those icy deserts by the precarious sustenance to be derived from the chase!

" It is, indeed, a wonderful and a painful thing to behold how eager a certain class of writers in the present day, including not a few men of most unquestionable talent and even piety, ever show themselves in seizing the most flimsy pretense for casting discredit upon the grand and simple verities of the written Word. The avidity with which the discovery of the supposed 'flint implements' in the valley of the Somme has been pounced upon by these gentlemen as affording incontrovertible proof of the existence of pre-Adamite man is an instance of the spirit which we deplore. But so eager are they to create a theory that they overlook the most startling difficulties in the way of the acceptance of their creed. They will swallow the largest camel that can be found, if brought before them under the auspices of the Geological Society, but turn with horror from a tiny gnat that even *appears* to have settled on the first page of the Bible, although all the rest of the world can see that it is nothing but a speck of dust on their own eyelash."

This last illustration reminds me of a fact that occurred in General Ford's barn, in Hoosic, New York, some forty or fifty years ago. One of his hired men, a stupid fellow, had been out with a gun, and taking refuge from

the rain in an old barn or hay-rick that had little or nothing in it, he saw on one of the topmost beams an owl, at
which he fired. The solemn bird sat still, and he fired
again. A third shot never disturbed the slumbers of the
night bird. Beginning to be a little alarmed, he put up
his hand to his eyes, and as he raised the eyelash he
found that a l—— was resting quietly there, and he had
mistaken it for an owl at the top of the barn. So with
many of our modern skeptics : blazing away at the owls
which they fancy to exist in the Bible, they are fighting
nothing but a maggot in their own brain. Our writer goes
on to say :

"Some of these theorizing gentlemen suggest in despair that there must have been a great trade carried on
in this neighborhood ; that Abbeville was, in fact, a kind
of Birmingham or Sheffield of those days. But can it
be that in a country like France, in which chalk, with
flint, occupies an area of forty thousand square miles, and
where the raw material for such an important manufact-
ure (!) was every where abundant and redundant, any
local trade without a circulating medium could have existed? or was theirs a foreign commerce, carried on by
ships made with chipped-flint implements, made without
planks, without iron, without cordage, and navigated without sails or compass? But in what country, geologically,
could such manufactured articles find a market? In the
countries occupied by the Secondary and Tertiary formations and the Drift-beds there could have been no buy-
ers ; the article was every where under their feet ; it
would have been, in common parlance, 'sending coals to
Newcastle.' And in the lands of the older rocks, stone
tools of a superior form are ready made by nature. The
carbonaceous grits of North Devon are split by divisional

planes and cleavage into more effective arrow-heads and chisel points ; and the pebble ridge of Northam would supply an unlimited amount of magnificent stone hammers. There could have been no demand for such manufactured tools ; and we can only infer that the commercial and speculative savages embarked in a trade which proved a perfect failure, and in their disgust cast away innumerable specimens of beautifully made tools, which therefore bear no marks of having been used, and with others so utterly rude and unformed that it requires the 'practiced eye' to discover the marks of human workmanship ; and thus the good and the bad, the raw material and the manufactured article, are mingled in one chaotic mass—a record of disappointed hope, mortified ambition, and speculative commercial despair. Surely this is philosophy in sport or science run mad. Was this the commerce—those the ships whose flag braved for unknown years the battle and the breeze, when 'the arts remained stationary for almost indefinite periods?' This is more like an Oriental romance, more akin to the history of a pre-Adamite Robinson Crusoe, than the deductions of legitimate science. It is a resuscitated Daniel Defoe who writes, and not the author of the Principles and the Manual of Geology."

X.

OCTOBER.

SURELY one who writes out-of-doors ought to take note of the seasons. Thomson wrote his poems in a rustic summer-house, no better than one within ten feet of my chair. I' was in it near Richmond Hill, and recollect the record on the wall :

"HERE THOMSON SANG THE SEASONS AND THEIR CHANGE." .

But he could not have lived in that charming spot when he began his career as a poet, for he first wrote his "Winter," and went from one publisher to another trying to sell the manuscript that he might buy for himself a pair of shoes. With success as a poet he obtained *patronage* and a place that gave him three hundred a year, which made him comfortable. His "Seasons" are among the pleasantest of all the English classic poems to read in the country. Parts of them are too sensuous for the more delicate tastes of our times, but Thomson had a soul to enjoy the beauties and glories of the country, and set them in his verse with a mellow melody delicious to read or hear.

It is now nearly the middle of the month, and so warm in this latitude that it is as delightful to sit out under the trees and enjoy a book or a pen as it has been any time this summer. In the spring we often think, if we do not say, that we would love to have such weather all the year.

But this October weather, such as we are now having, is more enjoyable than soft and genial May. It is cool and bracing. It invites to labor. Toil of mind and body suits the month. One feels like work, and springs to it with a will. To work is play when one's limbs are free, strong, and willing. It is a blessing that we are compelled to work, as our first parents were when they were put into a garden to dress and keep it, even before they dressed themselves. To have nothing to do is worse than to have nothing to wear.

The weather is so enjoyable that I am reminded of a letter I had a few days ago from an unknown friend, reproving me kindly for saying in one of my recent letters that my equanimity of soul would be disturbed if the wind should turn about into the northeast and a cold storm should set in. He says that, although he has had a life of sighing, he is never disturbed by the weather, and he thinks I ought, like the Shepherd of Salisbury Plain, to think that weather best which the Lord sends. And so I do. When bad weather drives me in, or gives me aches, or defeats my plans, I am afflicted; but it is good to be afflicted, and so I rejoice in adversity. I am disturbed when things go as I would not like to have them go, and I do not love trouble more than other men; but I know that He who orders all things, the weather as well as others, knows what is best on the whole, and therefore I take it as it comes. "When it rains, let it rain," is a motto that I have a hereditary right to wear under my coat-of-arms, for it was the motto of a father who never failed of an appointment on account of a storm, and always took the world as the Lord gave it, without a murmur or a frown. To be indifferent to the weather, or to disappointments or crosses or trials, is not virtue nor manliness. But to be patient when one's peace of mind is disturbed, to control the rising discontent, to refrain from sighing, to put on and wear a cheerful face, so that our vexation shall not vex others, this is virtue, and one who is always sighing has it not. It is easy for a man to make his family and his friends miserable by showing his own griefs and cares and little troubles that he ought to leave in his study or store, or out on the farm. When he is at home, let him be cheerful and bright, and good-tempered and patient, as becomes the head of the house, the sun in whose light and warmth all the plants should rejoice and shine.

But where were we? October: it is not likely that we shall forget it, for the evidences are all around us that the days of autumn have come. The chestnuts are dropping around me as I write, though as yet we have had no frost to open the burrs, which do not wait for that, but burst when the nuts are ripe and ready for harvest. The squirrels are busy for their share, and we suffer no disturbing stone or gun to dispute their right to all they can get. Two wild pigeons just now came into the tree under which I am sitting—beautiful birds; and after holding a short conversation, they flew away. Thousands of them are now on the wing to a warmer clime. They need not hasten, for the weather is mild enough for them yet, and they can fly to the South in a single day whenever they choose to make the journey.

Many of the forest trees have already put on their proud autumnal dress; the maples and beeches and oaks have begun to change. The second growth of late summer and early fall, which is rarely noted but is always observable, is now losing its distinctive hue. Along in July a fresh impulse seems to be given to the sap in shrubs

and trees, and you will see that a new growth starts up
with a tender, delicate green like early spring; and this
lies, another color, like a streak of sunshine on a darker
brown of the other foliage.   It is now all alike.   And
how radiant is that maple-tree in its scarlet robe !   And
here is a tree that was lately a deep green, now suddenly
clothed in yellow from the ground to its crown.   Some
of the very fanciful landscapers have endeavored to produce wonderful effects of beauty by setting out trees in
regular succession of autumnal colors, to have them in
the order of the spectrum as nearly as may be, improving
upon the arrangement of nature.   The effect is far from
satisfactory.   To paint the lily or the rose would be as
wise as to make a forest of colors by any law of the
schools.   As the heavens declare the glory of God, so
the mountains and forests display his taste and skill.
He makes them living pictures ; arranging the lights and
shades and hues with infinite art, himself the artist whom
no rival can reach.   To paint like him would be too
much glory for any man.   To be like him is more ; yet
this is what the humblest may.   To see his beauty in
these autumn leaves is great.   Yet we may have more ;
we shall be like him, for we shall see him as he is.

XI.

A FRIEND'S VISIT.

WE have just parted from a friend who has been spending a few days with us under the trees. Poets have sung the pleasures of solitude, and if there were any place in the world where a man might be alone, yet not alone, it would be this secluded woodside, where the sky looks down on us as a constant benediction of Providence, and the river lives and moves and smiles continually at our feet, and the old trees lift up their branches in perpetual psalms. This is solitude in the midst of nature's voices, with God all around us in his unwritten word, speaking in the sunshine and the showers, the flowers, the fruits, the growth of every thing, and now in the ripening and the fall of leaves that tell us autumn has come and winter is nigh. Solitude is scarcely solitary here, where every blade of grass and every oak and pine are companions, as well as the little rabbit that sports in the walk and flies at my coming, as he would not if he knew me better; and the squirrel who shares the nuts, and establishes his dwelling among them to make sure of his portion. With all this company, and that other "bliss of Paradise that escaped the fall," I had been longing for the sight and voice of a friend whose presence is always like that of the sun.

And so he came. Thanks be to God for friends. Thanks be to him for one friend; for one with whom

sweet counsel can be taken in the retirement of one's
own house and heart; one friend to whom you may tell
all your plans and hopes and fears; who will share his
with you, and make the world brighter and life's burden
lighter, because his sympathy and his experience and his
wisdom make up for your weakness and want of faith.
It is a grand error, too, that friendship is less sweet in
later life, and even in old age, than in the sunny times of
youth. Two of the early pieces of Latin that I had to
write into English were Cicero on Friendship and on Old
Age, and the fine philosophy that glowed in those beautiful pages has been a life-long pleasure. Nothing in the
poetry or prose of man's life on earth is more lovely than
a virtuous old age cheered with the friendship of the wise
and good. And why should any sensible man be averse
to old age, and strive to hide from himself and others that
he is advanced in years? If his days are crowned with
goodness, and his mind is a storehouse in which the har-
vests of successive years have been garnered, and the law
of kindness is on his lips, and love throws its arms around
him, or plays at his knees, and hope opens heaven on his
eye, and peace dwells in his soul—a foretaste of the rest
that remains for him when his pilgrimage is closed—why
should not old age be the happiest, cosiest, loveliest season of the life on earth ? The heart never grows old, and
out of the heart are the issues of life. The soul never
grows old, and the soul is the man. This poor, aching
frame of ours is not the thing that is to be, and not the
thing that is, if we reckon by the power to be, to do, to
suffer, and to enjoy. The life in us is the life of the soul;
that loves, learns, hopes, rejoices in the smile of God and
friends, and lives the most "when this poor stammering
tongue lies silent in the grave."

Our friend who came to see us you would not dare to call an old man.   Even the hand of time has dealt so tenderly with him that not a wrinkle furrows his brow, and his hair is brown as a boy's, though he tells us he was born in the last century, and we are bound to believe him, as he is the soul of truth.   Yet why not speak of him as old, for he has all that helps to make a man revered, and years enough to make him venerable have flown over him, if they have not shed the frosts of their winters on his head.   It has been summer with him always, and his heart is warm now.   He brought with him whatever makes life a charm and blessing.   Genial, cheerful, social, his mind is stored with all manner of pleasant memories of men and places, things and scenes, in the Old World and our own, for few men have read more, traveled more abroad and at home, met more of those men and women whom the world loves to talk of and remember; few have written more, and as reading makes a full man, writing a correct man, conversation a ready man, and society an accomplished man, our friend should have brought with him the means of enlightening the darkness and enlivening the dullness of our woods; and he did. And over all the charms of intercourse with one so richly furnished with the stores of learning and gifts of graceful culture, the higher and purer beauty of religion shone in every word and way.

How sweet the hours, the days, in such society!   How rich the flow of thought and feeling that came from his lips like a river of delight, as he spoke of former times, of great and good men now conversing with the angels in heaven; of books, that inexhaustible fountain of instruction and delight when congenial minds wander without method from one to another, over the fields of ancient

E

and modern times; yes, and of books that are to be, or
that might be and ought to be, that the world is waiting
for, and would welcome with favor if the man to make
them would come and do the work; of art, whose plastic
hand has made beauty a household treasure, and adorned
the world with fair creations that delight the eye of taste,
and stand from age to age the monuments of genius; of
nature lying in her loveliness all about us, her summer
garments just now exchanged for the richer robes of autumn; the grand old trees stretching their protecting arms
abroad, as if they loved to fold us in their embrace; rich,
ripe fruit pendant from many a vine and branch, telling
of the bounty of the Universal Father, blessed forever,
whose love and skill appear in every leaf and ray; of
friends, and those who are bound to us by sweeter names,
whose love is the balm of all life's sorrow, and the fullness,
in itself, of life's every joy.

In such discourse the hours went swiftly by, till the
time for his departure came. Too soon, but still it came.
And when he left us, it was as if half the world had gone,
so great the void and our regret.

> "When one that holds communion with the skies,
> Has filled his urn where these pure waters rise,
> And once more mingles with us meaner things,
> 'Tis e'en as if an angel shook his wings;
> Immortal fragrance fills the circuit wide
> That tells us whence his treasures are supplied."

He has left precious memories. We are glad that he
has been here, even while we miss him from these familiar seats and walks. His form, his smile, his words of
wisdom and affection are now linked with all we see.
Here he sat, there we walked; here he told us of one
whom we had known in another land, now in another

world, and here we laid out work for future years. Each
step and tree and scene will remind us of him. He is
part of us and ours. And when he was away out of
sight and hearing, I sat down in an old rustic chair that
he had been sitting in an hour before, and I said—

"What are meetings here but partings?
    What are ecstasies but smartings?
    Union what but separations?
    What attachments but vexations?
            Every smile but brings its tear,
            Love its ache and hope its fear;
            All that's sweet must bitter prove;
            All we hold most dear remove!

"Heavenward rise! 'tis Heaven in kindness
    Mars our bliss to heal our blindness;
    Hope from vanity to sever,
    Offering joys that bloom forever.
            In that amaranthine clime,
            Far above the tears of time,
            Where nor fear nor hope intrude,
            Lost in pure beatitude."

XII.

CONVERSATION.

THE savor of his conversation lingers so pleasingly. He has the happy faculty of saying the right thing at the right time, and that is high art. It is the art of conversation, a rare accomplishment, attained by few because it is thought to come of itself, and not to be sought, studied, and cultivated, as music or dancing is by those who would excel in either. Probably it does come of itself, but only to one who is well read, ready, and full of practice. It grows upon a man doubtless, unconsciously to himself but not to his friends, and they delight in him when he is quite unaware of the pleasure he is conferring.

Our friend who has just left us has had the best opportunity of becoming perfect in this art. He has read much, written much, traveled much, met the best, wisest, and greatest men in our own and other lands, listened to them, talked to and with them, and remembers every body and every thing, so that he illustrates his conversation with frequent anecdote and incident, quotes correctly sentences from speeches, sermons, and books, imitates the manner of the speaker admirably, giving a passage from Everett or Robert Hall, Channing or Webster, so that you might imagine the orators themselves before you, and this discourse, flowing easily from lively to severe, is seasoned with salt, sometimes Attic, always to the taste of the company, never flagging, never wearying, always rest-

ing when others have any thing to say, and listening with
graceful attention when they speak, and—but this sen-
tence is long and must come to an end.

We have traditions and records of men who were great
in conversation, as Dr. Johnson and Coleridge, but they
were not strictly conversationists. The idea of con-vers-
ing is a mutual interchange of thought, a reciprocation of
ideas ; there is little of this in Johnson, who was so dog-
matical as scarcely to allow any one else to have an opinion, certainly not to express it in his presence without rebuke. He was a tyrant among his friends, autocrat of
the dinner-table, and a bear always. Goldsmith said of
him, " If his pistol missed fire, he knocked you down with
the butt end of it." Yet some of his contemporaries tell
us that he led people about him to talk of the matters
with which they were the most familiar, and so became
possessed of their information. In this way he pleased
them, by making them think they pleased him.

Coleridge discoursed rather than conversed. His conversation was like the handle of the teapot, all on one
side. Dr. Dibdin, dining at the same table with him, describes his manner : " He rolled himself up, as it were, in
his chair, and gave the most unrestrained indulgence to
his speech ; and how fraught with acuteness and origi-
nality was that speech, and in what copious and eloquent
periods did it flow ! The auditors seemed rapt in wonder and delight, as one observation more profound or
clothed in more forcible language than another fell from
his tongue. He spoke for nearly two hours with unhesi-
tating and uninterrupted fluency. Thinking and speaking were his delight, and he would sometimes seem, during the most fervid moments of discourse, to be abstract-
ed from all and every thing about him, and to be basking

in the sunny warmth of his own radiant imagination."
This is not the art of conversation—it is the art of speaking. It is not the entertainment of the social hour, but
the very thing for the lecture-room. It justifies the reply
of Charles Lamb to Coleridge, who said to him, "Did you
ever hear me preach?" Lamb replied, "I never heard
you do any thing else." Coleridge began public life as a
preacher. He soon left the pulpit, but he continued to
discourse daily while he lived. Perhaps no man ever ex-
celled him in the power of expressing great thoughts in
the happiest manner without premeditation.

Of all the men whom I have had the pleasure of meeting in social life, no one has conversational powers superior, if equal, to Mr. Kinney, our late Minister at Turin,
when Italy was not as now under one king. Without
dogmatism or pedantry, he gives expression to the stores
of a richly furnished mind in language at once simple
and eloquent ; fluently putting forth his thoughts in
the readiest but best chosen words, with energy, yet
with courtesy and deference. His earnestness is infec-
tious. He rouses those about him to speak as well as to
hear, and thus his discourse soon becomes the animated
and delightful converse of the social circle. One evening — I remember it well — a shallow free-thinker in a
brilliant circle in Florence had been speaking lightly of
some of the truths of religion because to him they were
unintelligible ; he added, " I will never believe any thing
that I can not understand." "And pray tell us," said
Mr. Kinney, "what you do *understand?*" The man was
confounded by the suddenness of the demand, and Mr.
Kinney proceeded with great calmness but with a wealth
of illustration and logical force to show that we understand little or nothing of the simplest and commonest

things which we do not hesitate to believe—the relations of mind and matter—the phenomena of the world of nature—even principles in art, by which grand results are reached, and which we do not refuse to apply, are all beyond our power to comprehend. Yet this rebuke and instruction were conveyed in terms so graceful and engaging that the pleasure overcame our pity for the man who had invited such a criticism.

There is this marked difference in conversation among cultivated people abroad and at home, that here the opinions of others are challenged with greater freedom and opposed with more bluntness, while abroad dissent is rather implied than asserted. Here men oftener discuss than converse. There the interchange of opinion and information is made as if all were on the same side, and each was seeking to learn rather than to teach. Yet this is not peculiar to conversational circles. Social intercourse has much less friction there than with us. Society is tolerant of opinion, and policy controls the words of men and women more than it does here, where every man thinks he is as good as his neighbor, if not a little better. Chesterfield is supreme in the law of manners abroad, and a sin against good-breeding is worse, in many of the higher spheres, than a crime in morals. The advantage is with us on the score of honesty, frankness, sincerity, but with them in the matter of ease, gracefulness, and social pleasure. We ought to reach perfection in both and all. It is a pity that civilization tends in any way or degree to make society insincere. But the more that men learn to regard language as intended to "conceal their thoughts," the less honest they become, and more like politicians and diplomats than statesmen, scholars, and friends.

·Of the social circle he is the life and charm whose mind is stored with knowledge of matters and things in general, conversant with the past and present—history, poetry, and philosophy ; who has a memory ready to answer instantly every call, with anecdote to illustrate, wit to enliven, and fluency to speak ; is patient of contradiction, and full of gentleness, goodness, and truth.

XIII.

AUTHORS.

NEXT to reading good books, we enjoy reading about the authors of them. It is the next best thing to knowing them. Indeed, it is often better. For we are sometimes so sadly disappointed when we come to meet people of whom we have read and heard much, that we are rather sorry than otherwise we have had "the pleasure of their acquaintance." Even St. Paul anticipated this when he spoke of his "weighty" epistles, and his bodily presence "weak and contemptible." Something in the style or something we have heard helps us to an image of the author's person, and then of his manner, and it is painful to have this illusion dispelled. At the annual Literary Fund Dinner in London, I met a large number of eminent authors. I was disenchanted. Many of them were totally different from the ideal. The little child who was held up to a window in Newport to look in at George Washington, expressed the almost universal feeling on one's first sight of a hero, "Why he's only a man."

And men are not always the same, so that the accounts we have of them are as diverse as their sketches. M. Ampere says of M. de Tocqueville, who was remarkable for the purity of his language in the most familiar conversation : "While sitting on the rocks around Sorrento, I might have written down (and why did I not?) all that escaped his lips in those moments of friendly intercourse."

It so happens that I have enjoyed familiar converse with
the same illustrious author, philosopher, and statesman,
M. de Tocqueville, and, singularly indeed, under similar
circumstances; we were sitting, not "on the rocks around
Sorrento," but on a rail fence overlooking this Hudson
River; and then and there the French author referred to
the identical scenery he was perusing when M. Ampere
and he were conversing, for he said to me, "We will except the Bay of Naples out of deference to the opinion of
the world, but, after that, I never saw a more beautiful
scene than this." I was not impressed by the style of
his conversation, as Ampere was, but it was doubtless
owing to the fact that he spoke with me in English, while
he and Ampere were of course using their own beautiful
language.

Guizot says of Gibbon that his great conversational de-
feet was a studied arrangement of his words—that he talked like a book. I have heard Guizot talk, and his words
flow as readily as if they were in his memory, and not to
be found for the occasion. The most learned men are
not the most fluent in conversation. Christopher North
ridicules a dinner-table distinguished by the literary type
of its guests. "Even poets," he says, "are a sulky set, and
as gruffly and grimly silent as if they had the toothache
or something the matter wi' their inside." Sir Walter
Scott could not endure the "little exclusive circles of
literary society." "He often complained," says Jacox,
"of the real dullness of parties where each guest arrived
under the implied and tacit obligation of exhibiting some
extraordinary powers of talk or wit."

Emerson is one of the profoundest thinkers, but he is
very simple in his conversation; he is childlike in his
simplicity, or, to use his own words speaking of another,

he is "grandly simple." I have listened to him wondering that while the depths are so great there is so little on the surface, yet that little so beautiful.

The most learned woman it was ever my good-fortune to meet, and probably the most learned woman who ever lived, was Mrs. Somerville, the mathematician, astronomer, and philosopher. In fact, she was encyclopedic. She but recently died at the age of about ninety, for she was born in 1780. It was in 1853 I met her in Florence, and she was therefore then seventy-three years old, and in the prime of life and mental vigor. Her bust in marble had before that time been placed by the side of Sir Isaac Newton's, and no one more justly deserves the honor. But she was as simply natural and as easily graceful in her conversation as if she had never calculated an eclipse since she was the reigning belle in Scotland, admired for her beauty and accomplishments, but not suspected of genius or learning, and unthinking of fame.

Horace Walpole quotes with fondness the remark of one of Fanny Burney's friends : "I made a resolution early never to be acquainted with authors—they are so vain and so troublesome." And Jeffrey said of London society, "The literary men, I acknowledge, excite my reverence the least." It is often the case that the very pressure both of wisdom and knowledge shuts the mouth. To say any thing worth saying is far more of an undertaking for a wise man than a fool. Fools rush in, or out, where angels fear to tread. Mrs. E. B. Browning says: "How many are there, from Psellus to Bayle, bound hand and foot intellectually with the rolls of their own papyrus —men whose erudition has grown stronger than their souls." But Mrs. Browning was herself an illustration of the truth that one may be full of thought, reading, and genius, and as readily social and agreeable as if she were no greater than those with whom she conversed.   Thus she appeared to me in society, when poets and artists hovered around her, and again in her own Casa Guidi, with a few friends near her, her only child at her knee, looking up reverently into her sad face.

One of the most genial and pleasant old men I ever met of the race of authors was the poet James Montgomery.   He was so old when I saw him in his own house in Sheffield that I would not have looked for vivacity and humor in his conversation, but he was very lively in his manner; and when he gave me his birthday, and it proved to be mine also, and then his age, which was the double of mine to a day, the coincidences were welcomed with mutual and great delight.

Ready writing is written down as one of the greatest accomplishments, and yet it is a serious question whether it is in the long run as desirable a talent as the want of it.   When a great painter, whose name is now almost unknown to fame, was boasting of the celerity with which he dispatched his work, Zeuxis, whose name still lives among the arts, replied, " If I boast, it shall be of the slowness with which I finish mine."

Preachers who write their sermons gain little and lose much by dashing off their discourses with railroad speed. Haste makes waste, and a dreary waste it is that is spread out before a people whose teacher brings to them on a Sunday that which has cost him nothing through the week.   A minister neighbor of mine was in my house until nearly bed-time Saturday night, and when he rose to go, remarked: " I've half a sermon yet to write for to-morrow; don't you feel sorry for me?"

"Oh no," said I, "not for you ; I was thinking of the people."

The Rev. Dr. Sprague is the only man I ever knew who can write his best, and that first rate, and at the same time with great rapidity. As reading makes a full man, conversation a ready man, and writing a correct man, he is always full, ready, and correct, and the words flow from his pen in one steady, easy, pellucid stream. He rarely changes a word. I have had hundreds, perhaps thousands of his pages of manuscript under my hands for publication ; they were the first draft, and very rarely was the beauty of the page marred by an erasure or emendation. He began his great work, " The Annals of the American Pulpit," ten octavo volumes, when he was fifty-seven years old, and in the midst of the duties of a large pastoral charge, he never slighted a discourse, and once or twice a year he visited every house in his parish.

Dr. Griffin was one of the most eloquent preachers in the American pulpit. Dr. Sprague edited his sermons and wrote his biography. Dr. Griffin was the exact reverse of Dr. Sprague in composition : writing slowly, and correcting with much labor and care. When I was a boy in college he was its President, and my puerile compositions were laid upon the table before him, while he without pity blotted them with a broad-nibbed pen, until there was no likeness of the original page to be seen. He kept two pens at hand, one to strike out with, the other to restore. " The great art in criticism," he would say, "is to blot." And if a pet curl adorned the fair face of my essay, he without remorse and with apparent pleasure cut it off and cast it from me as if it were an offense. The late Dr. Murray (Kirwan), whose head came to the same block before mine, has left his testimony to the value of

Dr. **Griffin's** butchery as a critic and example as an author. " Young gentlemen," Dr. Griffin often said to us, "learn to stop when you are done."

Southey was a rapid writer, but found that what he gained in time he lost in polish and correctness. When one of his poems was finished, he would not give it to the printer, but wrote : " I am polishing and polishing, and hewing it to pieces with surgeon severity. Yesterday I drew the pen across six hundred lines." And again he says : " It is long since I have been a rapid writer ; the care with which I write, and the pains which I take in collecting materials, render it impossible that I should be so."

Dr. Johnson advised every young man beginning to compose, to do it as fast as he could, to get a habit of having his mind start promptly—" so much more difficult is it to improve in speed than in accuracy." But Dr. Johnson was one of the most unwise wise men that ever lived. He was a bundle of contradictions, and said a great many things for the sake of contradiction. " I would say to a young divine," says Dr. Johnson, "' Here is your text ; let us see how soon you can make a sermon.' Then I'd say, ' Let me see how much better you can make it.' Thus I should see both his powers and his judgment."

"Easy writing is very hard reading." And it is the easy reading, that which gives the most lasting as well as immediate pleasure to the reader, which has cost the writer the most labor. If he have the art to conceal his art, so that what is read or heard with the greatest delight seems to have leaped like Minerva from the brain in full dress and strength, so much the better ; but as a general rule in the matter of writing, as in all other of the works of man, that which costs nothing is worth nothing.

Milton's "Lycidas" was rewritten again and again; his biographer says he hovered over the "rathe primrose" passage with fastidious fondness, touching every color and fitting every word till he brought it to its present perfection of beauty.

The fastidiousness of authorship is ridiculed by some, like Cobbett, who said, "Never think of what you write; let it go—no patching." And Niebuhr's rule was, "Try never to strike out any part of what you have once written down." But such advice never made an author immortal. It may have helped him to sudden fame, and perhaps fortune, but usefulness and the "monumentum ære perennius," for which the best of men may strive, are not to be achieved without patient work, painstaking—labor limæ; and the reward is worth all it costs.

XIV.

DOGS.

We have been in mourning, if not in tears to-day. My son left us yesterday to go to Europe, and a favorite dog of his, a little fellow, "took on" dreadfully when his master went away. For several days, while preparations for the journey were in progress, the dog manifested great anxiety, watching the packing and listening to the conversation with evident uneasiness. The day of departure came. The dog was shut up in a room alone, and howled dolefully. Night came, and he wandered about the house, up and down stairs—though his rug was lying ready for him as usual by his master's empty bed. He had disturbed me in the early part of the night by his whines as he sought his master in vain. In the morning I went into his room, and found him asleep on his rug. He never awoke again. The dog was dead.

After breakfast we buried him under the trees, and a feeling of increased loneliness has settled on the house. We miss them both, and the thought of the love the dog had for his master—love stronger than life—touches us tenderly. We hope to see the son return. The dog had no hope, and died.

General Webb gave a little dog to the child of one of our neighbors, a friend of his. The child and the dog became tenderly attached to each other. The child was taken ill. The dog lavished its affections on its friend, caressing him constantly, and showing the strongest anxiety. The child died. The dog walked away from the bed to the other side of the room, lay down and died also.

My father had a small and beautiful dog who rejoiced in the name of Fidelity. He differed from other good dogs only in being better than others, and in manifesting something that resembled religious sensibility, or a peculiar attachment to religious places, people, and services. He attended family worship with a punctuality and regularity that the other members of the household might well have imitated, and certainly did not surpass. If a stranger were present—and much company visited our house— the dog's attention to him was regulated by his taking the lead or not in the religious worship of the household. If the visitor at my father's request conducted the worship, the dog at once attached himself to his person, and when he departed the dog escorted him out of the village; sometimes going home with him to a neighboring town, and making him a visit of a few days. If the visitor did not perform any religious service in the house, the dog took no notice of him while there, and suffered him to depart unattended and evidently unregretted.

Such a dog was, of course, an habitual attendant on the public services of the church on the Sabbath. It required extraordinary care to keep him at home. Shut up in a room, he dashed through a window and was at church before the family. He was once shut up in an outhouse that had no floor. He dug out under the sill of the door, and was at church before the first psalm was sung. In church he occupied the upper step of the pulpit within which his master ministered. He lay quiet during the service unless other dogs below misbehaved, in which case he left his seat, and after quieting the disturbance

F

resumed it.   He was equally devoted to the weekly
prayer-meeting which was held from house to house, the
appointment being announced on the Sabbath.   He remembered the evening and the place, and was always
present.   As it was not agreeable to have a dog at an
evening meeting in a private house, he was confined at
home.   The next week he went early, before the family
had thought to shut him up, and waited for the hour and
the people.   He knew the names of the families where
the meetings were held, and where they lived, and could
have gone to any one of them on an errand as easily and
correctly as a child.   And the only knowledge he had of
the place of meeting he got as the others did, by hearing
the notice on Sunday.   These habits of the dog were not
the fruit of education.   On the contrary, pains were taken
to prevent him from indulging his religious preferences.
He did not manifest a fondness for other meetings, or for
any individuals out of the family circle except those
whom he recognized by their habit of praying, as the people in whom he was especially interested.

My father was wont to relate many other anecdotes of
this remarkable animal, and the relation of them always
caused his eyes to fill with tears.   He had a strong impression that there was something very mysterious about
this propensity of the dog, and being himself a sternly
orthodox divine, he never ventured to express the opinion
that the dog had moral perceptions.   But I always thought
he believed so.

I have heard and read many stories of dogs that go
to show a moral sense.   Dr. Guthrie, the great Scotch
preacher, relates some incidents in the life of his dog
Bob :

" Though but a dumb companion and friend," he says,

"I must devote a few lines to the memory and affection and sense of my dog Bob, who, lying often at the head of the pulpit stairs, occupied a place on Sundays nearly as conspicuous as myself. He was a magnificent Scotch dog of great size, brave as, or rather braver than a lion. He expressed his respect for decent and well-conditioned visitors by rushing to the gate as if he were bent on devouring them, and gave them a welcome both with tail and tongue. Beggars, and all such characters, he wasted no wind on; but, maintaining an ominous silence, stuck close to their heels, showing a beautiful set of teeth, and occasionally using them; only, however, to warn the *gangrels* to be on their behavior.

"He had but one bad habit when I had him—to see a cat was to fly at it. This ended in his worrying to death a favorite grimalkin belonging to a neighbor, and the catastrophe raised a formidable commotion. I saw that I must part with Bob or impair my usefulness; so, with many regrets, I sent him to Brechin, fifteen miles off.

"There, early on the following Sunday morning, Bob was observed, with head and tail erect and a resolute purpose in every look and movement, taking his way from my brother's house. My brother's wife, struck with his air, said to one of her daughters, who laughed at the idea, 'There is Bob, and I'll wager he is off to Arbirlot!' Whether he had kept the road, or gone by some mysterious path across the country straight as the crow flies, I know not; but when I was leaving the church, about one o'clock, I was met by the beadle, with his old face lighted up with an unusual expression of glee, and exclaiming— for my dog and Johnny had been always fast friends— 'You manna put him awa', minister, though he should worry a' the cats in the parish!'

"On going to the manse, I found Bob outside the gate, as flat, prostrate, and motionless as if he had been stone dead. It was plain he knew as well as I did that he had been banished, and had returned without leave, and was liable to be hanged, drowned, shot, or otherwise punished at my will. I went up to him, and stood over him for a while in ominous silence. No wagging of his tail, or movement in any limb; but there he lay, as if he had been killed and flattened by a heavy roller, only that, with his large, beautiful eyes half shut, he kept winking and looking up in my face with a most pitiful and penitent and pleading expression in his own.

"Though I might not go the length of old Johnny Bowman in making free of all the cats in the parish, there was no resisting the dumb but eloquent appeal. I gave way, and exclaimed in cheerful tones, 'Is this you, Bob?' In an instant, knowing that he was forgiven and restored, he rose at one mighty bound into the air, circling round and round me, and ever and anon, in the power and fullness of his joy, leaping nearly over my head.

"What his ideas of right and wrong were I dare not say, but he certainly had a sense of shame, and apparently also of guilt. Once, for example—and the only occasion on which we knew him to steal—Mrs. Guthrie came unexpectedly on Bob sneaking out of the kitchen with a sheep's head between his teeth. His jail-like and timorous look displayed conscious guilt; and still more, before she had time to speak a word, what he did. The moment he saw her, as if struck with paralysis, he drops the sheep's head on the floor, and, with his tail between his legs, makes off with all haste, not to escape a beating, for she never ventured on that, but to hide his shame."

P. G. Hamerton is an English author of fine taste and

accomplishments, who discusses the subject of intellect in dumb animals with much ability and fine illustration. Some very able papers have recently appeared in foreign reviews on the same question. Mr. Hamerton has a paper on dogs, which he prefaces with a note: "There is so much in this paper which must naturally seem incredible;" and then he pledges "his honor" for the truth of what he tells. He then gives a detailed account of two performing dogs that had been trained by a man who had been a teacher in a deaf and dumb institution, and had thus been led to inquire how far similar education might reach the intelligence of dogs. These dogs would spell any common word proposed to them; would give the plural of a word when the singular was proposed. They would give the French for any English or German word in which the same letter did not occur twice; they would detect an error in any word spelled incorrectly, and point out the wrong letter, and bring the right one to go in its place; and questions in mental arithmetic were solved with correctness. The master left the room, and Mr. Hamerton proposed questions which were promptly answered by the dogs. The two dogs played a game of dominoes; and when unable to match, drew from the bank with great reluctance and went on.

The Rev. Dr. Wickam, of Manchester, Vermont, has told me of a dog which belongs to a good deacon of that place.

"At the stroke of the bell each Sabbath morning, unless forcibly restrained, this dog would hasten with all speed to the church, and take his position on the broad stair of the steps ascending to the pulpit, and there recline at his ease, remaining quiet during the public service. By the kind sufferance of the minister who then occupied the pulpit, he was never disturbed. But on the accession of another to the pastorate, to whom the proximity of this animal was unwelcome, he was once and again dislodged by a kick from his position as the minister ascended the pulpit stairs. Upon the repetition of this indignity he came no more, but regularly as the Sabbath returned passed by the door of the church he had attended to another of a different denomination nearly two miles distant from the former. He continued to do this for the space of nearly three years. At the end of that time, on the accession of a new minister, he was seen in his old position on the pulpit stairs. Being undisturbed, though his church-going habit remained, he went no more to the distant church ; but for the residue of his short life punctually attended where he had done before, and where his owner and family were stated worshipers."

The Rev. Mr. Buckingham, of Ohio, is my authority for the following :

" A few days after my third child was born (July, 1845), a little boy brought as a present to the child a black puppy. As he grew he became exceedingly playful, full of fun and life, barking at every thing and every person that came about the house. A mutual attachment was formed between the dog and the child. At nine months of age the child was taken with spasms. As soon as ' Coly' (that was the name we gave the dog) knew that the child was sick, his whole demeanor changed. He seemed sad, would not eat as usual, and ceased to notice those who came to the house. We never heard him bark after he knew the child was sick. During the sickness of the child (about forty-eight hours) he often came into the room where she was lying, would go to the cradle, and, putting his front paws upon the side of the cradle, look over into her face with the deepest interest, and then go out and lie down upon his rug at the door sorrowful. When the child died and was dressed for the grave, 'Coly' came into the bedroom, licked the cold face of the child, and then went out, lay down in the corn-crib, refused to eat or drink, and in a few hours I found him dead.

"In the fall of 1836 I started from my father's, in Newark, Ohio, to go to Circleville and Chillicothe—to Circleville on a courting expedition, and to Chillicothe to preach in the First Presbyterian Church. My father had a large yellow dog, who persisted in making the trip with me. I reached Chillicothe on Saturday afternoon, and put up at a hotel. Sabbath morning, fearing that my dog would follow me to the church, I requested the landlord to shut him up. He was confined in an outhouse. At tea-time he was safe, but when I returned to the hotel after the evening services I found the dog gone. I saw no more of him until my return to my father's, where I found him. On inquiry, I learned that he was found in the stalls on Monday morning, the day after he escaped from the hotel in Chillicothe. The distance between the two places is some seventy miles."

A Virginia gentleman tells me of three remarkable dogs:

"In 1850 odd my brother (still living in New Orleans) was a lieutenant in the United States Army, stationed at one of the forts in Boston Harbor. He was presented by the captain of a coaster, trading at that port, with two dogs—one a bull-terrier, named Dinky, and the other a beautiful Newfoundland (or Nova Scotian) dog, which he named Junot, after the French marshal. Some one else presented him with a splendid mastiff, which he named Duroc, after another of the marshals. During a leave of absence, he brought these three dogs with him to

Richmond, Virginia, where his father and a large family
resided. Dinky was milk white all over, and though
beautifully made as to his body and limbs, could not be
considered handsome about the face and head — a deficiency of beauty common to his tribe. When Dinky
was presented to my brother, he had just emerged from
a mortal combat with a dog much larger than himself,
in the course of which his side was torn open. The
captain was much attached to him ; but despairing of his
life, and landing at the wharf of the fort, parted with him
to my brother on condition that he saved his life. He
carried him in and invoked the services of the surgeon
of the fort (Dr. Murray, I believe). Dinky was laid on
the operating table, his wounds dressed, and his side
sewed up. Though he suffered greatly from the operation, he seemed to appreciate it, and endured it both
patiently and, apparently, gratefully. In due .time he recovered, but he never became a Quaker. His belligerency
was universal. He fought bulls, boars, dogs, snakes, bees,
wasps, hornets, the streams of water from fire-engines, or
any thing else that came to hand, without the slightest
regard to odds. It was the most irresistibly laughable
thing to see him surrounded by bees, wasps, or hornets—
his eyes blazing, his jaws snapping like castanets perpetually ; and, though stung all over, indomitably standing
his ground, until the spectators would leave and call him
away for his own sake. He would then consider the battle ended ; otherwise he seemed always to prefer death to
defeat. In the course of his life he killed, as I have been
told, several dogs with which he engaged in casual fights,
and he himself was often in the hands of the surgeon ;
but he was never, to my knowledge, engaged in a dog-pit
or the like. And yet with all this, his affection for his

human friends, who treated him kindly, and for Junot alone, of the dog kind, was enthusiastic, and sometimes even affecting. In truth, strange as it may seem, he was the most fascinating dog I ever saw. So much for Dinky.

"But Junot, what shall I say of him? With long, silky, curly blue-black hair, with a noble head, out of which looked soft, chestnut-brown eyes—brave, dignified, affectionate, intelligent, and accomplished—he was the peer of any dog. His accomplishments were numerous. He would shut the door; ring the bell; bring his tail in his mouth, turning in a circle as he came; hold a piece of savory meat on his nose when he was hungry, with his mouth watering, until the word of command, when he would throw it up and catch it; sit in a chair, etc., and all this without signs, but merely at command. He would dive off a wharf into deep water, the end of his tail waving a moment above the water as he disappeared, and bring up any thing thrown in, amid the shouts of spectators, who were always attracted by his performances. He would find any thing you had lost. He would bring slippers, gloves, clothes-brushes, etc., from the chambers to the dining-room or parlor when ordered.

"On one occasion, a young lady on a visit at my father's attended an evening party. It was her first party. She was adorned with the jewelry of a married lady in the house. On her return from the party late at night, in the midst of relating the novel pleasure she had enjoyed, she suddenly paled, and putting her hand on her arm, said, 'There! I have lost one of the bracelets.' She had walked home. I inquired the route by which she had come, and taking the other bracelet, showed it to Junot. He was eager for the hunt. It was so dark that I could scarcely see my hand before me—but Junot found the bracelet.

"He formed the most devoted attachment to my father. During his last illness, he insisted on being in his room, and would furiously resent any attempt to remove him, uttering low growls of deep meaning. I alone could remove him with safety, though with difficulty. While in the room, he would from time to time stand by my father's bed with yearning affection and interest, and oc-casionally lick his hand. The family never thought him like himself after my father's death.

"But Duroc furnished an instance of canine reasoning which, if it differ from that of our superior race in de-gree, can not be distinguished from it, by me at least, in quality. When he was brought to Richmond by my brother, he was just grown. His proportions were ma-jestic, and he was very amiable. Not long after, there was a clustering of the scattered members around the old family altar. Junot was privileged, and always had the run of the house. Dinky and Duroc were under greater restrictions. But on this occasion Duroc participated in the general festivities, and followed Junot about among the family. Junot had been repeatedly sent into the chambers of the young men, and had as often brought something or other—hat, slippers, clothes-brush, etc. Du-roc had watched him for some time with glistening eyes, tail erect, and a bark which indicated good-natured rivalry. But little notice had been taken of him, while Junot had been covered with caresses and applause at each of his successes. At last Duroc marched off, and returned with head erect—thrilling all over with the pride of conscious triumph—and with a tooth-brush in his mouth, the brush end on his tongue! He received what he had fairly won

—unstinted praise. He had never been taught any thing. Now was this reason or not?"

Did you ever inquire into the meaning of that question of God in his Word, "Who knoweth the spirit of man that goeth upward, and the spirit of the beast that goeth downward to the earth?" Does *upward* mean immortality, and *downward* destruction? Is the spirit of man the breath of the Almighty, and is the spirit of the beast his creation, to have an end with all else that has a beginning?

XV.

THE ADIRONDACKS.

LEAVING these trees, I have been in the deeper shades of the Adirondacks. One night on the river and half a day by rail brought me to Glenn's Falls.

Here we mount four-horse stages, each of which stages was loaded with about twenty passengers, outside and in, and set out for Lake George. At the Half-Way House we stop to water the horses, and the landlord graciously recounts to the passengers the names of the drinks he would gladly furnish them. Milk-punch is the favorite beverage, the ladies expressing their delight in drinking it, the gentlemen saying there was a great deal of milk in it with very little rum.

The scenery on the ride to the lake is fine, and every moment enjoyable. It becomes wilder and more picturesque as we approach, and at noon we are pleasantly deposited at the hotel. For quiet beauty, without the magnificence of some of the Swiss lakes, this Lake George is unsurpassed. As I sat upon the piazza and looked out upon its placid waters, its many isles, the mountains gently rising from its very shores, in the far distance the domes of many hills like temples touching the bending skies, I readily believed that a lovelier lake could not be found.

Near by sat a small party bewailing the loss of a trunk. Two young ladies and their aged mother, or grandmother, were the sufferers. It was the old lady's trunk that was missing, and she refused to be comforted even when told of another good old woman who had met with a similar loss, and who was heard to exclaim, " I shall never see that trunk again—at least, not in this world !" A young man came out of the telegraph office, and having taken from the young ladies a description of the lost trunk, assured them he would try to look it up by asking for it at the different stations on the route from Albany to the lake. In half an hour he sent word to the young ladies that the trunk was at Fort Edward, and would come up on the next stage. Their delight was beautiful to see. " Go, thank him," said one of them to her fair sister, who rose to go for the purpose ; " thank him ; *smile* on him—BEAM on him !"—which she fondly imagined would be the young man's highest reward.

In the far North huge and fearful clouds gathered, and out of them fierce lightnings gleamed, as if the prince of the power of the air were marshaling his forces for battle. The distant roar of thunder was like "the footsteps of the dreadful God, marching upon the storm in vengeance." A week afterward, in the wilderness of the Adirondacks, I passed the ruins of a mighty pine-tree shivered by lightning, and the guide told me that it was struck in the afternoon of the Friday previous ; being the very storm that had traveled down till it burst upon us on the piazza of the hotel, a hundred miles south of the spot where the big pine was shattered.

On the loveliest lake, on the morning of the loveliest day. It was cool and bright ; the mists still clung to the mountain sides, but the sun was pouring his golden rays upon them, and they were absorbed in the glory of his coming.

Islands, at least three hundred and sixty-five, bestud this lake. Its waters are translucent to a great depth. Its shores are lined with wooded hills, and in sunny nooks peaceful hamlets and frequent villas are nestling. Thirty-six miles long is this charming lake, one stretch of beauty from shore to shore. When the lower, that is the northern end is reached, we find stages waiting to transport us four miles overland to Lake Champlain. This stage ride is a great feature in the journey. Outside seats are reserved for those who get them first, and a general scramble ensues, in which ladies are the most vigorous and successful. Four or five stages, carrying twenty passengers each, are filled. Half way across we pass an extensive building with a large sign upon it, "Graphic Lead Factory," where pencil lead is made. One man sitting behind me said to another—

"What is it that is made there?"

"Plumbago," was the answer.

"Plumbago!" exclaimed the other; "I thought that was something the matter of your back." He had probably suffered with lumbago in his time.

The manager of this stage line goes with every excursion, and as the stages arrive at the ruins of Fort Ticonderoga, he calls the whole procession to a halt, dismounts, and, taking a stand by the roadside, makes an oration to the listening and greatly amused passengers. On this occasion he was very eloquent. He drew a glowing picture of the scenes that had made this spot memorable in the history of man. The blood of warriors, savage and civilized, had consecrated the soil; Abercrombie and Montcalm, Ethan Allen and Arnold, had been made immortal by their deeds on the ground we now survey; and, waxing magniloquent as he swayed his arms like a windmill, he pointed to the future of this great country, and exclaimed: "The glorious bird of Freedom, his beak a bill of rights, and his claws just laws, shall spread his wings from the coast that is gilded with the rising sun to the western shore, whose waves are amber and whose sands are gold."

Bowing low to the applauding company, he resumed the reins, and in a few moments we passed the old fort and were on the banks of another and noble water. From the quiet beauty of Lake George, we came upon the broader and more magnificent Lake Champlain. On the eastern shore, away under the horizon, lie the Green Mountains of Vermont, and the loftier peaks of the Adirondacks support the western sky. Large islands often rise before us, and their names are identified with important events in the history of the country.

I landed at Port Kent. This has long been the grand port of entry to the wilderness. The railroad from Plattsburg now makes that point the more desirable place to land. At Port Kent is the residence of Winslow C. Watson, Esq. His father was Elkanah Watson, of Revolutionary memory, born in Plymouth, Mass., of the Winslow family, whose stock was in the *Mayflower*. He was in France during a large part of the war of the Revolution, in active co-operation and correspondence with all our great statesmen of that day. He came to the State of New York after the war, and entered ardently into schemes of internal improvement to develop the resources of the country. His sagacious mind was the first to conceive the grand idea of uniting Lake Erie and the Hudson River by canal, and he lived to see it done, though, as in many other instances, the credit of the invention has been generally given to another. He bought vast tracts of land on Lake Champlain, and settled at Port Kent, having in his mind the splendid conception of uniting the lakes of the Adirondack region with each other and then with Lake Champlain, so that four hundred miles of interior water communication would be opened up through a region whose mineral wealth and lumber are incalculably valuable.

His son, Winslow C. Watson, settled in Plattsburg when he was twenty-one years of age, and has acquired great distinction in the field of law, politics, history, and literature.

Such a man (I have enjoyed his friendship nearly forty years) met me at the landing, in the midst of a pouring rain, and in a few moments I was by a cheerful fire on the third day of August in his hospitable house, in the midst of his delightful family. His house is on a bluff, overlooking the lake at its widest part. It is fifteen miles to the Vermont shore, in a bay before us ; but the city of Burlington is only ten miles off, its spires and towers in full view. To the south, as far as the eye sees, lies the broad lake and the Green Mountain range, with Mount Mansfield and the Camel's Hump towering high above all the rest. I enjoyed a few days in such a spot, with books and friends, by the wells of philosophy and history, while the waters of the lake and the silent majesty of the mountains were speaking constantly to the soul ; a wild, romantic, and exciting region of country near, and inviting me to explore its mysteries.

Within two and a half miles of Port Kent, on the way to Keeseville and the Adirondacks, is the most wonderful chasm or gorge that is to be found in North America. Such freaks or works of nature are not unknown in Scotland and Switzerland, but I do not know of any thing like this in our country.

" The passage of the Au Sable River along its lofty and
perpendicular banks and through the chasm at the high
bridge is more familiar to the public mind than most of
the striking and picturesque features of that romantic
stream. The continued and gradual force of the current,
aided perhaps by some vast effort of nature, has formed
a passage of the river through the deep layers of sandstone rock, which are boldly developed above the village
of Keeseville, and form the embankment of the river, until it reaches the quiet basin below the high bridge. In
the vicinity of Keeseville, the passage of the stream is
between a wall of fifty feet in height on either side ; leaving these, the river glides gently along a low valley, until
suddenly hurled over a precipice, making a fall of singular beauty. Foaming and surging from this point over a
rocky bed until it reaches the village of Birmingham, it
there abruptly bursts into a dark, deep chasm of sixty
feet. A bridge, with one abutment upon a rock that divides the stream, crosses the river at the head of the fall.
This bridge is perpetually enveloped in a thick cloud of
spray and mist. In winter the frost-work incrusts the
rocks and trees with the most gorgeous fabrics : myriads
of columns and arches and icy diamonds and stalactites
glitter in the sunbeams. In the sunshine a brilliant rainbow spreads its arc over this deep abyss. All these elements, rare in their combination, shed upon this scene an
effect inexpressibly wild, picturesque, and beautiful. The
river plunges from the latter precipice amid the embra-
sures of the vast gulf, in which for nearly a mile it is quite
hidden to observation from above. It pours in a wild
torrent, now along a natural canal, formed in the rocks in
almost perfect and exact courses, and now darts madly
down a precipice. The wall rises on a vertical face upon

G

each side from seventy-five to one hundred and fifty feet, while the width of the chasm rarely exceeds thirty feet, and at several points the stupendous masonry of the opposite walls approaches within eight or ten feet. Lateral fissures, deep and narrow, project from the main ravine at nearly right angles. The abyss is reached through one of these crevices by a stairway descending to the water by two hundred and twelve steps. The entire mass of these walls is formed of laminæ of sandstone rock, laid in regular and precise structures, almost rivaling the most accurate artificial work. The pines and cedars, starting from the apertures of the wall, spread a dark canopy over the gulf. The instrumentality which has produced this wonderful work is a problem that presents a wide scope for interesting but unsatisfactory speculation.

"At the foot of the stairway is a platform, separated by a narrow, deep chasm from what is called the Table Rock. Through this passage the river, compressed into a deep and limited channel, rushes with the impetuosity of a mill-race. The Table Rock was formerly reached by walking upon a log over the chasm, and was a favorite but somewhat dangerous resort of picnic parties, until a tragic event arrested the habit. A Mr. Dyer, an Episcopal minister, was, some years ago, in the act of leading a lady across this log, when, suddenly losing his balance, he fell into the rushing torrent, and never rose to the surface, nor was his body seen by the horror-stricken spectators until days afterward, when it was found far below upon a shallow in the river."

Coming up out of the chasm, awed by the grandeur and majesty of this mighty cleft in the rocks, an agreeable surprise awaited us. The ladies of Port Kent had come out to this romantic spot, and in the shadows of the pine groves had spread a bounteous table, to which we were invited. A feast "under the trees," and in the society of new-found friends, was a welcome addition to the pleasures of the day.

Then we rode up the river to successive rapids and falls, one of which would be famous if it were in Switzerland. A grave-yard which we passed is noteworthy only for one of those queer epitaphs which betray a streak in human nature so inconsistent as to be next to incredible. It is in these exact words:

> "Sally Thorne lies here, and that's enough;
> The candle's out and so's the snuff.
> Her soul's with God, you need not fear.
> And what remains lies interred here."

Halleck's Hill was not in our way, but we rode some miles around to cross it, for the sake of the view from its summit. The plain, as well watered as any Moses saw from Pisgah, stretches away and away to the St. Lawrence; frequent church spires and villages shone in the distance, and a world of wealth, prosperity, and contentment appeared to be reposing in this vast Vega.

Some years ago a Baptist minister in this quarter gave his whole mind to horseshoe nails, and when a man gives his whole mind to any thing, something comes. So in this case. If the good man failed to make good points to his sermons, he made points to nails; and the wisest of preachers said that good words are like nails fastened by the masters of assemblies. Perhaps this analogy led him to invent his machine to point horseshoe nails; and, having perfected it, he has retired from preaching, and derives a large income from the royalty paid him by the company that uses his patent. The village of Keeseville, on the Au Sable River, flourishes with numerous manu-

facturing establishments.   Besides its twine and wire
works, the horseshoe-nail factory presents a wonderful
specimen of power and beauty in mechanical labor.   In
this thriving and beautiful village of Keeseville I spent
the night, enjoying the hospitalities of H. N. Hewitt, Esq.

The stage called at six o'clock in the morning for me
at the door.   It was cool and exhilarating, and the ride
to the Point of Rocks was exciting and delightful.   Some
of the views on the Au Sable River were picturesque and
exceedingly beautiful.   We rode pleasantly on, and came
to Au Sable Forks, where some sportsmen halted from
the stages, with rods and guns and dogs, to spend a day
or two in the woods and streams.   Here and at Black
Brook village beyond we found the vast iron-works of
J. & J. Rogers, whose mines are mines of untold wealth;
and the mountain on our right, as we ride on, is honey-
combed by the miners' toil, taking out the bowels of the
hills and bringing them down to be roasted and tortured
into the thousand uses of man.   The recent death of the
son of Mr. Rogers, a young man who had charge of the
out-of-door business, was talked of wherever we stopped
as a calamity universally deplored.   He had endeared
himself to the thousand laborers and their families by his
manly bearing, indefatigable energy, and gentle kindness.
I think, from what I heard of him, that he was a hero—
young, great, and good ; powerful to do, and yet loving as
a child.   He overtasked his strength, began to run down,
sought recovery in a milder clime, failed to find it, came
back and died at home, among the people who loved him,
and who wept over his grave as if their leader and brother
had fallen.   It is something to know that in the midst of
the woods and mines and furnaces such a life is seen and
felt in our matter-of-fact day.   He was doubtless impru-

dent and over-earnest in his work ; but to die at twenty-four, with the benedictions of the sons of toil upon his dying head, is noble and blessed compared with an old age enriched by the ill-requited service and loaded with the reproaches of the poor.

High on the hills the charcoal burners pursue their carbonic work, and we frequently meet their long, black, huge vans, dragged along toward the furnaces, loaded with coal. By the roadside kilns are built, to which the wood is drawn and carbonized, and in one place we passed an extensive manufactory of creosote. All the industries of the country are such as relate to lumber and minerals. These are apparently inexhaustible. The pressure of demand will gradually compel better ways, for now we are riding over the ruins of a plank road, and worse going can hardly be found, unless the corduroy patent is worse on which Governor Marcy met with that accident to one of his garments for which he brought the State of New York into his debt to the amount of fifty cents.

My fellow-passenger on the front seat sought to be social. He was kind enough to inform me that he was from Boston. He was bound for the woods and camp, and his implements of sport—tools of trade—lying and standing about him, showed that he had purchased his outfit regardless of expense. Alas! for my judgment by appearances. We halted to water the weary and heated horses at a trough filled from a sweet spring. The youth anticipated the horses, and drawing from his bag a large bottle of whisky, poured some into a tin dipper, and adding just a trifle of water, pronounced it with a big oath to be good, and drank it off. He handed the bottle to the driver, who had hastened to his side, and greedily did

likewise, excepting that he did not add water. He said
he never liked to mix his drinks. After they and the
other animals were refreshed, we got under way again ;
the young man was more loquacious than before ; the
driver and he to their profaneness added vulgarity, a
mixture less disagreeable to both than even whisky and
water. They could not wait till they came to another
watering-place before they refreshed again, but, taking the
bottle by the neck, they guzzled, turn about. At every
spring to which we came they both descended and fra-
ternally drank, with coarse jokes, laughter, and swearing.
The only decent thing about it was that they did not invite me to join them in a drink. These frequent pota-
tions soon began to tell upon them, and they grew livelier
and more boisterous in their jollity. The Bostonian
punched the horses with the butt of his rifle to make
them go faster, while the muzzle of it was often pointing
fearfully toward my part of the stage. This was great
amusement. Then he took out his revolver, and let the
driver divert himself by firing it off at the trees by the
wayside as we rode along. A rifle in the hands of one
and a pistol in those of another intoxicated fellow were
making my situation unpleasant, and I began to fancy
that the dangers of the wilderness were upon me much
sooner than they were anticipated. I could have managed a bear or two, but these drunken ruffians, each of
them sporting with fire-arms, were unbearable. How
soon they might be tempted to take a pop at me, or what
might happen from an accidental shot, I could not tell;
but it would not have been strange if something serious
had occurred at any moment. The long forenoon wore
away in these exciting exercises. The rough plank road
became rougher as we proceeded. Nothing on it was

kept in repair but the toll-gates. Jolting on, pitching about, turning out to get by a bad place, we picked our way through the woods, till at last we reached Franklin Falls, where we were to stop for dinner. This over, and the horses being rested or exchanged, we resumed our seats. The dinner and the liquor made the youth and the driver stupid. The one stretched himself at full length upon a vacant seat in the stage, and was soon sleeping soundly. The other resisted the coming drowsiness a little longer ; but after a while, having no one to talk to him, fell asleep with the reins in his hands, and the horses took their own way—a very slow one always, and now a little more so. We crept on, gradually rising, the scenery more and more wild and weird and gloomy.

At Bloomingdale I left the stage which had thus far brought me on. Mounted upon the high seat in the front of the stage that bore upon it the name of Paul Smith, I rode a couple of hours from Bloomingdale right into the woods; now and then a clearing improved by culture met the eye, but it was plain that we were passing away from civilization and plunging into the wilderness. Suddenly we emerged from the dense forest on the margin of a lovely lake, and a short turn in the road brought us in front of a large, handsome hotel. Its broad piazza was filled with genteel guests, ladies and children, apparently at home ; and yet we are now in the lake country of the Adirondacks. The name of this place is Paul Smith. That is the name of the house—also of the proprietor and landlord. He was named Apollos Smith, and submitted to that name until he was long and widely known as Pol Smith, and then the heathen name gave place to the Christian, and Pol became Paul. As Paul Smith, he began to keep a little tavern on this lake, to give shelter and liquor to

travelers; but my good friend, Thomas H. Faile, Esq., encouraged him to drop the liquor, and the loss proved a
great gain.   He began to flourish forthwith.   His tavern
grew larger and larger every year.   He built new wings
and raised the roof, and stretched the verandas, until
now his house is by far the greatest and best in this whole
region, and Paul Smith does more business than all the
rest of the hotels together.   His house is on the margin
of the lower St. Regis Lake, bright mirror of the St. Regis Mountain, that stands in full view of the hotel, and
within easy reach by boat.

The first friend to greet me was Dr. McCosh, of
Princeton College, who was here quietly domesticated.
One could hardly imagine a more decided change for a
great philosopher and teacher than to leave college clois-
ters, and find the long-drawn aisles of these forest temples, with the woods, the waters, and the skies for his only
studies.   The seclusion is profound in spite of the company.   He had just returned from Mount St. Regis, to
the summit of which he and his family, including three ladies, had walked, making a journey of ten miles up and
down a mountain, and all were as fresh as the morning
when they returned.   After supper, and in the cool, late
evening, he and I went out into the middle of the lake in
a little boat, and sat under the stars.   It was an hour for
thought and recollection, and naturally we recurred to
scenes we had enjoyed together in other years and lands.
He visited this country ten years ago, and the day after
his arrival we went to the Falls of Niagara, and there,
while he was studying that wonder of Nature, I was studying a nobler work of God.

DEER SHOOTING.

There was great excitement on the piazza of Paul Smith's Hotel. The ladies were excited. The gentlemen were astir. Even the children were alive to the matter that now absorbed the attention of all hands. They were drawing lots! Lots for what? A grand hunt for deer was to come off the next day. To shoot a deer in the Adirondacks is a deed to be proud of, to boast of with that modest self-complacency which hangs around all truly great sportsmen. They go home from their summer campaign in the wilderness laden with spoils of victory. Their spear and their bow, or rather rifle, got them the trophies that now adorn their halls; the branching antlers of a noble buck are stuck upon the wall of their dining-room, and perhaps the skin has been made into an elegant mat that stretches itself before the fire. Admiring friends, who have never been in the woods, listen with mute wonder while the proud host relates the perils of the forest in which he pursued the monarch of the herd, and brought him low with the unerring aim of his trusty gun. Perhaps there is no pleasure in this world superior to that of the gallant hunter retailing to unsophisticated listeners his triumphs in the field.

The brave, hardy, eager gentlemen from New York and other cities were now prepared to go out the next morning to renew the chase. They go two or three times a week, and as the hunt is attended with great expense, exposure, and fatigue, and many are to share in it, it is just that each should have a fair chance to bag the game and glory of the day. The shore of the lake is laid off into sections, and each section has its point of observation. These points are some considerable distance asunder, and lots are drawn by which the station of each one going to join the hunt is determined. This allotment is made overnight, that when early morning comes, each brave deerslayer repairs to his post, and with all the patience he may possess awaits the issue. With him, in a light boat, is the guide, who rows and knows the spot to which his man is assigned. The boat soon reaches the point, and nothing is to be done but to wait, in it or on the shore, as the wary and anxious sportsman pleases. Thus the lake is environed with the watchful picket guardsmen.

In the mean time a real huntsman—a paid and experienced man of the woods—enters the forest, with a leash of hounds, some six or eight, attached to his belt. Well in, he lets off a dog, trained to the service and eager to have a run, who begins at once to run in a circle, widening constantly as he seeks to get upon the trail of a deer. The hunter goes on and lets off another dog, and then another, until he has started his whole pack, who, running in circles, scour the whole forest, and seldom fail to scare up a buck. The moment the dog strikes the scent he begins to bark, and the glad sound meets the distant ears of the waiting watchers on the lake. The deer, alarmed, instinctively takes to the water, as the only way to break the trail and deprive the dog of his scent, by which he is keeping up the chase. The noble animal rushes through the forest into the lake to swim across. He is the prize of the boat nearest to which he takes the water. The guide rows in pursuit of him, and being able to row far more rapidly than the poor beast can swim, has no difficulty in overtaking him. When he has come so near that the merest bungler with a gun, who could not hit a barn door across the road, can now put the muzzle of the gun into the ear of the animal, if he please, the gallant

Nimrod blazes away with his new rifle, lodges the bullet in the brain of the beast, and the work is done. If the deer, however, will not keep still long enough to be shot in this way, the guide takes him by the tail and holds him while the accomplished sportsman shoots him in the head. It sometimes occurs that even then, with the buck thus held by the tail at one end and the rifle in the hands of an excited shooter at another, the ball goes all abroad and the game is not hurt. Then the guide, with an oar or with his own stalwart arms, manages to get the animal's head under water, and so drowns him. But in the best of the business, it requires the same amount of science, skill, valor, and endurance to kill a deer that it would to go out to the barn and kill the cow. Give the cow the run of the yard, and it would be more of a feat to bring her down with a rifle than to slay a deer in the Adirondacks.

Before the present plan of laying off the lake into stations was hit upon, the rule was that whoever got within rifle-shot of the deer in the water first should fire. One of my friends was out with a party hunting ! When the deer took to the lake the boats started from their several points, and the gentleman in the first fired and missed. Then came up the second, and his aim was equally bad. The deer now belonged to the third, whose right there was none to dispute. He came on, and having his son, a lad of twelve years, with him, laid the boat alongside of the swimming buck, which the guide kindly seized and held fast by the tail while the boy delivered the charge into his head and made him dead.

The slain deer is now towed to the shore and transported to the hotel in triumph. All the ladies shake hands with the successful hero of the day, who is congratulated upon his heroism and prowess as a hunter. He is the champion of the woods until the next hunt comes off, and some one else, going through the same fearful. scenes, comes home with the spoils of the chase, to be greeted with the applause of admiring women and crowned with the laurels of the latest victory.

This evening a distinguished divine was the hero, having brought in from the last hunt the trophies of the field, a noble pair of antlers and the skin of a fat buck. It is not probable that he will be equally successful to-morrow, for you observe that it does not depend upon the skill or patience or power of the sportsman; but the simple matter is, whether the frightened animal flees into the lake near one boat or another. It is death to him to go into the water any where, for the lake is lined with rifles ready to do him execution. It is only a question of chance as to whether this or that man, the banker or the baker, the lawyer or the divine, shall have the pleasure and the glory of letting out the life-blood of the pride of the forest.

It is quite essential to the good standing of a gentleman who comes here to shoot that he should kill at least one deer. The ladies enter so heartily into it that a man fancies he loses somewhat in the eyes of his own wife if he fail to assassinate one or two bucks during the season. Not long ago a clergyman from the city of New York, who was equally anxious and unlucky, having heard that a guide had a pet deer of his own, bought the beast, and hired the man to take it out slyly in the morning and tie it to a tree. The reverend hunter followed, shot the poor thing and brought it home to his wife, who rejoiced with him as one who had taken great spoils.

There are other ways of taking deer here, such as

watching for them by night at favorite places where they come to the lake for drink, and shooting them there ; but this requires work in the dark, and keeps a gentleman out of his bed when he prefers to be in it. The more common one I have described, which is attended with no fatigue nor exposure, as the valiant hunter can take his lunch and an umbrella with him, and hunt a deer to the death without rising from his seat. So far as I know, this is the most luxurious mode of enjoying " the chase " that is at present practiced among accomplished sportsmen. Nothing could be safer and pleasanter, unless you sit in an arm-chair at the menagerie and fire at the beasts in their cages.

Hence we view : 1. That the killing of a deer in the Adirondacks is no very great exploit. 2. That the least said about it the better. 3. That the killing of deer is in itself right and proper, for the animal is good for the food of man, and all that are killed are duly eaten. We are fond of venison, and the Creator doubtless provided it for our use. It is quite proper that ministers and laymen should take a hand in purveying for the table, and the zest of the hunt is a pleasure to be enjoyed by those who like it. Because I have no taste for the sport, I will not infer that it is foolish or wicked for others. Let them enjoy it. But the romance of deer-stalking and the renown of the successful huntsman somewhat fade as we contemplate the picture of two men in a boat, the one holding a beast in the water while the other shoots him. It is right, but it is not great.

But there is glory up here. There is one glory of the woods, and another glory of the lakes, and another of the mountains. And the heavens cover the wilderness with their glory. And nature is untutored, wild, luxuriant, free,

jubilant. You can shout as loud as you like, and sing
and laugh, and nobody with store clothes or city ways
will hear you. You breathe freely and expand your chest,
and forget there is a book in the world, and don't care
if there is never to be another, and then take a strong pull
at the oar, and get tired and hungry before you go in to
eat and sleep and rise up to play.

If thinking is your mood, there's nothing here to hinder.
It is the most subdued, quiet, solemn solitude that my
soul was ever in. I have seen no signs that the aborig-
ines were ever here. No one is here but the strangers
who come and go. And the Invisible ! The Great Spirit
is here dwelling in the forest temples, riding upon the
circle of the heavens, speaking in the wind and thunder.
It is good always to be in the midst of him ; to feel this
strong wholesome air to be his love—an unseen sea, in
which we float and bathe and rejoice continually ; to look
down into this mirror in which his blue sky is reflected,
and to see in that beautiful concave tokens of his providence, care, and kindness, a loving Father over all and in
all, and we in him, now and always. We will get health
and strength in these wild woodlands, and then go down
to use them all for him, and those he bids us love and
serve. Life is good. Work is good. It is all very
good. Even play is good. And by-and-by rest. No
more toil. No pain. No misunderstanding. But peace,
rest, love, praise.

FISHING IN THE LAKES.

I flatter myself that I am lineal successor of that apostle who said, " I go a-fishing ;" or of one of those six who
said, "We also go with thee." From early childhood I
have been in that line. If half the time spent by the

brookside fishing had been given to study, I would have more book-lore to-day. Perhaps, also, less of nature, less of health, less of the world. The late Rev. Dr. Bethune was one of the ardent lovers of the rod, the fly, and the stream, a thorough enthusiast in the art and science of fishing; and when I asked him where he first *learned to love* it, he said that when he was a boy at school in Salem, N. Y., a man who was known as Fisher Billy was often sent up there from Cambridge—the town below—to go upon the limits of the jail—the limits were a mile every way from the jail, and a debtor had the freedom of the limits. Fisher Billy, always in debt, for he would go a-fishing when he ought to be at work, would bring his rod and lines and whip the brooks about Salem. Young Bethune fell into his company, and was then and there inspired with love of this gentle art. "The very man," I replied, "who first taught me." And so it proved that Fisher Billy, in jail at Salem, was fishing with Bethune; out of jail, Billy and I followed the running brooks together in Cambridge.

It is more of an art and more of a science now than it was then. And all the brooks and lakes within easy reach of the cities have been hunted and whipped and worried till trout—the only fish that true amateur fishermen seek after—have become as rare as gold eagles or silver dollars. Up here in these lakes and streams of the Adirondack region, there is as yet comparative retirement and peace. It is only a term of some thirty or forty years since these primitive wilds were invaded by the sportsman. The hundred lakes and rivers and rivulets are too many and too vast to have been sensibly affected by these years of spoil. All the lakes are not inhabited by trout. Some of them are infested with lizards, that

leave nothing else alive within their domains. They
would devour all the eggs that fish would lay if there
were any on such employment bent. Seth Green could
not propagate trout where pickerel abound. In fact,
trout are such good eating that they eat one another.
And many of these waters are therefore as clear of fish
as the lakes in Central Park. Others swarm with them.
All the fishing of the amateurs produces no perceptible
reduction of the number. Only a few of the thousands
who come here catch any. The rest go a-fishing. But
fishing is one thing, catching fish is another. I have
done a good deal of both in my day, and though now not
much addicted to the sport, and rarely finding time in the
course of a year to indulge in the passion of younger days,
I can tell you how to fish with a fly.

Fly-fishing ranks among the graceful arts. A fly rod
should be twelve feet long, light, very flexible, and yet
strong. English anglers adhere to heavy rods. American sportsmen regard a seven - ounce rod the perfect
weight for trout, and are yearly decreasing the weight of
their salmon rods.

The line should be braided silk, or a prepared silk line.
Hair and silk intermingled make a line highly recom-
mended by the dealers, but wholly rejected by experienced anglers. For trout-fishing the line should be about
a hundred feet long. The leader, or, as some call it, the
casting-line, should be nine feet long. The reel should
be as light as possible to hold the hundred feet of line.
There are so many persons to whom fly-fishing is a mystery that it may be well to explain it.

Imagine, then, the reel in its place on the light rod,
the silk line passed through the rings to the tip, where
the casting-line, of silk worm-gut, is attached. On the

casting-line, at equal distances apart, are looped two or three artificial flies. Grasping the rod in the right hand, the angler pulls off two feet or so of line from the reel with his left hand, and then gently, but with great skill, throws this increase of length through the rings and off from the end of the rod, steadily and gracefully increasing the length of line with each wave of the rod, until he has given out as long a line as he intends to cast. This length of cast will depend on a variety of circumstances; it may be only the length of the rod, or it may extend to nearly or quite a hundred feet. The casting-line which carries the flies falls on the water, lying out straight at the end of the line. Then the angler lifts the rod in his hand, thus drawing the flies along near or on the surface of the water. He draws them only a few feet, and if no trout rise to seize the fly, he lifts the line from the water with a slight jerk of the rod, throws it back over his shoulder, and again forward to the surface of the water, again drawing and lifting and casting. The object is to draw the flies over the surface of the water in various directions, and thus "whip" all the water in which trout are apt to be.

The trout, seeing the fly, rushes up from below, and generally strikes it with a swinging blow of his tail, at the same instant turning his open mouth to seize it. A slight movement of the angler's wrist strikes the hook into the mouth of the fish, and then it only remains to land him. A light fly rod is never used to lift a fish from the water. A landing-net is needed, unless the angler is well used to landing fish with his hand. The rod must be always held so that it bends, and thus the spring of the rod keeps the hook tight in the mouth of the fish. If the rod be light, this bend and spring will generally prevent the breaking

H

of the line or the tearing out of the hook. The fish struggles to get free, but the angler gradually reels in the line
until there is only the nine feet of casting-line beyond the
tip. Then, if the fish be well tired out, he lifts him to the
top of the water, places the landing-net under him, and
takes him out.

It is a meditative amusement. Fly-fishing is more exciting than the vulgar way of bait, though I regard the latter as the more honorable of the two. In both cases you
deceive the fish, but with the fly you mock him with the
semblance of the insect, and he jumps for it and is caught
with a bare hook; in the latter case he takes the veritable food he needs, and dies at his dinner. The question
is not worth debating, but I rather prefer the worm. All
real sportsmen despise fishing with bait where it is possible to cast the fly. I have a brother to whom all my love
for piscatory pleasures passed at his birth. Certain it is
that on or about the time of his coming into the world
my fondness for it ceased, and has never returned, while
he grew up with a passion for the sport, which has grown
with his growth. I have fished in his company this summer, finding far more excitement and enjoyment in seeing
him throw a line sixty or seventy feet long and pick a
trout up at that far distance from the boat than to both-
er and blunder about it myself. He came up here before
me, and you will not be surprised that the receipt of such
a letter as the following stirred within me the slumbering
fires of youth, fires that made me take to the waters.

MY BROTHER'S LETTER.

PAUL SMITH'S, *June* 18.

"*Dear Brother:*—My health and strength continue on
the gain, through constant exercise and exposure in the

open air. Rain or shine, I am out from morning till
night, and I sleep serenely. Last Saturday I fished the
Osgood River, through the 'burned ground,' and brought
in ninety-three trout, many very fair-sized, and all good
fish. It is plain that large fish are not to be found here
as plentifully as in old times. I recall my first visit to
this spot some fourteen years ago, and the numbers of
large trout that rose to my flies in the bay, at the mouth
of the Weller Brook. Now they are rare. Yesterday
morning I had for the first time an hour's sport which
reminded me of old times. I went out just at daybreak.
My guides, John and Frank, had not yet put in their
morning appearance, and I took a boat and went alone
around Island Point into the bay. Off the point a low
fog covered the water — a sure sign that no trout would
rise there; but I was glad to run out of it as I entered
the bay and found a clear, soft morning, with a slight rip-
ple on the water from a rising breeze. For three weeks
past I have been searching the bay for trout. I have had
no doubt whatever that there was a point of rendezvous
somewhere in the semicircle whose radius is over a fourth
of a mile. But I have cast, morning and evening, over
what seemed to me every inch of its surface, and found
only a few small fish.

" As I emerged from the fog and looked ahead (I was
pushing, not pulling my boat), I saw a good trout break
the surface two hundred feet from me ; and, shoving swiftly forward, I threw two flies over the spot before the concentric waves which he had made had wholly vanished.
The tail fly was a dark jungle-cock, and the bobber a
scarlet ibis. Imagine my satisfaction, as the flies struck
the water, at the sight of a fine trout going out into the
air and coming down, head first and mouth open, on the

scarlet ibis. No need to strike him. He was hungry, and hooked himself tight and firm; and the first rush he made—bending my Norris rod in a semicircle as I gave him the spring of it—told me that he was a strong fish for his weight, which turned out a trifle over two pounds. We don't kill trout now, as we used in our boy sports. What is there that we do now as then? Do you know of any thing? Many a trout I have landed with a home-made fly on the end of a short linen line, tied to a birch or a hackmatack rod, by guiding him in the current of a brook till I could suddenly rush him down stream and out of the water on some gravel beach, where sometimes (when I was a very small shaver—the trout very large) I would literally fall on him, and surround him with my arms and legs. All that was ages and ages ago; and now I am fishing with a rod that cost sixty dollars, a reel that cost twenty, and a line that cost six, and flies that cost two and three dollars a dozen, and—oh, that I had known the use of it when we were boys—a landing-net, the cost of which I can't tell, for I have used it ten years, and in repairs during that time it has passed through several generations of distinct existence in each separate part of it. And with all this tackle do I kill more trout than when I was a boy? Yes, fourfold. All the twaddle about country boys and country tackle beating the city sportsman is nonsense. I speak from thorough knowledge of both. In a mountain brook where the trout are small and plenty, give me bare legs, a birch rod, and a short line. But in lake fishing where large trout are not over-plenty, the costly fly-rod and tackle, in the hands of a knowing sportsman, will do the work. By long casts and rapid, easy work, he covers in a short time a vast extent of water, and thus finds the fish that would be slow to find a baited hook. You should see the working of one of these six-ounce Norris rods. It is a beautiful piece of machinery, and a fish once fairly hooked is as good as landed.

"When I struck that two-pounder, had he been on a line fast to a birch pole, his first rush would probably have torn the hook from his mouth, or broken rod or line; and if I had tried in the old-fashioned way to lift him out of water, the chances are ten to one I would have lost him. But my Norris rod bends tip to butt without breaking, and when he started I threw the rod back over my shoulder, and the tip, thin as a knitting-needle, was out before my eyes pointing to the fish—the spring of the rod serving to keep the hook gently pressed in its place, and the reel paying out line as long as the trout continued his rush. One, two, three rushes, and then he turned and began to swim in a circle, and, yielding to the pressure, approached the boat as I reeled in. Then he swam around me, rushed under the boat now and then, made some sharp, short dashes, and after three or five minutes of struggling gave it up, and allowed me to bring him where I could put the landing-net under him. As I tried that he made one quick plunge, but he was in the net, and then in the boat. I cast my flies again instantly, and two fish rose, one seizing the bobber, and the other the tail fly. This time each fish struck the fly with his tail, and, turning sharp, seized it with his mouth. Both were hooked, and both landed. So it went on, and in an hour or less I had killed nine trout, which weighed eleven and a half pounds. This is nothing, in point of size, compared with what we do in Maine and Northern New Hampshire; but the fish are strong. This is the best hour's sport I have had, and I have given you rather a

longer account of it than you will care for.   But come up
here, and see or do the thing yourself.   I love angling so
well that I always like better to see another take fish than
to take them myself.   And I know no other place where
one can live in so good a hotel and find plenty of trout.
I shall be here till the first, and if you can not come till
I have gone, I can trust you to the tender mercies of
Paul, and by that time you will find plenty of sportsmen
here.   Just now, I have the house pretty much to myself."

ON THE LAKES.

Early in the morning Paul Smith stood upon the shore
of the lake near one side of a light skiff, and Dr. McCosh
by the other.   I was in it, and alone, except the guide,
who was to be my oarsman, and to conduct me through
many of the lakes of the Adirondacks.   The landlord of
the hotel and the President of Princeton had done me
the great honor of rising with the larks to see me off.   As
I pushed out into the waters of the Lower St. Regis, a
sense of solitude began at once to come over me.   The
venerable Doctor had given me his blessing as we parted,
and I felt it was good to have it.   The morning mists
disappeared before the sun coming up in his strength,
and the loveliness of a cool day in August ; a bright,
bracing atmosphere lay around and over me, possessing
my veins and filling me with the rich sensations of high
animal enjoyment.   This is the luxury of living, of simply
being a thing with life, rejoicing in taking a long breath,
shouting, rowing, or leaping.   We do not know much of
this in town, certainly not in hot weather.   It marks the
difference in nations, and tells on character, religion, letters, and art.   It is climate : not half enough studied in
its bearings upon society and the progress of the race.

A quarter of an hour took me across the lake into the "slew," through which the guide poled the boat cautiously among the fallen trees and snags into Spitfire, a lakelet with a name that does it justice, and then by a narrow pass into St. Regis Lake, the upper. This is nearly on the summit of the lake region, 1500 or 2000 feet above the sea, its waters flowing off to the north, and the lakes into which we are soon to come discharging themselves eastward, and then northeasterly into Lake Champlain.

A sense of exquisite beauty filled me as the skiff glided gracefully into the midst of this lovely sheet of water. The sun was now well up in the blue, cloudless sky. Many isles lay around on the bosom of the lake. They and the shores were covered with dense pine and spruce trees. The water was like a polished mirror of steel. The islands were reflected. So was the heaven above me. Sometimes over the forest shores the distant ranges of mountains told me there was a world beyond and out of the limits of the bowl in which I was floating. But the lake seemed as a little sea of glass, clear as crystal, brilliant in the sun, skirted with living green, evergreen, and the feeling of the place was that of perfect isolation from "the world and the rest of mankind." During all the tour of these and three or four lakes yet to be mentioned, I did not see a boat or the face of a man, or any thing to intimate that one had ever entered this charming desert before. No voice, no gun, no bark of a dog in the all-surrounding forest disturbed the deep serenity of the scene. Now and then the scream of a loon, fearfully like that of a human cry, would pierce the ear and increase the stillness as it ceased. But for my guide, who happily was stupid and said nothing, I was the only man there. It was a natural paradise, and I was as solitary as Adam before Eve appeared. Charles V. said of the cathedral of Burgos, such was its beauty, it should be put under a glass case and kept for show. It was almost painful to me that the loveliness of this scene is lost to the world. Why is such a waste of glory here? The sun shines on nothing more charming to behold. Here it lies, and the summer dies away into winter; and then the spring clothes it with resurrection beauty again. Perhaps the angels see it. But why was so much glory spilled where so few mortals, out of millions, ever see it?

We touched the southern shore of the lake and stood in the margin of a dense forest, apparently impenetrable, certainly gloomy, damp, and cold. Out of the thicket emerged an old man, in many-colored and patched raiment, with long and matted beard and hair, who was not far above his companions of the woods, and this queer old fellow had with him a horse and a sled. Without words, for his business was understood by the guide, who knew where to meet him, the little boat was pulled out of the water and hoisted upon the sled, and we three trudged behind it as the beast drew it along over the damp, swampy way that had been made for this purpose. This is called a "carry." It might have been avoided by taking a passage around it by what is called "the nine carries," so many little lakes with slight separations, over which the guide drags or lifts his boat. As this is harder work for him, he said nothing to me of that route, and as the rule of the country is to get all the expenses, as well as the $2 50 a day to the guide, out of the traveler, the guide has clear gain by making his passenger pay the dollar, which is the fare on this overland ferry; then you pay him another dollar to come back over it the next day, which he saves for himself by going through the "nine carries " to-morrow. The old ferryman proved to be a character, a Frenchman, whose first name was Moses. His other name was to me unintelligible, though he and the guide took turns in pronouncing it for me. He is a trapper in winter, and makes game of the beavers and otter and mink, whose furs pay him better than toting boats across the land in summer. The walk was through a low and wet pathway in the woods, and I was quite ready to suppose we had made a long two miles' march when Moses lifted up his voice and cried, " Half-way !"

Another half-hour brought us to the border of another lake, at a clearing where stands the solitary cabin of Moses the Trappist; for he might well be one of that order, his business being indicated by the title and his solitude befitting the monk. About his abode were all the tools and signs of his craft. And a barrel of cider on skids, with a junk bottle inserted into the bung-hole, told me that however smart he might be in catching muskrats, he does not know how to make vinegar. Take the bottle out; leave the bung out; let the barrel be half full of cider; shake it thoroughly three times a day, and it will be vinegar in ten days. The bottle keeps the oxygen out; shaking gets it in and does the business. "What I know about farming " is very little, but I can make vinegar, though well aware that more flies are caught with molasses.

At the door of the cabin of Moses the Trapper we embarked on Big Clear Pond, a round lake, with no islands in it, and four miles in diameter. The wind had now risen, and as the little skiff danced about merrily, my dull guide sought to entertain me with narrow escapes he had made on former excursions, when he had ladies for passengers, who had been frightened greatly on this very lake, which has a fine sweep for the wind, and easily makes a great swell. As we approached the other shore, he gave a shrill whistle to summon a man to the " carry." In some stages of the water we could follow the " slew " between this and the next lake ; but now it was too shallow, and we were obliged to resort to horse-power. At the beach a boy was waiting with a horse and cart. Upon the latter was hoisted the boat, which was fastened in its place with pegs, and as the stretch was some three miles across—a longer walk than was agreeable—I resumed my seat in the boat on the cart, and was jolted and tumbled over the horrible pass, into the densest forest and through marshy ground, that made the ride any thing but enjoyable. Nor was the comfort of the journey increased by the heavy thunder that now rolled over us, presaging rain, from which the only protection would be the boat turned upside down, with myself on the wet ground underneath. Happily the clouds passed over, and when we emerged from the forest the sun came out also to meet us. On the edge of the lake to which we had now come stood a neat hotel, to which we were urgently invited ; but the time for rest and refreshment had not come, and we launched our tiny craft once more, and now we were on the bosom of the Upper Saranac.

This is the queen of the lakes. It is nine miles long, with irregular shores, wooded points putting out and making lovely nooks and bays, with frequent isles floating, as it were, on the surface. Some of these islands have traditions hanging around them, and one of them will be pointed out for years to come as the scene of a tragical event that happened upon it this very season. At the close of a very fine day last spring, a man and his wife had rowed out to the island, and were sitting near the shore enjoying the sunset. A gentleman out on the lake with his guide and boat espied something white on the island, and the guide insisted that it was a loon. The gentleman was not satisfied, but the guide took his rifle and fired, killing the woman on the spot.

A map of this wilderness country will show a hundred and more lakes to the west of the one we are now pass-ing through, and weeks as easily as days might be spent in going from one to another; but the journey would be-come tedious perhaps from sameness. Sweets cloy. This chain of lakes is " linked sweetness long drawn out." It is a system of lakes, rather than a chain. Raquette Lake is the largest of them all, with a shore of ninety miles, and it is 1800 feet above the sea, and the Blue Mountain rises east of it 4000 feet high, with a lake of the same name at its foot, esteemed the Pearl of the Wilderness. Raquette River enters Long Lake, sixteen miles long, and coming out of it, is navigable for thirty miles, and then enters Tupper's Lake, more celebrated for its picturesque beauty than any of the many around it. When the river leaves this lake again it rolls its augmented volume out of the wilderness into the fertile fields of St. Lawrence County. Thus the whole length and breadth of this strange country may be traversed by boats so light as to be easily carried on the shoulders of a man. When I had reached the lower end of the Saranac Lake, my guide drew the boat upon the land, and taking a yoke fitted for his shoulders and neck, put it across the middle of the boat; then, lying upon the ground, pulled the boat over so that the shoulder yoke came to its place, and, rising up, had the boat over his head and slanting down his back ; he walked off with it a few hundred rods, and deposited it in the Saranac River.

Here is Bartlett's, a very comfortable hotel—a great resort for sportsmen. It is not approached by any land

carriage—its only path being through the lakes by boat.
I dined here alone, the company being all out in the
forests and on the waters. The dinner was splendid:
trout, with egg sauce that any hotel in New York might
be proud of, and venison such as Sydney Smith's epicu-
rean neighbor never tasted.

Launching our boat upon the Saranac at its first issue
from the lake, we shot down the stream. It would be a terrible journey, but how grand to pursue it through lakes and
rapids, and cataracts and mountain gorges and fertile
plains, in the midst of millions of lumber rushing amain
down, till at last, after a descent of 1500 feet, it empties
into Lake Champlain away off at Plattsburg. We were
carried along but a few miles into Round Lake, and
through that into the broad, deep, swift current of the
river, which, with little aid of oars, swept us rapidly on.
After touching at the shore to drink from a spring which
was indicated by a board, on which was written " Jacob's
Well," we were soon ushered into the Lower Saranac
Lake. A steady pull at the oars, at the close of a long
day's rowing, when my guide might well be well worn,
brought us in an hour to the eastern end of it. Just as
I emerged from the lake, and at the verge of the forest,
I encountered a bear. Instantly he rose upon his hind
legs and thrust out his fore-paws, as if he were seeking a
prime dinner. I thought of my revolver, but it was fifty
miles away; of my rifle, but it was in my study at home.
He would not bear with me while I sought them to bore
him. Just as he made a plunge toward me, a chain that
went from his neck to a tree restrained him. That chain
of circumstances saved me, and made me sure that he
was not a beast to be feared. We are often frightened
at bears as harmless as this.

AMONG THE GUIDES.

The bear was at Martin's. I spent the night at Martin's. It is the largest hotel, except Paul Smith's, in the Adirondacks. Sportsmen and others often make this the first point on coming to the woods. Paul Smith's is the more civilized. This is rougher, but very comfortable.

An outer court—a covered passage between the house and the offices, quarters for the guides and dogs—affords a breezy lounge, and here in the cool of the day the company, tired with the day's work, enjoy the air and rest. One of the guides having been suddenly taken sick on the lakes, was brought up in the arms of his comrades, and a crowd pressed about him. No physician being on hand, I took the case, but the regular practice—a stiff glass of brandy—anticipated my prescriptions, and the man was better in the morning.

This incident led one of the guides to sit down on the steps at my feet and beguile the evening with information about the country, with which he had been familiar from his childhood. He thought but very little of it as a resort for consumptives, though many of them come here and go away nothing better, but a great deal worse. He told me a sad story of a young man brought in by his father, who doted on him with the "love of a mother"—as if that is more than a father's, as it is not; he tended the sick boy in camp, and ministered to him as well as he could, but the rough life of the woods is not for sick people. It makes well ones better; men who have been worn down with work at home, brain work especially, they come here and recruit splendidly. But the sick boy went home to die, and sick people would do well, if they do not get well, by staying away from these woods and waters. And then my talking friend very easily wandered on to telling me of a family in his native town, in Essex County, who had the consumption as a family inheritance, and he dwelt tenderly on one of them —"She was only seventeen years old, as bright as a silver dollar and as pretty as a doll; her lips were *white*, and her hair was yellow, and her eyes were blue, and we did not want her to die. And she did not want to, but she said it would be just as well, and she would not fret; but the sweet little thing kind o' melted away like, and just went to sleep and never waked up ag'in."

"Will she never wake up again?" I said, softly.

"Well, now, Mister, you put it to me, I know she will; but it was a good many years ago, when I was a younger man than what I am now, and she has slept on, and it has never been as light in the world to me as it was before she went out. But the minister said at her funeral —and I never forgot how it sounded, as he stood by the coffin, and said—'The maiden is not dead, but sleepeth.' Do you think she will ever come to us ag'in?"

"I think she is not far from you now, and that she is happier when you are good; and that by-and-by you will pass away into the spirit world where she is, and, if you are pure and true, that you and she will be perfectly blessed forever. Did you ever hear these words, 'He that liveth and believeth shall never die?'"

"To be sure I have; but we shall *all* die."

"And yet not perish: die as these lakes and woods die in winter; but spring comes, and every lake laughs in the noontide sun, and every woodland and meadow bursts into living beauty. You have seen it a score of times."

"Yes, and more; and I do like to hear you talk."

"But you brought it on; now go on with your own story. What good does any one get from coming here?"

"Rheumatism gits cured. The guides never have it— I ought not to say *never*, for I had it once myself, and I put a heap of balsam branches over the live coals of fire, and lay down on it and went to sleep, aching to kill with the rheumatism. The boughs did not blaze, but they burned some, and the smoke came up through, with the smell of the balsam, and it steamed away all the aches and pains, and I never had a touch of it after that."

"You think it does a man good, then, to sleep in a swamp when he has the rheumatism?"

"Not as a general thing; but if he will sleep on pine boughs, spruce, hemlock, balsam of fir, and such like, and keep dry, he will git over the rheumatism, sure."

This friendly guide talked to me an hour or more, in the dark, and seemed pleased to have a ready listener. He told me much of the agricultural productions of the lower country, and of his hopes to be done with guiding travelers and going back to guiding the plow. It was a curious group by which I was surrounded: rough but intelligent men, some lying flat on their backs, others half reclining, and some sitting on the steps, all attentive to the talk. In the course of it I managed to say some things they may think of afterward.

Late, even for me, I went to bed. It had been a long and crowded day. Seven distinctly marked and beautiful lakes, deep, primitive, forests, with all the wondrously novel scenery of this strange wilderness, were now in my mind. As I was floating through it, the day seemed to me more like the dream into which I was sinking than any land or water journey I had ever made. But the dream was brighter, just as the ideal rarely fails to exceed the real. I slept, and was among the isles of the blest.

AMONG THE MOUNTAINS.

At six in the morning, after a hasty but hearty break-fast, I mounted a stage wagon, and was brought down into the town of North Elba, made famous as the resi-dence, and now the grave, of John Brown. This lies off the road, and the stage sometimes goes out of its way to enable travelers to view the spot. We were behind time, and the driver declined the extra mile.

North Elba has a little village on a wide plain, with such surroundings as no other village may boast. An amphitheatre of mountains, some of them the highest in the State of New York, with an arc of sixty miles ·in ex-tent, forms on one side the magnificent framework in which this lonely hamlet sleeps. The gigantic group of mountains is the Adirondack region proper. Mounts Seward and McIntyre and McMartin can be seen from almost any point, and Mount Marcy—the loftiest of them all — towers in its vast proportions, well deserving the name which the Indians gave it—*The Cloud Splitter.* It is 5467 feet high. A spring is on the very pinnacle, near a rude monument raised to Mr. Henderson, of Jersey City, whose death is still remembered and mourned by a wide circle of friends. He was a noble Scotch gentle-man, son-in-law of Archibald McIntyre, and while en-gaged in the exploration and development of this iron re-gion, he was killed by the accidental discharge of a gun. The little lake by which the ,tragic event occurred is named *Calamity,* and a beautiful monument, wrought far away, was brought at great expense, and erected upon the spot where Mr. Henderson met his lamented death.

In this town of North Elba is Lake Placid, which is celebrated as one of the most lovely of all the waters, and for a very remarkable lakelet that is close by, and joined by a narrow channel; through this channel the water flows two or three minutes from the lake into the pond; an interval of five seconds follows, with no apparent motion of the water; after this it flows back into the lake for two or three minutes, and this ebbing and flowing continue perpetually.

The Au Sable River, after leaving Lake Placid, forgets its source and becomes raging and rapid, actually tearing its way through the mountains, and by finding or making a passage, gives to the traveler the White Face Pass, or Wilmington Notch, one of the grandest objects in nature. The narrow road by the side of the river is horrible. But on each hand a precipice, almost perpendicular, rises two thousand feet high. At noon we passed through it, and even at that hour we were in deep shadow, awed by the grandeur of the scene. In successive ages huge rocks have been hurled from these towering heights; perhaps the earth itself has trembled till they fell; the bolts of heaven have shattered them into fragments, and sent them tumbling into the abyss; but the battlements still stand in silent majesty, impregnable and enduring as the globe. White Face Mountain is easily and constantly ascended from Wilmington, and from its summit the best view of the region can be obtained. My days for climbing are over. My ambition is satisfied. No steeple tempts me to aspire. I do not expect to climb another "while life and breath and being last."

But the mountain region is the glory of this country. More than two hundred distinct peaks may be counted. And they are so compacted that their bases sometimes touch. So wildly disjointed and irregular is the system of mountains, it stands as though an ocean tossed by tempest had been suddenly congealed, and these strange heights had in ages following become clothed and in their right mind. It has been only partially explored, but some of the passes have become famous, and they are more and more frequently visited by tourists. Many who have come here from Switzerland and New Hampshire are in ecstasies over or under the Adirondacks. One of the best of guides descants on the region a few miles only from Wilmington—Keene Flats—a point which the tourist to the mountains should be sure to make :

" There is not another place in the state, and probably but a few on the globe, where there is so great a variety of scenery in so small a compass as is unfolded from the lower end of the Keene Flats to three miles above the Upper Au Sable Pond. In no equal space can there be found so great a variety of soil and climate which will yield any fruit grown North of Albany. Then its abundant groves of elm and maple, and the clear, cool fountains, render the whole surroundings a perfect summer bower, six miles long and one wide.

" If one want a little exercise, let him climb Baxter Mountain, and he will see the whole Flats as if he looked from a high balcony upon the street below. If his taste incline him to streams, cascades, and waterfalls, he can find them in almost every form, from one foot to three hundred feet high. If he is desirous to ascend mountains, there is a trail to Hopkins's Peak, the Giant, Camel's Hump, and Hurricane. If he wish to ascend Mount Marcy, he can go through the woods by John's Brook and trail some eight or ten miles, or by the Ponds twelve miles, and only six of this distance by walking. If he is disposed to make the round trip (as many never do), he will go to the Ponds, thence over Marcy to Lake Colden,

and by a side trip to Avalanche Lake and back to Colden ; thence by Calamity Pond to Upper Adirondack.
Rest there a day or two, if required, and then through
the Indian Pass to Blin's or Scott's. The course may be
reversed, but from North Elba it is more difficult and uncertain as to boats.

" I have made this trip in four days, and have taken
twelve. The trip embraces the most wild mountain and
gorge scenery in the region — Lower Pond, Panther's
Gorge, Lake Avalanche, and Indian Pass. It also takes
in the most beautiful lakes—Au Sable Pond, Lakes Colden and Avalanche, Calamity Pond, Lakes Henderson
and Sanford, and as many other wild scenes as he can
imagine."

A stage ride through the White Face Notch has in it
some of the elements of the sublime, for the road is terrible. It is better in this, the dry season, than at any other
time, and now it is as bad as bad can well be. Wrecks of
wagons by the narrow roadside told us the fate of travelers who had preceded us. Two young ladies, the day
before, had been obliged to tramp four miles in the blazing sun of noonday, while the driver rode the horses to
Wilmington, leaving the dilapidated vehicle in the Notch.
Our ride was safe, but slow. The horses had a long pull
of it, and a strong pull, but brought us to the Point of
Rocks in season for the five o'clock train for Plattsburg.

To take a seat in a comfortable car on the rails, after
having been ten hours jolted in a rough wagon over the
roughest road that bears such a name, was a relief too
great for words. But the ride was through a grand region
of country, the scenery richly repaying the traveler for his
toils. To me it was but pleasant exercise, the fatigue
being speedily forgotten, while the memory of the magnif-

icence of nature remains as a perpetual refreshment and delight. As I drew the contrast continually between this wilderness, out of which I had come, and that artificial wilderness of shops and palaces where I must soon resort and abide, the oft-quoted lines of Dr. Beattie, in the " Minstrel," would come to me, and I repeated them aloud—

> " Oh, how canst thou renounce the boundless store
> Of charms which Nature to her votary yields ?—
> The warbling woodland, the resounding shore,
> The pomp of groves and garniture of fields ;
> All that the genial ray of morning gilds,
> And all that echoes to the song of even ;
> All that the mountain's sheltering bosom shields,
> And all the dread magnificence of heaven—
> Oh ! how canst thou renounce and hope to be forgiven ?"

For I had now seen somewhat of the lakes and mountains of the Adirondacks, and had endured no more hardship than attends all mountain travel : had slept every night in an excellent hotel, had three civilized meals every day, had worn the same clothing that I wear at home, had not been bitten by a musquito or a fly, had encountered none of the horrors of the wilderness described by preceding tourists—the only bear being chained—and had been less than a week in performing the journey. It is true I did not assassinate a deer. That exploit I shall not be able to boast of at the social board during the coming winter. My brethren of the pulpit and the press, who know how to draw a longer bow than I, have all the honors of the chase.

They who have not visited this region of our own country, as I had not, but have been over all Europe and into Asia and Africa in search of the beautiful and the sublime, have left yet unseen and therefore unenjoyed some of the

most singular and interesting scenery in the world. The
mere map of the country is a curiosity. It lies before
me with the mountains piled up on one side of it, and the
one hundred lakes on the other half of the sheet, with the
many rivers streaming among the hills. But the forests
are not on the map, and the sun does not light up the
world and make all these woods and waters marvelous in
their native solitude and grandeur. No such loneliness
ever dwelt around me : a pleasing, sacred, holy peace, not
a painful solitude, as if lost or far from friends ; but as if
the Lord God were walking in his garden unseen of man;
and I alone, yet not alone, because he was there. Just
about the smallest nonsense in the wide world is that
which ignores God as a living, present, pervading Being
and Power in the midst of his own creation. There
might be some excuse for it in the city which man is said
to have made. This great Babylon had a builder, and
men saw him, and they called him a god. Art confesses
and proclaims an artist. No fool was ever so much an
idiot as to suppose that Venus in the Florentine tribune,
and Apollo in the Vatican, sprang from the Parian quarry
without hands, and clothed themselves with beauty that
charms the sense and makes their memory a lifelong joy.
Our living artists paint Niagara and the Yosemite Vale, and
no one dreams that the paints came into color by elective
affinity or chance, and then meandered along the canvas
into forms of majestic beauty that bear some faint image
of the forests of the Almighty, his rainbow and cataracts.
Yet these admiring art critics, and others greater than
they, will walk in the midst of nature, radiant with loveliness and glory, compared with which this art work is but
the sport of children playing with brush and chisel, and
pretend to believe that all this comes of itself: that no

great Architect planned and spanned the arch of the heavens and set the sun in the firmament; that no skill of the artist painted these lilies with living white and green, and bathed these mountains and lakes, forests and shores, with exquisite loveliness, whose only but sufficient end appears to be the pleasure of those who come to see and admire. The sense of sublimity has not indeed possessed me so fully as that of beauty while here, and awe has not shadowed the soul in the midst of the wondrous loveliness of wild woodland scenes; but so little of man's work is around, and so much of God's, that I have again and again fallen back upon Coleridge in the "Vale of Chamounix," and rehearsed his great psalm as the only fitting interpretation of the believing soul when Nature, in naked majesty and beauty, stands before it, and it longs for words in which to float as part of the living universe praising its animating Maker. Read this with me, and our tour among the mountains, lakes, and waterfalls of the Adirondacks will be closed:

"Awake, my soul! not only passive praise
Thou owest! not alone these swelling tears,
Mute thanks, and secret ecstasy! Awake,
Voice of sweet song! Awake, my Heart, awake!
Green vales and icy cliffs, all join my hymn.

"Thou first and chief, sole sovran of the Vale!
O struggling with the darkness all the night,
And visited all night by troops of stars,
Or when they climb the sky or when they sink:
Companion of the morning-star at dawn,
Thyself Earth's rosy star, and of the dawn
Co-herald: wake, O wake, and utter praise!
Who sank thy sunless pillars deep in Earth?
Who filled thy countenance with rosy light?
Who made thee parent of perpetual streams?

"And you, ye five wild torrents fiercely glad!
Who called you forth from night and utter death,
From dark and icy caverns called you forth,
Down those precipitous, black, jagged rocks,
Forever shattered and the same forever?
Who gave you your invulnerable life,
Your strength, your speed, your fury, and your joy,
Unceasing thunder and eternal foam?
And who commanded (and the silence came),
Here let the billows stiffen, and have rest?

"Ye ice-falls! ye that from the mountain's brow
Adown enormous ravines slope amain—
Torrents, methinks, that heard a mighty voice,
And stopped at once amid their maddest plunge!
Motionless torrents! silent cataracts!
Who made you glorious as the gates of Heaven
Beneath the keen full moon? Who bade the sun
Clothe you with rainbows? Who, with living flowers
Of loveliest blue, spread garlands at your feet?—
God! let the torrents, like a shout of nations,
Answer! and let the ice-plains echo, God!
God! sing ye meadow-streams with gladsome voice!
Ye pine-groves, with your soft and soul-like sounds!
And they too have a voice, yon piles of snow,
And in their perilous fall shall thunder, God!

"Ye living flowers that skirt the eternal frost!
Ye wild goats sporting round the eagle's nest!
Ye eagles, playmates of the mountain-storm!
Ye lightnings, the dread arrows of the clouds!
Ye signs and wonders of the element!
Utter forth God, and fill the hills with praise!

"Thou, too, hoar Mount! with thy sky-pointing peaks,
Oft from whose feet the avalanche, unheard,
Shoots downward, glittering through the pure serene
Into the depth of clouds, that veil thy breast—
Thou too again, stupendous Mountain! thou
That as I raise my head, awhile bowed low
In adoration, upward from thy base

Slow traveling with dim eyes suffused with tears,
Solemnly seemest, like a vapory cloud,
To rise before me—Rise, O ever rise,
Rise like a cloud of incense from the Earth!
Thou kingly Spirit throned among the hills,
Thou dread embassador from Earth to Heaven,
Great hierarch! tell thou the silent sky,
And tell the stars, and tell yon rising sun,
Earth, with her thousand voices, praises God."

XVI.

WITH THE OLD MAN OF THE MOUNTAINS.

LEAVING the Adirondacks, crossing Lake Champlain and Vermont, I sought the White Hills of New Hampshire. By rail to Wells River Junction, and then to Littleton, was a charming ride.

That brother of mine who was fishing in the Adirondacks so marvelously a month before was waiting with his carriage for me at the foot of the mountains. Leaving the stages to come at their leisure, we wound our way along and up, easily beating them two hours in twelve miles. Nearly half-way we pass through the straggling village of Franconia, where the mercury falls lower in winter and gets higher in summer than in any other place in the country. It has been sometimes supposed they have thermometers of peculiar construction, to produce such remarkable results; but they claim to use Fahrenheit only, and to reach 40° below without much inconvenience, when at Boston or New York the coldest inhabitant can not boast of any thing below 10°. The village bears the same name with the Franconia Mountains, separated from the White by a narrow defile; but, in fact, the Franconia and the White are parts of the same system of hills, called often the Switzerland of America by people who never saw the Alps. We are now ascending the heights. Six miles of a winding, narrow, wooded road, toiling upward, we beguile the way with gentle discourse.   I pull out a book and read of the joys that are before me.   The gushing Eastman, who has illustrated the region, chants the praises of Franconia in such glowing words as these :

" Here is rest, here is comfort.   Beneath the shadow of these mountains the weary soul finds composure." [Just the place for poor worn-out writers to seek.]   " Selfishness and worldliness are rebuked."   [Of course, the bears and bulls of Wall Street will not come here to be rebuked.]   " The most thoughtless are hushed to reflection, and a better understanding of life grows up in the midst of Nature's grand instructions."   [I can not develop such thoughts out of the scenes around me, and must keep on quoting.   Our guide continues—he means you and me now, when he says]—" We do not suppose our tourist is in quest of mere pleasure : we believe him to be a better and nobler man than to spend his days thus. He is open to every good influence that will make life more rich and beautiful and fair.   There is no better influence than that of which he will be sensible in the still retreat of Franconia."

And with such soothing and, at the same time, cheering assurances, we reached the strange plateau on which, in the midst of Franconia Notch, stands the Profile House. A plain of a few cleared acres in extent, in a gorge that admits the passage of a narrow carriage-way, mountains two thousand feet high rising almost perpendicularly on each side, with two lovely lakes lying under the hills and skirted with forests, has been chosen as a summer resort and the site of a magnificent hotel, in which five hundred guests find refreshment and a cool retreat from the torrid heats that blight the world below.   It is never hot at the Profile House.

It is not always fair weather up here.   To say that it does not rain frequently would not be an honest report if one were keeping a record of the season.   Indeed, there is a great tendency in the direction of rain, and the rain has a decided tendency to come down.   Clouds rarely get into this cool gorge without being condensed into showers.   But they are short, and the bright shining after the rain is more enjoyable always than if it had not rained at all.

The huge crag at which we are gazing as we sit upon the piazza is called Eagle Cliff, and one never wearies of its contemplation.   Like the ocean, mountains are ever new to one who thinks while he sees.   They would be moral teachers, if human nature could be reached by such influences.   It is probably never touched by them.   So far as the tables show, there is no marked difference in the moral character of people who live in and out of such scenery as this.   Climate has its effect, but the scenery none.   Yet the thought is led up by these mountains to the everlasting, as the sea speaks of the infinite.   Both are sermons.   " Thy righteousness is like the great mountains," exclaimed the Jewish bard, who had never seen any thing greater than Carmel or Horeb.   And there is a little of the superstitious mingled with the sentiment that is inspired by the profile of the Old Man of the Mountain, the presiding genius of this Notch and the grand feature of the place.   I have seen the Sphinx by the side of the Pyramid of Cheops—a solemn, majestic, human face looking over the valley of the Nile, as if within the stone resided the divinity of that mysterious land. But the Sphinx was carved by the hand of man.   It had a maker like ourselves, and we are therefore greater than the Sphinx.

But there, away up against the clouds, nearly two thousand feet in the air, out upon the crag that terminates
Canon Mountain, itself the utmost precipice, far away
from the reach of human ingenuity or human daring—solitary in repose, sublime in its awful elevation—there is the
mighty human face, with every feature as distinct and
perfect and symmetrical as if Thorwaldsen had come to
Franconia, as he went to Lucerne, to carve a rock into an
everlasting monument.   One's emotions are strange as
he looks upon it for the first or the hundredth time.
Has the Old Man, as the face is called, been there always?   Does he think?   At the beginning of this century, when the path was cleared through the Notch, the
face of the Old Man was seen, looking away into the East,
and down into the Pemigewasset Valley to the rising
sun.   His countenance is fixed, for it has never changed
in the century.   Millions of people have come and gone;
the natives have disappeared ; civilization has set in upon
the forests ; and the bears have yielded to the incoming
of the luxury of cities, but the Old Man says—" None of
these things move me."   Often the clouds hide him in
impenetrable gloom.   Again the mist depends from his
chin like a heavy gray beard, and the wind sweeps it
back from his forehead as if his hoar locks were streaming in the gale.   Then the sun lights up his face with a
smile of amazing brightness and beauty, and his lips appear to be parted, as though he were about to address
the nations.

The awe abates when we go to another point of observation, and see that the face is not carved or even
formed by the peculiar shape of any one precipice or
rock, but is the accidental result of the happy location of
several crags some distance apart, which happen to come

into such lines and relations that at one particular point of observation they are so blended as to form the outline of the human face. Then the wonder becomes greater that it should be a face at all, but the sense of its presence as of a human head is dissipated, and we smile at the delusion whose strange fascination we had felt before.

"It is good for us to be here," said a disciple to the Master, on the top of a mountain. It is good to be any where with him. Let us stay here a while and rest. We are above the world while in it. By-and-by, all too soon, we will go down to work.

The luxury of nothing to do becomes irksome after a while. We do not seek it as much as we ought. Perhaps we ought not to work so much and so hard as to need it. But two or three hundred men in the mountains, shut up in a tavern for a month or more, find time heavy on their hands, and must resort to some means to kill it.

Here, at the Profile House, we have few out-of-door amusements. The mountains are so close upon us, pre cipitous and craggy, that no ordinary mortal man will find entertainment in carrying a rifle and climbing in search of game that has long since fled to parts unknown. The fishing is good in the little lakes that are close by the house, and a few of the guests are devoted votaries of the rod. Out of these lakes the waters find their way through awful gorges, wild ravines, huge rocks, making barriers over which the torrents tumble in their dark and mad plunges toward the sea. The adventurous fisherman, in love with the sport, not counting his life dear, but daring all things for the sake of what he calls sport, follows these mountain streams adown the deep abysses, crossing them

at times astride a fallen hemlock which spans a deep
gulf far beneath this giddy bridge of a single, shaky, rot-
ten tree ; or he leaps boldly across the chasm, as did the
priest with the maiden on the St. Gothard Pass in the
Alps ; or he slides down the slope of a long declivity, too
steep for him to walk, too far for a jump, and brings up
below, all standing on the flat of his back.

These dangers and hardships have their exhilarations,
and those with nerve and muscle to endure them are re-
warded, not so much by the beautiful fish they take under
such difficulties, as by the health and strength they gather for the sterner conflicts which, as fishers of men or
workers in some other field of useful labor, they must en-
counter when the play-spell is over.

But the most of us are not equal to such amusements.
We could not, if we would, attempt them, and probably
would not if we could. To sit on the piazza, with one's
heels on a level with his head, smoking a cigar and talking politics or stocks with a friend, is the chief amusement
of the average American taking his summer vacation.
Two or three times a day the stages arrive with loads of
new prisoners, and their arrival is a new topic of talk for
five or ten minutes. Perhaps a live judge, or a governor,
or a candidate has come, and diverts for a moment the current of conversation, which soon resumes its channel, and
flows on as languidly as the Passaic seeking the sea. A
few, to whom talk is tedious, or whose talk is tedious, cul-
tivate whist. In the middle of the day, and day after day,
and all day long, a learned judge, a learned lawyer, a successful broker, and a portly railroad president sit at a little table and silently, solemnly, and earnestly amuse themselves matching bits of pasteboard, on which are grotesque
pictures. My knowledge of the art and science of cards

is just equal to that of the courtier of whom the king asked—

"Do you not play cards?"

"No, your majesty, I can not tell a king from a knave."

The end of the season was approaching, and the few days remaining must be enlivened with something to make a stir in the. mountains. Practical jokes had been exhausted. Bogus news had been repeated till general skepticism prevailed. It was now announced that the "circus" was coming, and, more remarkable, would be exhibited in the grand parlor of the Profile House. A circus in the parlor was a novelty—indeed, without a parallel. The handbills were issued in flaming capitals and characters.

The performance far exceeded the promise. It is quite impossible to imagine fifty (some of them) grave and venerable men, all of them intelligent and cultivated people, by means of picturesque, burlesque, and comical dresses, shawls and feathers, bear and buffalo robes, converting themselves into the most amusing representations of animals. At the appointed hour the parlor was seated with elegantly dressed ladies and gentlemen and children, four hundred in number, in concentric circles, leaving the centre of the long room, a hundred feet, clear for the performance. At the sound of the trumpet the cavalcade entered: the elephant led by four keepers; then the bear and giraffes, and Dr. Darwin followed, leading his ancestor, the ape; and then the whole retinue, as advertised; and the several parties performed their *rôles* to the unbounded entertainment of the applauding assembly.

At another time it was announced that Horace Greeley was to arrive at 8 o'clock in the evening, and would be received with appropriate honors in the parlor. The stage arrived at the time, and in the centre of it sat a man with a mask head of Greeley on his shoulders, twice as large as life and twice as like. An escort of colored citizens and Indians in costume attended him. The band played "Hail to the Chief," and the populace greeted him with cheers. He was led to the parlor, where a platform was erected, and upon it stood the Governor of the State of New York, not a sham, but the genuine Governor, who in his summer travel, fortunately, was a guest at the Profile House when this reception occurred. The Greeley being presented, thus the Governor began :

"Mr. Greeley,—It was expected that Governor Straw, of New Hampshire, would be here to-night to welcome you to this one of your many birthplaces. But he is absent— straws show which way the wind blows—and it devolves upon me, the Governor of the state next to New Hampshire in resources and population, to bid you welcome to the freedom of this house, from the offiee to the bar. This ceremony, it is understood, has no political significance; indeed, like a modern popular sermon, it has nothing to do with politics or religion. I was out this afternoon looking at the Old Man of the Mountain, and seeing a benevolent smile upon his face, I asked him what pleased him so, and he replied, 'Horace is coming.'" [Great applause.]

In this pleasant way the Governor discoursed to the imaginary Greeley for a few minutes.

As this burlesque was performed in the midst of the presidential canvass, and included among its performers men of all sorts of political relations, it was evidently appreciated and enjoyed as a fitting epilogue in the great farce then convulsing the nation.

In such sports as these the dwellers at the Profile

House amused one another during the last days of their sojourn among the mountains. They had a mock trial, at which one of the best judges presided, and near him, with all gravity, sat one of the judges of the Supreme Court of the United States, while eminent lawyers made as desperate efforts to amuse the audience as they ever did to clear a rogue at home.

Sunday came. And then it was good to see that rest, such as the Sabbath invites, does not require amusements to make it thoroughly enjoyable. The same grand parlor, which the evening previous had been given up to innocent play, was now filled with the same audience, reverently assembled to worship God. They were of all religious *persuasions*, but I do not know that one in the house was absent because of the faith of him who was to conduct the service. It was the wish of the company that I should take this duty, and it was pleasant to lead such a multitude, all away from home, unknown to each other, and nearly all of them so to me, but all children of the same Father, and seeking the same home in his house. And with what fervor did we sing that morning, and again in the evening, when we met for social praise, the old familiar hymns, some that had rung out from the lips of martyrs, and all of them the joy of saints whose feet now tread the higher courts and whose voices make the melodies among the heavenly hills :

"They stand, those halls of Zion,
 Conjubilant with song,
And bright with many an angel
 And all the martyr throng.

"The Prince is ever in them,
 The daylight is serene;
The pastures of the blessed
 Are decked in glorious sheen.

K

"There is the throne of David,
    And there, from care released,
The song of them that triumph,
    The shout of them that feast.

"And they who with their Leader
    Have conquered in the fight,
Forever and forever
    Are clad in robes of white."

XVII.

MEMORIES OF ITALY.

LYING here under the trees, my soul often goes away
to other lands, and lives in the climes and scenes it has
enjoyed in years gone by. I have often looked on the
face of a man asleep, and its vacuity suggested the idea
that his soul was on its travels elsewhere. And as I recline beneath these deep shadows, in the heat of this summer day, though my eyes are open, I dream, and the dream
is of Italy. I will tell you what I saw when there, and
what is as vivid now as if we were yesterday in the Land
of the Beautiful.

It was nine at night when we had reached Florence
and supped, and then it was time to go to bed ; for we
had made a long day of it. What with getting ashore at
Leghorn ; running the gauntlet of all sorts of officials
and non-officials ; having our luggage twice searched and
plumbed to go from one town to another in the same kingdom ; then coming up to Pisa, and stopping there under
the shadow of that wondrous Leaning Tower, which leans
as it has leaned for six hundred years, and, as it seems to
me, leans still more than it did years ago, when I swung
myself out from the iron rail around the ninth story of it,
and tried to see the base from the summit, and could
not ; having toiled up the winding stairway that Galileo
so often ascended and descended in the pursuit of science
—for here he tested the velocity of falling bodies—and

then walking through the Cathedral, where still hangs,
and sometimes swings, the lamp which set the same grand
philosopher on the track of the pendulum, whose constant
movement, silent and steady, in every palace, hall, and
home in the civilized world has, perhaps, been and will
be as useful to mankind, in teaching the measure and value of time, as any thing they will learn this side of eter-
nity ;. and then looking into the Campo Santo, not less
memorable for the great and good who are buried in it
than for the genius and fame of the painters whose works,
once thought to be immortal, are even now fading from
the eye that strains its vision to catch departing beauty,
as if the figures were angels fast disappearing ; and sculpture so ancient, rescued from distant tombs, that the names
of the mighty makers have long since been buried beyond
the sound of the trumpet of fame, which is no resurrection
trump, but only heralds the names of those whom the
world will not let die ; and the very ground of the Campo
Santo was brought from the Holy Land, and perchance
may be itself the dust of patriarchs and apostles, as the
ground we daily tread once lived ; I was saying we had
paused at Pisa, and spent the balance of the day in the
midst of these old monuments and wonders of science
and art, and, wearied with seeing and thinking, had turned
away and come on to Florence in the evening.

All around, not alone in the palaces of the Medicis and
the Pittis, nor in Santa Maria Novella, the Bride of Michael Angelo ; nor in Santa Croce, where is his tomb, by
the side of Dante's, and face to face with Galileo's ; but
all around us in the streets and the piazzas, and on the
bridges over the Arno, were forms of beauty whose presence makes an atmosphere of art, filling Florence with a
fragrance that belongs to no other city on earth ; and we

could not go to sleep till we had walked out in the midst
of them, even if we could catch but the graceful outlines
of these creations of other days. We walked up the Arno
to the Uffizi, and under its arches and along the terrace
passed between rows of statues of great men gone, and
into the Piazza della Signoria, and there the handiwork
of Michael Angelo in David, and Bandinelli's Hercules,
and the Sabine woman, by John of Bologna, were lumi-
nous in the dark, as we greeted their familiar forms. Yet
we walked on, pilgrims from a land unknown when Cimabue found Giotto tending sheep hard by this fair city
that now glories in being the early home of both, and
treasures their works among her priceless crowns of art.
We went on looking upward to catch sight of the Duomo,
and soon we were on the spot where Dante was wont to
sit, and gazing on the wondrously suspended and supported dome of this great cathedral, whose architects, Ar-
nolfe and Brunelleschi, now sit here in stone, as if sur-
veying their own stupendous work. And there rose to
the near heavens—for in the night its crown was hardly
visible—there rose the Campanile, so massive, majestic,
and sublime in its proportions, as it is beautiful beyond
comparison, by daylight, in its marbles of every color—
the most perfect bell-tower in the wide world. We could
not see the bronze doors of the Baptistery, the early
works of Ghiberti, who spent upon them forty years of
his life, and left them as his monument; but we reserved
these, and all we had only caught glimpses of, and this
whole cityful of ancient and modern art, to be studied
and enjoyed in successive days and weeks at hand.

This was enough for one day. In the morning on the
sea; in the afternoon, with the weight of centuries on us,
at Pisa; in the evening wandering along the ways of

Florence, so often pressed by the feet of old poets and
world-famed statesmen, and artists that neither Greece
nor Rome, in the palmiest days of their art triumphs, ex-
celled ; now, as midnight drew near, standing midway of
the Arno, on the Santa Trinita, which has stood, just as
it now stands, for three hundred years, adorned with four
statues as its corners, representing the four seasons of the
year ; and thence looking at the long lines of lamps on
either hand, reduplicated in the waters, above and below,
as far as the city stretches on both sides of this silver
stream, was it strange—willing as the soul might be to linger and dream away the night in the first joy of the embrace of so much loveliness and glory—that the flesh was
weary ?   And so we entered our hotel, on the bank of
the river by the Ponte Alia Carraja, and were soon at
rest.

And yet not at rest.   For here, into this very house,
the first time I was in Florence, I had come with a young
friend, on whom sickness laid its fevered hand almost as
soon as he came, and day after day he faded away from
the life and joy of the beautiful Florence he had sought
with me, till at last, while a dear friend held one hand of
the dying and I the other, death came and bore his spirit
to the better land.   The frightened Italian servants, looking in at the window from the balcony, said inquiringly,
" Morto ? morto ?" and we answered, " Yes ; dead, dead."
And from this house, in a chill November morning, before
eight o'clock, as the laws of the country then required, we
bore him out to his far-from-home grave.

It was hard to sleep in a room haunted with such memories ; yet with thoughts of better rest and fairer scenes,
and bliss that knows no weariness, decay, nor night—
beauty in everlasting spring, and a crown that fadeth not

away—I slept sweetly, and awoke with a heart and mind and frame rejoicing, with every string of the thousand of this wondrous harp in tune, to enjoy the harmonies of art and song in Florence the Beautiful.

The time was when Florence had the reputation of being the pleasantest and the cheapest place to winter in. It is not so pleasant, and it is not so cheap as it once was, and the reason why you will learn by degrees, as we did. Still it is, as compared with any other capital in Europe, both pleasant and cheap, and in many respects the most attractive. What it once was, it will not be again ; yet it has riches of beauty, and monuments of genius, and trophies of art, and memories in story and song, that will make it sacred and glorious in the eyes of all with taste to appreciate its treasures. And to many its charms are ravishing. "See Naples and die," was the old-time saying ; but, having seen Naples and Florence and, midway, Rome, I would rather see and enjoy what is in Florence than all in both her rival sisters.

With a list of " apartments to let," we set out the first morning to find a home for the few weeks we had to stay ; and, after running and riding some hours, were so fortunate as to find just the quarters of all others that we would most desire.

Casa Guidi is one of the historical mansions of Florence. It is on the Piazza San Felice, just where it opens on the Pitti Palace, the late residence of the Grand-Duke of Tuscany, and the later residence of Victor Emanuel. Casa Guidi is our home in Florence. For many years past, like many other old palaces in this city, it has been "let" in apartments, and so distinguished have been some of its modern tenants that it has become more famous as their residence than as the house of the Guidi. It was in this palace that Mrs. Elizabeth Barrett Browning resided for many years. Here I made her acquaintance in the year 1853. Here Mrs. Browning wrote some of her best poems, and to one of the most spirited and feeling she gave the name " Casa Guidi Windows," for out of these windows she saw the scenes therein portrayed, and which predicted to her prophetic spirit the future glory of Italy. Here she died. With her husband and only child she had come in from the country, in feeble health, but with no expectation of approaching death. The good woman who now lets the chambers was with her then, and told me the incidents of her last days. She was called suddenly at the last, but went away cheerfully, to sing sweeter songs with the angels. The city of Florence has caused a marble slab to be placed over the portal of this mansion, on which is inscribed in Italian—

" Here wrote and died
ELIZABETH BARRETT BROWNING,
Who in the heart of woman combined the wisdom of the learned and the spirit of poetry, and made of her verse a golden ring uniting Italy and England. Grateful Florence placed this memorial, 1861."

In the room where I was writing, and at the same table, wrote Mrs. Jameson, whose works on " Sacred and Legendary Art," " Legends of the Madonna," " Italian Painters," and " Loves of the Poets," etc., are text-books for students and travelers in Italy. A few doors below, Sismondi wrote his history ; Motley, our American historian, had his chambers ; Hawthorne was a little way on the other side ; and Miss Mulock, and how many more I have not time to write. The Machiavelli house is close by, and I have been up and down its stone stairway a score of times, wondering always how many statesmen and priests and women have been there before me. We have rooms on the first floor—that is, up one flight of stairs, looking out on the Square and the end of the Pitti Palace. Our parlor, eighteen by twenty feet, and as many high, is handsomely furnished, and the bed-chambers adjoining are supplied abundantly. The greatest inconvenience we endure is from the cold, for the idea of an American stove, or a modern civilized fire-place, has not reached this capital of science and art. Our fire-place is indescribable. The wood that costs us half a dollar would not last us a day, if we kept the fire going; and if it go out, we must go out, too, and get warm. Many of the palatial residences and thousands of the humbler dwellings have no fires in them, and no chimneys. Ladies sit all day with an earthen kettle in their laps or at their feet, filled with hot embers, and ofttimes they upset them; and some carry them in the street, and enjoy them when they make calls. They are called *scaldini*, and are very poor comforters, even when wrapped up and put to bed, as they are sometimes in place of our ancient warming-pans. Lady Morgan, in her charming volumes of travel in Italy, speaks of a visit she made, in November, at a villa near Florence :

"The evening was intensely cold, and we were struck upon this occasion, as upon many similar ones, by the insensibility of the Italians to the influence of cold. For our accommodation a wood fire was lighted in one of the few hearths which this large villa contained, but no one ventured to approach it but ourselves. When the Russian Czar, Paul the First, visited Florence, he went shuddering about from sight to sight, observing, 'In Russia, one sees the cold ; in Italy, one feels it.' The common people of Tuscany only approach fire for culinary purposes, and females of all ranks move about with their *scaldini* hanging on their arms. When seated, they place it under their petticoats; and this, in the extremest cold, is the only artificial heat they resort to."

So Lady Morgan says; and I have seen all she describes. I learn also that judges, when they enter court and take their seats on the bench, bring their *scaldini* with them, and warm their fingers, to soften their own trials. A lawyer, one day, leaped up, in great wrath, to reply to something, and flourished his earthen kettle of coals in his furious gesticulation.

Every step to be taken in the city of Florence has a story to it. History has done much to preserve and transmit the interest that invests the palaces, monuments, bridges, public squares, and private houses. Poetry has done more. It is a city of the Muses. It is itself almost a poem. Its air is full of song. Tradition has been more busy with the stones of Florence than the pen or pencil.

It is hard to say which are the most numerous, tales of love or tales of blood, in this beautiful Italy. It is a singular feature in human nature that the love of the beautiful and that of the tragical is so often blended in the same breast. I went to see an exhibition of the recent works by native artists. Its object is similar to that of our National Academy's annual exposition. And the greatest picture—that which attracts the most attention, elicits the warmest eulogies, and holds the most conspicuous place in the gallery—is a story of love and blood. A wife, still young and beautiful, detecting the secret admiration of her husband for a former rival of hers, has contrived to get her into her power, has cut off her pretty head, and, having nicely arranged it in a basket of flowers, with the yellow locks of hair lying neatly among them, she is bringing the precious present to be offered to her husband when he comes home. It reminded me of a similar incident, the scene of which is also laid in Florence. A wife is sitting in front of her mirror, and her pretty maid is arranging her hair. Her husband is just leaving the room to go on a journey, and as he passes out of the door the wife detects in the mirror a look which he gives to the maid, and it rouses the fire of jealousy in her burning heart. He goes. She says nothing ; but before he returns she has led the poor girl, perhaps more innocent of evil than herself, to the cellar of the palace, and into a recess in the wall, where solid masonry soon consigns her to a living grave and lingering death, a wretched victim of a wife's jealousy and hate. In the St. Luke Gallery at Rome is a solemn picture that shows a vestal virgin sitting in a dungeon ; thus immured, a small lamp burns at her feet, while she waits for that release which death only can bring.

Every day we are passing the square called the Piazza Santa Trinita. The City Hall stands upon one side of it, and in the centre is a granite column, once in Rome, in the Baths of Antoninus, and which Pius IV. presented to Cosimus I., the first of the Medici, who won the title of Father of his Country. It is surmounted by a statue of Justice, who, like the one on our City Hall in New York, holds in her hand a pair of scales. A few steps farther on is a famous palace, that of the Strozzi, built in 1489. Severe as its principal front is, its great cornice, by Cronaca, is justly regarded as an admirable work even in this city of art triumphs. Many, many years ago—so long ago that it is not important to fix the date—one of the ladies of the household lost her diamond necklace. The maid who had charge of her toilet was suspected of the theft, and when accused protested her innocence. It seemed to be impossible to account for the loss in any other way, and to make the girl confess her guilt she was put to the torture, and the awful secret drawn out of her by rack and fire. It is common for the victims of this inquisitorial process to confess, and probably the innocent confess more readily than the guilty. The hardihood of crime may endure when sweet innocence sinks under suffering. The hapless maiden, when her joints are drawn asunder by the tightening ropes and wheel, will accuse herself of any crime in the sad hope of speedy release by pardon or the finishing stroke of death. Perhaps this poor Italian maid was thus made to confess. At any rate, she was condemned to die for the dreadful crime of robbing her mistress. This was law then, and many years have not passed since it was law in England. She was put to death at the foot of this granite column, on which the statue, a female divinity, was standing, and, as if in mockery, holding out the scales of justice. It is not related that the statue wept or groaned in sympathy with the cruel tragedy enacted in her name and at her feet. It is not even said that the beautiful mistress was unwilling to look out from her palace window upon the scene, when the young life of her fair maid was crushed out of her in the midst of a crowd that always relishes the sight of blood. But it is recorded that, shortly after the tragedy was over, a thunder-storm arose, a flash of lightning struck the scales in the hand of Justice, and down fell the nest of a jackdaw, and out of that fell the diamond necklace, for the theft of which an innocent girl had just suffered a cruel death. The scales still swing in the statue's hand, but the goddess has no power to call back the poor creature who was thus first robbed of her good name and then of her life.

It is a short walk onward to the Piazza della Signoria. But it would be a long story to tell you of the half that is in it and around it—more of art glory than illustrates any other square in Europe. In the middle of it is an equestrian statue of Cosimus I., the one to whom the historic column was presented, at whose base the poor girl was killed of whom we have just been speaking. John of Bologna made this statue—a great work—and the grim man on the horse looks as if the story of him I am about to tell might be true. He had two sons, one of them just of age, the other a year or two younger. The two young men were out together hunting, and the older one was killed. When the younger returned with the dead body of his brother, too well did the stern father read in the eye and voice of the ambitious boy that his brother's blood was on his soul. Down into the deep recesses of the palace dungeons the father led his son—now his only son; and there, with a candle in one hand and a knife in the other, charged him with the crime; and while the guilty boy knelt before him, and begged for mercy with screams that might have made the huge walls melt with pity even for a fratricide, the proud duke plunged the knife into his heart, and went up childless to his bed.

It would not be strange if some of these tales and many more were done in smooth verse in Rogers's "Italy." If so, you may be sure that there is history as well as poetry to verify the stories. For he, unlike other poets, gives his authorities and deals only with facts. With one exception. He makes a note at the bottom, and confesses to this invention—the old story of Ginevra, the bride of the mistletoe-bough. Rogers lays the scene of it in one of the streets through which he passes on that journey which, in the manner of Horace, he has put into pleasant verse.

He describes the house where the picture of Ginevra may be seen, and then with words of tenderness he tells the story of her love and bridal—how she playfully ran from the wedding banquet and bade her new spouse follow her: he pursues and loses track of her as she flies up the stairs and through the chambers, and search for her is all in vain ; and night and day, and weeks and years wear away, and no bride appears ; and when at last the " old oak chest " in a garret is removed, the jeweled skeleton falls out, and Ginevra is found.   The story is told of a house in England, probably of half a dozen ; it is just as true of several in Germany ; but Rogers puts it into his poem of " Italy ;" and although he adds a note that indorses it as pure fiction, so credulous is the world that they have found the house he describes in the locality he indicates, and the rush of travelers to see the hypothetical picture has become so great that the persecuted proprietor, for the sake of getting quiet enjoyment of his humble home, has been compelled to put up a " notice " on his gate that no such picture is there, and never was.   But this only makes the matter worse.   His notice is regarded as a mere ex- cuse for not opening his doors to anxious strangers, and it may be that he will have to burn his house down and build another elsewhere, or get a picture of some ideal bride and hang it on his outer wall, that people may be- hold and go on their way content.

Until we had been to the two great galleries, it was not possible to feel that we had actually come again to Flor- ence.   Every moment there was the present consciousness that within a few steps was the perfection of human art and genius, shedding its beauty continually, but not for us, and time was more and more precious as it passed, and these glories of the old masters were yet unseen.

In the possession of statues and paintings Florence is richer than any other city in the world. Critics may dispute this remark, but the fact will remain. And when Paris and Berlin, and Munich and Dresden, and Rome and even Madrid have been exhausted, the lover of the beautiful will delight himself here as he has not elsewhere, and then will carry away impressions to abide among the brightest and sweetest that linger in the evening of his life.

In the midst of the Uffizi Gallery stands the statue that not only "enchants the world," but is the model of beauty in the studios of painters and sculptors. To see it is an essential part of a liberal education. It is surrounded by other works of art scarcely less worthy of study, and thither tend the feet of the pilgrim as he enters this temple, as if there were the high altar for his first worship. The portico of the temple is adorned with twenty-eight statues, but these are passed without notice, as the traveler hastens to ascend the stone staircase, and enters at once the halls that were founded by the Medicis three hundred years ago. This proud and powerful family, whose virtues and vices are alike illustrious in the annals of Italy, and whose name will be immortal in art, have their statues in the vestibule among those of Mars and Silenus, Bacchus and Hecate. But these effigies of the real and ideal do not detain us. Nor can we stop in the second vestibule, and study a horse in marble, so instinct with life as to suggest the idea of danger in his presence, as also in that of the famous marble boar, on the other side. Enter the first corridor: Pompey, Julius Cæsar, and Augustus, Julia and Tiberius, are here in marble, while the warmer painting introduces you to the earlier stages of the art, and thus prepares you to appreciate and enjoy the luxuries of the higher developments beyond. Cimabue and his shepherd-boy pupil, Giotto, are represented here in their works. They are all of the sacred school : the Virgin and Child, chiefly, with a picture of *a soul flying* into the arms of the Saviour. Twelve angels of rare love-liness surround the Virgin Mother and her Son, the Wise Men are adoring the infant Jesus, and the next picture introduces us to the Nuptials of Perseus, disturbed by Phineas. Is it from want of religious sentiment that we soon weary of these endless repetitions of sacred scenes, and find relief in a picture or a statue that by contrast is called profane ? We are in haste to get on, and St. Francis and St. Lawrence, nor even the Birth of Venus, nor Moses defending the Daughters of Jethro, nor the Creation of Adam, the Rape of Ganymede, the New Spouse, the statue of a Nymph extracting a thorn from her foot, nor a thousand more must demand of us more than a passing glance, for there is something that calls us on-ward, and we can not pause by the way, even to dwell for a moment on these works, which alone would be the ad-miration of mankind.

It will check our ardor for an instant to read the notice of the chamber into which we are about to enter. The author of the catalogue has essayed, in English, to inform the reader what he is expected to feel as he beholds the mysteries of this place. He says :

"*Tribune.*—This pretty octagon saloon, known under this name, is one of the rarest wonders of the art, one of those sanctuaries which can not be looked upon without being amazed by a respectful and moving sentiment."

Entering this sacred chamber, whose atmosphere is loaded with beauty, and whose every work is one of the masterpieces of masters to whom all other masters are

proud to do homage, one is instantly struck with the un-
desirable change that has come over the face of things
here since the Grand-Duke was compelled to quit these
walls.   In those severer days these wide and splendid
apartments were hallowed by and to art.   Silence and
study and admiration and worship filled them.   One took
off his hat instinctively when he came into the Tribune,
and though many guests were there from many lands,
none spoke except in whispers, and it seemed a desecra-
tion of the place to be gay or rude.   But now the free
and easy bear rule.   Soldiers lounge and laugh loudly
behind and before the statues.   Copyists fling their jokes
across the chamber to each other, and it was hard to be
content with the fact that, with the boon of greater liberty,
the people were evidently losing their appreciation of the
beautiful and reverence for the glorious in works of art.
But the truth, sad as it is, meets the eye and the ear, on
the street and in the gallery, wherever men mingle, and
we must reserve the philosophy of it till we get out of
this radiant chamber, where we can converse more calmly than here.

For we are now in the presence of the loftiest conceptions of what mankind for three centuries at least have
been agreed in regarding the most worthy of admiration
in the picture and the marble.   An inscription on the
base of the statue of the Venus de Medici ascribes the
work to Cleomene, the son of Apollodorus, the Athenian
sculptor, and there is no doubt that the Greeks conceived
and produced it.   But it was found in the ruins of Hadri-
an's villa at Tivoli, near Rome, and brought to Florence
when Cosimus III. was lord of the city.   Rich as Florence is in marbles, the most of its ancient treasures
came from Rome ; and the wealth and power of the

Medicis made this their city rich at the expense of its
greater rival. To those who have a higher idea of the
loveliness that lies in the soul, and laughs in the eye, and
finds expression in the voice when words come up from a
fond heart and out from a cultivated mind, than the ancient Greeks or Romans had, or than any Oriental race
now has, this statue would be more beautiful if it had
no head. It may have been designed by its sculptor for
a Venus, but it has not intellect enough, nor room for
intellect enough to make a respectable woman of any
kind, not to speak of a goddess, who should be at least
equal if not vastly superior to the divinities of the human
race of ladies. Yet this was and is the ruling sentiment
of the ancient Greek mind and the Roman, and perhaps
of every race, however cultured, without the revelation
of that religion which brought to light the true glory and
power of woman. We then study the statue simply as
the marbleized idea of a physically beautiful female form:
not of a Venus, not a goddess of beauty, not a portrait or
copy from a model, but the production of one's idea of
what perfection would be if it were put into flesh or stone.
And here the consent of the centuries must be taken in
evidence, and there is no use in writing an argument to
show that they have all been mistaken. There it stands.
And if you had stumbled upon it in the ruins of Karnak
or Persepolis, you would have been entranced. To see
such a work and be unmoved is to be more or less than
a man. The beauty that covers it as with a garment, for
it has no other covering, is so radiant from every limb
that he would be very foolish who should try to say
wherein its chief excellence lies as a work of art. Perhaps the exquisite proportions of the form and limbs are
such as to prevent the attention from being fastened on

any single feature as more perfect than another. It is
harmonious. It sings melodiously in its silent loveliness,
ravishing the eye year after year, age after age, without a
rival or a peer. Why can not others, standing on the
height to which this statue beckons and lifts them, think
out and carve something higher and better. They have
done it in the intellectual and moral application of art to
marble; but they have no forms more perfect than this, no
lines more graceful, no limbs so fitly tapered, proportioned,
and harmonized that the spectator is lost in mingled wonder and delight as the marble floats in the air, cheating
his senses into the half delusion that a thing of life is
there before him. It is not a modest statue. The
pose of it is the attitude of one who is " naked and not
ashamed," because innocent like Eve and ignorant of
evil. And the whole question of the moral influence of
undraped statues would come under discussion if we were
now speaking of this from any other than the stand-point
of art, to judge of it only as the lithograph of some great
master's dream of beauty.

Day after day it is a joy to come into this chamber,
take an arm-chair, removed from contact with others, and
give one's self up to the gentle flow of soul that moves on
with the harmony of these fine creations. They are the
works of man, but what work of God is greater than the
mind capable of conceiving such things as these? And
if God taught the fingers of David to fight, and gave his
right hand cunning to play on stringed instruments, how
much more of the infinite wisdom and skill was imparted
to him who composed and achieved these marble portraits of ideal loveliness. It is worship to look through
nature up to God, and higher and profounder worship
still to see the hand of him who painted the rainbow

and the rose, and set the stars in constellations of beauty, revealed in the works of instruments he made to produce these grand results. Art is therefore only nature in school: the fruit of the seed that Infinite Wisdom planted, the up-growth of that divine and immortal nature of which man was made a partaker when he was born in the likeness of God. How it has been debased by sin! Even here in these holy places the evidence is all about us. This Venus is an illustration.

Near to her, in strong contrast, the Wrestlers show the development of muscular strength, and then the Dancing Faun, attributed to Praxiteles, and a boy Apollo, and above all an ancient statue of a man apparently sharpening a knife—a noble work to exhibit anatomy in stone. All these works have their separate and distinctly defined attractions, few more exciting than the voluptuous and meretricious charms of the marble goddess who stands like a queen of beauty among them. And each one is a study on which criticism has been exhausted. From them all ideas have been drawn that are again produced in the works of other artists, unconsciously for the most part, but as distinctly as the words or thoughts of one author sometimes find their way into the works of another, who has no recollection of their foreign origin. Thus the beautiful and the great are wisely and widely diffused. Passing from one gallery, or studio, or country to another, we meet in the modern production what is in part a reproduction of the ancient; and so far from reproaching the copyist as a plagiarist, which he is not consciously, we do well to be glad that his mind was large enough to receive, his taste capable of appreciating, and his hand cunning to render in oil or in clay the charm that delighted us in the work of the older worker. It is genius only that can imitate the perfect. A great actor is a great artist. The faults of others may be parodied by a clown; but to interpret the thoughts of others in words, in gesture, on canvas, in bronze or marble, this is a labor not to be successfully achieved without at least a portion of that genius which originally wrestled in the creation.

The paintings in this chamber are not less worthy of study than the statues. Some great artists pronounce Titian's Venus the best coloring in the world. Many admire it as the most perfect painting of the human figure, as the statue before it is the most perfect copy in marble. Here, too, are the best pictures, or, if not the best, some of the most celebrated works of Domenichino, Andrea del Sarto, Guercino, Van Dyck, Raphael, Perugino, Fra Bartolomeo, Correggio, Rubens, Giulio Romano, and one by Michael Angelo. Each painting is a masterpiece. Most of them, yet not all, are sacred themes. Raphael's Fornarina certainly is not a very sacred subject. But besides this portrait of a frail beauty, whom he loved, there is also his "Virgin of the Goldfinch," as it is called, a painting scarcely less admired than those other Madonnas of his which have been copied and recopied until it would seem that the world itself would not contain them.

Reluctantly leaving this charmed spot, we wander from room to room, through all the various schools of painting, thus readily catching the peculiarities of each, as we would not if they were hung promiscuously. The Tuscan easily holds the pre-eminence. It was a wonderful outburst of nature, or rather a remarkable gift of Heaven, that bestowed the five greatest painters that ever lived upon this little city of Florence within the same short period of twenty-five years. And here they shine from these walls, living in their works—dead, but speaking. In the hall of portraits we have the likeness of all the great masters of all countries, most of them painted by their own hands; and thus a double interest is imparted to the pictures. Thus they looked. And thus they drew their own ideas of themselves. Wonderful men! Is the race extinct forever?

It certainly is not, because in some lines of art we have men now who surpass these who are honored as the old masters. There are no painted landscapes in Italy superior, none equal to the glorious works of our quite modern American school. There are no paintings of animals more true to nature than Rosa Bonheur's, and she is not an "old master." But when we come to that higher region of· thought, and of power to paint it, such as the "Descent from the Cross" required in Rubens, and the "Transfiguration" demanded of Raphael—who died while the canvas was yet under his young but mighty hand—or as the "Communion of Jerome" reveals in Domenichino, and at least a thousand others exacted of their authors, whose works—on the walls, in fresco, or on panels or canvas—remain for the imitation of the coming generations of disciples, who will be lifted up by their contemplation, then we are constrained to confess that these men of the fifteenth and sixteenth centuries still remain without rivals in these realms of art.

After we have spent a few days in the various halls of this Uffizi Gallery, the names and numbers of the apartments being more than can be mentioned here, you will walk with us by a new yet very ancient path to another gallery of richer beauty. It is a new, but very ancient way. On the other side of the River Arno, which divides the city of Florence, stands the Pitti Palace, for several hundred years the residence of the Grand-Dukes of Tuscany, and afterward the palace of the King of Italy. Between this Pitti Palace and the old palace a secret gallery was built some three hundred years ago, extending along the tops of houses, across streets, and, following the Ponte Vecchio over the river, making a promenade of nearly one thousand feet in length, and about twelve feet wide. This long passage has been exclusively reserved for royal footsteps. In these passing centuries the Florentines and strangers have known that such a passage joined the distant palaces, but none knew what treasures of art were there enshrined, nor what mysterious pleasures would be revealed if the tide of ordinary humanity were allowed to ebb and flow along its silent pavement. In course of time, when Victor Emanuel came into quiet possession of the seats of the grand-duke, he threw open this long and long-closed gallery to the public; and now a stream of life flows through it daily. For it is rich in stores the existence of which was quite unknown to the common world. Its walls are hung with Gobelin and other tapestries of surpassing excellence of workmanship, more admired by many than the most exquisite paintings. Tables and shelves are loaded with gems of precious stones, mosaics, cameos, and curious coins, and thousands of interesting and rare productions from ancient museums and former civilizations in this and other lands. And perhaps more to be prized than all else in this unique collection is an almost endless number of simple sheets of paper, on which are the first sketches of the great works of those mighty sons of genius whose labors we have just been beholding, and of others whose fame has filled the earth. These are autographs that thrill one as he thinks that Michael Angelo

put with his own hand, and perhaps his old hand, these
lines on this sheet; drew with bold yet cautious strokes
this rude outline of a group which grew in his mind and
underneath his touch till it blazed into a painting that
now, when his hand has been dust for three hundred
years, is still one of the joys of an admiring and appre-
ciative age.   And there is scarcely a man whose fame is
world-wide as a painter or a sculptor of the last four or
five centuries whose infant works are not preserved under
glass in this royal mausoleum of genius.

Midway of the bridge the windows of this hanging gallery are enlarged, and a saloon is furnished with seats,
where a wearied guest may sit and muse among the
present and the past.   The Arno flows beneath him.   Its
swollen waters, confined within walls, rush below the bal-
conies of old palaces, each one of which has a history full
of romantic interest.   On either hand the fairest works
of art are lying, inviting him to be wise and happy in the
good and the beautiful.

The story of this Pitti Palace is familiar.   The head
of the family that built it, in 1440, wished to eclipse the
splendor of the reigning house, and boasted that he would
rear a palace in whose court the house of the Medici
might stand.   He did.   But by one of those little ups
and downs in life that are quite as common in old countries as new, it came to pass that the Pitti family went
under, and the Medici, instead of putting their palace
into the court of the Pitti, put themselves into the Pitti
Palace; and it has remained the royal residence down to
this day.   And when the grand-duke went out in haste,
leaving his effects behind him, Victor Emanuel came in
and took possession.   These royal gentlemen in Europe
are wide-awake to the ticklish tenure by which they hold

their palaces and power; and it is their practice to make to themselves friends of the mammon of unrighteousness, by hiding away, in other countries than their own, nice stores of gold and silver, which are very useful when they find it necessary to be up and moving to foreign parts. Thus the ex-King of Naples, without a crown, has more crowns at the bankers, it is said, than almost any other man in Europe; and he lives right royally at Rome, or any where else that it pleases him, except at home. The former Grand-Duke of Tuscany is a private gentleman in a beautiful villa in Austria; and in one of his establishments in Florence there are ninety elegant carriages belonging to him, which he is at liberty to send for and take away.

On the upper floor of this palace, and extending the whole length of it, is a gallery of pictures. Beneath are the royal apartments. The stone staircases leading up are detached entirely from the household entrance, and the stone floors of the long corridors of paintings are impervious to the sound of footsteps, so that the gallery, open daily to the public, is as secluded from the residence of the king as if it were in another part of the city. It includes about five hundred pictures; but the number, though smaller than that of the Uffizi, embraces more works of transcendent merit, and, as a whole, is vastly superior. The ceiling of the saloon where we begin to study the pictures in order has a moral that one may well learn, even from heathen mythology: it is a lesson the young are slow to take; but they never come to much of any thing in this world till they do learn it, and for the want of it thousands go astray. The painting is by Pietro da Cartona, and represents Minerva taking a young man from Venus and conducting him to Hercules. There is no need of pausing here to preach a Christian sermon from this Pagan text. There are several texts in the Proverbs of Solomon teaching the same idea. Minerva is the goddess of wisdom, Venus of sensual love, and Hercules the god of strength, energy, power. Wisdom takes a young man away from sensual indulgence, and inspires him with force to do and conquer in the battle of life. And it is just this that makes the difference in the success of men.

All the great painters of the last four hundred years are now near us in some of their finest compositions. The freshness of the coloring, too, often tells us that rash hands have been permitted to retouch some of these mas-terpieces. " Fools rush in 'where angels fear to tread." It is even easier now than ever for an ambitious young artist to get an order from the authorities to take down one of these pictures and restore (!) it. It is also much less difficult than formerly to get permission to remove a painting from its place to make a copy of it. In this process the original often suffers injury. And the thought that a profane hand has touched one of the works of these men of old is painful. They ought to be above suspicion.

Raphael's Madonna della Seggiola, in this gallery, has been more frequently copied and recopied by every proc-ess of art known to men than any other picture in the known world. From the breastpin of a maid to the glorious tableau that adorns the hall, the pencil and brush and sun have multiplied it, until there are few who are not familiar with the young woman's face as she sits in a chair with the babe nestling on her shoulder. And that is about all you can make of it. It is not the Mary who gave the infant Jesus to the world, and one looking at it would not suppose that she thought so herself. The same may be said of the same great artist's Madonna of the Balcony, and also of the Goldfinch. If the old masters failed ever, they all failed in that which more frequently than any thing else employed their powers—the production of a just idea of the Mother of our Lord. Yet they were not unmindful of the obvious truth that the one grand idea to be embodied and made visible in the countenance of the Virgin Mother is this—the consciousness of the fact that she herself was mysteriously the mother of Immanuel. Others might *believe* it; her own husband might, because he had been told so in a dream, and his Mary, whom he loved, had often whispered in his amazed and trembling soul the awful secret that "that which was conceived in her was of the Holy Ghost." But she only, of all the world, *knew* it was so. Jewish maidens and mothers longed and prayed that it might be so with them. But now it was hers. The angel of the Annunciation had brought her the joyful tidings of its coming. The Messiah, of God begotten, had leaped in her womb. He was born of her and laid in a manger. The sages of the East had worshiped him with gifts of incense and gold, as he lay by the side of his spotless mother. What to her, in the hope and glory of that triumphant hour, was the world's opinion of her or this wondrous child? He lived and grew, and her mother heart swelled daily with the knowledge of the future redemption to be wrought for Israel through her fair boy. All this and more were in the soul of Mary as she hugged the child Jesus to her bounding breast. Could not a great artist put somewhat of it in her radiant face? These old masters do not appear to have made the attempt. To attempt was with them to succeed, and thus we know they did not try. Their Madonnas, for the most part, are only nice young women;

but never could have been in the royal line, like her who
was called to be the Mother of the Son of God.   If there
is one exception, it is to be found in the gallery we are
now visiting.

When I was first in Florence, a friend informed me that
the grand-duke had in his private apartments, and hanging by the side of his bed, a Madonna by ·Raphael, pronounced by all who had seen it to be the most perfect
realization of the idea, and that no other would compare
with it favorably.   We obtained permission to visit the
chamber, and the result more than answered my expecta-
tions.   It has not all that belongs to the Virgin Mother ;
but it has more than any other in the world.   So highly
was the painting valued by the grand-duke that he had
it with him in his carriage when he traveled, and it rested
near him wherever he slept.   Its history is remarkable.
In this city of Florence, some years ago, one of the old
and decayed families, whose only treasure left was an inherited picture, unable to pay their rent, which was only
forty dollars, offered to the landlord this painting for the
debt.   As it was all he could get, he took it.   The new
possessor showed it to the father of the last grand-duke,
who was then in power.   He appreciated it, and insisted
on retaining it, giving the owner six hundred dollars, which
he probably regarded as a high price.   It is now beyond
value in gold, for the richest king could not buy it.   The
grand-duke left it in his flight, and has sent for it as part
of his private property ; but the present government
chooses to regard it as belonging to the public collections
of art, the property of the crown, and so retains it.   It is
the crown of the gallery now.   So recently has it been in
the reach of the public that few copies have been made
of it.   But daily groups of silent spectators pause before

it, arrested by the solemn thoughtfulness, the calm conscious dignity, the majestic womanly beauty of the blessed
Mother with her divine child.

You would be surprised on coming for the first time to
these and other collections in Europe to see how large a
part of the labor and genius of the great painters of three
and four hundred years ago was expended upon pictures
of the Holy Family, and more than all others on the Virgin Mother herself. The sentiment of the age may be
traced in the art of the age. The world owes more to
the Church of Rome for the works of art which her sentiment has produced and preserved than for aught else
she has done for mankind. Protestantism never protested
against art ; but its higher spiritualities rejected the visible and material, and holds communion directly with the
unseen and eternal. The doctrine of justification by faith
only, drawing the soul to the ascended Saviour, and uniting it to him in a communion that admits no intercessor
or mediator, left no place for the images or pictures of
saints or virgins, or even of the human body of the once
crucified but now glorified Redeemer. It is not important that we regard the making of these likenesses a
breach of the second command, in order to understand
the reason of their absence from the Protestant idea of
worship. They are an element indispensable to the Roman Catholic system, because from the early departure
of that Church from the simplicity of the Gospel it sought
and taught salvation through the intervention of saints,
and the great intercessor between man and the Saviour
was held to be his Virgin Mother. The intelligent
teachers of this Church tell us, and we will not question
their candor when they say they do not worship the picture or the graven image of the saint or the Madonna.

But they use them as aids to devotion. In them they see what they must otherwise conceive, and the feeble mind of the multitude is incapable of reaching, in the pure ideal, such conceptions of the holiness, tenderness, love, and power of these intercessory agents as the genius of a great artist portrays in oil or in stone, and leaves for the use of the Church, or for the edification of the private, perhaps secluded Christian in after-ages. This was the sentiment that gave birth to these great works of art. Some of them were painted expressly to be placed over the high altar in magnificent churches. When the artistic taste or the pride of possession has inspired an emperor or a pope with the desire to add one of these glorious pictures, like the "Communion of Jerome," to his palatial gallery, the individual altar which it was designed to hallow with its mysterious power has been despoiled ; but in place of the picture an annual revenue of gold has been secured to the Church. Running on in the line of this thought, further than we have time to pursue it, we see that the Roman Catholic idea of the way of life was the inspiration of art in those years that gave to the human race such hands as those of Michael Angelo, Titian, and Raphael.

So many times, as we pass from hall to hall, do we see the story of the Cross on these walls, that we will not stop to speak of any one of them as more worthy of study than the others. They who need it, or they who love it, may find employment or profit in the contemplation of the blessed Saviour's agony. Here they may come and learn what art has done to paint the Man of Sorrows in every stage of his existence in the world he came to redeem. The darkness of the stable his little body illuminates. In the Temple he stands, self-poised, and teaches the doc-tors with words of wisdom wondrous from a child. Every miracle he wrought, every scene that he passed through, is here. He sweats as it were great drops of blood in Gethsemane. He is betrayed by a traitor's kiss. He stands before Pilate's bar. His bare back is cut with the sharp blows of the scourge. He sinks beneath the weight of the heavy cross—ah, how much heavier than any of ours, poor, sinful followers afar of that divine, majestic, glorious sufferer, going of his own free will to the Mount of Martyrdom. And then the crucifixion! Again, and again, and again, till the very repetition tires, is this scene of all scenes with every form and feature of mortal agony drawn. Each one of the old masters has exhausted his art upon some of these passages in the life and death of the Lord of life and death. And not less often is the tenderest of all the stories told: how they come with pious, woman love, and gently—as if the dead, yet still divine, might suffer—take him down from the cross. How lovingly does the Mother Mary hold his sacred feet, as if she would receive them in her bosom, and warm them back to life! Here on another canvas they are laying him in the tomb. There the guards are flying while the God is coming forth from the burst sepulchre. And now a conscious Saviour reveals himself in that one word, "Mary," and she beholds her Lord. The walk to Emmaus is here. And why need we tell of the numberless scenes on the Hill of Ascension—the stricken disciples, the glorified, rising Redeemer, the clouds, the heavens opening, the work of redemption finished.

Some of these scenes it is well to study even in pictures. Yet there are few devout minds unable to form an ideal of the Saviour and his passion more edifying than art can put in colors. And it is not a part of our holy and happy religion to be made holier and happier

by the study of the physical sufferings of our blessed Saviour.   It does not make one love him more nor love
him less to see his sacred head bleeding under the crown
of thorns.   But we may for the time separate ourselves
from the relation in which we stand to the original of
these Oriental scenes, and study them merely as works of
high art, and then their true excellence will appear.   We
are too wise and too orthodox to use or to need them as
aids to holy living.   Perhaps we are too irreverent to regard them with the sacredness of contemplation which
their subjects demand.   But, in any aspect of the question
they awaken, they are the great boons of Romanism to
mankind ; and as such, as well as for the moral and intellectual power that is in them to instruct, exalt, and inspire
humanity, they will be prized even by those whose religious system rejects them from among its means of grace.

The whole Scripture history may be found illustrated,
Old and New Testament alike.   From the creation of
Adam, and the rising from his side of Eve, to the opening
of the seals of prophecy, every thing has been seized upon
as a theme for the painter's skill.   Titian's Mary Magda-
len is here, whose golden tresses fall in luxuriant waves
around her, and Mazzolini's adulterous woman, and every
bloody scene that rises into the dignity of history and
justifies the expense of time and paint.   Judith holding
by the hair the bleeding head of her slain enemy is often
copied, and groups of people are always taking delight
in its study.   Classic history is ransacked for subjects.
Heathen mythology, Roman and Grecian poetry and
prose yield rich material for the artist's toil; and he who
masters the story and the picture will go away with a
cultured intellect, and stores of beauty to admire in the
retrospect, so long as memory performs her office.

XVIII.

A NIGHT AND A DAY IN THE ALPS.

I was on the great road that leads over the Alps into Italy by the famous Pass of St. Gothard. A party of students, seven from Germany and two from Oxford, joined us, and we resolved to hire a carriage to Amsteg, two hours onward, and there to begin the ascent and the pedestrianism together. When we were set down at that village, with a walk of five hours before us, and all the way up the mountains, I confess to a slight sinking at the heart, and my courage oozed out gradually at the end of my toes. At the inn of Altorf, one of these German students attracted me by the gracefulness of his manner, the delicacy of his features, and the pleasant expression with which he conversed. He attached himself to our party, and we walked on together, pilgrims as we were, bound to see Switzerland, and rejoicing in the power to take leave of all modes of traveling but that first and best which nature had provided.

The River Reuss comes dashing along down with the fury of a young torrent, pouring over rocks and whirling around precipices with a madness that brooks no control. The Bristenstock mountain towers aloft into the regions of snow and ice, and nature begins to grow wild and dreary. The soft meadows on which the maids of Uri were making hay have disappeared, and the green pastures with frequent herds are now the only hope of the shepherd.

M

The road is no longer a straight path, but in its toilsome way upward it crosses again and again this foaming river, and bridges of solid masonry, built to resist the flood when it bears the ruins of avalanches on its bosom, and spreads them in the spring on the plains below.

We crossed the third bridge and came to a gorge of frightful depth, through which the river rages furiously in a maddened torrent too fearful to look upon without awe. It is called Pfaffensprung, or the Priest's Leap, from a story which no one will believe who stands here, that a monk once leaped across the chasm with a maiden in his arms. I have no doubt a monk would do his best under the circumstances, but I doubt the possibility of his clearing thirty feet at a bound over such an abyss as this, even for the sake of the prize he is said to have carried off. We had been beset by beggars under all sorts of guises, and here a miserable old woman—alas, that a woman could come to this—appeared with a huge stone in her hands, which she hurled into the deeps, for us to see it leap from rock to rock and finally sink into the raging waters far below. A few cents she expected for this service, and she received them with gratitude ; when an old man, perhaps her husband, came on with another rock, which he was willing to drop for a similar consideration. As I turned away from the scene, a carriage came up in which an English gentleman was riding, with two servants on the box. I walked by the side of his carriage and fell into conversation, when he invited me to ride with him. I found myself with a member of the London bar. He knew public men whom I had met, and was well acquainted with all subjects of international interest, so that in fifteen minutes we were comparing minds on those questions in which England and America are so much concerned. We stopped at the little village of Wasen for refreshments. I insisted on paying the reckoning, when he stopped me with this remark: "Sir, you are my guest to-day; when I meet you in America, I shall be happy to be yours."

We rode on and upward, the road now assuming the character of a mighty structure of mason-work, through a savage defile, only wide enough for the carriage-path, and for the torrent of the Reuss, which no longer flows, but tumbles headlong from one cliff to another, while for three or four miles the lofty precipices hang fearfully on high. In the spring, the rage of this mountain river, swollen by melting snows, and bringing down ice and rocks in its thundering fall, would tear away the foundations of any common pathway, and this must be built to defy the fury of the fiercest storm. It is scarcely to be credited that twenty-five or thirty thousand persons cross the Alps by this route every year; and to secure this travel, which would otherwise be carried off to the other passes, the cantons of Uri and Tessin built a road here which has twice been swept away by the avalanches; but one would think that the present might stand while the mountains stand. So rapid is the ascent that the road is made often to double on itself, so that we are going directly backward on the route; a foot-passenger may clamber across the doublets and save his time, but the carriage must keep the zigzag way, patiently toiling up a smoother and more beautiful highway than can be found in the most level region of the United States of America. Not a pebble in the path: the wheels meet no other obstruction than gravitation, which is sufficient to be overcome only by the strongest of horse-power. Yet through this very defile, long before any road like this had been built, three armies—

the French and the Russians and the Austrians—have pursued each other, contesting every inch of this ground, and each one of these rugged heights, and disputing the possession of dizzy cliffs where the hunter was afraid to tread.   Never did the feeling of nature's awful wildness so take possession of my soul as when night was shutting in upon me in this dreary pass.   Sometimes the road is hewn out of the solid rock in the side of the precipice, which hangs over it as a roof, and again it is borne over the roaring stream, which in a gulf four hundred feet below is boiling in its obstructed course, and, making for itself an opening, it leaps away over the rocks, and rushes down while we are toiling up.   In the daytime it would be gloomy here ; it will be terrible indeed if the darkness overtakes us before we reach our resting-place for the night.

More than five hundred years ago an old abbot of Einsiedeln built a bridge over an awful chasm here, but such is the fury of the descending stream, the horrid ruggedness of the surrounding scenery, the smoothness and solidity of the impending rocks, the roar and rage of the waters as they are tossed about and beaten into spray, and so unlikely does it appear that human power could ever have reared a bridge over such a cataract, that it has been called from time immemorial the Devil's Bridge, and so it will be called probably till the end of time.   It was just nightfall when we reached it.   It was very cold, so far up had we ascended, and my English friend and I had left the carriage and were walking to quicken the blood, when the roar of the waters rose suddenly upon us, the spray swept over us, and we were in the midst of a scene of such awful grandeur, and with terror mingled, as might well make the nerves of a strong man tremble.

The River Reuss, at this stage of its course, makes a sweeping leap—a tremendous plunge at the very moment it bends nearly in a semicircle; while the rocks, as if by some superhuman energy, have been hurled into the torrent's path, so as to break its force, but not to withstand its power. No words will describe the terrific rush of waters underneath the bridge which spans the dark abyss. Two bridges, indeed, are here; for when the old road was swept away, the bridge defied the storm, and now this, more solid and of far greater span, has been thrown high above the other, which is left as an architectural curiosity in the depths below.   And long before that was built another one was there; and when the French in 1799 pursued the Austrians over it, and while the embattled hosts were making hell in a furious fight upon and over this frightful gorge, the bridge was blown up, and the struggling foes were whelmed together in the devouring flood. A month afterward, and the Russians met the French at the same spot. No bridge was here, but the fierce Russians bound timbers together with the scarfs of the officers, threw them over the chasm, crossed in the midst of a murderous fire, and drove the enemy down the pass into the vales below.

It was dark before we were willing to quit this fearful place. The strength of the present bridge is so obvious, and the parapet so high, that the scene may be contemplated without fear; but the clouds had now gathered, hoarse thunder muttered among the mountains, spiteful squalls of rain—cold, gloomy, and piercing—were driving into our faces, and we were anxious to find shelter for the night. We left the bridge, but in another moment plunged into utter darkness as we entered a tunnel called the Hole of Uri, where the road is bored one hundred and

eighty feet through the solid rock, a hard but the only
passage, as the stream usurps the rest of the way, and the
precipice admits no possible path over its lofty head.
This was made one hundred and fifty years ago, and before that time the passage was made on a shelf supported
by chains let down from above. It was called the Gallery of Uri, and along it a single traveler could creep, if
he had the nerve, in the midst of the roar and the spray
of the torrent, and with a hungry gulf yawning wide below him. Emerging from this den, we entered a vale—
yes, a valley five thousand feet above the sea: once
doubtless a lake, whence the waters of the Reuss have
burst the barriers of these giant fortresses, and found
their way into more hospitable climes. No corn grows
here, but the land flows with milk and honey, by no means
an indication of fertility, for the cows and the goats find
pasture at the foot of the glaciers, and the bees their nests
in the stunted trees and the holes of the rocks. We drove
through it till we came to Andermatt, where the numerous lights in the windows guided us to a rustic tavern.

By this time it had commenced raining hard, and I began to be anxious for my young friends behind. But I
could do no more for them than to send a man to watch
on the highway till they should come up, and lead them
into the house where I was resolved to spend the night,
whether we could find beds or not. These rural inns in
Switzerland are rude and often far from comfortable.
But travelers must not stand upon trifles. The house
was designed to lodge twenty travelers, and thirty at least
were here before us. A large supper-table was spread,
and around it a company of gentlemen and ladies, mostly
Germans, were enjoying themselves right heartily after the
day's fatigue was over. The London lawyer and myself

had a separate table laid. We soon gathered on it some of the good things of this life, which you can find almost every where, and had made some progress in the discussion of the various subjects before us, when my traveling friend and Heinrich arrived, nearly exhausted with their toilsome walk. They had a dreadful tale to tell of the storm they had met, which we just escaped, and barely that. The lightning filled the gloomy gorge, lighting up for an instant the mighty cliffs and hanging precipices, while the thunder roared above the sound of the torrent, and the rain drove into their faces, disputing with them the upward pass. But they were young men, and strong. They told me that I never could have borne the labor and the exposure of the walk. Two travelers and a guide had given out, and taken lodgings in a hamlet we had passed, and the man whom we had employed to bring on our light bags had also halted for the night, and would come up early in the morning.

After supper the landlady led us up three pairs of stairs, under the very roof, into a low garret bedroom, with one window of boards which could be opened, and one small one of glass that could not, and with three beds. Worn out with their hard day's work, but free from all anxious care, my young friends were asleep in five minutes, while I coaxed the candle to burn as long as it would—fastened it up with a pin on the top of a candlestick—and tried to write the records of the few past hours. It was amusing to hear my companions, one on each side of me, talking in their sleep, Heinrich in his native German and the other in his English, showing the restlessness of over-fatigue, while I sat wondering that I, so lately a poor invalid, should now be in this wild region, exposed to such nights of discomfort and days of toil.

In the morning I met an American gentleman returning from the summit of the St. Gothard Pass, and he advised me strenuously not to go farther up, unless I were
going into Italy. The most wonderful of the engineer-
ing in the construction of the road I had already seen,
and there was nothing else of interest above. The same
savage scenery, in the midst of which the Reuss leaps
down two thousand feet in the course of a two·hours'
walk, is continued, and the dreariness of desolation reigns
alone. A house for the accommodation of travelers has
been maintained for hundreds of years, destroyed at times
and then restored; and a few monks have been supported
here to extend what aid they may to those who require
their assistance. I resolved to pursue my route through
the Furca Pass, one of the most romantic and interesting
of all the passes in Switzerland. A long day's walk it
would be over frozen mountains and by the side of never-
melting glaciers, and no carriage-way. Nothing but a
bridle and foot path, and a rough one, too, was now before
us; and if we left the present road, and struck off over
the Furca, it would be four or five days at least before
we should reach the routes which are traversed by wheels.
Our baggage, though but a bag apiece and blankets, was
too heavy for us to carry if we walked, and I proposed
to my companions that we hire a horse, put on him our
three bundles, and take turns riding—or, more elegantly,
ride by turns. Heinrich had never heard of the mode
of traveling called "ride and tie," and he was greatly
amused when I described it to him over a very comfortable cup of coffee. An idle group of guides and tavern-
hangers were gaping around, and a party of Germans and
English were looking on when I bestrode the horse, and
took my seat in the midst of bundles rising before and

behind, like the humps of a camel. Behold us now upon our winding way. We are yet in the vale of Urseren, not more than a mile wide, and lofty mountains flanking its sides. The mountain of St. Anna is clad with a glacier, from which the "thunderbolts of snow" come down with terrific power in the spring; and yet there stands a forest in the form of a triangle, pointing upward, and so placed that the slides of snow as they come down are broken in pieces and guided away from the village below. The great business of the people in this vale is to keep cattle and to fleece the strangers who travel in throngs over the Pass of St. Gothard. Hundreds of horses are kept for hire, and nothing is to be had by a "foreigner" unless he pay an exorbitant price. Even the specimens of minerals are held so high that no reasonable man can afford to buy them. But we are now leaving Andermatt; and on the side of the road not long after leaving the village we saw two stone pillars, which need but a beam to be laid across them, and they make a gallows, on which criminals were formerly hung, when this little valley, like Gersau on the lake, was an independent state. The pillars are still preserved with care, as a memorial of the former sovereignty of the community. We reached Hospenthal in a few moments: a cluster of houses about a church, and with a tower above the hamlet which is attributed to the Lombards. I was struck with the exceeding loneliness and forsakenness of this spot. It seemed that men had once been here, but had retired from so wild and barren a land to some more genial clime. Hospenthal has a hotel or two, and it is a great halting-place for travelers who are about to take our route over the Furca to the Hospice of the Grimsel. Here we quit the St. Gothard road, and winding off by a

narrow path in which we can go only in single file, we
are soon out of the vale, and slowly making our way up
the mountain. The hill-sides are dotted with the huts
of the poor peasants, who have hard work to hold fast to
the slopes with one hand while they work for a miserable
living with the other. The morning sun was playing on
the blue glacier of St. Anna, and a blue waterfall wandered and tumbled down the mountain; yet this was but
one of many of the same kind that we are constantly
meeting as we go through these defiles of the high Alps.
The vast masses of snow and ice on the summits are
sending down streams through the summer, and these
sometimes leap from rock to rock, and again they clear
hundreds of feet at a single bound; slender, like a long
white scarf on the green hill, but very picturesque and
beautiful. At the foot of this mountain are the remains
of an awful avalanche, which buried a little hamlet here
in a sudden grave, and a sad story of a maiden and a
babe who perished was told me with much feeling by the
guide as we passed over the spot. The peasant men and
women were bringing down bundles of hay on their heads
and shoulders from the scanty meadows which here and
there in a warm bosom of the hills may be found; and as
they descended I recalled the story of Orpheus, at whose
music the trees are said to have followed him, and I
could readily understand that such a procession as I now
saw on these mountains might be taken or mistaken for
the marching of a young forest. We are still following
up the River Reuss toward its source, and though it is
narrower, it is often fiercer, and makes longer strides at
a step than it did last evening. We cross it now and
then on occasional stones or on rude logs; but we have
now come to a passage where the bridge was swept away

last night by an avalanche of earth and ice, and well for us that it came in the night before we were here to be caught. An old man with a pick-axe in his hand had been working to repair the crossing, and had managed to get a few stones arranged so that foot-passengers could leap over, and the horses, after slight hesitation and careful sounding of the bottom, took to the torrent and waded safely over. I held my feet high enough to escape a wetting, but I heard a lady of another party complaining bitterly that the water was so deep or her foot so far down, I could not tell which; but it was evident that very much against her will she had been drawn through the river.

At Realp, a little handful of houses, we found a small house of refreshment, where two Capuchin friars resided to minister to travelers; and this was the last sign of a human habitation we saw for some weary hours. We were now so far up in the world that the snow lay in banks by the side of the path, while flowers—bright, beautiful flowers—were blooming in the sun. It is difficult to reconcile this apparent contradiction in nature. The fact is not surprising here, where we see such vast accumulations of snow, and remember that a short summer does not suffice to melt it; but it is strange to read of flowery banks within a few feet only of these heaps of snow. I counted flowers of seven distinct colors, and gathered them as souvenirs of this remarkable region. On the right the Galenstock Glacier now appears, and out of it vast towering rocks like the battlements of some old castle shoot 10,900 feet into the air. It was a glorious sight. There was brightness, strength, majesty, beauty, but it was nothing compared with what we saw before the sun went down. We are now among the ice palaces of the earth.

We were just making the last sharp ascent before reaching the summit of the Furca, when I overtook a lady sitting disconsolately on the wayside. She cried out as soon as I came up, "Oh, sir, my guide is such a brute—the saddle turns under me, and I can not get him to fix it—my husband has gone on before me—I can not speak a word of German, and the dumb fool can not speak a word of English. What shall I do?" "Madam," said I, "my guide shall arrange your saddle in an instant, and I will conduct you to the summit, where the rest of your party will doubtless wait." She overpowered me with her expressions of gratitude; and while the man was putting her saddle-girths to rights we crossed a vast snow bank together, climbed the steep pitch, and in ten minutes reached the inn at the top of the Furca. Distant glaciers, snow-clad summits, ridges, and ranges, named and unnamed, stood around me—a world without inhabitants, desolate, cold, and grand in its icy canopy and hoary robes of snow.

The descent was too rapid and severe for riding, and giving the horse into the charge of the guide, we walked down, discoursing by the way of things rarely talked of in the Alps. My young German friend was a philosopher of the sentimental school, with all the enthusiasm of the French character joined to the mysticism of his own nation. He was well read in English literature and familiar with ancient and modern authors, so that we had sources unfailing to entertain us as we wandered on; now sitting down to rest, and now bracing ourselves for a sharp walk over a rugged pass. I became intensely interested in him, though I had constant occasion to challenge his opinions, and especially to contrast his philosophy with the revealed wisdom of God. We had spoken of these

things for an hour or more, when I asked him if he had
ever read the " Pilgrim's Progress ;" and when I found he
had not, I told him the design of the allegory, and said,
"We are pilgrims over these mountains, and have been
cheering one another with pleasing discourse, as the travelers did on their way to the celestial city. They came
at last in sight of its gates of pearl."

"But what is that ?"

We had suddenly turned the shoulder of a hill, and a
glacier of such splendor and extent burst upon our view
as if to fix us to the spot in silent but excited admiration.
It was the first we had seen near us. Others had been
lying away in the far heights, their surface smoothed by
the distance, and their color a dull blue ; but now we
were at the foot of a mountain of ice. We could stand
upon it, walk on its face, gaze on its form and features,
wonder, admire, look above it and adore. This was the
Glacier of the Rhone. That great river springs from the
bosom of this glacier with a strong bound, as if suddenly
summoned into being, works its way through a mighty
cavern of ice, and then winds along the base, till it
emerges in a roaring, milky-white stream, and rushes
down the valley toward the sea. This glacier has been
called a "magnificent sea of ice." It is not so. That
description conveys no intelligible idea of the stupendous
scene. You have stood in front of the American Fall,
not the Horse-shoe Fall, of Niagara. Extend that fall
far up the rapids, gradually receding as it rises a thousand
feet or more from where you stand to the crest ; at each
side of it let a tall mountain rise as a giant framework on
which the tableau is to rest ; then suddenly congeal this
cataract, with its curling waves, its clouds of spray, its
falling showers of jewelry ; point its brow with pinnacles

of ice, and then let the bright sun pour on it his beams, giving the brilliancy, not of snow, but of polished ice to the vast hill-side before you, and you will then have but a faint conception of the grandeur of this glacier as I saw it that afternoon.

Heinrich cited Burke's definition of the sublime, and said that all the elements of sublimity were here. I replied that it was impossible for me to have the sensation of fear, and scarcely of awe, in looking upon the scene before us; it rather had to me the image of the outer walls of heaven, as if there must be infinite glory within and beyond, when such majesty and beauty were without. And then these flowers skirting the borders of this frozen pile, and smiling as lovely as beneath the sunniest slope in Italy, forbade the idea that this crystal mountain was of ice. It must be an illusion of an hour; and if we return to-morrow, will it not have disappeared?

No, not at all. These glaciers are the great reservoirs that feed all the springs and fill all the rivers of the continent; they are placed away up there where they yield only to the heat of high summer, and send down their waters to supply the fountains that otherwise would be dry; and thus, in all their coldness and apparent uselessness, they are among the greatest blessings of the human race.

I must pass rapidly over the remainder of that day's journey: the game at snow-balling which we had on this glacier; my interview with a man who had fallen into one of the many crevices of these glaciers, and from the depths of seventy feet had cut his way up with a hatchet, and thus rescued himself from an icy grave. I shall not even speak of the ascent of the Grimsel, but ask you to come with me at once to the summit, where there is a lake called the Dead Sea, or the Lake of the Dead, into which the bodies of those who perished in making this journey were formally cast for burial.   Heinrich and I left the path and climbed to a cliff, where we looked down on the pilgrim parties on horse and on foot, winding their way along the borders of this dark lake, and a more romantic sight I have not seen.   We sent our guide onward to engage beds for us at the Hospice of the Grimsel, and resolved to spend the rest of the day (the sun was yet three hours high) in this wilderness of mountain scenery.

We could now look down into the valley of the Grimsel, a little valley, but like an immense caldron, the sides of which are sterile naked rocks, eight hundred feet high. On the west they stand like the walls and towers of a fortified city, and in the bottom of the vale is a single house and a small lake ; but a flock of one hundred goats and a score of cows, with their tinkling bells, are picking a scanty sustenance among the stones.   The scene was wild, savage, grand indeed, and had there been no sun to light it up with the lustre of heaven, it would have been dreary and dismal.   Heinrich had been very thoughtful for about an hour.   He had discovered that my thoughts turned constantly to the God who made all these mountains, while he was ever studying the mountains themselves.   He sat down on a rock, and said :

"Here I will commune with Nature."

I replied, "And I will go on a little farther and commune with God."

"Stay !" he cried ; "I would go with you."

"But you can not see him," I said.   "I see him in the mountain and the glacier and the flower; I hear him in the torrent and the still, small voice of the rills and little waterfalls that are warbling ever in our ears. I feel his presence and something of his power. I beg you to stay and commune with Nature, while I go and commune with God."

I left him and wandered off alone, and in an hour went down the mountain, and to my chamber in the Hospice. I was sitting on the bedside, arranging the flowers I had gathered during the day, when Heinrich entered, and, giving me his hand, said to me—" I wish you would speak more to me of God."

He sat down by my side, and I asked him if he believed the Bible to be the Word of God.

He said he did, but he would examine it by the light of history and reason, and reject what he did not find to be true.

"And do you believe that the soul of man will live hereafter in happiness or woe?"

" I doubt," was his desponding answer.

I then addressed him tenderly: "My dear young friend, I have loved you since the hour I met you at Altorf. And now tell me, with all your studies have you yet learned how to live? You doubt, but are you so well satisfied with your philosophy that you are able to look on death among the mountains or by the lightning without fear? My faith tells me that when I die my life and joy will just begin, and go on in glory forever. This is the source of all my hopes, and it gives me comfort now when I think that I may never see my native land and those I love on earth again. I know that in another land we shall meet."

" How do you know that you shall meet?"

" My faith tells me so. I shall meet all the good in heaven. I am sure of one child, an angel now."

"And where are your children?"

"In America, and one in heaven. I had a boy four years ago—earth never had a fairer. His locks were of gold, and hung in rich curls on a neck and shoulders whiter than the snow; his brow was high and broad like an infant cherub's; and his eyes were blue as the evening sky; and he was lovelier than he was fair. But in the budding of his beauty he fell sick and died."

"Oh no, not died."

"Yes, he died here on my heart. And that child is the only one of mine that I am sure of ever seeing again."

"I do not understand you."

"If my other children grow up to doubt, as you doubt, they may wander away on the mountains of error or the glaciers of vice, and fall into some awful gulf and be lost forever. And if I do not live to see my living children, I am as sure of meeting that one now in heaven as if I saw him there in the light of the setting sun. Heinrich, have you a mother, my dear friend?"

"Yes, yes," he cried; "and her faith is the same as yours."

I had seen his eyes filling, and had felt my own lips quivering as I spoke, but now he burst into tears and fell on my breast. He kissed my lips and my cheeks and my forehead, and his hot tears rained on my face and mingled with my own. "Oh teach me the way to feel and believe," he said at last, as he clung to me like a frightened child, and clasped me convulsively to his heart. I held him long and tenderly, and felt for him somewhat, I hope, as Jesus did for the young man who came to him with a similar inquiry. I loved him, and longed to lead him to the light of day.

N

This was more than twenty years ago. My young friend wandered with me among the Alps for some weeks longer, and then returned home—and I went into the East. He is now a learned, able, and excellent teacher of Christian theology in one of the great universities of Germany. I often hear from him, and love him yet.

XIX.

A NIGHT AND A DAY IN THE DEEP.

IT was just the length of time that Paul said he was afloat, when recounting the hardships he had endured. Doubtless he was in far greater danger than we, and had not half so good a ship as ours in which to weather the storm. But ours was a very small affair of a steamer, and is not to be ill spoken of, as we are now safe on shore.

We came from Florence to Leghorn by rail in the middle of the day: a cloudy, rainy, but very calm, dull day; just the day of all others when you would think the sea would be smooth. We had bought our tickets in Florence for the steamer of that evening from Leghorn to Genoa. On reaching the port we learned that the steamer for that evening was the *Francois Marie*, lying nearly a mile off in the harbor, in the midst of scores of other vessels, and of course indistinguishable from the pier. A little row-boat took us and our baggage out to it. Probably had we seen it at the shore, we would have been disposed to lose the passage money and wait for another ship. It was a small iron steamer, a screw, of two hundred tons, very narrow, and by the side of others near she looked very diminutive, and, being very dirty, was decidedly repulsive. She was taking in her freight—bales of hemp raised in the northern part of Italy, and now shipped to Marseilles. Her hold was filled to its utmost capacity, and some freight was left for which there was no room.

We knew that we were " heavy laden." Then some kegs
of specie arrived. This was encouraging, for money is
not usually sent by doubtful carriers. Then came the
mails. This was even more assuring. It was the regular
mail line : every night from Leghorn to Genoa.

We went down into the cabin. It was just wide enough
for a table, and a passage between it and the state-rooms.
There were but two or three of these on a side, but they
were sufficiently numerous, as we two were the only passengers. By-and-by a·Maltese gentleman came on board
and raised the number to three. The sea was placid.
The rain had ceased. The sun had gone down in a
dense black mass of cloud that in our country would
have presaged a storm, but the rough captain assured us
that we should have a beautiful night, and be in Genoa
before daylight. Eight hours was the usual passage. We
were to sail at five. Five came, and the freight was not
on board. Six, and they were still at work taking in
more. The lazy, easy, good-for-nothing way they hoisted
the bales was amusing, if we had not been anxious to get
off. But an Italian never cares, never thinks, how long it
takes him to do any thing. The only thing in the world
he has enough of is time. He can spend as much of that
as he pleases, and have plenty to spare. It often takes
half an hour to get a draft cashed at the banker's. The
old clerk, or the old banker himself, looks at your letters,
goes and consults one or two others in the room, sits
down at his desk, takes a pinch of snuff, comes and asks
how you will have it, in gold or paper ; returns ; reckons
his commission of half per cent. ; thinks the matter
over a while ; gives his nose a tremendous blast with a
silk handkerchief; and finally, after you have given two
signatures of your name, he gives you a ticket to the

cashier, who with a small shovel scoops up the gold, and it is yours. The same indolent habit of business prevails in every department of life, from the banker to the boat-man and stevedore. Passengers' time is nothing. The advertised time of sailing is of no account. They go when they are ready, and they are ready when it suits their convenience to work and get ready. Seven came, and there were no signs of sailing. The captain came down into the cabin, took up a trap-door, and into it went a dirty little boy of his—more like a son of Vulcan, so black with coal and grime he was. To him was let down the specie; he stowed it away in some place known only to him and the captain. The trap-door was then closed and the money considered safe. Eight o'clock came, and the freight was all in. Dinner had been served to us in the cabin, for which we were charged extra, after having paid an enormous fare—$6 apiece—for the eight hours' run. Nine o'clock arrived, and soon after the grinding of the screw gave sensible notice that we were under way. Smoothly we passed out of the harbor, and wearied with a long and tedious day of waiting, and with no anxious thoughts about the night, we went to bed and to sleep.

"The cradle of the deep" is favorable to sleep. Many sleep more soundly at sea than on shore. Even in storms, the motion, if somewhat uniform, does not always disturb, and the berth is the best refuge for one addicted to the sickness of the sea. About midnight a crash in an empty room roused us from sleep; a shaky berth had given way in a sudden lurch of the ship. We were rolling out also. The next moment we were rolling in, and quite over the other way. The crash of the waves against the vessel, the roar of the wind, the unsteady roll and pitch of the ship, told us very plainly that a gale was on us, all the

more unpleasant as it was sudden and unexpected. My
traveling companion, decidedly more aquatic in his tastes
and habits than I, clambered up the stairs to take ob-
servations. It was a night when the blackness of darkness was on the face of the deep. Rain poured in torrents in the very thick of a furious gale. All hands
were at work lashing every thing fast, and putting the
little craft into condition for the worst that might come.
For us there was nothing but to wait. In a better ship
we would have had no fears of the results. Doubtless
the vessel had gone through many worse nights than
this, and why not again? Then came the suggestions of
faith, hope, and the sweet experience of other dangers
passed safely; and as hours dragged themselves slowly
and drearily along, we used all these sources of comfort
and found them good.

At such times one studies the things around him to
form some estimate of the rising or subsiding of the gale.
The lamp in the centre of the cabin swung freely, and
this was a pendulum to mark the length of every roll.
Soon its motion became too swift for pleasant contemplation, and the glass shade was smitten by striking the
ceiling. Now we were in total darkness. The steward
rigged another lamp, but it soon went over and out.
Every moment the sense of danger became more apparent, yet there was nothing for us to do but to wait.
The hours wore on slowly, but the longest and darkest
and dreariest night in the world has a morning to it, and
we knew there was one to ours. A tremendous shock, as
if some new engine of destruction had hurled a mountain
against the ship, and for a moment she seemed to stop in
her course, to shake herself from stem to stern, trembling
and uncertain what to do; and then the steady screw

screwed on and on, and the brave little vessel emerged from the wave that had smitten and covered her and moved on as before. Again and again, in the thick darkness of this tempestuous night, was the shock repeated, and as often we paused, hesitated, and then plunged along. "And oh, how welcome was the morning light!" I crept up in my berth to the port-hole above, and looked out on the boiling sea; it seemed to be rushing up from some horrid gulf in the bowels of the earth, and making sport of the vessel, that danced and rolled and pitched like an eggshell on the hissing and seething caldron of waters.

At this juncture word was brought down to us that we had better get ready for the worst, as it was impossible to say what was before us. But there was no preparation necessary, as the ship was the safest place, and one part of it was as safe as another. In a few moments we were reassured. No danger was apprehended. Land was in sight. We knew where we were. That was some comfort. But we were farther from Genoa, our destined port, than when we started ten hours ago. In the darkness of the night it was safer to keep off the coast; we had stood out to sea, had shot by the port, and now took the back track and toiled on, the storm increasing in fury every hour. The headlands were familiar to the Corsican captain, a rough fellow, who did his duty as well as he could under the circumstances, and kept sober, to my great comfort. It was in the afternoon when the City of Palaces—Genoa the Superb—burst upon our sight. The gale had not abated, but the rain had ceased; the sun was struggling through the clouds, and a blessed, beautiful rainbow was spanning the city with its arch of hope. In 1492 a son of Genoa discovered America. Not to him was the sight of our land more grateful than that of his native city was to us from the land he found. Our sailors shook hands, laughed, leaped, and danced for joy. Above the roar of the winds and waves I heard *Grazie a Dio*—thanks to God—and my heart echoed the praise. Two hours more and rougher sailing brought us safely into port, and a few steps into the snug harbor of the Hôtel d'Italie.

This storm swept the sea from Naples to Gibraltar. Between Naples and Leghorn more than fifty vessels were driven ashore or lost at sea. A great number of lives were lost. For weeks afterward the newspapers had reports of wrecks all along the coast. The day after we got into port the steamers that attempted to leave the harbor were compelled to give it up and return. For many days not a sail was to be seen on the sea. Between several of the ports navigation was suspended for a week.

XX.

A PARSON'S STORY.

IT is not a romance. It is a narrative of facts, which I give you as nearly as possible in the words of the village pastor:

I.

She was gasping when I came in. Her sickness had been sudden and severe, and before we were prepared for the terrible event, we knew that death was at the door.

The house in which Mrs. Bell had lived for twenty years was an old-fashioned mansion on the hill overlooking the village and the bay, and a wide expanse of meadow that stretched away to the water's edge. On the side toward the sea was a long piazza, a favorite resort of the family in summer, when the weather was pleasant. I was walking on it, and now and then looking off upon the world below, but with my thoughts more turned upon the scenes that were passing within.

I had been sent for a few hours before, and to my consternation and grief had found Mrs. Bell already given up by her physicians, and her life rapidly rushing to its close. Her disease was inflammatory. Its progress had defied all human skill, and two days had brought her to this. It was hard to believe it. But why should I be so distressed with the result, when others were suffering anguish which even my sympathies could not reach to relieve? Exhausted with my vain but earnest efforts to soothe the heart-rending grief of those who clung to the dying, I had left the chamber.

Mrs. Bell was a member of my church. Mr. Bell was not. He was reputed to be a man of means, and was known to be living easily, doing but little business, and apparently caring for nothing in the future. No one suspected that this indifference had resulted in the gradual wasting away of the property he had inherited: mortgages covering all the landed estates he was known to possess, till even the homestead was in danger.

But the pride of my parish was in this family. Two daughters, with only the difference of a year in their ages, and now just coming up into womanhood, were the only children of Mr. and Mrs. Bell. Sarah was the oldest, and her blue eyes and yellow hair were like her mother's, and the younger, Mary, had inherited from her father a radiant black eye, and locks of the raven hue. They were sisters in heart, soul, and mind, though a stranger would not have taken them to be the children of the same mother. Such love as bound them was wonderful to me, who, as the pastor of the family, was often there, and knew them well. I had watched its growth for ten years, and frequently had remarked that it exceeded in tenderness and devotion any thing of the kind that had ever fallen under my notice. Mrs. Bell had a thousand-fold more opportunities of putting it to the test, and of seeing it tried in the daily and hourly intercourse of the family, and she had told me that she had never known a moment of failure in the season of childhood and of youth, when the temper is often tried, and children are called on to make sacrifices for one another in little things, far greater tests of love than the struggles of after-life. She had observed, and had mentioned to me, a mysterious sympathy between them even from very early years. Their minds were turned at one and the same moment toward the same subject, when there appeared to be nothing suggestive of the train of thought engaging them both. A secret thread seemed to connect their souls, so that what was passing in one's mind was often at work in the other's. Instead of provoking dissension, as such a coincidence would naturally produce, it was rather a bond of union, leading them to love the same pleasures, and to study and labor to promote each other's joys. This was the more remarkable as their natural temperaments were unlike. The eldest was sanguine and cheerful, a sunbeam always shining in the house, glad and making glad—the brightest, happiest, gleefulest girl in my parish. Mary was sedate. Like her father, she was not inclined to action. Even in her childhood a tinge of melancholy gave a coloring to her life. She was fond of reading and retirement. When alone, her thoughts were her own. Her love for Sarah, and her filial love, made her faithful as a sister and a child; but there was a trait of character in which her sister, with all their sympathy, did not share. It was requisite, this contrast, to make them two. There was individuality, notwithstanding the kin-tie of spirit binding them as one, in a deep, earnest, true-hearted love that knew no break or change. But I am dwelling on these features of the children while the mother is dying. I was walking up and down the piazza, thinking of the awful work death was making in this house; of the wondrous love that bound mother and daughters, now to be no barrier in the way of this fell destroyer, half wishing I had the power to stay his arm, and drive him out of the paradise he was about to blast with his breath, when a servant summoned me to the chamber.

She was gasping as I entered. The fever raging in her veins had suffused her cheeks with crimson ; the rich hair, which, according to the custom of the times — for this was many, many years ago—she had worn in a mass sustained by a comb on the back of her head, now hung in great ringlets on her shoulders, and her eyes, sparkling with the last light of life, were fixed on her daughters kneeling at the bedside, giving vent to their bitter grief in floods of tears, and sobs they strove in vain to suppress.

Yet she knew me. She raised her hand as I came in, and said to me as I approached, "I know that my Redeemer liveth." Before I could find words, she added : "My children — the poor girls — be kind to them — be a friend to my dear husband." It was her last effort. While I had been out of the room she had taken leave of those dearest in life, and was now breathing away her spirit calmly, for she was not afraid to die—peacefully, for the pains of death were past.

It was all over. The stricken daughters were borne from the room by kind friends. The husband, betraying less emotion than we thought he would show in the midst of such a scene, retired, and I was for a moment alone with the dead. Wondrous the change that an instant had wrought! Out on an unknown sea the soul had drifted, and left this wreck upon the shore—a dissolving hulk—a heap of clay that would soon be loathsome to those who an hour ago were hanging over it with intensest love, covering it with kisses, and folding it in their arms. They call this awful work by the name of death. But this is not the last of Mrs. Bell—the lovely, living Mrs.

Bell. She is not dead. This is not the wife, the mother, the friend. She is not here. And as she is not here, we can do nothing more for her.

A few days afterward we laid her in the grave. She was a great favorite among our people, and they were all present at her burial. The grief of the daughters was for the present inconsolable ; it was kindness to let them weep freely, and have their own way in the first gush of their great sorrow. Perhaps time would do something for them. Religion would shed a soothing influence over their crushed and bleeding hearts, but now it was better to let the streams of affection flow along in these gushing tears, for there is a medicine in weeping that is the first remedy of grief.

II.

Mr. Bell died in less than a year. He was seized with a fit of apoplexy while sitting on the piazza after dinner, and died without a word.

The daughters were not at home, but were sent for in haste, and arrived just as I did, being called again to the house where so recently I had seen the fairest and fondest of mothers expire. The body of Mr. Bell, dressed as he died, was lying on the same bed which I had last seen when the corpse of his wife was there. It seemed but the day before. Not a change had been made. The same Bible lay on the same stand, near the bed, and I had heard that he read it oftener since the death of his wife. The same bureau with drawers and covered with a white cloth, a few choice books standing on it, was on the other side of the room, and a large easy-chair stuffed and clothed with dimity, and a few simple but very convenient articles completed the furniture of

the apartment. But instead of the pale form of my gentle friend, Mrs. Bell, lovely even in death, there was lying
on that white counterpane the large and now blackened
corpse of her husband. The physician, who had been
early on the ground, had found him dead. The case was
a plain one. Indeed, he had been often warned of such
an event, but his habitual fondness for putting things off
had led him to neglect all means of improving or pre-
serving his health, and he had been cut down in the midst
of his days.

But the daughters. They were orphans now. They
clung to me as to the friend on whom they might lean,
and who would not forget the dying request of their saint-
ed mother. They had loved their father with all the earnestness of their nature, and all the more since the death
of their mother had made him dependent on them for a
thousand nameless acts and arts of kindness which he
had ever received from his faithful wife. And the loneliness that now lay before them was so appalling that
they feared to look into the future. They had no brother, no relative to whom they might turn. It was not
strange that such thoughts pressed on them, even at the
side of their dead father, and that in the midst of their
anguish under this sudden and overwhelming blow they
should every now and then cry out, "What shall we do?"
And who could answer the question?

If it were a sad and fearful inquiry while as yet we
believed that Mr. Bell had left behind him a large and
handsome property, it was more distressing still when a
few weeks after his death it was discovered that he was
hopelessly involved in debt, and after the claims of his
creditors were but partially satisfied, it would leave nothing—not a cent, not the homestead, not the house, not

even the furniture—to his daughters. He was a bankrupt, and had been for a long time past; but he had no energy to meet the calamity, and death came on him just as his affairs were reaching a crisis that put further concealment of the state of his affairs out of the question. Perhaps the coming disclosure hastened the blow that killed him. But the facts could no longer be hid even from those whom they must crush. Poor girls! In every sense that makes the word *poor* a term of pity, these girls were now poor indeed. Had it been possible for me in my circumstances to have assumed the burden, I would gladly have taken them to my own home, and made them sharers with my children in the weal or woe in store for us all. This I could not in justice do. But something must 'be done, and that with no delay. The estate was administered upon in a few weeks, and as there were no funds to meet the debts, the law took its course, and the orphans were homeless.

Their education had been domestic. Mrs. Bell had been their teacher. They were well-read girls, but not fitted to teach others. So that door was not open to them. Sarah particularly, with a fine imagination and a decidedly poetical turn of mind, was familiar with the literature of her own language, which she was accustomed to read with her mother. Many of her letters are now in my possession, and they are clothed in language at once graceful and rich, and some of them are beautiful in style and thought. Mary had less taste for reading, yet she thought more and felt deeper than her sister. In the retirement of that home circle the mother and daughters, with an industry more common perhaps in those days than it is in the present, had made needle-work their chief employment; and it was natural that the girls should

turn to that in which they were the most expert as the
means on which they must rely for their main support,
now that they were thrown upon their own resources or
upon the charity of the world.   They had too much self-
reliance and too much confidence in God to trust themselves to the kindness of friends who, in the impulse of
sudden sympathy, might offer to do for them what would
soon prove to be a task and a burden.   No ; they would
meet the emergency with the energy of faith and hope,
knowing that God helps those who help themselves.
They gave themselves scant time for mourning.   They
left the home of their infancy and childhood—the third
great sorrow of their lives.   But now that father and
mother were both gone, even the honeysuckle that climbed up the piazza, and the beds of flowers they had planted and tended with their own hands, and the fruit that
hung in rich abundance in the garden, lost half their value—they served rather to remind them of days when in
happy youth they had enjoyed them all with the parents
they had lost ; and it was almost a relief to turn their
backs upon the home they had loved, and seek a humble lodging in the village. . ·

III.

For they are sewing-girls now.   It was nothing that
they were young and pretty and well-bred.   They must
have food and raiment and shelter, and they could earn
all by the labor of their hands.   They were not the girls
to shrink from the contest with pride and opinion, and the
thousand and one mortifications to which this new and
trying life would lead.   Sarah led and Mary followed.
They had no words about it.   Sarah proposed it, and
Mary had been thinking of the same plan.   It was the

only one before them. And it was not so hopeless as it might be. They had many friends. They would find work, plenty of it, and it would be sweeter to live on the bread of honest industry than to ask the charity of any one, or to receive it without asking. It was a noble resolution. They consulted me before coming to a decision, and I could not oppose their scheme, though I had no heart to counsel them to go on with it. The future would be so unlike the past. These sensitive natures—these children as they were to me, who had known them so long as children only—to be exposed to the rough-and-tumble of the life of orphans, was bad enough under almost any aspect of the case. But to be harassed by the daily vexations, and wearied by the daily toils of the life of a seamstress, was more than I could think of without tears ; and I admired the fortitude with which they addressed themselves to the work they had assumed.

Mrs. Benson was a friend indeed. She was of one of the most influential families in my flock, and had been the bosom friend of Mrs. Bell while she was yet with us. Mrs. Benson offered the girls a home, and when they declined her generous proposal, she insisted on their looking to her as to a mother in the future, whatever might be the issue of the new and untried experiment they were about to make. We shall, however, overrate the heroism of the girls if we measure it by the sacrifice of feeling which such a mode of life would require at the present time. In our rural village of a thousand inhabitants the girls would not be the less esteemed by any of the better sort of people for their new employment. On the contrary, the door of every house would be open to them, and every voice would be one of kindness to greet them when they came.

O

"I shall die, I know I shall," said Mary, as they were alone in the snug parlor of the old homestead for the last time. "I feel it here"—as she laid her hand on her side, and pressed her beating heart. "I can never leave it, and feel that it is to be no home of ours again."

"But, Mary dear," said her more hopeful sister, "we could not be at home if we stayed here. It is all gloomy now, and what there is to love will be as much ours hereafter as it ever was. These walks will be here, and these trees and flowers, and we will often come and look on them; for whoever lives here will never deny us the privilege. And we are to do for ourselves now. It is too soon to be discouraged. God will help us, and that right early."

"Yes, Sister Sarah, I know all that, and more, but I am afraid. It is dreadful, this going out into the world alone. It looks so dark. My head aches when I think of it. A great black cloud seems to be hanging over us; and sometimes I think I am growing blind, every thing is so dark before me. Tell me now, truly, have you had no such fears?"

"But I will not give them room in my thoughts for a moment. They do come to me as to you, and sometimes they frighten me, but I drive them away, and look to God for strength. Fearful thoughts never come from him. He is our Father now more than ever, and has promised that he will never leave nor forsaké us."

Mary was silenced, but not satisfied. Sarah could thus reason her into resignation, but it was still very dark and trying; and to her desponding nature there was something in store for them more terrible than they had yet experienced. The presentiment was dim and might be idle, but it was deep-seated and absorbing. She said it was in her heart, but it was in her brain. She often pressed her hand hard on her forehead, and then thrust her head into Sarah's bosom, not weeping, but asking her sister to hide her from the terrible fate that gathered about her, and threatened to blast them both in the morning of their grief.

IV.

"What will George say?" had been a question often on Sarah's mind when coming to this decision, that she must be a seamstress. George had never told her that he loved her, but he had been kind and attentive, and a thousand nameless acts had given her the assurance that he was more to her than a friend. She was not insensible. Sarah would have loved him had he sought her love. Happily for her own peace, he had made no advances; and when he learned that she and her sister were not only orphans but poor, he discovered that he had no particular regard for either of them, and with no words left them to their fate. Perhaps this blow to Sarah's hopes, for she had hopes, was necessary to complete the misery of her portion. A noble, faithful friend to stand by her in such an hour would have been like life to the dead. There was no such stay for her now. And the two sisters, finding that few friends are born for adversity, prepared to go forth hand in hand, and trusting only in God, to do what they could for themselves.

Mrs. Benson was always ready with plenty of work for them when they had nothing to do elsewhere. She made it for them, not that she had need of their aid, and so cheated them into the belief that they were indispensable for her comfort, while she was only ministering to theirs.

V.

Mrs. Flint was the housekeeper of Mrs. Benson. She had now held this situation for many years, never gaining the confidence of the lady whose domestic affairs she had superintended with so much zeal and discretion as to render herself indispensable to the house. But she was very far from securing the affections of any of its inmates. A married daughter of hers in the village was even less a favorite than she in the family of Mrs. Benson. Perhaps the evident partiality which Mrs. Benson had exhibited for the young ladies, who were now her *protégées*, and her failure to interest Mrs. Benson in her daughter, may have been the occasion of a feeling of enmity which she had cherished toward these girls ever since they had become the occasional members of the family. Yet it is needless to speculate upon the causes which led to the indulgence of such feelings. A bad heart affords the only explanation of the phenomenon ; for such it certainly appears to any one who came to the knowledge of the fact that a woman could cherish in her heart a desire to injure two unprotected orphans, whose helpless situation and exceeding innocence of character won for them the universal love and confidence of the community. Without stopping, therefore, to speculate upon the causes of her enmity, it is enough to say that she conceived and carried into execution a plan for the destruction of their character. She accused them to Mrs. Benson of having purloined many articles of clothing ; and when the declaration was made, and was received by Mrs. Benson with indignant exclamations of incredulity, she demanded that the basket which they had brought with them should be searched, and expressed her willingness to abide by the result of the examination. She dèclared that she had seen one of them coming from the wardrobe in the morning, and under circumstances that left no doubt upon her own mind that she had been there for no proper purpose.

More for the sake of convincing her housekeeper of the innocence of those whom she had so recklessly accused than with any idea of making a discovery that should even awaken suspicion in her own mind, Mrs. Benson consented to the search; and while the girls were engaged upon their work below, Mrs. Benson and the housekeeper proceeded to the apartment which had been occupied by the girls, where Mrs. Flint immediately produced from the bottom of the basket the articles, of no great value, to be sure, but enough to fix upon them the guilt which Mrs. Flint had already imputed to them. Still Mrs. Benson was not satisfied. The confidence of years was not to be destroyed, even by such a disclosure as this. But what could she say? Mrs. Flint, with vehemence, insisted upon calling up the girls, setting before them the evidence of their shame, and compelling them, with the proof before their own eyes, to confess their guilt.

Bewildered by the painful circumstances for which she was utterly unable to account, and hoping that they would be able to make some explanation of the unpleasant facts, Mrs. Benson consented to summon them to the chamber, and to hear from their own lips such explanation as they might be able to offer. At her call they came bounding into the room, with conscious innocence in their faces, and wondering at the occasion of being called at such an hour to meet Mrs. Benson in her own room. She held up before them what would appear to be indisputable evidence that they had been seeking to rob their best friend; and with trembling voice and tearful eyes she begged them to tell her by what means these evidences of their wrong had thus been secreted. To her astonishment, they both received her inquiries and disclosures with a ringing laugh. This could mean only utter unconscious-ness of evil, if it were not the evidence of a hardened de-pravity inconsistent with their previous history.

When they came, however, to view the subject in a more serious light, and to perceive the necessity of giving some account of the circumstances in which they were involved, they could do nothing more than to declare their utter ig-. norance of the way and the manner by which they had so suddenly come into possession; and looking at Mrs. Flint, whose eyes fell to the floor when they attempted to catch her. attention, they united in the declaration that some evil-disposed person must have secreted the articles among their things for the purpose of fastening upon them the suspicion of theft. Mrs. Flint declared that no one excepting herself and Mrs. Benson had been in the house, or had any access whatever to their apartments, and it was quite impossible to suppose that these things could be found there without hands; and if not without hands, whose could they have been, unless those of the young la-dies in whose possession these things had been so *prov-identially* discovered?

"But how came they to be discovered?" demanded the girls.

This was a question for which Mrs. Flint was unpre-pared; but recovering herself, she said that for some time past her suspicions had been excited by having missed various articles, which she had never mentioned to Mrs. Benson, and which she was resolved not to men-tion until she should be able to account for their disap-pearance; that, accordingly, she had kept her eye upon

the girls since they came into the house, and having no-
ticed one of them that morning under circumstances that
led her to suspect all was not right, she had taken the
liberty, in their absence from the room, of examining the
apartment—and this was the result.

Roused by a sense of the great injustice which had
been done them, yet scarcely able to believe that so much
malice could be in the human heart, unable to imagine a
reason that could prompt any human being to devise and
execute such a plan of mischief against them, they, nevertheless, in conscious innocence, united in charging upon
Mrs. Flint, with courage which injured virtue always sum-
mons to its own defense, with having contrived this de-
testable scheme for their ruin; and throwing themselves
upon the mercy and upon the neck of Mrs. Benson, they
begged her, for the sake of their mother, now in heaven,
for their own sakes—helpless and friendless as they were
in the world—not to believe this terrible charge, of which
they declared themselves to be as guiltless as the spirit
of her who bore them.

Mrs. Benson believed them. With all the confidence
of a mother, trusting in the purity of daughters whose every word and action she had known and loved from infancy, she took them to her heart, and assured them that,
however dark the circumstances might appear, however
difficult it might be to explain them, she would believe
that God would yet make it plain, and that whatever others might think, she for one would cherish no suspicion.

This was a dark chapter in the history of the orphans.
Hitherto misfortune had followed fast upon the heel of
misfortune. The "clouds had returned after the rain;"
but the sorrows which they had experienced had been
such as left them in the enjoyment of that priceless treas-

ure—a character above reproach or suspicion. Now the cloud that hung over them was darker than any which had ever yet obscured their path. For they began to feel how vain would be all their own efforts to stem the tide of adversity, unless they had not only the present consciousness of virtue, but the sweet assurance of the respect and confidence to which it would entitle them.

It was a cheerless circle that surrounded the table at Mrs. Benson's that evening ; few words were spoken, but every heart was full of its own reflections upon the events of the day, and their probable influence upon the parties interested. Mrs. Benson's mind was made up as to the course it was her duty to pursue with reference to the woman who, she had no doubt, was the evil genius in her house, and to whose malignant jealousy of the orphans she was compelled to attribute this fiendish attempt at their ruin. Still she desired so to manage the affair as to prevent any future mischief resulting to them from the tongue of Mrs. Flint, when she should dispense with her services in the house.

In the retirement of their chamber the sisters wept together over this new sorrow ; they sought strength from God, to whom alone they had learned to look for help in extremities ; and hour after hour, as they lay in each other's arms, they sought to cheer one another with words that did not speak the feelings of their hearts ; and it was not until long after midnight that disturbed sleep gave them a brief and imperfect respite from the grief now thickening around and upon them. It was impossible to escape the apprehension that Mrs. Benson's confidence in their integrity had been shaken ; and they could not but feel that, were she lost to them, all on earth was lost ; and then, so often had they already been compelled to experience the failure of all earthly friendship, they would seek to persuade themselves that, even in the last and most trying circumstances to which they could be subjected, there was One ever above and near them to whom they might flee for succor, and whose promises, made to their mother in her dying hour, would never fail.

A few days afterward Mrs. Flint left the house of Mrs. Benson, going to her married daughter's dwelling, which she made her home for the future. It was not long before the sisters found that her tongue was busy; that she had correctly interpreted the reason of her dismissal; and now, more than she ever had done, sought to work their destruction for the sake of revenge. Whatever might have been the deficiency of motive in her case when she first meditated mischief, she had now abundant excitement in the fact that the failure of her scheme had wrought her own injury. Stung by the mortification of her own discharge, she sought to expend the violence and bitterness of her own feelings in circulating, with malicious expedition, the story which would serve at once the double purpose of injuring the orphans and accounting for her own retirement from the service of Mrs. Benson.

The girls saw the effects before they heard the cause. Friends in whose doors they had been welcomed now received them with coldness. Those who had sought their services fell away, and they soon found themselves entirely dependent upon their truly maternal friend, Mrs. Benson, who alone, of all the circle in which they had formerly been received, stood by them. So widespread is the mischief which an evil report occasions. It was in vain that Mrs. Benson asserted her belief in the innocence of the sisters. The community took the side of her whom they believed to have been unjustly accused, and to have been discharged when all the evidences of wrong were against the parties whom Mrs. Benson had sheltered with what they believed an overweening confidence.

VI.

So strong became the prejudice against these unfortunate girls that their employment gradually fell off, until it became evident that they must be dependent upon Mrs. Benson for their daily bread, or must seek in some other place a more favorable opportunity of sustaining themselves. Their friend and patron kindly assisted them in establishing themselves in a neighboring village, where it was believed they might be able to pursue their work, and by degrees gain the confidence of the community. But with a vindictiveness rarely to be found in the female sex, and painful to be contemplated wherever observed, Mrs. Flint followed them to their new home, and soon spread widely, where they were now seeking to establish for themselves a character, the report that they had been compelled to leave their native village under suspicions of dishonesty. They struggled heroically against this new dispensation of evil, but in vain. A few weeks had scarcely elapsed before it became evident that they would be utterly unable to make progress in this new field, and that the few friends whom they had made were not proof against the insidious effects of slander, which was now undermining them. Indeed, so strong became the popular feeling of indignation against them, as suspicious and dangerous young women who had come into the place because they were unable to live in another where they were better known, that the house in which they lodged was surrounded by a mob, and demonstra-

tions of violence were made. When they heard the
alarm which came up from the street, and were told that
they were the occasion of the disturbance, trembling lest
they might be the victims of personal violence, their fright
became insupportable. Mary, the less excitable of the
two, sat moody and speechless.

"They are coming!" she exclaimed at last; "they are
coming for us. We shall be driven out; perhaps we shall
be killed. What shall we do?"

Sarah, more excited, but always more hopeful, strove to
allay her alarm, beseeching her not to lose her trust in
God, but to hope for the best. Through the help of the
man whose house they were dwelling in, Sarah succeeded, after a while, in inducing the rioters in the street to
retire, after having given them the assurance that they
would on the next day return to the village from which
they had come.

But they had to be taken there. And it was a month
before that could be done. The fearful presentiment of
some greater sorrow—the great black cloud—was made
real—Mary was laid upon a bed of suffering with a brain
fever, and Sarah was by turns a gentle and then a raving
maniac. God help the orphans.

VII.

A year in their native village passes by.

They are now hopelessly deranged. Wandering in
the streets, singing loose and ribald songs—a source of
intensest grief to all those who had known them in the
loveliness of their childhood and youth—they were objects also of the tenderest compassion; and had there
been at this time any provision for the care and cure of
the insane, doubtless they would have found a refuge in

some such asylum.   Human skill had not yet contrived
such institutions, and the insane were only prevented
from doing injury to others by being confined among
the most miserable and degraded of the public poor.   As
the girls manifested no disposition to do violence to others, and were cheerful rather than gloomy in their madness, they were suffered to go at large; and many sought
by kindness to win them back again to a state of quiet-
ness and peace.   Often, when led by the hand of friendship into the houses of those who would care for them,
they were known to leap from the window into the street,
as if apprehensive of being confined.

As yet they were never, even in their worst state, insensible to the voice of love.   My own house was freely
opened to them as a home, where I sought, by all the assiduity which my affection for their parents could suggest, to administer the balm of comfort, if I could not
furnish the balm of healing, to their wounded minds.

One instance occurs to me of peculiar interest.   They
were invited, as not unfrequently they had been before,
to spend a social evening with some of the young people
of the village ; and in the midst of the lively associations
of the evening, their spirits seemed to revive.   Something
of their former gentleness and loveliness began to return.
Yet now, so far had the work of ruin gone on in the minds
of these young girls, that they not only had forgotten
many of their early friends and associates, but, strange to
say, they had forgotten the relationship between themselves.   They knew each other only as companions.   At
the close of the evening they were invited to spend the
night at the house where the entertainment had been
given ; and after retiring to bed, and lying in each other's
arms, soothed by the pleasures which they had been en-

joying, and the circumstances of comfort by which they
found themselves surrounded, a calm serenity of mind
stole over them, fond memory came back with all its
sweet influences, and gradually the truth broke in upon
their souls that they were sisters.   In mutual recognition, and in the fullness of that affection which had been
uninterrupted from infancy, they spent the most of the
night in delightful union of spirit, forgetful, of course, of
all that had occurred in the hours and months of their
delirium; yet remembering that some great sorrow had
once shed its gloom over their minds, and that they were
now in the midst of friends and pleasures which it was
their privilege to enjoy.   They arose in the morning refreshed by a night, not of sleep, but of sweet peace.
Alas! it was but for a night.   Before the day was gone
the cloud gathered over them once more; delirium seized
them; they rushed forth from the house of their protect-
or and friend, and again in the streets of the village renewed their wild mirth, piercing the ears and the hearts
of those who heard them.

VIII.

It was now late in the summer.   Mrs. Flint had been
for some weeks confined to her bed with a wasting fever.
I was sent for to see her, and was out in the country visiting a parishioner some miles from my home.   I had seen
her several times during her sickness, and was well convinced that her disease would have a fatal termination.
As soon as I returned home and learned that I had been
sent for, I hastened to the cottage; as I entered, a scene
of strange and thrilling interest was before my eyes.   The
woman was dying, and kneeling at her bedside were
these two wild girls.

I soon learned the facts that had brought them there under such strange and exciting circumstances. They had been wandering, as usual, through the streets; and when the sound of their mirth broke in upon the hearing of the dying woman, she inquired what it was. Being told that Sarah and Mary Bell were carrying on as they were accustomed to, she started at the mention of their names, and begged that they might be called in. They came at the call, and without hesitation approached the bed on which their enemy and destroyer was now stretched, in hourly expectation of death.

"I did it!" said Mrs. Flint; "it is all my work; and here, as I am now about to leave this world and go into the presence of God, I would not go without clearing these girls of that great sin which I laid to their charge, but which God knows they are as innocent of as the angels in his presence. I did it—I did it; it was all my work."

The girls were evidently affected deeply by the sight before them, and by the tones of her voice; and as she repeated again and again her asseverations of their innocence and her own guilt, they began to comprehend the nature of the scene that was transpiring. It pleased God to give them just at this hour, and doubtless through the influence of the communication which they were receiving, at least a temporary deliverance from the darkness and delirium in which they had so long been lost. He restored peace and a measure of strength to their minds, enabling them to receive and to understand the blessed truth that evidence was coming, though from the verge of the grave, to deliver them from the wrongs they had suffered. They took her extended hands in their own; they knelt upon the floor by her side; they assured her, even in their wretchedness and their ruin, that they would forgive her ; and they prayed Heaven to grant her forgiveness ere her soul should take its departure.

It was at this juncture that I entered the room. The moment Mrs. Flint caught my eye she renewed her protestations of the innocence of the girls, told me how for years she had carried the pangs of remorse in her own breast, how often she had desired to do them justice, and to seek peace for her own conscience; but her selfishness and her pride had always overcome her better resolutions, and she had witnessed month after month the dreadful fruits of her sin, and feared continually that the judgments of God would overtake her. Here, on her sick-bed, and in view of death, when no other considerations than those which attended preparation for the grand event which was just before her were allowed to have any power upon her mind, she had been driven to this last and dying confession, which, while it would relieve her own mind of the burden under which she was sinking, would restore to those unhappy girls the priceless treasure of a character which they had lost ; though she believed, as I did, that it was too late to hope that the restoration of their character would bring them back the treasure of reason, which there was too much cause to fear was irretrievably lost.

What could I add to this revelation, than which nothing could be more solemn and affecting? Here were all the accessaries of a sublime yet painful drama. The dying woman, with her sharp, haggard features, her piercing, agonized eyes, looking now at the girls, and now upward as if she would look into the other world, striving to read the destiny upon which she was about to enter,

now turning to me with imploring glance, and asking me
to direct her, even in her extremity, to some way by which
she might find forgiveness and peace, now seeking to re-
assure the helpless daughters of sorrow yet kneeling before her that God would be their father and their portion,
saying that she could die with contentment if she could
believe that her death would be the means of giving back
to them the life which they had lost.

In vain was it for me to offer a word of consolation.
Indeed, there was none to be spoken. I directed her, as
I would any lost sinner in the hour of calamity, to the
only refuge, and besought her to seek in the Saviour the
only source of peace.

When the girls arose from their knees, and were about
to leave the house, she begged them to remain, and even
required from them a promise that they would not leave
her while she lived. With gentle kindness they began to
perform the part of nurses around the sick-bed, and with
unaccustomed ministries they soothed her sufferings, and
gradually seemed to bring her to the enjoyment of something like peace of mind. But this was temporary. Soon
the paroxysms of anguish came back with redoubled force,
and in words too strong to be repeated, and such only as
dying pains extort from consciences ill at ease anticipat-
ing greater anguish near at hand ; fearful of the present,
and more fearful still of that which is to come, she cried
again and again, "It was I that did it—it was I that did
it ; it was all my work." And so she died.

IX.

I took the girls home with me, and embraced this present lucid interval to make an earnest experiment, in the
faint hope of securing their permanent restoration. Noth-

ing had occurred since their derangement which afforded such good ground to believe that there might be a basis laid for a permanent cure. They could be assured that all suspicions formerly resting upon their character were now removed, and they would enjoy the universal confidence and love of those who had been their friends, and their mother's friends, in the days of their prosperity and joy. I told them that my house was to be their home; I gave them their chamber; I gave them such light work as would occupy their minds, and in the cultivation of flowers in the garden, in the pursuit of such studies as they were always fond of, and in the society of kind and genial friends, I sought to surround them with those pleasant influences which would cheer and console, and gently aid in their perfect recovery.

Among the many friends who were in the habit of visiting at my house from the city of New York was a merchant of large means and extensive business. His wife had died a year after their marriage, and he had led a single life for five or six years. It was not among the remotest of my suspicions that he should think of finding a second wife in my house, and in one of these unfortunate yet lovely young ladies.

But there is no accounting for tastes or sympathies. Mr. Whitfield was a man long accustomed to think for himself, and not given to asking the opinions of others till after his own mind was made up. Then it was too late to shake his resolution, whatever the force of the motives urged against it. He knew the story of the Bells, and that story had first awakened his sympathy, his pity, and prepared the way for love. When he broached the subject to me, I begged him to dismiss it at once and forever from his mind. But he respectfully declined, telling

P

me he had counted the cost, and was prepared for the risks.

Although there had been great improvement in the health and appearance of both Sarah and Mary since the death of Mrs. Flint, they were still liable to returns of the fearful malady; and Mr. Whitfield had his resolution put to the severest test as soon as he ventured upon the experiment of making known his intentions to Sarah, the object of his choice. He had invited her to ride with him. They drove out of the village, passing the door of the house in which Mrs. Flint had died. Sarah had never entered it since that terrible hour when she and her poor sister closed the eyes of the wretched woman. The memories of that scene, and of all they had passed through in the years of their former struggles and trials, came rushing upon her mind, and she began to talk wildly, and then madly; and soon she became frantic, and strove to leap from the carriage, and would have done so but for the main force of her friend and companion, who trembled at the brink on which he was standing.

Still he was not disheartened. He hastened back with his charge to my house, and told me of the excitement into which Sarah had been thrown, and the danger from which she had been rescued. He was deeply affected. He was in trouble. "And yet," said he, "in spite of all this, I believe that if she were once more in a home of her own, and surrounded with the duties and pleasures of the household, her mind would become settled, and she would be restored to the enjoyment of health and reason."

I assured him that, next to my own children, I desired their happiness before all others, but I could not advise him to take a step which might make him miserable, without adding to the enjoyment of her who could not be a wife such as he desired unless God should give her back the permanent possession of her once cultivated and now disordered mind.

He returned in a week or two, with his purpose unchanged. He asked Sarah again to ride with him; and this time she seemed to enjoy the world around her, and to enter into the spirit of nature as its beauties met her eyes. The birds were happy, and she spoke of their gladness as she saw and heard them. The fields seemed to clap their hands. Sarah was joyful in the midst of a world of joy. They rode to Passaic Falls, at Paterson, in the State of New Jersey. The deep roar of the waters as they approached was a solemn music that subdued and stilled her soul. They walked out upon the wide, flat rocks through which the river makes its broken plunge, and, instead of being terrified, she gloried in the excitement of the scene. She spoke of the spray as a cloud of incense rising from those eternal altars, and ever praising Him who sits in the heavens, and listens to the music of all his works. They came to the edge of the precipice, and Mr. Whitfield pointed out to her the very spot where, a few months previously, a bride had fallen from the side of her husband, and had been dashed to pieces on the rocks below. She looked down with steady nerves, and said that it was a fearful fall, and more fearful to him who remained when his bride was gone.

He led her cautiously and by a winding path to the bottom of the ravine, whence they could look up to the brow of the black jagged rocks, from which the white waters were tumbling through the green fringes of stunted trees and bushes that clung to the sides of the clefts.

And here, in the roar of the fall, as she was rejoicing

in the wonderful beauty of the scenes around her, he began his declaration.

"You are not serious, surely," she cried, in mingled fear
and surprise, as he intimated that he desired her love,
and would be only too happy to give her his fortune and
his hand. "You do not know my story, or you could not
dream of such a proposal."

"I know it all; it was that story which first led me to
think of devoting my life to yours; and if you will cast
in your lot with me, you shall find that I will be parent,
brother, husband, all in one."

"It is altogether out of the question," she returned.
"I do not love you; I do not know that I could love.
This thought of love is one that I have not known since
those happy days before the clouds came. You did not
know that I ever loved?"

"Yes, I have heard that one all unworthy of you once
sought you, and that he fled when the day of your adversity came. I would come to you in the midst of your
sorrow, and win you to a home of peace and joy. I have
the means of surrounding you with all that you can desire, and my life shall be spent in making yours as happy
as you ever dreamed of being."

"But you have not counted the cost; you know not
what you are proposing; I am a poor, weak thing; and
I have even been told that my sister and I are sometimes
deranged. I do not know what it is, or why it is, but I
have strange, dreadful thoughts sometimes; and these
have been more frequent and more terrible since the time
when Mary and I were accused of a crime of which we
were altogether innocent. You will not be so rash as to
think of taking such a wild, thoughtless woman as I am
to your home, even if I could assure you that the affec-

tion you promise could be returned in all its sincerity and strength." .

Still he pressed his suit. In the honesty of his heart he felt he had now committed himself, and even if he had been staggered in his purpose by the serious objections she had so rationally raised, and urged with so much earnestness, he was bound to go forward. And never did the girl appear to him more lovely than when, with such delicate appreciation of his motives, and tempted as she must be by his proposals, she still resisted his appeals, and left him an open door to retreat. He renewed his entreaties.

"But there is my sister Mary, who was with me in our childhood, the companion of all my sorrows—I will never, never leave her."

"And you shall not leave her. She will go with us to our own home, and be my sister as well as yours. Instead of losing a sister, she will find a brother."

Sarah was deeply affected. It seemed to her that God was in this thing, and that the dark clouds which had so long hung over her were now clearing away, and a new light was breaking upon her path. Yet she could not yield to the offers so pressed upon her till she had consulted her friends, and she finally promised to be governed by my advice in the matter. She was calm and cheerful as they came home together that evening. I should not have suspected that any thing unusual had passed between them. But after the sisters had retired for the night, and I was left alone with Mr. Whitfield, he told me of the events of the day, and begged me to aid him in procuring Sarah's consent to their union. He knew well that I had already advised him against the proposal; but now he was more than ever infatuated with the conviction that

the restoration of the sisters to the calm pleasures of a
home they might call their own would be the means of
getting them health and peace.   To all prudential considerations he turned a deaf ear ; and I was obliged to tell
him that it was impossible for me to object, if he were
willing to take the responsibility upon himself.

With a new and an admiring sense of the ways of divine
Providence, I looked upon the change that was about to
take place in the situation of these poor sisters, and said
to myself seriously, as I thought over the ways by which
they had been led, is there, indeed, any thing too hard for
the Lord?   Who would have believed that such a door
of deliverance from poverty and suffering would be opened?   Who would have thought that one of these orphans,
a few months ago wandering in the streets, and raving in
the wildness of delirium, would now be sought after by a
man of character and wealth, laying his fortune at her feet,
and offering to share his home with her sister, so that both
should be equally the recipients of blessings which Heaven
is so kindly bestowing?   Here was the promise of God
most strikingly fulfilled : " Leave thy fatherless children
—I will keep them alive ;" " When my father and my
mother forsake me, then the Lord will take me up."
There had been many long and painful years, when it
might be feared that these promises had been forgotten.
So deep had been the extremity of their destitution, and
so hopeless their condition, I had looked forward to their
death as the first release they could have from sorrow.
Such a termination was far more probable than that one
of them should win the love of a noble-hearted man who
would take her to himself, and surround her with the
sweets of social and domestic life.   But if all this is, indeed, in store for these orphan sisters, far be it from me

to say a word, except to pray God to bless them both, and give them a respite from the miseries which have so long been their portion.

During the interval of three months that followed this eventful day there was a daily and marked improvement in the sisters. The vivacity of childhood, without the levity of their wandering years, returned : they were themselves again. And when Sarah at length gave her consent, and stood up before me to be joined in marriage to the man who had thus nobly called her to be his own, I said to him, " I give you Sarah to be your wife, and Mary to be your sister." And he replied, " I will be faithful to both until death shall separate us."

If any part of this narrative has had the appearance of romance, much more like it is that which is now to be recorded. But if I have not already given the assurance, it may be well to say here that I am following out the events of real life, and there are many now living who will read and attest, if needful, the truth of these strange facts.

Among the guests at the marriage of Sarah was a younger brother of her husband, his partner in business, and with the same bright prospects. He stood up by the side of his brother, and Sarah was supported by her sister. In less than a month from that time the order was changed, and the young Whitfield and Mary stood side by side, and plighted their vows in the presence of God, and surrounded by a glad and admiring circle of friends, who could not conceal their grateful recognition of a merciful providence in the marriage of these two sisters under circumstances of such extraordinary interest.

A short time afterward I saw them settled in their new homes. They lived in adjoining houses in one of the pleasantest streets of the city, then quite down town, where now the march of business has driven out the old settlers, desecrated the firesides hallowed by a thousand sacred associations, and converted the sanctuary of love into temples of Mammon.

X.

And here I would be willing to close this record, and leave my young friends in the bliss with which at length their lives are crowned.

"It is wonderful," Sarah said to me as I called to see her in her beautiful mansion. "It is wonderful. How strangely God has led us; and now we are as happy as we have ever been miserable in the years that are past. Do you believe that my dear mother knows what we have passed through, and what we are enjoying now?"

I told her I had often indulged the idea that the spirits of the departed were conversant with our spirits—that they are indeed ministering spirits to those whom they loved while in the flesh, and it was not impossible that her mother had followed her in all her eventful and mysterious history. Even now she may be near and rejoicing that peace and joy had at last visited the hearts of her daughters, and out of great tribulation they were already brought to happiness they had never dreamed of.

It was a short year after Mary's marriage when the birth of a child promised to fill the cup of her thanksgiving. Others rejoiced, and yet she did not seem to be happy in the prospect, nor when it was laid in her arms did she give it more than a melancholy smile of satisfaction. Instead of fondling it with the yearning tenderness of a young mother, she looked on it calmly, but with a fixedness of interest that was more full of anxiety than affection. Days and weeks went by and this moodiness increased. She was able now to sit up, and when the infant was lying on her knees or in the cradle by her side, she would sit by the hour and watch it steadily, without a word, but often sighing as if some great sorrow was in the future of her child's history, into which she was looking. Slowly but steadily, and in the lapse of weeks and months, she sank into melancholy gloom. No art of medicine, no kind devotion of a faithful husband, no sweet ministries of a large and loving circle of friends could raise her up, or dispel the cloud that gathered over her spirit. The child was removed from her sight, but it was all the same to her. She never asked for it, seemed never to think of it unless it were in her sight. Foreign travel was proposed, and Mr. Whitfield earnestly strove to prevail on her to go with him abroad. But to all such invitations she was indifferent. She must have been carried by force, or she would never have been taken from the room where in profound reverie she sat day after day, without interest in the world around her, or even in those nearest to her fireside.

Sarah was not careless for her sister's state, but alas, by that strange fatality which had hitherto followed them both, making them one in suffering as they were also one in the few joys that were theirs in life, she too began to show signs of returning madness. What was the secret principle thus linking their destinies? In childhood they had been as one in love and innocence. In youth they had been crushed, together and by the same blow. In womanhood they had both found loving hearts, fraternal hearts, that gave them a shelter, a home, and all the sympathies of a noble conjugal affection. And now, when the great struggle of life was past, and they were in the midst of joys that even in the dreams of childhood they had never thought of, the darkness is coming on again, and other hearts besides their own are to be shrouded in the approaching gloom.

Mary's child died in its first year. Mary did not shed a tear. It was no more to her than the child of a stranger. She was now silent and sullen. She never complained, but it was gradually apparent that disease was making progress. She took to her bed, and a slow fever wore out her life. She died three months after her child, and less than two years after her marriage.

Sarah's malady had a widely different development. Naturally more excitable than her sister, she had in former days been more wild and gay in the seasons of their derangement. Now she was wilder than ever. She became uncontrollable by the friends who surrounded her. There was no asylum into which she could be placed: the insane at that time were confined only among paupers or criminals, or in hospitals under circumstances the most unfavorable to their recovery. Her faithful husband, as tender in his affection and devoted as when he first won her, sought to restrain her by gentle assiduity, striving to conceal from others, when he could no longer hide from his own mind, the terrible fact that she was mad. But her madness wore a humorous rather than a mischievous type for some months. She would enter the parlor while he was on his knees conducting the devotions of the household, and leap on his back as if in the exuberance of childish spirits, and frolic there, laughing while his heart was breaking. They put a strait-waistcoat upon her, but she would contrive to get it off and throw it through the window, and threaten to leap out herself if it were ever put on her again.

The hospital in Broadway at the head of Pearl Street was then new, and after long hesitation, and acting under the advice of the best physicians, Mr. Whitfield was at last prevailed upon to consent to her removal there. He obtained the most desirable apartment, on the southeast corner, in one of the upper stories; and having furnished it with every appliance for her safety and comfort, he consigned her to the medical men of that institution when it was no longer possible for him to keep her in any comfort at home. But he could not rest in his own mansion while the wife of his bosom, whom he so tenderly loved, was in a public hospital, alone and crazed. Night after night he walked the street in front of the building in which she was confined, looking up at the window in her narrow chamber, sometimes fancying that he saw her struggling to force her way through, and expecting to see her plunging headlong from that fearful height. By degrees her strength gave way; and when she was no longer able to be violent in her paroxysms of madness, he had the melancholy satisfaction of again taking her to his own house. Directly over his own bed-chamber he had an apartment prepared for her, and thither she was conveyed, and watched by suitable attendants. When by the silence of her chamber he knew that she was asleep, he would often steal up from his own room, and sitting down in a large easy chair near the bed, he would look upon the wreck of his lovely bride, weeping over the change, and praying that even now, in her hopeless and helpless state, the power of God might be revealed for relief and restoration. The first sweet year of their union would then come to his memory, when something whispered to him of his rashness in linking himself to one whose mind was shattered, whatever might be her virtues and her charms; and he thanked God that it had been his privilege, even for that brief period, to make her a home, and fill her heart with peace and joy.

One night he was sitting there, and musing, perhaps somewhat encouraged by having been told that through the day she had been calmer, and at intervals apparently rational. Now she was sleeping, more sweetly than he had known her in many months. And as he leaned his head back in the chair, wearied with long and anxious waking, he fell asleep. When he awoke, his wife was sitting on his knees; her arms were around his neck. She pressed her lips to his, and said to him, "My dear, dear husband." It was the first recognition of many long and awful months. He pressed her warmly, convulsively to his heart.

"Sing to me," she said; "sing to me one of those Sabbath-evening songs."

"I can not sing, dearest," he replied; "it is enough that you are mine again, and here, here on my breast, dearest, sweetest wife." Her head fell on his shoulder, and he poured into her ear the glowing words of his love.

"Oh, these months of wretchedness, when you could not know that I loved you, and longed to bless you, dearest, as I will, if God will spare you, as he has restored you to my arms. Kiss me again, sweet wife."

She did not speak. "Kiss me, love." Her head still rested on his shoulder. He raised her up to press his lips to hers. She was dead.

XXI.

PROPHETS AND PROPHETESSES.

A WOMAN has just gone, and I will tell you why she came. She was past middle age, not very comely, her voice sharp, clear, and decided. She stood, and was beginning to speak, when I rose and asked her to be seated. She sat down and was quiet for a moment. Presently she began :

"I have come to you with a message from the Lord."

"Ah, and did you bring a letter of introduction?"

"What did you ask?"

"I asked if you brought your credentials with you : any token by which I may be assured that you are authorized to speak to me in the name of the Lord. You are a perfect stranger to me, and there is nothing (pardon me) in your appearance to indicate the divinity of your mission; so that, before I hear your message, I ask for your authority. If you have brought no testimonials, give me a sign."

"A sign! What sign do you ask?"

"Any sign—a miracle or a wonder—that shall convince me of your supernatural endowment to make known to me the mind of the Lord. Here is a letter lying before me undirected. I was on the point of directing it when you came in ; now tell me to whom it is to be addressed, and I will know that you have meat to eat that I know not of."

"I don't pretend to have any such inspiration as that;

but I have studied the prophecies, and have been taught
of God to know who the Two Witnesses are that are
spoken of in the Revelation, and I have come to make
it known to you, and you must teach it to the Church.
The Two Witnesses are—"

"Stop, if you please, madam; I do not care about hearing what you have to say; I have forgotten more than
you know about the Two Witnesses—"

"But you must hear me, you shall hear me, and the
whole Church is bound to hear me. I have been praying and reading and thinking about these things twenty years, and it has all been opened to me now, so that
the Church is no longer to be in any doubt about them.
Commentators have differed: scarcely any two of them
think alike; but it is all plain now.   The Two Witnesses
are—"

"I tell you again, madam, I will not listen to you unless
you give me a sign.   You are either deranged or you are
divinely inspired to reveal the Word of God.   It needs
no revelation to me.   All that is needful for my instruction and comfort and hope is as plain to me as the nose
(pardon me again) on your face; and what things I do
not understand I leave to Him who gave them to make
them plain in His own good time and way, if He would
have me to understand them."

"Certainly; and He has sent me to tell you who the
Two Witnesses are, and I have come to tell you that they
are—"

"And I tell you, madam, that I am not going to hear
you.   I know who the Two Witnesses are as well as you
do, and do not care to be instructed on the subject."

"Well, now, tell me.   I'll hear what you have to say.
I don't believe you have the least idea who the Two Wit-

nesses are, and you never will know unless I tell you. Come now, who are they?"

"Why, if you know who they are, and I don't, what is the use of my trying to teach you. It would be better for us both to go about our own work, and let the Two Witnesses alone."

She now rose, and with fierce invective denounced me as slow of heart and unwilling to hear the truth ; and as I was resuming the pen—the sceptre here—she withdrew. She is one of several demented women who go about persecuting the Church, and annoying those unfortunate men who have means of reaching the public ear. They ought to be tenderly cared for by their friends, and detained from these peripatetic teachings.

VISIONS AND OTHER NOVELTIES.

One of the most curious chapters in philosophy might be written by any one who had the facts in regard to the delusions of the human mind on religious questions.

A few days ago I received a letter of which the following is a passage :

"Now is the time for the Dark Ages to pass away. He who openeth, and no man shutteth, and shutteth, and no man openeth, is about to shut the door of the Dark Ages and open the door to his Kingdom of Light. His name shall be known as God alone, as he has foretold by all his prophets. Come and see me. It is very easy to be great like the Almighty, but it is very hard to be humble like Jesus. Do gladden his heart by letting him see *one* humble man in these worldly, self-seeking days. I have been humbled to the dust, and you can bear to talk with me, for I assure you for some years past. I have received *visions* from God revealing these wondrous truths. If it is God's will, you must come. My present address is," etc.

I was very busy, but there was something in the letter which made me think that I might do wrong if " I were

not obedient to the heavenly vision." In the parlor of one
of the most fashionable houses in this city I was received
by a genteel and very ladylike woman, who said, in very
gentle words—

"I knew you would come; the Lord made it known
to me that you would, and I have a message to you. He
has appeared to me in the person of a little child, whose
mouth was opened to say the most wonderful things, and
it was given to me to know that they came directly from
the Lord, who—"

She had not as yet given me the chance of a word, and
probably did not care whether I spoke or not, as she evidently proposed a conversation in which she was to do
all the talking. That is the case generally with people
who have a religious maggot in their brain, and come to
other people for aid and comfort. But when she had run
on until an opening for a word appeared, I said—

"You tell me that you have a message from the Lord
to me; what proof do you propose to give me that he is
speaking to me through you?"

"Oh, I know he does; I feel it and see it; and you
would not doubt it for a moment if you would hear what
this dear child has said to me, and what she never could
have dreamed of if it had not been given her of the
Lord."

"Pardon me, madam, I have had many men and women
coming to me with revelations, and I invariably ask them
for a sign—something to signify to me that they are ac-
credited from the court of heaven. If a strange lady
should come to me and tell me that the Queen of England
had sent her to me with a message of great importance, I
should ask her for credentials—some letter or other token
by which she could make me certain that the queen had

deputed this unknown lady to be her representative. In old times monarchs intrusted a seal ring to the keeping of a secret messenger, that it might be evidence of the authority by which he was to speak; or some password which might be understood between the king and his absent general, and when that was mentioned, the claim of the messenger was recognized. God gave his prophets and apostles power by which they wrought signs and wonders, and men knew that such could come only from him who was King over all. What can you do?"

The good woman was not in the least disconcerted by this address, and when I closed with the direct personal inquiry as to her ability to prove her mission from heaven, she was as quietly ready to begin again as if I had merely spoken of the state of the weather. Indeed, all she wanted was a chance to speak. What a wonderful safety-valve and source of pleasure is the gift and chance to talk! Especially to people who have but one idea. Only one class of people talk more than those who have only one idea, and that is the class who have no idea at all. Put a man on a hobby, and he rides forever without stopping. Let him become absorbed with one idea, and he can talk without ceasing till the ears of the hearers are heavy; he is as fresh as the morning, when they are ready to die of his discourse. This is peculiarly true when a man imagines he has had a new religious experi- ence or revelation. Having left all other doctrines and precepts of the Word of God, as of very little account compared with his pet theory, he spends his time in drilling other people into his views. I am the hapless victim of numberless male and female revelators, who assure me that if I only listen to them they will show me the truth, and then I can write about it and do good to thousands.

Q

Ah! how often have I, in a moment of weakness, yielded
to the flattering suggestion, and permitted the bore to
have the use of my ear! Talk—a stream of talk—
shallow, of course, for only still' waters run deep; that
no barrier can arrest, flows on, until that divine virtue,
patience, ceases to rule, and I have to beg, with painful
countenance, to be excused from further instructions.
This can be done when the orator is a prophet. But
when it is a prophetess, escape is more difficult.

The lady in the parlor was fluent, voluble, and sin-
cere. She had one idea, and that was absurd. She could
not speak two minutes without self-contradiction twice.
And when I put the contradictions before her, she was
just as well pleased as if I had assented, and rushed on
with the unending, overwhelming chatter. Doubtless the
gift of speech is good—but, oh, how much more good
when sense is given with it!

At last I was obliged to interrupt my fair teacher by
saying that I could not hear her message without some
evidence that it was from heaven, and, as I had several
little matters to attend to, she must pardon me for saying
" Good-afternoon."

The year 1842 was marked by the sudden rise, and
1843 by the fall of the Millerites, a sect who had been
deluded with the notion that the Lord Jesus Christ would
come in visible person on a certain day in the latter year
to receive his saints, to destroy his enemies, and to establish his throne on the earth. They took their name from
William Miller, a Baptist minister in the northern part of
this state, who had studied the prophecies until he knew
nothing about them, and by a process in arithmetic peculiar to himself had hit upon the year when the final catastrophe was to occur, to the confusion of the wicked and

the glorification of all who were found waiting for the coming of the Lord. It is wonderful with what avidity this delusion was received. Its dupes numbered thousands. They were not of the more intelligent classes— indeed, very few educated people were led astray—but of serious-minded and unlettered multitudes who composed the great mass of the community at that time. The sudden converts to Millerism were many. One reason that operated rapidly upon this sort of people was the shortness of time allowed them to make up their minds. They were told that the end was at hand. First the year was fixed; then the month and the day. And to make a sure thing of it, they thought the safest course was to believe, and if the crash came at the appointed time they would be all right, and if it did not they would be no worse off than before on account of their faith in the figures of Miller. And I am inclined to think that Miller's name, having an apparent analogy to Millenarianism, helped to faith in his calculations. Thousands of excellent Christian men, scholars, divines—some of them men of wide repute for learning and religion—are Millenarians; believing in the future personal reign of Jesus Christ upon the earth, and in his speedy coming to set up his throne. But they do not set the time. Some writers of this school have found in the figures of the Prophet Daniel a starting-point and a period, and have therefore ventured to fix the year when the King might be expected to appear in his glory; but in all such cases the march of time has compelled them to find errors in their calculations by which the great event was necessarily postponed.

But in the Millerite year the delusion took the form of an epidemic or a panic. The leaders of the sect perambulated the country with immense tents in which to hold public meetings, and these were crowded for days and nights in succession by excited congregations, whose prayers and songs and cries bordered on the delirious. Many became deranged. Lunatic asylums reported this delusion as the cause of insanity in many cases.

One night, very late, a man came to me with a message from God that I must believe in the speedy Advent, and teach it to the people. He would not be put off with the excuse that it was nearly midnight, and that I could not listen to his discourse at such an unseasonable hour. He said that nothing was so important as the revelation he had come to make, and that it was high time I heard it. Then he began with his figures. He added, subtracted, and divided, piled up dates from history and prophecy, told of the "abomination of desolation" that was to be set up and that was set up, and started off from that date and calculated the downfall of the Roman Empire and the death of Napoleon, and brought out 1843 as neatly as the most accurate mathematician could desire. Out of breath at the end of his computation, and triumphing in the result, he demanded my assent to his conclusion.

I looked up at him and quietly asked, "And what do you make of the two sticks?"

"Sticks—what sticks?" he said.

"Well, sir," I replied, "if you are an expositor of the prophecies and do not know the two sticks of which the prophet speaks, you must excuse me from receiving any messages from you as coming from heaven." He soon left me to my fate.

Some of the Millerite societies were so sure the end was at hand that they put their individual possessions, which were usually very slender, into joint stock, in imitation of the early Christians, who had "all things common." In Oneida County, New York, a well-to-do farmer, being converted to their doctrine, came to join their meeting, and, on being told of this rule, said he would think of it a while, and pray over it. He went away sorrowful, for he was very rich. At the next meeting he appeared, and, upon being called upon for his answer, he said he had received a message from heaven, and was prepared to obey. "While engaged in prayer for divine direction," said he, "I have had one passage of the Bible so powerfully impressed upon my mind that I know it is from God, and I shall do as I am commanded."

The brethren and sisters were in breathless expectation of the tremendous sacrifice he was about to make. The elder bade him be of good courage, and declare the message. And the rich man said—

"The passage which came to my mind, and which I am resolved to obey, was in these words—'Occupy till I come.'"

When the appointed time arrived, thousands of them were ready as far as their white raiment could be regarded as readiness for such an event. So purely carnal and earthly were all their views of this great spiritual change, that they made linen garments called " ascension robes," with which they arrayed themselves. Some of them, in cities, took their seats upon the edges of the house-tops. Others, in the country, ascended hills or climbed into trees, and sat as patiently as possible, while their locks were wet with the dews of the night. They thought they would see the Lord descending from the sky, and that they would rise to meet him in the air. It was easy to believe that a mistake of a day, or even of a month, had been made in reckoning thousands of years, and many therefore thought the advent was still at hand,

though they had not hit upon the identical day. Others
gave up to wild despair. Many were made faithless in
Scripture when they found they had been duped by false
teachers. I never heard that any were made more charitable, more patient, humble Christians. The prominent
trait of character in the Millerites was their censorious
and denunciatory spirit toward those who would not
adopt their arithmetic. But their end came when they
thought the world was coming to an end. The awful
day came. The sun rose, shone as usual, and set just as
it was in the habit of doing. And then the moon made
its quiet tour among the stars, and died away in the light
of another day. And all things went on as from the beginning.

Two or three other dates were fixed upon, and previous
errors of calculation were explained, but the end would
not come any way they could fix it. Miller subsided into
his farm. Elder Himes, who had been the fidus Achates
of Miller, and had blown the trumpets in advance of the
coming King, blew on, but, as before, it was all sound and
fury, signifying nothing. And now, after the lapse of a
quarter of a century, there is here and there only a ves-
tige remaining of a faith that took possession of thousands,
and had its disciples in almost every city and village and
rural parish of the Northern, Eastern, and Middle States.

In the month of January, 1854, I found a miserable,
half-starved colony of this sect in the Holy Land. Their
delusion had received the additional article of faith that
the Lord would set up his kingdom in Palestine, and
reign again in the city of the Great King. They had
gathered what earthly possessions they had, and fiuding
their way across the ocean and through the Mediterranean
Sea, had landed at the ancient Joppa, where dwelt, once

on a time, that Simon the Tanner to whom Cornelius
sent his messengers. Near this city they had bought a
little land, which cost them but a trifle; they had reared
cottages, and were there waiting. Poverty came, but the
Lord did not. Loneliness, homesickness, disease, but no
signs of the Healer and Saviour. Some of them lived to
be brought away by the hand of charity, and some of
them died there, and their bodies will rest in the grave
until the resurrection, when they shall be raised up, let us
hope, in glory.

But it is no false report that the Lord is coming. Not
in a coach and four, and with soldier guards attending.
I do not look for such an appearing. But I see the signs
of his advent, as when I stood on the Rigi in the early
morn and saw the eastern mountain-tops tipped with fire
as the king of day in his chariot of glory was riding up
the steeps. I knew he was at hand. And he came.
Peak after peak was on fire, and the ice plains "caught
the flying joy." The valleys glowed with the sunbeams
and the world rejoiced in the coming of the king. It was
all gloomy when I came out of my lodgings, but it was all
glory now. And just so—yes, just so—do I see the signs
of the coming of the Sun of Righteousness, the advent of
the Son of Man. Brighter than the eastern sky when the
sun is there, is the promise of that reign of peace and joy
which is sure to come, when the chains of superstition and
error and vice are stricken from the soul of humanity, and
the race rejoices in the liberty of those whom Christ the
Lord enlightens and makes free.

Professor George Bush was a man of wide reputation
in his lifetime, though he has signally dropped out of the
world's memory. He was born at Norwich, Vermont, in
1796, graduated at Dartmouth in 1818, studied theology

at Princeton, and, entering the Presbyterian ministry, went out as a missionary preacher to Indiana. With tastes for scholastic studies rather than the pulpit, he finished his Western ministry in four years, returned to the East, and devoted himself to Biblical science. Becoming a thorough Hebrew scholar, he was elected in 1831 to the professorship of that language in the University in this city. His duties there must have been nominal, and his income the same, for he was in great straits for means of support, living in the midst of his books, and picking up what he could by contributions to the press. He had accumulated a vast store of ancient volumes, to which the shelves of his study were inadequate, and they covered the tables and chairs, and lay around in heaps on the floor. It was hard to find a seat, and harder to get about in his narrow quarters. He was the personification of a book-worm. Prematurely aged and wrinkled, poring with spectacles of large power over his misty and antique volumes, spending his days and nights in a dimly lighted and ill-ventilated apartment, which was rarely cleansed of its dust, he was the representation of the ideal Rosicrucian searching for wisdom. Social when in company, genial and good-tempered, patient under contradiction, and tolerant beyond the toleration of greater men, he was a pleasant neighbor, with whom I had much intercourse. He had already published his " Life of Mohammed," and a " Treatise on the Millennium," which he held to have passed by long ago, and a Hebrew Grammar, and a big volume of " Scripture Illustrations." Then he started a periodical which he called the " Hierophant," in which the types, symbols, etc., of the Bible were interpreted in his way; and then came his "Anastasis" in 1844, in which he brought out an original notion of the resurrection which nobody understood, and I never heard of but one man who professed to adopt it. It is not likely that his disciples ever reached the number of two.

This publication separated him in a large measure from the orthodox community, and shook confidence in the soundness of his religious opinions, essential to the circulation of his " Commentaries on the Scriptures," which he had issued in successive volumes.

As early as the year 1844 he became bewildered by the phenomenal representations of animal magnetism and mesmerism, and soon afterward he very naturally wandered into the faith of Swedenborg, who may be called the father of technical spiritualism. One hundred years ago this Swedish philosopher professed to be in daily converse with departed spirits, and a tradition says that he predicted a general reception of his curious doctrines in eighty years after his death, which would be 1851. Professor Bush was almost every day in my study, and with great simplicity spoke of his wild beliefs, especially of the wonders of mesmerism. He said that he could read the character of a person he had never seen by passing his hand over his manuscript. His explanation was this : " You see there are spheres evolving from the mind of every living person, and these spheres roll also from the record of the mind as a manuscript ; and when I pass my hand over the writing, my spheres come into harmony with the other person's spheres, and I thus become acquainted with him ; you understand." " It is just as clear as mud," I assured him. And he marveled at my little faith. Months passed by after his adoption of the Swedenborgian delusion, and he made a public profession of it in a course of lectures in this city. He then wrote with his own hand the following notice, which was published :

"Professor Bush is now delivering a course of Sabbath-evening lectures in this city on 'The Future Life, as disclosed by Swedenborg.' His audiences have been large and respectable, attracted probably in great measure by the novelty of the subject as viewed in such connection, and by the boldness and emphasis of tone in which the Professor announces his faith in the revelations of the Swedish seer. His first lecture, we learn, was devoted to a general view of the evidences which he considered as sustaining his divine mission, drawn principally from his representations of heaven and hell, which he makes to be the ultimate realization of certain moral *states* of the soul, determined by the influence of the *ruling love* for good or evil. The second was announced in the daily papers as offering proof that 'all angels are human spirits,' in which, we understand, he fully took the ground that the existence of a superior race of beings to man is not only unscriptural but impossible, inasmuch as creation in the *image* and *likeness* of God is affirmed of man, and the highest angel can not be any thing more. Men and angels are the same race of beings in different stages of existence. The third announced a somewhat singular subject for pulpit discussion, to wit, 'The Relation of Mesmerism in its Higher Phenomena to the Doctrines of Swedenborg.' The lecturer asserted that Swedenborg's psychological state was altogether of a higher order than that produced by mesmerism, and that the belief of his followers was wholly independent of the truth or falsehood of the alleged mesmeric developments. The mode in which he brought the two things into connection was this : In the mesmeric state the spirit predominates, for the time being, over the body. The bodily sensations are suspended while the soul is awake and active, though mysteriously influenced by the operator. Its state therefore approximates to the state of a spirit dislodged from the body. A new condition is developed, especially as far as the laws of mental intercourse are concerned. This lays the foundation for a comparison of the phenomena displayed with the professed disclosures of Swedenborg relative to the facts and laws of spiritual communication in the other life. The result Professor Bush undertook to show to be such a striking coincidence as to force upon the mind the conviction that if mesmerism is true, Swedenborgianism is true, for the revelations of both showed that they belonged to the same great system of spiritual manifestations. This he held to be the more remarkable as Swedenborg died ten years before Mesmer was heard of. From the relation in which Professor Bush has hitherto stood to the

Christian community, we have deemed it our duty to make our read-ers acquainted with his present position. We believe he makes no reserve himself of the fact that he has come to entertain a full con-viction of the truth and authority of Swedenborg's mission. This might perhaps have been anticipated from the tenor of his recent publications on the Resurrection and its kindred subjects. We are ready to give him credit for sincerity and honesty in his convictions" [and the editor added, " however much we may regret that a man of his erudition should thus make shipwreck of the faith, and plunge headlong into the abyss of error "].

He became the leading writer and teacher of the sect; went to Rochester, and died there. It was in Professor Bush's room that I met Andrew Jackson Davis shortly after he began to talk spiritualism—an ignorant young man of talents, who has since become an apostle of spir-itualism, and the source of larger books with nothing in them than any other man of the age. At the house of the President of the United States I was present when the disquisitions of Davis and some pretended communi-cations from dead statesmen were under discussion. The volumes were produced and passages read, while the question was seriously asked, "What is all this but the merest platitude, of which a living sensible author would be ashamed?"

Hon. Waddy Thompson, United States Minister to Mex-ico, a very prominent Southern politician, was in Wash-ington at that time, and I met him at Gadsby's Hotel. He said to me, " You will be pleased to learn that I have been led from the utter darkness of atheism to believe in spiritual religion, and all by the influence of spirit rap-pings." He then informed me of the specific revelations that had been made to him. The Rochester Fox women were then giving lessons in spiritualism in Washington, and many public men were converted to their school. Mr. Thompson said :

"I knew a man who had killed his friend in a duel, and was afterward afraid to sleep in a room alone. He finally died. I called for him when the rappings were going on, and very soon I heard a clawing and scratching (rising and putting his hands against the wall, he scratched down), as if a wild beast were clawing a bar of iron." This he gave me as evidence that the man was actually in the midst of torment for his awful crime.

Professor Bush would not let me go with him to any of the circles where the mesmeric experiments were to be seen, for he held that so obstinate an unbeliever would interfere with their success. His view was that the consent of the will of all present was essential. Why of those present only, he never explained. But when the Fox women came here from Rochester, they proved to be such efficient manipulators that faith was not required to make miracles. They could bring the spirits into conversation with any body for a dollar.

I spent an evening with one of them, and had the best possible opportunity of testing for myself the spirituality of the conversation. I was directed by Miss Fox to write five or six names of departed friends, and to touch each name, saying, "Is this one present?" I had no difficulty in having the assenting rap made at any name I pleased —for in this and several other trials, when it was required that I should write and ask "Is it this?" if I allowed my voice to tremble a little, or to be specially firm in utterance, the rap was sure to come. Paper and pencil were put on the floor under the table, but I was not allowed to look under; and a scrawl was found upon the paper, which might have been written by the toes or smuggled there. Fifty experiments were performed, none of which were satisfactory, and the young woman expressed her regret at the total failure of the evening. I was convinced that the whole affair was a mixture of delusion and imposture.

There are some facts at present inexplicable to unbelievers, as there are in the feats of necromancers or dealers with the dead. And some of the simplest tricks of jugglers are beyond the reach of ordinary ingenuity. There is also an unseen force of mind on mind, the laws of which are not yet understood. And the subtle power to which we have given the name of magnetism has its influence over material objects and living bodies in a way that we have not yet discovered. But since the world was made, the soul of no dead man has made signs to a live one of what is going on in the world of spirits; and apart from what we know of the spirit world from the book of Revelation, the veil is unbroken, and beyond it all is mystery. Bodily senses are not the media of spiritual communications; and between the living and the dead a great gulf is fixed.

Rev. Dr. Edward Beecher made a book on the pre-existence of the human soul. I can not state the doctrine, but it was the ancient Eastern tenet of the life of the soul in a state of being prior to its union with the human body. I never saw a living man who believed the doctrine, though the book has been before the world some twenty years. And the nearest that I ever came to seeing a dead man who had believed it was in Syria, in Mount Lebanon. I was admitted into the sacred tomb of a man reputed to have been wise, who had been buried a thousand or two years ago, and who had been a believer in the doctrine of Dr. Beecher's book. The author and this old Pythagorean philosopher are the only two men whom I was ever near who held to the transmigration of souls.

And other men have spent their strength for naught in attempts to make truth more simple, and have succeeded only in leaving it as they found it, if they did not darken it by their words without knowledge. A very eminent divine of the Presbyterian Church, a professor of metaphysics, and who knew almost every thing else better than he did metaphysics, made a book to explain the "existence of evil under the government of a benevolent God." He brought it to me in manuscript, and I endured the hearing of tedious pages and chapters long drawn out. I assured him candidly that he had not thrown one ray of light on the subject, and his book would do nobody any good. But he printed it, and then begged me to read the whole of it. Incredible as the statement may appear, I did. Again he came to know the effect, and I told him frankly that " if I knew any thing about the subject before reading his book, I was now helplessly in the fog."

"The trouble is," said he, "you have not a metaphysical mind."

"Very true," I answered ; "but if I have the average or ordinary intelligence of the human family, and you have made a book that I positively can not make head or tail of, what good will it do?"

His book was published and reviewed (I doubt much if the critics read it), and to this day I do not know of another man who went through as I did, with the heroism of a martyr, that mysterious and muddy volume, that was to make all things clear, even the deep things of God.

A rural clergyman, quite innocent of the ways of the trade, brought to me a huge manuscript, " The Revelation of St. John Revealed." He had discovered the full meaning of the mysteries of the Apocalypse, and if he could find a publisher who would print his work, that wonderful portion of sacred writing, so long baffling the critics and commentators, would be as simple as the songs of Zion. Would I put him in the way of making the acquaintance of a publisher who would bring out this important volume? I was frank, and warned him that he was on a vain errand; he could not get a publisher in New York to look into his book, and I did not believe he would do any good by printing it. But he was not discouraged; all he wanted was to get into print.

"Well," said I, at last, "you take the book to any publisber you please, and tell him from me that if he will publish the work in good style, you will bring the first copy to me, and I will read it, and if it enable me to understand the book of Revelation, I will pay the bill for the publication of the whole edition." The good man went away, and I have never heard of him or his book from that hour.

Another popular preacher came to me with an immense manuscript. Fearful to relate, it was an epic poem in ten books, of the size of Milton's "Paradise Lost." And thus the poet pastor spoke:

"I have written a poem. It has been the labor of the last twenty years. I have obeyed the injunction of Horace in his "Ars Poetica," and have written it over from beginning to end nine times, and intend to write it again after having submitted it to Professor Wilson, of Edinburgh, Bryant, Longfellow, and yourself (!). When will it be convenient for you to hear me read it, or would you prefer to take the work and peruse it in your study?"

To whom I: "Have you reflected upon the magnitude of the undertaking—an epic poem? But one has been a success in the English language ; and he must be bold who offers to make the next."

"I am aware of it," he replied. "Only one epic poet can be in any age ; there has none appeared in ours, and it remains to be seen if I am not the man."

I made answer : "You may be the poet of the century, but as I shall have to sit in judgment upon your work after it appears, you will perceive that my judgment will be biased by reading it now, and you must excuse me from the service to which your partiality has invited me."

His poem was handsomely published, but no man has confessed that he read it. It died and made no sign.

It was on the edge of the evening, when I was told that a woman at the door wished to speak with me. A plainly dressed person she was, and evidently of the Irish element, sober and very civil spoken. She began at once with her errand, and with less of an introduction than is common with the men or women of her country, she said :

"Please your reverence, and I want to be turned."

"I do not understand you. What do you say you want?"

"And I want to be turned !" Still assuring her that I did not get hold of her meaning, and that she must be more explicit in her request, or I should not be able to do any thing for her, she made another and vigorous attempt to make me understand what she was seeking, and this time she was completely successful. She said :

"I am a Catholic, sir, and I want to be turned into a Protestant, sir ; and I was told your reverence was one of them that turns the Catholics into Protestants, and I come to get myself turned, sir."

The simple earnestness with which the woman stated her case divested it of the ludicrous, which it wears to one who hears the story told, and can not see, as I did, that the poor woman had come for a purpose which she now frankly stated; and when I said to her, "Why do you want to change your religion and become a Protestant?" she was ready with a reason, which she gave with great freedom, and I presume with perfect candor and truthfulness.

"My husband is a Protestant, your reverence, and I am a Catholic, and we fight a great deal about it—we can never agree at all, at all; and I just thought if I could be turned into a Protestant too, that then we would be both one way of thinkin' like, and we would have nothing to fight about at all, at all; and would your reverence be so good as just to turn me into a Protestant, and I'll bless you the longest day I live."

Finding that she was really and truly set upon making a change of base and taking a new departure, I sought, in simple words and few, to explain to her what was required of one who would sincerely embrace the faith of Protestant Christians, and turn away from the Church of which she had been a member. And I told her that I could do nothing for her—that she must go directly to Him who had promised to be the Saviour of all who believe on Him; and that to be a Protestant it was necessary only that she should receive Christ as her Saviour, and not rely upon a priest to say mass, nor a Virgin Mary to intercede for her. She did not get into the sense of this, and insisted that she must then and there, before she went again to her home, become a Protestant, and be able to tell her husband so. To satisfy her, and to do as well by her as I could, I then went to my library and, taking a folio volume, wrote a renunciation of every evil way, and a pledge of faithful obedience to the command-

R

ments of Christ, by faith in whom salvation is to be found. Armed with this volume, I came again to the woman and read in her hearing the words I had written, explaining their full meaning to her as I read.

"That's it," she said; "that's just what I want: now we won't fight again."

She could not write her name to the deed of renunciation, but she made her mark with a bold and steady hand, for her mind was made up, and she knew what she was doing. The deed was done, and she was going away with many blessings on me for turning her into a Protestant, when she stopped on the steps and said:

"And I'll come to you to confess."

"No, no, my good woman, you are not much of a Protestant if you are coming to me or any other man to confess your sins. Tell all your sins to God, and he will forgive you for Christ's sake, and then sin no more; but don't come to me to confess."

"But I will," she said as she disappeared from the door. I never saw nor heard from her again. It was a blunder of mine not to take the number and street where she and her husband in time past had their battle-ground, for I might then have followed her up, and perhaps strengthened her resolutions of reform, and done some good to her husband, who, Protestant as he was, was probably quite as much to blame for the fighting as the wife. And it is very certain that if he were as much disposed to avoid quarreling as she was, the reign of peace would have been perpetual in that house. As it takes two to make a bargain, so it always requires at least two for a fight. It was certainly a great shame that "Betsey and he" should be "out" on the subject of religion, just the last thing in the world about which people should quarrel. But the subject-matter of dispute is of very little importance in families or states; if the disposition to quarrel exist, there is no loss for an occasion. Out of the heart come fightings. Even those who love one another may get into a fight if there is not a disposition in each party to let the other have his or her way and the last word. The old story of the rat and the mouse is older than mine of the woman who wanted to be turned, and like that story will bear being told once more.

A loving, newly married couple sat down to tea for the first time in their new home. Happy as a pair of birds, they were billing and cooing to each other, when seeing something run out of the chimney corner, they exclaimed—one of them, "Oh, see that rat!" and the other, "Oh, see that mouse!"

"Oh no, it was a rat."

"No, it was a mouse."

"Not at all, my dear; I saw it, and I am sure it was a rat."

"And I saw it too, and I know it was a mouse."

"I say it was a rat."

"I say it was a mouse."

"'Twas a rat." "'Twas a mouse." "'Twas a rat." "'Twas a mouse." And they kept it up till both were in a passion, and finally the bride in her tears and her anger said she would go home to her parents; and away she went.

A few days or weeks of reflection showed them both their exceeding folly, and they readily yielded to the suggestion of friends that they were a couple of little fools, and had better come together again, which they did.

Once more seated at their cheerful tea-table in the cosiest of rooms, and happy in the thought that they were restored to their own sweet home, they looked across the table into each other's eyes, and one of them said laughingly to the other:

"Was it not foolish for us to make such a fuss about that good-for-nothing little mouse?"

"Why, dear, it wasn't a mouse—it was a rat."

"No, love, it was a mouse; I saw it myself."

"And so did I, and I am sure it was a rat."

And so at it they went again, one as positive and unyielding as the other, till they were as mad as they were before, and the wife went off to her papa, and that ended the story.

XXII.

ON LYING AND LENDING.

THERE is an art in lying, but you have no need to read any thing about it. That remark sounds as if you are so familiar with the art as to require no further instruction. Such is not the intent; but this: You are so free from tendencies in that direction, you so love, honor, and cherish the truth as the holiest of holies, that I need not spend time in giving you lessons in an art you will never practice nor preach.

Nor will I give lessons for any body in this art, which is so well understood as to require no books to teach it, no rules to govern it. It has its masters every where. They go astray, said the ancient poet, from the birth, speaking lies. It was lying that began the fall in Eden, and it has been growing ever since. In some countries it is so common, this telling of lies, that no one believes his neighbor. The Greeks are said to be great liars. In heathen countries very slight regard is paid to the truth. We are in the habit of saying that Roman Catholics regard the truth with less sacredness than we do. But I do not know that lying is any more common among them than among large classes of people who call themselves Protestants. Take the money-making men, who get their gains by the rise and fall of prices. Is it any strange thing for them to set on foot a lie to affect the market? Being myself in the newspaper line, I would be very

slow to intimate that newspapers ever say any thing that
is not strictly true.   But when two of the daily papers
get into a quarrel, the tricks of the trade sometimes
come out; and we have reason to fear that sometimes,
in default of news from the seat of war, there is a manu-
facture of "cable telegrams" and "letters from our cor-
respondents," which are palmed off upon the unsuspect-
ing public as veritable facts.   This is lying, and there is
great art in it.   A *littérateur* told me that he prepares a
weekly article for one of the city papers on the " Rats of
Brazil," or the " Cockroaches in Japan," or something of
that sort.   "Not that there are any," said he, "but I make
a sensational chapter on a subject that few can know any
thing about, and I get ten dollars for it.   That pays my
board."   Here was a specimen of the art of lying; indeed, it was elevated to the rank of the fine arts.   Certainly it becomes a fine art, when a painting is offered for
sale as an original which has been copied from a copy,
and half ruined to make it bear the marks of age.

There is another art that comes under the same head,
or on the same head, and that is the art of coloring the
hair.   One of my ministerial acquaintances undertook to
lie about his hair—that is, to dye it—and the chemical
compound that he used produced such a frightful color
that he was frightened with the fear of divine judgment
on his head.   I think dyeing is lying.   Whether a man
or a woman do it, the motive is a bad one: the intent is
to deceive, and that is the very essence of lying.   I am
told that one half of the men who go to our church dye
their hair habitually, and, if so, I shall run the chance of
giving offense to many whom I would much rather please.

You ask a mechanic to do a job for you.   It is his
trade; he wants to do it, and he gets his pay for it.   He

promises you it shall be done by Saturday night. Another customer and another comes, and he wishes to serve them all and get their money. He makes the same promise, well knowing that some of them must be disappointed. Job after job is thus engaged, and the same promise repeated, with the dead certainty that it will be broken. This is the art of lying applied to a trade. And it runs through a hundred trades. It destroys confidence in human nature. But it is the custom, and is as universal in Christian countries as in heathen. There is very little conscience about it. "Other people do so, and the job will go somewhere else if I do not promise;" and so it is taken, and the lie is told.

Borrowers are often great liars. There is less conscience in this than in almost any other matter. Many a man who would see a twenty-dollar bill lying on my table and never think of stealing it, will ask me to lend it to him and never pay it. Or, what is next door to the same thing, will not pay it when it was promised. I knew a clergyman who would get his check cashed after bank hours by a friend who would find the next day that the minister had no money in the bank, and never had. There is no true religion in a man who borrows and does not pay when he engages to do so. Misfortune may overtake him, and unforeseen circumstances prevent his doing his duty; such cases are exceptional. But borrowers are often great liars. I would there were more conscience in the matter of borrowing books. A friend gave me four volumes of a Latin classic with a French translation, elegantly bound in gilt calf. A Quaker friend asked me to lend him one volume of it for a special purpose, with the promise of its speedy return. Alas! he never brought it back; and when I sent for it, he said he had mislaid, lost it. The three remaining volumes are standing up before me this moment, silent witnesses that this friend was—well, what shall I call him? to say he was a liar or a thief is hard, but he injured me quite as much as if he had stolen my book. And he certainly broke his promise. If that were not the art of lying, it was the art of book-keeping, and I have the best of reasons to know that book-keeping is not one of the lost arts.

Truth between man and man is one of the cardinal virtues. It is at the basis of good character and of honorable success in life. It despises shams in public and private. Hating deception of every form and kind—all glosses, paints, covers, disguises, subterfuges, tricks, evasions, every thing that maketh a lie, that misleads or deceives another—it is always above-board, frank, manly, courageous, and faithful. In the Church and in the world there is an abundant lack of this vital element of honest truth. It is not always good manners to call a spade a spade, but to attempt to deceive is to lie, and for the want of a better word I use it. It was a great poet and good man who once said in haste, " All men are liars." I do not venture upon so broad and unwarrantable an assertion. I should be untrue, if I did. But with every desire to be charitable and within bounds, and not so hasty as the bard of old, I am constrained to say with Recorder Riker that "the practice is quite too common in this community."

I have met with something of a loss. Not money; I could, from bitter experience, write feelingly of that sorrow. Just now I am mourning the loss of a text of Scripture, and how it happened is in this wise: In the

Second Book of Kings it is written that the students of a theological seminary thought their quarters were too small, and proposed to the president, whose name was Elisha, that they should build something on a larger scale. He gave his consent, and they went to work. As they were cutting down a tree on the banks of Jordan, the axe of one of the students fell into the water and sank ; the loser cried out and said, " Alas, master ! for it was borrowed." Now, on taking up a new and learned commentary on this book by Dr. Kiel, I find that in his notes upon this text he says : " The word here rendered *borrowed* is *begged;* the meaning *to borrow* is attributed from a misinterpretation : the prophet's pupil had begged the axe, because from his poverty he was unable to buy one ; and hence the loss was so painful to him."

I had always valued that text as one left on long record, as a testimony that one man once lived who regretted the loss of a thing the more because it was borrowed than if it had been his own. To be sure, we have not the young man's name : like Lot's wife, he is an anonymous individual. But his virtuous exclamation of sorrow, his plaintive wail as the axe fell from his hand and sank beneath the wave, was to go down to all time as the fitting reflection of every right man when he loses any thing that he had borrowed. Dr. Jamieson, who has just made a new commentary on Kings, holds fast to the old idea of the translator, though he gives a mean kind of a reason for the young man's grief. He writes : " The scholar's distress arose from the consideration that the axe had been lent to him ; and that, owing to his poverty, he could not procure another." That is too bad. I supposed the young man was sorry that he had lost another man's property ; and, because of his own poverty, could not re-

place it.   But Dr. Jamieson thinks the boy was grieved
only because he could not get another axe.   Well, the
doctor has the idea of most borrowers, we must admit.
An habitual borrower has as little conscience as Dr.
Jamieson attributes to this student in Dr. Elisha's theological school.   He keeps what he borrowed, till he re-
gards it as his own; or, losing it, regrets the loss on his
own account only, and not the owner's.

A neighbor in the country who sends in every day to
borrow a little of this, and just a little of that, and a very
little of the other thing -- now it is milk, now eggs, now
sugar, now soap—is not a very desirable neighbor, except
as all afflictions, crosses, vexations, and trials, when properly received and enjoyed, are a sort of good to them who
are exercised thereby.   On this principle, such neighbors
are to be endured, perhaps prized as blessings in disguise.   Yet they would find it much more for their own
comfort to provide things honest for themselves, and cul-
tivate such habits of domestic economy as would prevent
the necessity of their taxing the faith and patience of the
saints who dwell near unto them.

To return to our books.   Book-keeping is a science ex-
tensively cultivated by borrowers, and there is probably
less conscience on this subject than on umbrellas.   He
who borrows the latter may feel that the owner is exposed without shelter to the pitiless pelting of a storm,
and such feelings may lead to penitence and restitution.
But no such salutary meditation disturbs the calm serenity of the wretch who has borrowed his friend's book.
He knew that his friend had read the book, and therefore he pretends to himself that it can not be wanted
again.   He reads it without remorse.   And when he has
read it, he beholds it from time to time standing in broad

daylight before him, a silent witness against him, but no sense of guilt steals on his senses ; no thought of regret for his own wrong, nor pity for his despoiled friend stirs the deeps of his depraved heart. Hardened by long indulgence in this course of evil-doing, he has been lost to all the gentler considerations of propriety, friendship, honesty, and honor ; until, from being a borrower, he has come to be a thief, and thinks it no ill.

A clergyman of my acquaintance was asked if he had read a new and valuable publication, and on his saying that he had not, the loan of it was at once offered to him. He declined it, with the remark that he did not read any books which he could not buy. Of course, he would not decline the aid of public libraries, where books are lent for hire, and every subscriber is part owner ; but he would not get his knowledge from borrowed books, nor sponge upon his friends.

Broken sets of books stand as memorials of my un-trustworthy friends. In an hour of weakness I permitted the books to go from the shelves, and the places that knew them once know them no more. It would be grate-ful to my lacerated feelings if the borrowers would return and take away the remains of the sets, or restore the miss-ing volumes to the empty space.

It is not possible to ask a man to return borrowed goods—books, money, or any thing else—without putting in peril the beautiful friendship on the strength of which he fleeced you. He was a wise man who said to his friend wishing to borrow : "You and I are now good friends—if I lend you money and you do not pay it, we shall quarrel ; if I refuse to lend you, I suppose we shall quarrel : there are two chances of a quarrel, and I think I will keep the money, rather than run the risk of losing it and you."

He had in mind the old saw :

> "I had my money and my friend,
>   I lent my money to my friend ;
> I asked my money of my friend,
>   I lost my money and my friend."

"The borrower is servant to the lender," saith the Bible.   That is so when the borrower has made himself liable to the law, so that the lender can put the screws
upon him when he does not come to time.   But in all
the petty concerns of neighborhood life, especially in the
rural districts, it is the lender who is the servant of the
borrower.   The inveterate beggar is not so great a pest,
because you can give him what he demands, and he is
off.   But the borrower lives near and on you.   Nothing
you have is too good for him to ask for.   Things you
prize the most, which you use only on rare occasions, and
then with extremest care—sacred in associations, or deli-   ·
cate, and therefore precious—the borrower asks the loan
of without scruple, and uses without fear, with the feeling
that, if injured, he is not the loser, for happily it was borrowed.   There is a beauty in good neighborhood.   That
help-one-another spirit which prompts to constant recip-
rocal kindness makes life in the country, among neighbors, charming.   But when it is like the handle of a pitch-
er, all on one side, this borrowing becomes a nuisance to
be abated by general agreement among the oppressed.

XXIII.

LITTLE TRIALS.

IT has been often said that it is harder to bear little trials than great ones, and many persons make the remark as if it were an excuse for being vexed at trifles, or for making trifles into mountains. Of all possible troubles in this world, perhaps no one source is more full of trial to the temper and the patience of mankind than disagreeable weather. It would certainly disturb the peaceful equanimity of soul which is this moment enjoyed in this old arm-chair if the wind should shift around to the east, as it did last week, and another cold storm should set in, and set down. It kept me in-doors for two days; and when I came out here to have a little penchat under the trees, the seat of the chair was a pool of water, and the trees themselves shed drops of grief, as if they were mourning in their solitude; and the ground was so damp that it was unsafe to be a man of letters out-of-doors, and I was obliged to give it up. And even then and there, or else by an open window, the change of air with the cold northeast wind might give one a touch of that most deplorable of all the *isms* that infest the state—the rheumatism—a trial to the faith and patience that may fairly claim to be equal to any other of which flesh is heir.

John Wesley was visiting a very wealthy gentleman, who was greatly annoyed by a servant leaving the door open, and he said to his guest, "You see what annoyances I am compelled to endure." Mr. Wesley took the occasion to preach him a little sermon on the duty of being patient under such trifling vexations of spirit, when he was surrounded with all the good things that heart could desire. And it is not likely that the possession of good things, by the thousand even, tends to make one patient under the infliction of a petty grievance. Rather it tends to create the feeling that money, or what money buys, ought to purchase exemption from the little troubles that are the necessary lot of the poor. "It is a great pity that I can not be comfortable," says the man of wealth and ease, "with all these servants about me, and this great house, and all this furniture." And the woman who flatters herself that a costly establishment, with a retinue of men and maids, will keep her from little trials, will find herself so sadly mistaken that she will often sigh for a cottage of three rooms in which perhaps she began her married life.

And these little trials, among the rich and the poor alike, are for the most part imaginary, or at most so nearly ideal that they are not worthy of being fretted at by an intelligent man or woman. Who has not seen a full-grown man, of average sense and fair reputation for virtue, out of humor because his dinner was not ready when he was, or not cooked to his taste when it was served? He could meet with the loss of a thousand dollars, and not speak of it at home; he could bear that in silence, with patience and serenity; but to be compelled to wait half an hour for a rail-train or his dinner would throw him off his balance, and provoke him to use such impatient words as hardly become a man of average self-control. His wife is a notable housekeeper, with an awful eye for dirt, and she can put up with any thing if the house is only clean. But a few specks on the windows or an undusted parlor will put her into fits, that nothing but cold water and rubbing—not of her, but of the windows and furniture—will cure.

Indeed, it is not unusual to see good people more disturbed by the little vexations of life than they are by real trials, such as come home to their hearts, and might reasonably be supposed to overwhelm them with sorrow. The reason of this inconsistency may be that the little trial is so insignificant itself that one scarcely thinks of calling in grace or philosophy to help in bearing it. Instead of resisting, the soul worries and frets till the trouble irritates and wounds and festers, and then breeds others. Seven evil spirits come home with the first, and the house is turned upside down by the fretfulness of the soul now under the power of the evil one.

If we had a higher sense of the greatness of our present comforts, and a deeper sense of our unworthiness to have them, we would be less disposed to repine when we suffer for a time the loss of some of them. He was wise who, when he had the toothache, was thankful that he had not a broken leg; and when the leg was broken, that it was not his neck. And if we compare our enjoyments with our trials, and take the balance as the sum that we have a right to make the most of, we shall discover that there is no reason in the world for being discontented with our lot. More than this, it is the testimony of Infinite Wisdom, confirmed, if confirmation is wanted, by the experience of all good men who have left their experience on record, that little trials and great trials are means to ends, and those ends are the greatest and best in the moral universe. When the young eagles in the nest where they were hatched have grown to be too large for it, however much they may love to stay in it and be fed by indulgent parents, the old eagle stirs them up and crowds them out, and compels them to do their duty in the sphere to which eagles are called. It will not be permitted to any one who has work to do, to dwell at ease in his nest and be fed all the time ; to take comfort, as we call it, forgetful of the duties of life and the calls of a world suffering around us. These little trials are to stir us up, and drive us out of ourselves. We would not mind them at all if we had our eyes and hearts on the great business for which we were put into this garden.

And nearly all these little crosses and vexations which we dignify by the name of trials, are not worth speaking of, and to-morrow they are quite forgotten, though to-day they seem to be intolerable.

XXIV.

TALKING TO MAN AND BEAST.

HAD I my life to live over again—how often we say or think these words, and it were well if they lead us to put what remains of life to better use—I would, with God's good help, never speak a harsh word to man or beast.

I have been in state-prisons, and studied the system and practical workings of the theories of various overseers and governors; and in reformatories and asylums, and houses of refuge and penitentiaries and jails, and also in Christian families and boarding-schools; and in all of them have earnestly, candidly, and anxiously sought to learn the best way to make men better; and the result of all this observation and study is that no good and only evil come of harsh speaking.

The other extreme, the milk-and-water system, coddling the wicked to make them good, coaxing a villain to induce him to be a saint, giving a child candy to stop crying, or hiring him to do what he ought to be required to do—this or the like of this is just as far from the right way of dealing with the wayward and refractory.

Children are not fools generally, and convicts are usually smart. They who are under parental government, or in the hands of the law, undergoing the penalty of crime, very soon get to know the measure of those who are over them, and act accordingly. They see the inconsistency and folly of the sugar system, and learn to despise those

S

who try it on.   Bribing or coaxing people to be good
makes them worse, for they are only corrupted by the
gifts or promise, and when the motive is not repeated
they are less than ever disposed to do what is required.

What set me upon this train of thought was a letter
calling my attention to the late killing of his keeper by a
boy in the House of Refuge, and I was asked to make
some inquiries into the system of discipline in that and
similar institutions, as one of the most important depart-
ments of philanthropic effort.   But I do not know that
the desperate act of a bad boy, or the murder of his keeper by a convict in a state-prison, would show any thing
respecting the general discipline of the establishment.
It is not unknown that children have murdered their parents, and where there are hundreds of men or boys together, all of whom are collected because they are bad,
there must be among them some so bad as to defy the influences that have restrained or changed others.

The best man, or the one who has just now the highest
and best reputation as a prison manager, believes in *pun-
ishing* prisoners — in making them feel that they are in
prison not only to be reformed, but to suffer a penalty
for crime.   He mingles firmness, justice, and kindness in
such proportions as to give him great power over the convict, and real success in promoting his reformation.

A wise governor of a prison or a school or a family
never scolds, never speaks a harsh or hasty word.   Indeed, the first requisite to the successful government of
others is self-government.   And no one expends words
upon others in tones of impatience or severity until he
has lost command of himself.

Rarey, the horse-tamer, gave us lessons in the art of
reforming vicious beasts.   I saw him subdue a horse of

whom it would have been said the day before that "no man could tame him." But there was almost magic in the art and science that rendered the fiery and fractious, the biting and kicking beast, as gentle as a lamb. He did not speak harshly to him, nor did he inflict blows. But he mastered him, held him, fettered him, and, by firmness and gentleness combined, subdued his will. The same treatment certainly ought to be better for animals with reason than animals without it. It is a question that is yet unsettled whether such animals as dogs and horses reason. They have some faculty so near to reason that they can be reasoned *with*. They learn also to understand words, so that they can be talked *to* to some purpose. They certainly have feelings, and far deeper than their hides. They notice our neglect and are hurt by it, as a human friend is. They rejoice in our kindness as one does whom we love; and because they are unable by words to tell us how they suffer, or to make excuse for the wrong they do and for which we punish them, it is our duty to be very tender and considerate in our treatment of them. No good man would do wrong to a dog or a horse any more than to a child, without being sorry for it. I have profound respect for Mr. Bergh, who has done so much to prevent cruelty to animals. He deserves an *equestrian* statue in the Central Park. It should stand at the principal entrance. If the proposal were made to the horses, there would not be a nay among them.

But I would not put up a statue to the pigeon-shooting men; they need to feel the force of statutes made and provided for such cases as theirs. Among them I see men whose names are respected in political and financial circles. It may be that these words from one so far removed from such circles as I am may reach them, and convey to them some faint impression of the regret and indignation they excite when for sport they shoot birds. It is small business any way, if that may be called small which involves the suffering and the life of any creature.

And I would like to have sporting gentlemen reminded that as a sparrow does not fall to the ground without the notice of the Infinite Majesty, so it is quite certain that when a pigeon, wounded, bleeding, and gasping, lies quivering before them, the good God is not pleased with the sacrifice, and will charge the murder to their account. Cowper would not keep on his list of friends the man who needlessly set foot upon a worm, and I do not care to be on terms with one who wantonly hurts a bird.

XXV.

LOVING AND DOING.

WHEN Dr. Franklin was American Minister to France, and residing at Passy, a small village near Paris, he wrote a letter to Dr. Mather, in which he said:

"When I was a boy, I met with a book by your father, entitled, 'Essays to do Good.' It had been so little regarded by its former possessor that several leaves of it were torn out, but the remainder gave me such a turn of thinking as to have an influence on my conduct through life, for I have always set a greater value on the character of a doer of good than on any other kind of reputation; and if I have been, as you seem to think, a useful citizen, the public owes the advantage of it to that book."

To one who has only the amelioration of the present or temporal condition of his fellow-men in view, the life of Franklin is a beautiful example of what one man may do who gives his life to humane, philanthropic, and judicious essays to do good. If Mather's "Essay" were the inspiration of Franklin, you see what the little book did; and if Mather made Franklin a philanthropist, you may be encouraged to be like the one or the other, or both. Franklin made no pretensions to Christian motives of action. Whitefield was coming to Philadelphia when Franklin resided there, and Dr. F. wrote to W. and invited him to be his guest during his stay. The great preacher wrote, accepting his invitation with thanks, and added: "If you

do this for Christ's sake, you will not lose your reward."
Franklin replied immediately that "he wished it to be
distinctly understood that it was done for Mr. Whitefield's
sake."

Franklin loved his fellow-men, there is no doubt of
that ; and lived, of course, to do them good.

Among the mountains of Switzerland, in a secluded vil-·
lage of the Canton of Appenzell, I made the acquaintance
of a philanthropist, who was using a large fortune, and all .
his time and strength, in doing good to others.   Like his
Master, he went about doing good.   He had asylums and
hospitals and schools and shops sustained by his money,
and over which he kept personal watch, going from door
to door, and seeing that every thing was done as it should
be.   He was a walking benediction, a peripatetic joy.
Little children left their play when they saw him passing
by, ran up and put their hands into his, and returned to
their sport.   He lived to do good.   And he told me that
it was not of himself at all: that some unseen agency im-
pelled him to do all this, and over the doors of some of
his homes for the suffering he had placed inscriptions
giving the praise to Him who had put him up to it.

In New York there is a good man dwelling, whom to
know is a great blessing ; to be able to call him your
friend would be an honor.   He was once in the Moravian
connection.   Now he is a minister of the Episcopal
Church.   For some years he was the rector of a free
church, and it was thronged whenever it was open by
multitudes eager to be led by him in the worship and
service of God.   By-and-by he founded and built St.
Luke's Hospital, and went into it to live among the pa-
tients, to be their pastor and comforter, day and night
and always.   For many years he has dwelt there, married

only to Christ and his work, doing good, and in that only finding his joy, or if not joy — for it is of no moment whether one have joy here or not—finding his good in doing good, and so getting out of life the best that life can yield. He has realized another of his many schemes for the comfort of others, in laying out a tract of five hundred acres in an adjacent county, where he has a retreat for the aged poor and invalids and orphans; and a home for the homeless, who find rest and peace in St. Johnland. Some years ago, he—that is, Dr. Muhlenberg—wrote a hymn which millions have sung, beginning—

> "I would not live alway,
> I ask not to stay;
> Where storm after storm
> Rises dark o'er the way."

He is known to the world better by that hymn than by his philanthropic and Christian work, but his work is more characteristic of him than the hymn. I have no doubt Job was honest when he said, "I would not live alway," but he said it under great trials and disappointments. And he who has the joy of seeing that his labors are prospered to the blessedness of others, so that he is able to say as Job could say before his calamities, "The blessing of him that was ready to perish came upon me; and I caused the widow's heart to sing for joy: I put on righteousness, and it clothed me; my judgment was as a robe and a diadem: I was eyes to the blind, and feet was I to the lame: I was a father to the poor; and the cause which I knew not, I searched out" — he may well be content to "stay" just as long as the good Lord is pleased to keep him here, and give him work to do. Indeed, the place we are in is our place, and all we have to do is to make the most and best of it for the good of those near us, and those to whom we can send the good we can not give with our hands.

The most thoroughly self-sacrificing man I ever saw was Dr. Guggenbuhl, in his school for idiots, away up on a mountain near Interlaken.   It nearly made me sick to see the Cretins around him.   He was a gentleman of culture and learning and skill and fortune.   He might have had his place at the head of his profession in any city.   But he was in the woods and among idiots, only to do good.   He died in the service.   It was a life beautiful in its devotion, and he had his reward.   But he did not set the reward before him as the end, the motive.   He loved to do good, and the reward came of necessity.

Pastor Heldring went to Hohenderlo, a miserable wilderness of a place, full of thieves and robbers, and he set about doing them good.   They had to go a long distance to get a drop of fresh water, for it had been found impossible to dig a well, and the good man worked till he overcame all difficulties ; and when he had caused a spring to spring up there, he soon had a school and a church, and by-and-by the wilderness blossomed as the rose.   You may not teach idiots, or dig wells in a desert, or found asylums, or write hymns ; but you are called to do good. There is a little world in which you dwell, and its name is the sweetest word perhaps of all. Its name is home. You may do a world of good in that little world.   It is the easiest thing imaginable to do good.   You may do it with words or without words.   You may do it by cheerful looks and kind, gentle ways ; by keeping your lips closed when an impatient, fault-finding expression is ready to escape ; by cheering those about you with perpetual loving words and little deeds of kindness, not worth mentioning, but worth more than rubies to the heart that feels their infinite power. And then all about you is this wide world, full of sore places for you to heal, dark places for you to lighten, rough places for you to smooth, sad places for you to cheer, wicked places for you to fill with the saving love of the dear Lord.

When Jesus became man, he made the whole human race his brethren, as we are brethren. And when he came unto his own, his own received him not. In that wonderful drama, drawn out in the twenty-fifth chapter of Matthew, and which has never had half the power and importance in the Church and in theology to which it is entitled, the great Teacher has given an outline of the Christian system. The moral grandeur of the scene is unsurpassed in the facts of history or the realms of poetry. In all the conditions there stated by the Judge in his awards, sympathy shown to those in distress is the chief if not the only ground on which he pronounces the word "come" or "go." "I was in prison," he says, "and ye came unto me." Was he there in the person of some saint unjustly seized and shut up among thieves? Or did he intimate that the wicked—criminals, convicts, outcasts—they who have broken the laws of God and man, and were justly suffering the punishment of their crimes, were objects of Christian kindness, persons to be visited in their cells with the words and deeds of divine compassion and holy love? And when he put himself between the wicked woman and the men who were disposed to be hard upon her as a grievous sinner whom their law would not suffer to live, he gave them a lesson never to be forgotten by men or women, that charity to the wicked, even the vilest of the wicked—for there is no vileness in the world more vile than such sin as this woman sinned—

that charity even to such as she, is the outflow of the spirit of him whose lips, dropping the sweetness of heaven, said, "Go and sin no more." And the whole science of Christian duty is set forth and illustrated and proved in those few sentences of the mountain discourse, when the Saviour says : "Love your enemies, bless them that curse you, do good to them that hate you, and pray for them which despitefully use you ; that ye may be the children of your Father which is in heaven : for he maketh his sun to rise on the evil and on the good, and sendeth rain on the just and on the unjust. For if ye love them which love you, what reward have ye? do not even the publicans the same ?"

Then comes the concluding, clinching, and exhaustive command, " Be ye therefore perfect, even as your Father which is in heaven is perfect." Look closely into the philosophy and the religion of those passages from the best of all sermons.

And when he came to die! He had lived among sinners ; he had done works of mercy for sinners ; he had been reproached for living so much among them ; and when he came to die, what then? He was hung between two thieves. Wondrous combination of facts, to make the death of the Saviour harmonious with his life. They who did it, meant it not so. They would crown his death with ignominy, and so they crucified him—and between two thieves. He came from glory to save sinners. He lived among them ; ministered unto them. He loved the lost, and sought them in their sins. And when he died in shame, he had a sinner, a thief—the one on his right hand and the other on his left, and Jesus in the midst.

Now when you think of the way in which our Lord lived and died, and when you are longing to be like him, and to be perfect as your Father is perfect, you will try to do good ; present good, temporal good—to sinners, to the wicked, to "cursing mothers and drunken fathers ;" and to that class of sinners from whom the most of Christ's people, and especially Christian women, turn away with mingled hate and scorn.

To do good for the sake of the reward may be the zenith of self-worship. · But there is no merit in doing good to those who pay us by their love and gratitude for what we do. To make a widow's heart sing for joy may be done in such a way as to make your own heart sing louder. And you surely do not expect any higher reward. The sweetest of all earthly pleasures is to be the minister of gladness to the sick or the wounded or the poor, who are themselves gentle and good and grateful. They praise you, and tell you what an angel you are, and you half believe them, and it makes you feel very happy. It is the cheapest way in the world to get a cheerful glow all over your heart. You are not much more like your Father, who is perfect, for having done the good deed. It was well. But nothing very great. It was nothing to speak of, and when you gave your dollar or ten to the female benevolent society, which hires good women to go about with baskets of charity, you did a good thing, but it was of no great account in the sight of him who poured out his blood for you.

Go yourself. Take the basket on your own arm. Visit the cellar, damp and dirty; climb the rickety garret stairs yourself, and with your own hands and pleasant words dispense the gifts of food, clothing, medicine, and care.

XXVI.

THE NEGLECTED GRAVEYARD.

RIDING out into the country some eight or ten miles yesterday (and these days are superb for driving over the hills and along the valleys), I came by an ancient and apparently forgotten graveyard. It was so far from the sight of the living, that the thought was natural, "the people are all here." But somebody must have buried them; and I soon discovered that it was only a mile or two from the village, and the whole country side was densely populated with the living, many of them doubtless the relatives and friends of the dwellers in this silent land. But what affected me the most strangely and sadly was the utter neglect and desolation that reigned among these tombs. It was easy to step over the stone wall, and I picked my way around and among the gravestones, some of them lying on the ground, others ready to fall, and most of them so hidden by weeds and bushes that it was hard to read the inscriptions, or to find the name they were set up to commemorate. Yet on many of those that I succeeded in reaching and reading were words of affection; lines that told me how tenderly once were loved the ashes that are now lying here unnoticed and perhaps unknown. On some of the old headstones the dates could be made out that went away back to the days of our Revolution, and it is very likely that in this changing world of ours, and very changing country, there is no one now living here who has the blood or the memory of these ancients in his heart. But here are inscriptions that have been made within the last twenty or thirty years, and they too seem to have been made by hands that are now cold, or to have been prompted by hearts that have forgotten.

It helps to humble us to take a walk in a neglected graveyard. We think that we are of some value to our friends, and they would grieve much if we were taken away. And we think rightly. But how very soon after the grave closes over us is the place where we sleep suffered to pass into oblivion! Perhaps a stone with a record of their estimate of our worth is set up; but even that is suffered to be overgrown with weeds, or to fall to the ground as we fell but a few years before. When a stone is thrown into a lake it makes a great commotion for a moment, but very soon the water is as placid as if its surface had not been disturbed at all. And when a great man dies, or one who was greatly beloved in the circle of his acquaintance, the heart of the community is stirred: we talk of the whole people being in tears. But a few months only and all is as if nothing had happened; and in a few years his name is rarely mentioned. His grave is neglected. The places that knew him, know him no more. It will be just so with us. We can not tell where we shall be buried; and a few years after we are buried how very few in all the world will know or care where we are sleeping! It is not very grateful to our pride to take this view of our future; but if we may judge by what we see here and every where, this oblivion awaits the most of us.

It is a mark of low civilization that the country graveyard is a forlorn and neglected place. Religion and refinement would both encourage us to guard it from the intrusion of beasts, and also to make it attractive, that the living may be led to come and meditate among its tombs. There is an excess even of floral ornament that tends to destroy the proper effect. I have seen cemeteries that were rather places of entertainment for the living than fitting homes for the dead. This is the tendency in rural cemeteries near the city, the resort of visitors who go to see how death can be cheated of its terrors, and his field of triumph made a holiday spectacle. Yet even these groves and drives and lakes and bridges and flowers innumerable and glaring monuments, costly whited sepulchres, are more becoming than this desert desolation that reigns in many country church-yards, and those not a hundred miles from the city.

They should have walks laid out between the rows of graves, and monthly roses ought to be planted on either side, with here and there a weeping-willow, and the cypress or pine—evergreens are emblems of immortality, and monthly roses speak of the Resurrection. Then it is well to keep the grass closely cut, and the weeds out altogether, for they are as much in the way in this garden of the Lord, where he watches the dust of his saints, as they can be among the vegetables. Up in old Cambridge, the graveyard was close by the "Old White Meeting-house," and on the Sabbath-day, during the intermission, it was common for the people—men, women, and children—to walk among the graves, families gathering around their own dead, and conversing with their neighbors of the departed. It was even in childhood an offense to me that Mr. Beebe would let his sheep run in the graveyard, but I was told he did so to keep the grass down.

On the continent of Europe and in England the rural

graveyards are better cared for than with us. I wandered into them in many countries, particularly in Wales, Germany, and Switzerland, and I do not recollect of seeing them any where so utterly neglected as some are here in Westchester County, in the focus of American civilization, wealth, and culture.

We do not have the yew-tree here as in England. There they grow to a great size, as in Stoke, where Gray lies buried in the country church-yard. That was the scene and theme of his elegy—a poem that has furnished more lines that have become familiar to mankind than any other poem of equal length. The third stanza is—

> "Beneath those rugged elms, that yew-tree's shade,
>   Where heaves the turf in many a mouldering heap,
>   Each in his narrow cell forever laid,
>   The rude forefathers of the hamlet sleep."

The sixth stanza is very fine :

> "For them no more the blazing hearth shall burn,
>   No busy housewife ply her evening care,
>   No children run to lisp their sire's return,
>   Or climb his knees the envied kiss to share."

The last line of the ninth verse is often quoted :

> "The boast of heraldry, the pomp of power,
>   And all that beauty, all that wealth e'er gave,
>   Await alike th' inevitable hour :
>   The paths of glory lead but to the grave."

And as I was walking recently in that desolate rural field of graves, another stanza of this elegy seemed very appropriate :

> "Perhaps in this neglected spot is laid
>   Some heart once pregnant with celestial fire ;
>   Hands that the rod of empire might have swayed,
>   Or waked to ecstasy the living lyre."

And then follows the most familiar verse, quoted oftener than any other :

> " Full many a gem of purest ray serene
>   The dark, unfathomed caves of ocean bear ;
> Full many a flower is born to blush unseen,
>   And waste its sweetness on the desert air."

In that country church-yard which Gray calls a " neglected spot," the poet was buried by the side of his mother, to whom he had erected a monument there.   But the
quiet beauty of that long, low church in the midst of those
graves has lingered with me these ten years or more, and
the signs of neglect, if there were any, have been forgotten.

XXVII.

WHENCE COMFORT COMES.

In the gray of the cold winter morning, the earth covered with its winding-sheet of snow, I was standing on the front step, and a solitary hearse came through the lane from my nearest neighbor's house, and passed the door. It was the saddest sight that had yet darkened my view. I knew what it was bearing away: the lifeless form of a lovely girl who, but a few days ago, was the life and joy of our little neighborhood. Taking cold, she was suddenly thrown into a fever, and now, after a week's sickness, was dead. Of all the children around us, she was the one who bid the fairest to live. Full of health and spirits, rosy and buoyant, she was the pride and sunshine of home and friends. She was as good as she was beautiful. Seeing her almost daily, we had never seen or heard what we wished otherwise. It is rare, indeed, that we can say so much as that, even of our own children, to whose faults parents are often blind. Yet this dear child, so fondly loved at home that the love of others is not to be thought of, was now dead.

The hearse was taking her away, and, joining the smitten household, we followed with the remains to the city, and to the house of God where the burial-service was read, and then to Greenwood, where we laid her down beneath the snow and the winter clods, till the spring-time of the Resurrection, when she shall rise again

T

with angelic beauty, and clothed with garments of immortality.

Now I do not know what there is outside of the Gospel
of Christ to sustain and comfort a bleeding heart in such
a sorrow as this. To our unaided reason, the blow that
crushes parental hopes by such a sudden and appalling
affliction is terrible and cruel. And why is a child permitted to live and develop into lovely girlhood, and win
the affection of friends, and taste the joys of young life
that knows no care, and look out on the future with every
prospect of giving and receiving pleasure with increasing
enjoyment as years increase, to be thus early blighted,
smitten, slain, buried, lost, gone forever from our arms and
sight and hearing, laid in the earth, to be enjoyed, to enjoy no more?

If there be no truth in the doctrine of our holy religion,
this event is simply a horrible disaster, against which reason revolts, and philosophy furnishes no antidote. But
the Gospel comes with a voice of tender consolation, and
gives the sweet assurance that even such a sorrow is not
without its own strong relief. Much of what has been
said in sermons and books by way of consolation to the
afflicted is drawn more from reason than from Scripture,
and therefore fails to satisfy the aching heart of sorrow.
The peace of God flows into the soul only by his Spirit
through the Word of truth. All that teaching which mag-
nifies the blessedness of the departed, and would persuade
us to be content because the one we love is better off than
here, is well enough for those who can not take higher and
broader views of the wonderful works of Him who doeth
all things according to the counsel of his own will, and
therefore must do them all well. It is a source of comfort to a mourning mother to follow with the eye of faith

her buried babe, as it rises into the form of an infant angel, and enters upon the praises of the heavenly state—
a redeemed and holy child among the redeemed and holy.
But this is only the comfort of compensation. There is
higher and better solace than this in the doctrine of the
good Word. And when the hand of God presses us
heavily—takes away our treasures, health, wealth, friends
—strips us of all that we love in life—puts bitterness into
the cup we are most fond of drinking—spreads a pall over
the nursery, and hangs the fireside with black, and makes
the house solitary and cold and dreary, that was last week
vocal with songs and shouts of young gladness and health,
and turns all our joy into mourning, our beauty to ashes,
and our home light to darkness—then comes the message
of the Gospel to the stricken soul, with its words of healing, saving power. Afflictions come from the love of our
Father in heaven. He pitieth us. He remembereth our
frame. He is kind in his dealings and infinite in his wisdom, knowing what is best for us and his kingdom. What
we know not now, we shall know hereafter. It is good to
be afflicted. We are to be made perfect through suffering. He does with us as with children whom he loves.
And this affliction will work out glory. I hear that sweet
voice, which gave words to a soul of infinite tenderness,
saying, " Let not your heart be troubled." I do not feel
ashamed to weep, for my Lord and Pattern, my Priest and
King, once stood by the side of a grave in a country village, and there wept over a friend that he loved. And so
because he wept, I will weep also when death takes away
those whom my soul loves. And because he said, in the
midst of mortal agony, " Not my will but thine be done,"
therefore will I bow down under the weight of the heavi-
est load that he in his holy wisdom and mercy lays upon

me, and sinking into the great depths of human woe, I will cry, " Even so, Master and Saviour, not as I will, but as thou wilt."

To believe in God is to get the victory over death—our own or of those dear to us. It is not Christ-like nor Christian, it is sinful and worse, to give way to unbelief, to repining, or to unconsoled grief. One joy is gone, but other joys remain. Duty to the dead is no longer required, but duty to the living is increased. As our grief was the greatest, so our comfort in believing was through grace the greatest, that we might be the minister of consolation to those around us in the same sorrow.

> "Oh, let my trembling soul be still,
>   While darkness veils this mortal eye,
> And wait thy wise, thy holy will,
>   Wrapped yet in tears and mystery.
> I can not, Lord, thy purpose see ;
> Yet all is well, since ruled by thee.
>
> "Thus trusting in thy love, I tread
>   The narrow path of duty on ;
> What though some cherished joys are fled ?
>   What though some flattering dreams are gone ?
> Yet purer, brighter joys remain :
> Why should my spirit then complain ?"

An aged minister, under the snows of more than seventy winters, having just buried the wife of his youth, wrote to me in his sorrow. One of the strangest but not the most thankless of the works to which we are often called is the ministry of consolation. But the poorest of all comforts in sorrow is human sympathy. It seems a sacrilege and offense to say so ; yet what can it do to mitigate grief or bring back joy to a desolate spirit? Still we love it, and seek it, and find it, and weep on. I wrote to the weary and smitten old pilgrim words like these :

"Were you young and thus bereaved, I would find other consolations than such as I bring you now. The days of your years are so far spent that, in the ordinary course of things, it will not be long ere you are again with her to renew your youth, immortal in union and love. It is, therefore, of no great moment whether you suffer or not, for at most it can not be very long, and then your joy will be forever.

"And if you have already attained to some good degree of union with God by love, so that you have learned to live for others more than yourself, you have thanked him several times, since your wife's departure, that you were permitted to live until her life on earth was finished. It was meet that she should die first. She leaned upon you even when you trembled with age. It is sad to be left alone in this world, all the friends of one's youth long since fallen asleep, and then at last the companion of half a century—whose arm has been a support, whose bosom a pillow, whose smile dearer than the sun, whose voice the sweetest music, and whose love a life-long joy— to pass away. It were better that she should go before you than for her to be thus left alone.

"And now the memory of a lifetime, like a meadow stream, flows along through your soul, with sweet, bright flowers on either bank: the sunny days, when you whispered softly in her ear the old, old story, and won her for your bride. Often in the daytime these scenes recur with tender beauty to the eye of your spirit; but mostly when the shades of twilight gather, and you sit, slippered and gowned, for a solitary evening by your one-sided hearthstone, then

"'Fond memory brings the light
Of other days around thee,'

and you revel in the recollections of youth and life and love, long time ago. Now you know how better far it is to have loved and lost, than not to have loved at all.

" And that leads me to observe it is only in a very restricted sense we can say that we have lost our departed friends. Thirty-six years ago a friend, who had just been bereaved as you are now, asked me for a single line to put on the tombstone of his wife. I gave him—

" 'NOT LOST, BUT GONE BEFORE.'

supposing it was original; but long before that time the poet Rogers had said it in lines that just meet your present want:

" ' Those that he loved so long and sees no more,
  Loved and still loves—not dead—but gone before,
    He gathers round him.'

And on the tombstone of Mary Angell, at Stepney, England, who died in 1694, the very line is written which I gave to my friend as an original in 1838. He put it upon a slab which still stands in the church-yard at Fishkill on the Hudson River; and he who placed it there has since been laid by the side of her who had ' gone before;' and he has found, in the glad life beyond the grave, that his wife's epitaph is true. The same enjoyment waits on you in that other state.

" A very thin partition, a veil almost transparent, separates you from her. It is a divine and wise arrangement that in the body our intercourse with human souls shall be through our senses only; and this makes the veil impenetrable, separating us from those gone before. They can not speak to us, nor we to them. But they may be near us always, and in ways unknown may be our ministers.   Never mind how it is.   Sufficient for us that they are blessed, and we

"'Soon their blessedness shall see.'

" For if they sleep in Jesus, they shall awake in him; and we, being in God by love, and one with them and him by love, shall be one with each other when those who sleep in Jesus are brought with him.   Blessed are the dead who die in the Lord. , The early Christians had a deeper consciousness of this union than we have.   The epitaphs on the tombs in the Catacombs of Rome, and the inscriptions on the old memorial marbles dug up from the repose of eighteen centuries, tell us that they had peace unspeakable in the thought that saints die in the Lord, rest in him, sleep in Jesus, are by death born into new life with God.

"'We a little longer wait,
But how little, none can tell.'

"Be patient, and tarry till the Master calleth for thee. All the days of my appointed time will I wait until my change come.   This is the fruit you are to bring forth in old age.   The out-of-door work of life is for the younger, who are strong.   Yours is to set an example of cheerful content, in the day when those who look out of the windows are darkened and all the daughters of music are brought low.   Be not like the bird that beats her breast against the bars of her cage and pants to be free.   But like one who sits all day long and sings, glad to go, yet content to stay.   And when the door is opened, step out and fly away.   The bride of thy youth, in whiter vestments than she wore on the day of her espousal, waits for thee.   Infant voices cry, ' Come, father, come.'   And He whose smile lights the universe with love, greets thee

on the threshold of glory with those words (Oh, God!
that we might hear them now) : 'Enter thou into the joy
of thy Lord.' "

The cup that Jesus took from the hand of his Father
was one of sorrow.   This expression—the cup—is often
used in the Sacred Writings for that which the cup con-
tains.   It may be of thanksgiving, of salvation, of joy, or
of sorrow.   It is even used to hold the displeasure of the
Father, whose wrath is sent upon the children of diso-
bedience.   This is the bitterest cup.   It is often de-
served.   But we are not always, nor often, to infer that
the cup of sorrow is given to us because the Giver is an-
gry.   It may be in great pity, with infinite tenderness,
and with a view to our highest good.   Now no chasten-
ing is for the present joyous.   The cup comes from the
Father.   The judge in Eastern countries and ancient
times condemned the criminal to drink the poisoned
draught—a mode of punishment, of execution—and the
condemned took the cup and drank it, and perished.   But
what father, if his son asked bread, would give him a serpent? or water, and would give him poison?   If my Father give me the cup, I know it is not the hemlock of
which Socrates drank and died.   It may be a very bitter
cup.   Medicine is not always pleasing to the taste.   But
it may be very important that you take it, nevertheless.
And if my Father tell me it is better for me to drink it,
bitter as it may be, my confidence in him is perfect, and
I will drink it to the last drop in the cup.   You have
seen children do so a hundred times.   And you have
seen them rebellious, and refuse to take it, and fight
against it, and sometimes they must be held firmly and
actually made to drink the unpalatable draught.   It does

not do them half as much good as it would if they received it willingly and drank it cheerfully. And I have
found it just so with every cup of sorrow that my Father
has put to my lips. If I resisted, and refused to admit
that there was any need of it, and felt offended that it
was pressed upon me, insisting that I knew what was
good for me, and did not require the proffered medicine,
and would be actually better off without it—the cup was
forced upon me by the higher will of my Father, and not
until my will was subdued, and the cup received as a
good child receives it, was it good for me to be afflicted.
Then, in the dust and depths, with a crushed and melted
heart, have I felt the infinite love of the Father, who does
not willingly afflict, who never lays upon us more than we
are able to bear, who is himself afflicted in all our affliction, who bore our sorrows, who became a man of sorrows, who knows every one of our griefs because he took
upon him our nature, and therefore knows just what to
put into the cup; and he will not add a drop of bitter
more than his unfathomable pity knows that we should
drink.

I know that the cup comes from his hand to mine; and
he is not only my Father, but my Heavenly Father;
therefore too wise to err, too good to be unkind; infinite
in his wisdom, goodness, and truth. And oh! so tender,
so loving, so full of all compassion; he holds worlds in
his hand, but he would not suffer a hair to fall from the
head of one of his little ones unnumbered. His tender
mercies are over all his works. If one we love is sick,
with what gentle care we minister to every want; how
tenderly we lift from the pillow the fevered head, and
hold the cup with cooling draught to the parched lips we
have so often kissed. Like as a father pitieth his chil-

dren, so the Lord pities us, his poor, weak, sick, suffering little ones. He holds our aching heads, heals our bleeding hearts, leadeth us into green pastures by still waters, and (blessed be his name) restoreth our souls.

And shall I not drink it? The cup that my Father hath given me! It is he who has raised up my head from this hot pillow ; I feel his soft hand upholding me ; my lips touch the cup, but his hand is putting it there, and I hear his voice speaking soft and low into my soul, and saying : "Fear not, for I am with thee ; be not dismayed, for I am thy God."

Yes, I will drink it, all of it. For as oft as I drink of this cup, I take the draught that my Father gives, and drink of the cup from which my Saviour drank. His was a cup of agony unspeakable. It was a cup of blood. I do not wonder he prayed—"If it be possible, let this cup pass from me." He did not love the taste. His soul was exceeding sorrowful. But he drank it all. What a privilege to drink out of the same cup with him ! To be baptized with his baptism. To be a partaker of his sufferings. And if we suffer with him, we shall also reign with him.

Give me, then, the cup, my Father ; hold it to my lips till I have drank so much as thy will directs. The cup that my Father hath given me, shall I not drink it?

XXVIII.

MY FIRST AND LAST GREAT SERMON.

I HAD never preached in Princeton. Often invited, it was easy to make an excuse, while the real one was the reluctance, not unusual with young preachers, to appear as a teacher of teachers. To preach in Princeton involved the necessity of being heard by the venerable and learned professors in the theological seminary and college, and the still more critical audience of embryo divines and philosophers in those institutions. But in the year 1849, being Secretary of the American Bible Society, I was requested to visit Princeton and "present the cause." As this was in the line of duty, I made the engagement at once, and commenced the preparation of a "great sermon."

Taking the best one of several discourses already prepared on the special topic, I determined to load it with all the lore within reach, and to astonish the scholars of Princeton by my familiarity with the original Scriptures. My text and introduction were in these or similar words:

"The 19th Psalm, 4th verse: 'Their line is gone out through all the earth, and their words to the end of the world.'

"Beautiful as this passage is in our translation, it is far from giving the force and grandeur of the original.

"If you consult the marginal reading, you will see that the word here rendered *line* is a rule or direction.

"If you turn to the Septuagint, you will find that the word is *sound:* their *voice* has gone out," etc.

"But go to the original Hebrew, in which this poem was written, and there the word *line* is a *string*, a cord, a harpstring, and the idea is that the heavens are a great harp, the cord of which is stretched from sky to sky, making music to celebrate the glory of God."

With this introduction, and a discourse to match, I went to Princeton, taking no other sermon with me, but armed with a serene consciousness that my first effort there would not be altogether unworthy of the place and occasion. The Rev. Dr. Schenck was pastor of the church, then, as now, a valued friend. With him I lodged, and as we were conversing upon the subject, I asked him to take down his Hebrew Bible and Septuagint, and listen to the introduction of my sermon. He heard it, expressed his satisfaction, and kindly admitted that he had not compared the readings before. It was arranged that the Rev. Dr. James W. Alexander, then in the noonday splendor of his rhetorical power, should preach in the morning, and all the congregations and institutions should be assembled in the evening, when the Secretary should "present the cause."

I modestly declined to go into the pulpit. Dr. Alexander, after an invocation, announced to be sung the 19th Psalm, first part. I said to myself, "I intended to sing that." Then he read as the morning lesson the 19th Psalm. I began to be anxious, as I expected to read that. Then he gave for the second singing, 19th Psalm, second part. My anxiety now suggested perspiration. With intense suspense I waited a few minutes, and the eloquent doctor rose for the sermon and thus began :

"The 19th Psalm, 4th verse : 'Their line is gone out through all the earth,'" etc.

"Beautiful as this passage is in the vernacular, it is far below the grandeur of the original. In the margin you will observe that the word here rendered *line* is rule or direction. In the Septuagint it is *sound*—and their voice is gone forth. But in the original Hebrew the word *line* is a *string*, a cord, a harpstring, and the figure of the inspired poet is that the heavens are a great harp, swept by the hand of the Almighty and celebrating his praise."

And then, with a wealth of illustration, fertility of imagination, depth and extent of learning, in the blaze of which my poor little bantling wilted and perished, he went on to celebrate the excellences of the Scriptures, their majesty, variety, wisdom, power, and glory, and all this with an ease that showed what he was saying to be only the efflorescence of his knowledge, whose fruit and root and richness were scarcely called into use to make this magnificent discourse. Fancy my feelings when I heard every thing I had thought worth saying a thousand times better said, and on the top of it all such profusion of learning and copious streams of eloquence that my labored dissertation appeared tame and insipid. At last, to my great relief, he stopped.

Before he left the pulpit, Dr. Schenck said to him : "You have used up the Secretary."

"Why, what do you mean by that?"

"He read to me this morning the introduction to his sermon for the evening, and you have preached it."

Dr. A. came down from the pulpit, and taking me by the hand, his fine face hiding and revealing a quizzical smile, he said, "You did not put all your eggs into one basket, did you?"

"Yes, I did," said I with a groan, "and you have put your foot into it."

Yes, he had. My "great" sermon had proved to be a small one, and of course, great or small, was not available for the evening. What did I do? It's of very little moment what I did, but I took the lesson severely to heart, was punished and mortified. In the evening the house was thronged in every part. The divinity students in one gallery, the collegians in the other, all the faculties of both institutions, pastors and people were before me—the most intellectual audience I had ever addressed. I "presented the cause" as well as I could.

That was my first and last "great sermon." And I didn't preach that. The lesson needs no enforcement, but young preachers will easily see the moral of it.

Some seven years before that adventure I was wandering in New England in a summer vacation. On Saturday afternoon I stopped at Andover, Mass., where I did not know a person. A country inn received me, and soon the Rev. Bela B. Edwards, D.D., found me, and with gentle force drew me to his house, where I spent one of the most delicious Sabbaths that earth ever yielded to me, or will. What peace, what grace, what chaste refinement in that home. Mrs. Edwards was the fitting complement of that accomplished man.

In morning worship he used the Hebrew Bible, and read the 19th Psalm, translating as he read. In the 4th verse he said, "Their cord has gone out."

"What's that?" I said. "That is new to me."

He read again—"Their cord, string, harpstring;" and then we pursued the word through various languages, and I went away the next day wiser than I came.

The learning which I had picked up so casually at

Andover I attempted seven years afterward to discharge upon Princeton; but, alas! they knew it all before I arrived.

How charming the memories of those men whose friendship and love are more precious than gold or ru-bies. Heaven has them now, but we will walk and talk with them yet again by the river side. We shall know more than books can teach us; and when we sing the new song, the harps of the stars will be silent, but the melody will be sweeter, and the music the voices of angels only, and the ransomed of the Lord.

> "Oh, may I bear some humble part
>   In that immortal song;
> Wonder and love shall tune my heart,
>   And joy command my tongue."

XXIX.

THE LAST DAY OF SUMMER.

I CAN not imagine any thing in nature more lovely than the scene that lies around and above me. It is a warm day—very warm. Out in the sunshine it is hot, and in the city it is an oppressive day. But I will tell you how the land lies about the trees under which I am writing, and you shall then have some idea of what a summer has just closed.

Last year I built a rustic sofa: built it with my own hands, to the profound astonishment of friends who had given me no credit for hammer-and-saw skill, and were quite unwilling to believe that I could get up a fancy settee of this sort. But here it stands the second season, as good as new, and likely to do duty many more ; and I am stretched on this seat, with pencil and paper, a strong south wind moving among the trees that hang over me in thick shadow, the atmosphere fragrant with flowers that skirt the hedge rows, and the river glistening through the leaves like a crystal sea, while the trees and shrubbery, the grass and vines, washed clean with the late rains, seem to laugh in their beauty, looking so fresh and sweet as if this were nature's holiday, and every leaf and blade and shrub and plant were on a frolic, to be glad while they may.

A friend near me this morning had remarked, " Nothing but heaven can be more beautiful ;" and the thought

carried me away to the glory of an everlasting summer
—the life-time day in heaven; and I have been thinking
while lying here of the scene that must break upon the
eye when it first opens in the celestial paradise.

> "There, on a high, majestic throne,
>   The Almighty Father reigns,
> And sheds his glorious goodness down
>   On all the blissful plains.
> Bright like the sun the Saviour sits,
>   And spreads eternal noon;
> No evenings there, nor gloomy nights,
>   To want the feeble moon.
> Amid those ever-shining skies,
>   Behold the sacred dove;
> While banished sin and sorrow flies
>   From all the realms of love."

I love this present world; God has made it all good—

> "Oh earth! thy splendor and thy beauty how amazing;
> Whene'er, anew, I turn to thee intently gazing,
> With rapture I exclaim, How beautiful thou art,
> How beautiful!"

Then I look away from it and cry out, so that the birds
in the branches overhead pause in their songs to listen
while I sing:

> "Oh, if now so great the glory
>   In the heavens and earth we see,
> What delight and joy forever,
>   Near His throne and heart to be!"

And then, changing the metre and the tune to one
more stately but not less jubilant, when an oriole had
finished his song, I began again:

> "Descend from heaven, immortal Dove!
>   Stoop down and take us on thy wings,
> And mount and bear us far above
>   The reach of these inferior things:

U

Beyond, beyond this lower sky,
Up where eternal ages roll,
Where solid pleasures never die,
And fruits immortal feast the soul.
Oh for a sight, a pleasing sight,
Of our Almighty Father's throne!
There sits our Saviour, crowned with light,
Clothed in a body like our own;
Adoring saints around him stand,
And thrones and powers before him fall:
The God shines gracious through the man,
And sheds sweet glories on them all.
Oh! what amazing joys they feel,
While to their golden harps they sing,
And sit on every heavenly hill,
And spread the triumphs of their King!"

We form our conceptions of the heavenly world from the descriptions of it briefly given in the Revelation, and by combining all the ideas of beauty which earth affords to aid us. The old poets, more indeed than the modern, delighted in the sensuous when they would paint the beauties of paradise, the finest of all of them being the

"Oh, Mother dear, Jerusalem,"

which I love to repeat, but can not write out on these flying leaves. I recall from Watts a stanza scarcely less realistic in its imagery than any thing in Dickson's "Hymn of Heaven:"

"Oh! the transporting, rapturous scene
    That rises on my sight;
Sweet fields arrayed in living green,
    And rivers of delight."

[Just the scene around me now.]

"There, generous fruits that never fail,
    On trees immortal grow;
There, rocks and hills and brooks and vales
    With milk and honey flow."

And there is another stanza that comes in so fittingly with this bright day and these joyous scenes :

> "There, all the heavenly hosts are seen,
> In shining ranks they move,
> And drink immortal vigor in,
> With wonder and with love."

Running water is one of the most common images in the poet's fancy when singing of heaven—

> "There the Lamb, our Shepherd leads us,
> By the streams of life along ;
> On the freshest pastures feeds us,
> Turns our sighing into song."

All those illustrations come from the twenty-third Psalm—the Shepherd, the water, and the pastures. And John says : " He showed me a pure river of water of life, clear as crystal, proceeding out of the throne of God and of the Lamb."

> "This stream doth water Paradise,
> It makes the angels sing ;
> One cordial drop revives my heart,
> Hence all my joys do spring."

"The Lamb is the light thereof." I have seen a picture in which a temple is lighted up by rays of light proceeding from the person of the Saviour—he is the Sun—they have no need of any other—

> "That clime is not like this dull clime of ours—
> All, all is brightness there ;
> A sweeter influence breathes around its flowers,
> And a far milder air.
> No calm below is like that calm above,
> No region here is like that realm of love ;
> Earth's softest spring ne'er shed so soft a light,
> Earth's brightest summer never shone so bright ;

One everlasting stretch of azure pours
Its stainless splendor o'er those sinless shores;
For there Jehovah shines with heavenly ray,
There Jesus reigns dispensing endless day."

Some people are often drawing contrasts between heaven and earth, not merely to the sad disparagement of the world they are living in, but to their own discomfort: fretting themselves into discontent, while they are growing no better fitted for this life or that which is to come. A cheerful spirit is at once the privilege and the duty of every Christian to enjoy, and heaven has far more attractions to one who has a heart to enjoy the good and the beautiful here than to one who goes with his head like a bulrush, and grumbles all the way through the world. The fact is — and we may try to evade the truth if we will—that the greatest difference in the opportunity of enjoyment between this world and heaven lies in the spirit that is in us, not in the circumstances around us. The soul is the man. Heaven reigns and shines, yes, and sings in the heart that is right. Poverty, sickness, bereavement, anguish even on the rack or in the flames of martyrdom, can not make the man miserable. Laurentius, or, as we call him, St. Lawrence, suffered more than any martyr that I remember now. Instead of lying on a rustic sofa such as this on which I am stretched, with the balmy air of heaven breathing on me, and the warm sun hid by these trembling leaves, and the birds and bees and flowers singing their hymns, he was laid out on a large gridiron over a slow fire; and when he had been there for some time, he called out to the Roman emperor, who was looking on while the saint was broiling, "I am done to a turn," or as the Latin has been rendered:

"This side enough is toasted,
    Then turn me, tyrant, and eat;
And see whether raw or roasted,
    I am the better meat."

And it seems to me that if a good man could take things so coolly while broiling on a gridiron, we may be quiet under the little trials that we endure while on our way to the heavenly rest.

XXX.

OUR FRIENDS IN HEAVEN.

So many of my friends have recently gone to heaven, it is quite natural that thoughts of them and their surroundings should be frequent. And certainly they are very pleasant. If there were ever a time when religion and death and the life beyond were subjects of sad reflection, to be indulged only as a duty, such a time has passed away. It is now as cheering and agreeable to think of friends (and the more loved in life the more pleasant) enjoying the pleasures of the heavenly state, as to hear from others traveling in foreign lands, rejoicing in scenes and associations that satisfy their longing desires. The wisest and best of Roman moralists and philosophers enjoyed such thoughts of their friends gone before them into the unseen and eternal, and they anticipated with fond emotions a blissful reunion and refreshment in the society of the great and good. And with life and immortality brought to light by Revelation, what was to those ancient pagans a dreamy speculation, scarcely worthy of being called a faith, is to us reality. Our faith is the substance of things hoped for, the evidence of things not seen. We have thus entered already upon the inheritance, so that we have the good of it and part of the glory, as the heir to a vast estate or a throne enjoys, long before he comes into possession, the reflected honors and pleasures awaiting him.

Names and faces and forms of friends who have within
the past year preceded me into their rest have been peo-
pling the cheerful chambers of memory this evening. It
is a rough night outside, and the day has been a weary
one ; but now a soft firelight fills the room, and the study ·
lamp is shaded, so that the silence and shadows invite
converse with the spiritual and unseen. And the departed of the year have joined themselves with the many who
finished their course before them, and are now in the
midst of worship and feasts and friendship in the mansions of the blessed. How pleasant their memories now !
How the heart gladdens with the remembrance of the
joys on earth and the hopes of higher in heaven !

A very few years ago I had some friends at dinner with
me—a larger number than are often gathered at my table ; but they were friends, valued friends, some of them
very dear. It was a feast of fat things, and six hours
flew away like so many moments, making an evening
never to be forgotten here or hereafter. And of that
dinner company, a score are now in another state than
this—their bodies resting in the ground, their souls with
God. Twenty of my companions, associates in business,
in the Church, in public and private life, personal friends,
eating and drinking with me in one company, and now
all gone !

I stopped just here, and took out a sheet of paper on
which is a diagram of the table and the seat that each one
occupied, with his name written in it. The links of memory are brightened, so that their voices, their pleasant-
ries, their very words of wit and wisdom, sparkling and
bright, come flashing and shining, as on that glad and
genial evening. At my right was the stalwart Edgar of
Belfast, and on my left the polished Dill of Derry ; and

just beyond was the elegant and eloquent Potts; and next to him the courtly and splendid Bethune; S. E. and R. C. and S. F. B. Morse, three years sundered by death, but reunited to be sundered never again; and there was Krebs, himself a host, my companion in foreign travel, and a most delightful friend; and Murray, "Kirwan," brightening the brightest with the humor of his native isle; and Cooke, who was with me in Switzerland; and that wonderful astronomer, Mitchell, who now looks down to study the stars; and Hoge, with love like that of woman; and my brother, Stevenson, and others as bright and good: a brilliant company; an acquisition to the skies—stars all of them; who finished their course with honor, and then entered into joy. It would seem that the earth could not spare all those men, and keep right on. But they are in fitting company, with the Lamb in the midst of them.

> "There is the throne of David,
> And there from toil released,
> The shout of them that triumph,
> The song of them that feast."

And there is a younger company. All these were heroes and prophets and kings, but the children who have gone up there are children always. Oh blessed thought! They were with us long years ago, and they are in our hearts the same playful little ones they were when the Father of us all asked them to come to his house. And they are his children and our children forever. That little one to whom David said he should go, is still the child of David, not an infant of days, for there are no days nor nights in heaven, but the saint-child radiant in immortal beauty.

"Oh! when a mother meets on high
    The babe she lost in infancy,
Hath she not, then, for pains and fears,
    The day of woe, the watchful night,
For all her sorrows, all her tears,
    An overpayment of delight?"

Heaven's floor is covered with them. Of such is its kingdom. They have been going there—flying before they could walk, carried there by the angels—all these thousands of years. There, did I say? We do not know where the place is, nor what a place is for spirits to dwell in. They may be near us, around us, ministering spirits sent forth to do us good, to strengthen us. It would be good, doubtless better, to be with them where they are, and with Him who has them near his face.

THE END.

FLAMMARION'S ATMOSPHERE. The Atmosphere. Translated from the French of CAMILLE FLAMMARION. Edited by JAMES GLAISHER, F.R.S., Superintendent of the Magnetical and Meteorological Department of the Royal Observatory at Greenwich. With 10 Chromo-Lithographs and 86 Woodcuts. 8vo, Cloth, $6 00.

HUDSON'S HISTORY OF JOURNALISM. Journalism in the United States, from 1690 to 1872. By FREDERICK HUDSON. Crown 8vo, Cloth, $5 00.

PIKE'S SUB-TROPICAL RAMBLES. Sub-Tropical Rambles in the Land of the Aphanapteryx. By NICOLAS PIKE, U. S. Consul, Port Louis, Mauritius. Profusely Illustrated from the Author's own Sketches; containing also Maps and Valuable Meteorological Charts. Crown 8vo, Cloth, $3 50.

TRISTRAM'S THE LAND OF MOAB. The Result of Travels and Discoveries on the East Side of the Dead Sea and the Jordan. By H.B. TRISTRAM, M.A., LL.D., F.R.S., Master of the Greatham Hospital, and Hon. Canon of Durham. With a Chapter on the Persian Palace of Mashita, by JAS. FERGUSON, F.R.S. With Map and Illustrations. Crown 8vo, Cloth, $2 50.

SANTO DOMINGO, Past and Present; with a Glance at Hayti. By SAMUEL HAZARD. Maps and Illustrations. Crown 8vo, Cloth, $3 50.

LIFE OF ALFRED COOKMAN. The Life of the Rev. Alfred Cookman; with some Account of his Father, the Rev. George Grimston Cookman. By HENRY B. RIDGAWAY, D.D. With an Introduction by Bishop FOSTER, LL.D. Portrait on Steel. 12mo, Cloth, $2 00.

HERVEY'S CHRISTIAN RHETORIC. A System of Christian Rhetoric, for the Use of Preachers and Other Speakers. By GEORGE WINFRED HERVEY, M.A., Author of "Rhetoric of Conversation," &c. 8vo, Cloth, $3 50.

CASTELAR'S OLD ROME AND NEW ITALY. Old Rome and New Italy. By EMILIO CASTELAR. Translated by Mrs. ARTHUR ARNOLD. 12mo, Cloth, $1 75.

THE TREATY OF WASHINGTON: Its Negotiation, Execution, and the Discussions Relating Thereto. By CALEB CUSHING. Crown 8vo, Cloth, $2 00.

PRIME'S I GO A-FISHING. I Go a-Fishing. By W. C. PRIME. Crown 8vo, Cloth, $2 50.

HALLOCK'S FISHING TOURIST. The Fishing Tourist: Angler's Guide and Reference Book. By CHARLES HALLOCK. Illustrations. Crown 8vo, Cloth, $2 00.

SCOTT'S AMERICAN FISHING. Fishing in American Waters. By GENIO C. SCOTT. With 170 Illustrations. Crown 8vo, Cloth, $3 50.

ANNUAL RECORD OF SCIENCE AND INDUSTRY FOR 1872. Edited by Prof. SPENCER F. BAIRD, of the Smithsonian Institution, with the Assistance of Eminent Men of Science. 12mo, over 700 pp., Cloth, $2 00. (Uniform with the *Annual Record of Science and Industry for* 1871. 12mo, Cloth, $2 00.)

COL. FORNEY'S ANECDOTES OF PUBLIC MEN. Anecdotes of Public Men. By JOHN W. FORNEY. 12mo, Cloth, $2 00.

MISS BEECHER'S HOUSEKEEPER AND HEALTHKEEPER: Containing Five Hundred Recipes for Economical and Healthful Cooking; also, many Directions for securing Health and Happiness. Approved by Physicians of all Classes. Illustrations. 12mo, Cloth, $1 50.

FARM BALLADS. By WILL CARLETON. Handsomely Illustrated. Square 8vo, Ornamental Cloth, $2 00; Gilt Edges, $2 50.

POETS OF THE NINETEENTH CENTURY. The Poets of the Nineteenth Century. Selected and Edited by the Rev. ROBERT ARIS WILLMOTT. With English and American Additions, arranged by EVERT A. DUYCKINCK, Editor of "Cyclopædia of American Literature." Comprising Selections from the Greatest Authors of the Age. Superbly Illustrated with 141 Engravings from Designs by the most Eminent Artists. In elegant small 4to form, printed on Superfine Tinted Paper, richly bound in extra Cloth, Beveled, Gilt Edges, $5 00; Half Calf, $5 50; Full Turkey Morocco, $9 00.

THE REVISION OF THE ENGLISH VERSION OF THE NEW TESTAMENT. With an Introduction by the Rev. P. SCHAFF, D.D. 618 pp., Crown 8vo, Cloth, $3 00.

This work embraces in one volume:

I. ON A FRESH REVISION OF THE ENGLISH NEW TESTAMENT. By J. B. LIGHTFOOT, D.D., Canon of St. Paul's, and Hulsean Professor of Divinity, Cambridge. Second Edition, Revised. 196 pp.

II. ON THE AUTHORIZED VERSION OF THE NEW TESTAMENT in Connection with some Recent Proposals for its Revision. By RICHARD CHENEVIX TRENCH, D.D., Archbishop of Dublin. 194 pp.

III. CONSIDERATIONS ON THE REVISION OF THE ENGLISH VERSION OF THE NEW TESTAMENT. By C. J. ELLICOTT, D.D., Bishop of Gloucester and Bristol. 178 pp.

NORDHOFF'S CALIFORNIA. California: For Health, Pleasure, and Residence. A Book for Travelers and Settlers. Illustrated. 8vo, Paper, $2 00; Cloth, $2 50.

MOTLEY'S DUTCH REPUBLIC. The Rise of the Dutch Republic. By JOHN LOTHROP MOTLEY, LL.D., D.C.L. With a Portrait of William of Orange. 3 vols., 8vo, Cloth, $10 50.

MOTLEY'S UNITED NETHERLANDS. History of the United Netherlands: from the Death of William the Silent to the Twelve Years' Truce —1609. With a full View of the English-Dutch Struggle against Spain, and of the Origin and Destruction of the Spanish Armada. By JOHN LOTHROP MOTLEY, LL.D., D.C.L. Portraits. 4 vols., 8vo, Cloth, $14 00.

NAPOLEON'S LIFE OF CÆSAR. The History of Julius Cæsar. By His late Imperial Majesty NAPOLEON III. Two Volumes ready. Library Edition, 8vo, Cloth, $3 50 per vol.

HAYDN'S DICTIONARY OF DATES, relating to all Ages and Nations. For Universal Reference. Edited by BENJAMIN VINCENT, Assistant Secretary and Keeper of the Library of the Royal Institution of Great Britain; and Revised for the Use of American Readers. 8vo, Cloth, $5 00; Sheep, $6 00.

MACGREGOR'S ROB ROY ON THE JORDAN. The Rob Roy on the

WALLACE'S MALAY ARCHIPELAGO. The Malay Archipelago: the Land of the Orang-Utan and the Bird of Paradise. A Narrative of Travel, 1854-1862. With Studies of Man and Nature. By ALFRED RUSSEL WALLACE. With Ten Maps and Fifty-one Elegant Illustrations. Crown 8vo, Cloth, $2 50.

WHYMPER'S ALASKA. Travel and Adventure in the Territory of Alaska, formerly Russian America—now Ceded to the United States—and in various other parts of the North Pacific. By FREDERICK WHYMPER. With Map and Illustrations. Crown 8vo, Cloth, $2 50.

ORTON'S ANDES AND THE AMAZON. The Andes and the Amazon; or, Across the Continent of South America. By JAMES ORTON, M.A., Professor of Natural History in Vassar College, Poughkeepsie, N. Y., and Corresponding Member of the Academy of Natural Sciences, Philadelphia. With a New Map of Equatorial America and numerous Illustrations. Crown 8vo, Cloth, $2 00.

WINCHELL'S SKETCHES OF CREATION. Sketches of Creation: a Popular View of some of the Grand Conclusions of the Sciences in reference to the History of Matter and of Life. Together with a Statement of the Intimations of Science respecting the Primordial Condition and the Ultimate Destiny of the Earth and the Solar System. By ALEXANDER WINCHELL, LL.D., Chancellor of the Syracuse University. With Illustrations. 12mo, Cloth, $2 00.

WHITE'S MASSACRE OF ST. BARTHOLOMEW. The Massacre of St. Bartholomew: Preceded by a History of the Religious Wars in the Reign of Charles IX. By HENRY WHITE, M.A. With Illustrations. 8vo, Cloth, $1 75.

LOSSING'S FIELD-BOOK OF THE REVOLUTION. Pictorial Field-Book of the Revolution; or, Illustrations, by Pen and Pencil, of the History, Biography, Scenery, Relics, and Traditions of the War for Independence. By BENSON J. LOSSING. 2 vols., 8vo, Cloth, $14 00; Sheep, $15 00; Half Calf, $18 00; Full Turkey Morocco, $22 00.

LOSSING'S FIELD-BOOK OF THE WAR OF 1812. Pictorial Field-Book of the War of 1812; or, Illustrations, by Pen and Pencil, of the History, Biography, Scenery, Relics, and Traditions of the Last War for American Independence. By BENSON J. LOSSING. With several hundred Engravings on Wood, by Lossing and Barritt, chiefly from Original Sketches by the Author. 1088 pages, 8vo, Cloth, $7 00; Sheep, $8 50; Half Calf, $10 00.

ALFORD'S GREEK TESTAMENT. The Greek Testament: with a critically revised Text; a Digest of Various Readings; Marginal References to Verbal and Idiomatic Usage; Prolegomena; and a Critical and Exegetical Commentary. For the Use of Theological Students and Ministers. By HENRY ALFORD, D.D., Dean of Canterbury. Vol. I., containing the Four Gospels. 944 pages, 8vo, Cloth, $6 00; Sheep, $6 50.

ABBOTT'S FREDERICK THE GREAT. The History of Frederick the Second, called Frederick the Great. By JOHN S. C. ABBOTT. Elegantly Illustrated. 8vo, Cloth, $5 00.

ABBOTT'S HISTORY OF THE FRENCH REVOLUTION. The French Revolution of 1789, as viewed in the Light of Republican Institutions. By JOHN S. C. ABBOTT. With 100 Engravings. 8vo, Cloth, $5 00.

ABBOTT'S NAPOLEON BONAPARTE. The History of Napoleon Bonaparte. By JOHN S. C. ABBOTT. With Maps, Woodcuts, and Portraits on Steel. 2 vols., 8vo, Cloth, $10 00. .

ABBOTT'S NAPOLEON AT ST. HELENA; or, Interesting Anecdotes and Remarkable Conversations of the Emperor during the Five and a Half Years of his Captivity. Collected from the Memorials of Las Casas, O'Meara, Montholon, Antommarchi, and others. By JOHN S. C. ABBOTT. With Illustrations. 8vo, Cloth, $5 00.

ADDISON'S COMPLETE WORKS. The Works of Joseph Addison, embracing the whole of the "Spectator." Complete in 3 vols., 8vo, Cloth, 6 00.

ALCOCK'S JAPAN. The Capital of the Tycoon: a Narrative of a Three Years' Residence in Japan. By Sir RUTHERFORD ALCOCK, K.C.B., Her Majesty's Envoy Extraordinary and Minister Plenipotentiary in Japan. With Maps and Engravings. 2 vols., 12mo, Cloth, $3 50.

ALISON'S HISTORY OF EUROPE. FIRST SERIES: From the Commencement of the French Revolution, in 1789, to the Restoration of the Bourbons, in 1815. [In addition to the Notes on Chapter LXXVI., which correct the errors of the original work concerning the United States, a copious Analytical Index has been appended to this American Edition.] SECOND SERIES: From the Fall of Napoleon, in 1815, to the Accession of Louis Napoleon, in 1852. 8 vols., 8vo, Cloth, $16 00.

BARTH'S NORTH AND CENTRAL AFRICA. Travels and Discoveries in North and Central Africa: being a Journal of an Expedition undertaken under the Auspices of H.B.M.'s Government, in the Years 1849–1855. By HENRY BARTH, Ph.D., D.C.L. Illustrated. 3 vols., 8vo, Cloth, $12 00.

HENRY WARD BEECHER'S SERMONS. Sermons by HENRY WARD BEECHER, Plymouth Church, Brooklyn. Selected from Published and Unpublished Discourses, and Revised by their Author. With Steel Portrait. Complete in 2 vols., 8vo, Cloth, $5 00.

LYMAN BEECHER'S AUTOBIOGRAPHY, &c. Autobiography, Correspondence, &c., of Lyman Beecher, D.D. Edited by his Son, CHARLES BEECHER. With Three Steel Portraits, and Engravings on Wood. In 2 vols., 12mo, Cloth, $5 00.

BOSWELL'S JOHNSON. The Life of Samuel Johnson, LL.D. Including a Journey to the Hebrides. By JAMES BOSWELL, Esq. A New Edition, with numerous Additions and Notes. By JOHN WILSON CROKER, LL.D., F.R.S. Portrait of Boswell. 2 vols., 8vo, Cloth, $4 00.

DRAPER'S CIVIL WAR. History of the American Civil War. By JOHN W. DRAPER, M.D., LL.D., Professor of Chemistry and Physiology in the University of New York. In Three Vols. 8vo, Cloth, $3 50 per vol.

DRAPER'S INTELLECTUAL DEVELOPMENT OF EUROPE. A History of the Intellectual Development of Europe. By JOHN W. DRAPER, M.D., LL.D., Professor of Chemistry and Physiology in the University of New York. 8vo, Cloth. $5 00.

DRAPER'S AMERICAN CIVIL POLICY. Thoughts on the Future Civil Policy of America. By JOHN W. DRAPER, M.D., LL.D., Professor of Chemistry and Physiology in the University of New York. Crown 8vo, Cloth, $2 50.

DU CHAILLU'S AFRICA. Explorations and Adventures in Equatorial Africa, with Accounts of the Manners and Customs of the People, and of the Chase of the Gorilla, the Crocodile, Leopard, Elephant, Hippopotamus, and other Animals. By PAUL B. DU CHAILLU. Numerous Illustrations. 8vo, Cloth, $5 00.

DU CHAILLU'S ASHANGO LAND. A Journey to Ashango Land: and Further Penetration into Equatorial Africa. By PAUL B. DU CHAILLU. New Edition. Handsomely Illustrated. 8vo, Cloth, $5 00.

BELLOWS'S OLD WORLD. The Old World in its New Face: Impressions of Europe in 1867–1868. By HENRY W. BELLOWS. 2 vols., 12mo, Cloth, $3 50.

BRODHEAD'S HISTORY OF NEW YORK. History of the State of New York. By JOHN ROMEYN BRODHEAD. 1609–1691. 2 vols. 8vo, Cloth, $3 00 per vol.

BROUGHAM'S AUTOBIOGRAPHY. Life and Times of HENRY, LORD BROUGHAM. Written by Himself. In Three Volumes. 12mo, Cloth, $2 00 per vol.

BULWER'S PROSE WORKS. Miscellaneous Prose Works of Edward Bulwer, Lord Lytton. 2 vols., 12mo, Cloth, $3 50.

BULWER'S HORACE. The Odes and Epodes of Horace. A Metrical Translation into English. With Introduction and Commentaries. By LORD LYTTON. With Latin Text from the Editions of Orelli, Macleane, and Yonge. 12mo, Cloth, $1 75.

BULWER'S KING ARTHUR, A Poem. By LORD LYTTON. New Edition. 12mo, Cloth, $1 75.

BURNS'S LIFE AND WORKS. The Life and Works of Robert Burns. Edited by ROBERT CHAMBERS. 4 vols., 12mo, Cloth, $6 00.

REINDEER, DOGS, AND SNOW-SHOES. A Journal of Siberian Travel and Explorations made in the Years 1865-'67. By RICHARD J. BUSH, late of the Russo-American Telegraph Expedition. Illustrated. Crown 8vo, Cloth, $3 00.

CARLYLE'S FREDERICK THE GREAT. History of Friedrich II., called Frederick the Great. By THOMAS CARLYLE. Portraits, Maps, Plans, &c. 6 vols., 12mo, Cloth, $12 00.

CARLYLE'S FRENCH REVOLUTION. History of the French Revolution. 2 vols., 12mo, Cloth, $3 50.

CARLYLE'S OLIVER CROMWELL. Letters and Speeches of Oliver Cromwell. With Elucidations and Connecting Narrative. 2 vols., 12mo, Cloth, $3 50.

CHALMERS'S POSTHUMOUS WORKS. The Posthumous Works of Dr. Chalmers. Edited by his Son-in-Law, Rev. WILLIAM HANNA, LL.D. Complete in 9 vols., 12mo, Cloth, $13 50.

COLERIDGE'S COMPLETE WORKS. The Complete Works of Samuel Taylor Coleridge. With an Introductory Essay upon his Philosophical and Theological Opinions. Edited by Professor SHEDD. Complete in Seven Vols. With a Portrait. Small 8vo, Cloth, $10 50.

DOOLITTLE'S CHINA. Social Life of the Chinese: with some Account of their Religious, Governmental, Educational, and Business Customs and Opinions. With special but not exclusive Reference to Fuhchau. By Rev. JUSTUS DOOLITTLE, Fourteen Years Member of the Fuhchau Mission of the American Board. Illustrated with more that 150 characteristic Engravings on Wood. 2 vols., 12mo, Cloth, $5 00.

GIBBON'S ROME. History of the Decline and Fall of the Roman Empire. By EDWARD GIBBON. With Notes by Rev. H. H. MILMAN and M. GUIZOT. A new cheap Edition. To which is added a complete Index of the whole Work, and a Portrait of the Author. 6 vols., 12mo, Cloth, $9 00.

HAZEN'S SCHOOL AND ARMY IN GERMANY AND FRANCE. The School and the Army in Germany and France, with a Diary of Siege Life at Versailles. By Brevet Major-General W. B. HAZEN, U.S.A., Colonel Sixth Infantry. Crown 8vo, Cloth, $2 50.

HARPER'S NEW CLASSICAL LIBRARY. Literal Translations.

The following Vols. are now ready. 12mo, Cloth, $1 50 each.

CÆSAR.—VIRGIL.—SALLUST.—HORACE.—CICERO'S ORATIONS.—CICERO'S OFFICES, &C.—CICERO ON ORATORY AND ORATORS.—TACITUS (2 vols.). —TERENCE.—SOPHOCLES.—JUVENAL.—XENOPHON.—HOMER'S ILIAD.— HOMER'S ODYSSEY. — HERODOTUS. — DEMOSTHENES. — THUCYDIDES. — ÆSCHYLUS.—EURIPIDES (2 vols.).—LIVY (2 vols.).

DAVIS'S CARTHAGE. Carthage and her Remains: being an Account of the Excavations and Researches on the Site of the Phœnician Metropolis in Africa and other adjacent Places. Conducted under the Auspices of Her Majesty's Government. By Dr. DAVIS, F.R.G.S. Profusely Illustrated with Maps, Woodcuts, Chromo-Lithographs, &c. 8vo, Cloth, $4 00.

EDGEWORTH'S (MISS) NOVELS. With Engravings. 10 vols., 12mo, Cloth, $15 00.

GROTE'S HISTORY OF GREECE. 12 vols. 12mo. Cloth.

HELPS'S SPANISH CONQUEST. The Spanish Conquest in America, and its Relation to the History of Slavery and to the Government of Colonies. By ARTHUR HELPS. 4 vols., 12mo, Cloth, $6 00.

HALE'S (MRS.) WOMAN'S RECORD. Woman's Record; or, Biographical Sketches of all Distinguished Women, from the Creation to the Present Time. Arranged in Four Eras, with Selections from Female Writers of Each Era. By Mrs. SARAH JOSEPHA HALE. Illustrated with more than 200 Portraits. 8vo, Cloth, $5 00.

HALL'S ARCTIC RESEARCHES. Arctic Researches and Life among the Esquimaux: being the Narrative of an Expedition in Search of Sir John Franklin, in the Years 1860, 1861, and 1862. By CHARLES FRANCIS HALL. With Maps and 100 Illustrations. The Illustrations are from the Original Drawings by Charles Parsons, Henry L. Stephens, Solomon Eytinge, W. S. L. Jewett, and Granville Perkins, after Sketches by Captain Hall. 8vo, Cloth, $5 00.

HALLAM'S CONSTITUTIONAL HISTORY OF ENGLAND, from the Accession of Henry VII. to the Death of George II. 8vo, Cloth, $2 00.

HALLAM'S LITERATURE. Introduction to the Literature of Europe during the Fifteenth, Sixteenth, and Seventeenth Centuries. By HENRY HALLAM. 2 vols., 8vo, Cloth, $4 00.

HALLAM'S MIDDLE AGES. State of Europe during the Middle Ages. By HENRY HALLAM. 8vo, Cloth, $2 00.

HILDRETH'S HISTORY OF THE UNITED STATES. FIRST SERIES: From the First Settlement of the Country to the Adoption of the Federal Constitution. SECOND SERIES: From the Adoption of the Federal Constitution to the End of the Sixteenth Congress. 6 vols., 8vo, Cloth, $18 00.

HUME'S HISTORY OF ENGLAND. History of England, from the Invasion of Julius Cæsar to the Abdication of James II., 1688. By DAVID HUME. A new Edition, with the Author's last Corrections and Improvements. To which is Prefixed a short Account of his Life, written by Himself. With a Portrait of the Author. 6 vols., 12mo, Cloth, $9 00.

JAY'S WORKS. Complete Works of Rev. William Jay: comprising his Sermons, Family Discourses, Morning and Evening Exercises for every Day in the Year, Family Prayers, &c. Author's enlarged Edition, revised. 3 vols., 8vo, Cloth, $6 00.

JEFFERSON'S DOMESTIC LIFE. The Domestic Life of Thomas Jefferson: compiled from Family Letters and Reminiscences, by his Great-Granddaughter, SARAH N. RANDOLPH. With Illustrations. Crown 8vo, Illuminated Cloth, Beveled Edges, $2 50.

JOHNSON'S COMPLETE WORKS. The Works of Samuel Johnson, LL.D. With an Essay on his Life and Genius, by ARTHUR MURPHY, Esq. Portrait of Johnson. 2 vols., 8vo, Cloth, $4 00.

KINGLAKE'S CRIMEAN WAR. The Invasion of the Crimea, and an Account of its Progress down to the Death of Lord Raglan. By ALEXANDER WILLIAM KINGLAKE. With Maps and Plans. Two Vols. ready. 12mo, Cloth, $2 00 per vol.

KINGSLEY'S WEST INDIES. At Last: A Christmas in the West Indies. By CHARLES KINGSLEY. Illustrated. 12mo, Cloth, $1 50.

KRUMMACHER'S DAVID, KING OF ISRAEL. David, the King of Israel: a Portrait drawn from Bible History and the Book of Psalms. By FREDERICK WILLIAM KRUMMACHER, D.D., Author of "Elijah the Tishbite," &c. Translated under the express Sanction of the Author by the Rev. M. G. EASTON, M.A. With a Letter from Dr. Krummacher to his American Readers, and a Portrait. 12mo, Cloth, $1 75.

LAMB'S COMPLETE WORKS. The Works of Charles Lamb. Comprising his Letters, Poems, Essays of Elia, Essays upon Shakspeare, Hogarth, &c., and a Sketch of his Life, with the Final Memorials, by T. NOON TALFOURD. Portrait. 2 vols., 12mo, Cloth, $3 00.